Praise for *Prairie N*

"Ivan Doig is a world-class novelist, and *
composition."

—*Seattle Weekly*

"With a wonderful feel for the wild Montana landscape, Doig deftly moves back and forth in time to fill in the past, and when the action moves from Montana to New York we are given an equally convincing bird's-eye view of the Harlem Renaissance."

—*The Boston Globe*

"[A] subtle, highly textured love story."

—*Booklist*

"Doig maintains a firm grip, aided by limber, burnished prose. A."

—*Entertainment Weekly*

"Doig does his usual splendid job of interweaving several time frames to bring alive American history and to chart the evolving relationships of thorny, independent people who love fiercely but never go easy on one another or themselves. . . . It all combines to create a compelling story that ends too soon."

—*Kirkus Reviews* (starred)

"[L]ike Doig's other books . . . *Prairie Nocturne* is a fine example of his ability to populate places and times with living, breathing characters."

—*The Oregonian*

"[Doig's] characters are unforgettable. . . . He embroiders them with history, myth, and sensuality."

—*San Jose Mercury News*

PRAIRIE NOCTURNE

· a novel ·

WITHDRAWN

IVAN DOIG

New York   London   Toronto   Sydney

To Dave Walter and Marcella Sherfy
for doing half the laughing
and damn near all the history

SCRIBNER
1230 Avenue of the Americas
New York, NY 10020

First Scribner trade paperback edition 2005

SCRIBNER and design are trademarks of
Macmillan Library Reference USA, Inc., used under license
by Simon & Schuster, the publisher of this work.

For information about special discounts for bulk purchases,
please contact Simon & Schuster Special Sales:
1-800-456-6798 or business@simonandschuster.com

DESIGNED BY KYOKO WATANABE
Text set in Garamond 3

Manufactured in the United States of America

1   3   5   7   9   10   8   6   4   2

Library of Congress Control Number: 2003050385

ISBN 0-7432-0135-3
0-7432-0136-1 (Pbk)

Author's Note

This work of fiction takes its cues from something once said by Peter Brook, who as a stage director has sought to imbue storytelling, as he phrased it to an interviewer, with "the closeness of reality and the distance of myth, because if there is no distance you aren't amazed, and if there is no closeness you aren't moved."

—I.D.

Overture

A story wants to be told a certain way, or it is merely the alphabet badly recited. At the right time the words borrow us, so to speak, and then out can come the unsuspected sides of things with a force like that of music. This is the story of the three of us, which I am more fit to tell now than when I was alive.

—on the flyleaf of the diary of Susan Duff,
discovered among the papers of the WW Cattle and
Land Company, Wesley Williamson Special Collection,
Harvard University, in the year 2025

AMENDED STAR

· 1924 ·

*"The evening, the evening,
The evening brings all home."*

THE LAST RINGLETED girl had finished off the ballad on a hopeful note—she would have given her ears for a praising word from Miss Duff—and night and quiet came again to the house on Highland Street. Regular as the curtain of nightfall was Susan Duff's routine in closing away her teaching day. Shoulders back, her tall frame straightening expectantly even though there was no one in the house to meet for the evening but herself, she shuffled sheet music into its rightful order, tallied the hours of lessons in the secondhand mercantile ledger she kept handy atop the piano, and cast an eye over the schedule of impending pupils, then the balky old doors of the music parlor were slid shut. Next a freshening of her face with a rinse of cold water; one adjusting glance into the mirror, never two; hairpins taken out, and her chestnut hair shaken down. Onward to her stovetop supper, which she raced through as though still making up for her father's interminable graces over expiring food. Now, with a pat to the kitchen and a cursory locking of doors and windows, she was ready to ascend.

As fixed as a star, the telltale glow of her gable window appeared over Helena at the last of dusk and burned on past respectable bed-time. You might think a woman of her early climb in life, singled out by her father's God for a soaring voice to lift His hymns and then cast-ing away choirsong for the anthems of a harsh young century, would find it a hard comedown to be faced with a nightly audience of only herself. You'd be as wrong as you could be, Susan would have you know in a finger snap.

This night, however, no sooner was she upstairs than she whipped to a halt in front of the alcove of window, her gaze drawn down the hillside to the state capitol dome, resting as it did on the center of the government of Montana like a giant's copper helmet. The dome still was alight with the festoon of bulbs that had greeted 1924 three months ago, which seemed to her uncalled for.

"Blaze," Susan addressed the civic constellation in the coarse-ground Fife burr she was born to, "see if I care."

She gave a throaty chuckle at herself and wended her way toward her desk. Pausing to choose a lozenge from the cut-glass jar there, she tasted it thoughtfully with the tip of her tongue, then swirled it in her mouth as if it would clear away beginner lessons and quavery approximations of high C; poor Flossie, last pupil of the day and absolute farthest from a worthwhile voice. *No recital there,* she reflected, *except what I'll hear from her mother.*

Still caught in thought, Susan automatically cast a glance around to judge the state of her housekeeping up here and reached her usual conclusion that she needed the availability of these spacious hours beyond dark more than the place demanded housecleaning. The attic-like room extended the full length of the house—loft quarters for a married pair of servants, this must have originally been—and she treated the expanse like a rambler cottage perched above the formal quarters of downstairs. The rolltop desk, a divan, a Victrola, what had been her father's Morris chair and footstool, onyx-topped side tables, a blue-and-black knitted comforter on the sill seat of the strategically aimed gable window, swayback sets of bookshelves, a spinet piano, a typewriter sitting composedly on a rolling secretarial table, a highly unreliable new thing called a radio set standing on a sturdy side cab-inet, the whopping Duff family Bible on a commemorative reading stand of its own, all populated what was in actual fact her bedroom.

This mob of comforts drew her up out of public day as if lifting her into a lifeboat, and Susan tallied the necessity of this each time, too. Liberal with the night, resourceful as she probably ever was going to be in what that Bible would have deemed her fortieth year under heaven, she held to the belief that she was most her reconstituted self in these upstairs hours, at this elevation where the minute hand did not count. The time of footlights and the song-led marches for the right of women to vote were tucked into the past as firmly as could be, and as to the tongues of the town down there beyond the base of the stairs, she could do nothing about those. But up here, what she could do was to get busy at life's amended version of Susan Duff. There were encouraging letters to be written to favorite former pupils. (Tonight's, which took lip-biting concentration, to the breathy young soprano whose recent *lieder* recital in Milwaukee had not found favor there; many a time Susan wished she could deal solely with the voices, shapes of sound standing free in the air, without the human wrappings.) This political city's newspapers to be devoured, Anaconda Copper's one for spite and the independent one for sustenance. Books in plenitude; currently she was trying to make her way through E. M. Forster and the murky doings in the Marabar Caves. Music, of course: her half-finished operetta *Prairie Tide* always awaited, always unnavigable; and the radio set sometimes brought in serenades from unimaginable distances and sometimes madly cackled out static; but the Victrola sang the songs of others perfectly on command, restorative in itself to a teacher of voice. Then too she still was secretary of the state chapter of the Over There Memorial Committee, which took her to a drafty meeting hall once a month and obliged her to see to official correspondence, clerical enough to cross the eyes, in between. Tonight, as always, she shifted workspots every so often, her tall solo figure suddenly on the move as if she were a living chess piece. Time did not lag here in her industrious garret; it was not permitted to.

When it was nearing midnight and she had just begun to salt away another day between diary covers, she faintly heard the turn of a key in the front door and then the rhythm of him coming up the stairs to her for the first time in four years.

* * *

"Susan? You might have changed the lock."

He arrived on the wings of that commanding smile. *The very model of a modern genteel major,* a line of hers teased somewhere back in that diary. The blue of his blood and the red silver of bayonet steel, those paradoxical flying colors by which he came through the war. Behind Wes, it was said, men would have charged Hell; in fact, men had.

Susan sat back hard in her chair at the desk, surprised no end to be confronted with him again after all this time. Even so she could not help but marvel at the presence with which Wes did most anything, as though the shadow under him were the thrust of a stage. Her emotions were more mixed about how little the years told on him. Poised there at the top of her stairs, wearing a fortune on his back—or more aptly, on the swath of chest where General Pershing himself had pinned the highest medal—as ever he looked ready to do a white-glove inspection. Civilian life, now that he was tailored to it again, was a continuation of duty by other means. Even his way of standing like that, the weight taken on his left leg to spare the right knee peppered by shrapnel at St. Mihiel, proclaimed the reliance that the world had wanted to place on him. Brave and wounded at the same time: the story of Wesley Williamson's life, as she was plentifully aware, on more than one kind of battlefield.

Voice training had unforeseen benefits. She thought she managed to sound in possession of herself—or at least within her own custody—as she spoke back to the immaculate invader:

"Evidently I saved you some shinnying, by not."

"Oh oh," Wes said, his smile dented but still there, "I guess I've been told."

He picked his way through the long room, interested as a museum-goer, to the perch nearest her, which happened to be the edge of her bed. "May I?"

You and your Williamson manners. In out of nowhere, walk uninvited into a woman's bedroom, then be solicitous about seating himself too near. Susan laughed to clear away her incredulity, and answered him in a tone that would have cut through bone:

"Sit yourself down, Wes, please do. I haven't had a good look at a family man in a while."

Wes ducked his head slightly in acknowledgment. *One thing about*

Susan, she doesn't just go through the motions of being riled. At least she had not put the run on him, quite yet. He settled to the very outside of the bed, accommodating his leg, and wordlessly looked over at her before trying to make his case. The woman there just beyond reach had an enlarged sense of justice, which had been one of the first passions that drew them together. He saw that their years apart had deepened the lines of her, accented the lean longstroke features that would never amount to outright beauty, quite, but summed up as an august well-carved attractiveness; a face that had always had character enough for the capacity of a stage. The old disturbance Susan caused in him gathered at the base of his throat as he sat there reviewing her. That laugh of hers which started somewhere down in the Scotch gravel of her family footing, then her voice finding its way to the heaven-given lilt: Lord, how he missed that. The snip and snap of talk with her, all the times of concocting their political mustard plasters for the world. The linear extra helping of her, the long-boned grace that had added so to their lovemaking. Topping it all, her cinnamon eyes that could put you in your place and make you like it. Everything was there to be missed, as he contemplated Susan across the frozen distance between bed and desk.

"Lost, are you?" she inquired. "I thought this was still your New York time of year."

"You make me sound like a migratory bird."

"If you show the feather . . ."

"Didn't I hear you've been to France again yourself?"

"Committee doings. That was two years ago."

"Four take away two," he mused as if maintaining his own special calendar of their time apart. "Halfway back to when the earth cooled."

"Wes?" She put down her pen as if pinning something beneath it. "Do I get to know why you're here?"

"I'm working on that." Reluctantly giving up his inspection of her, he let his eyes slide over the motley keepsakes in attendance around her, the brass paperweight shaped like a treble clef, the tiny mock strongbox which held pen nibs, the soldier photograph with its tint going drab, the silver letter opener with the maiden of liberty, one breast bare and glinting, in bas relief on its handle. His gaze lit on the open pages in front of Susan. The voices of paper were one of his specialties. Thinking out loud, not a usual habit, he said: "A woman armed with a diary. Not the best company for me to be keeping, I suppose."

She looked at Wes across the small white field of pages. Just looked at him. When you have cost a man a governorship, what further scandal does he think you are apt to inflict on him?

The silence stretched. At last he brought out:

"You know I couldn't."

"I know you wouldn't," she said as if correcting his spelling. They had been through this and through this. A proven hero who could not or would not undergo a tug-of-war with his church. *"Wes, the Pope has no need of the divorce law. But you do."* Who had broken his vows six ways from Sunday in half the countries of Europe and in this very room and then would not break his misbegotten marriage. *"She's not a well woman, Susan. That on top of the faith—I can't face leaving her when she's like this, it's against everything in me."*

Susan, from a family that had the stamina of sled dogs, held no patience for the delicate constitution and strategic indispositions of Wes's wife. She could not resist asking now:

"How is the tender Merrinell?"

For a start, his wife was under the impression Wes was in Minneapolis at this moment, buying grain consignments. He shifted a bit on the bed and reeled off that she was holding her own, at the Lake George place now for Easter break with the gold-dust twins, although they weren't especially twins anymore, only grudgingly even sisters. . . . Susan half-listened, fascinated as of old with the change of atmosphere he brought into a room with him. In the period before him, one of her beaus at musical evenings, a tippler, smelled of cloves. She could swear Wes always carried the scent of silk.

He broke off what he was saying and again regarded Susan as though taking the opportunity to stock up on her. "We both know you don't care a hoot in hell about any of that. Let's try you. How is the Lord's gift to the musically inclined?"

"Oho, this from the man who always told me he couldn't tell Paganini from page nine? This isn't like you, Wes. At least your word was always good. When we stopped throwing ourselves at each other—"

"—when you dropped me like a bushel of hot peppers—"

"—when we were this close to being the flavor on every gossip's tongue and I said I'd have no more of it if I couldn't have you, we agreed that was that."

Actually, he recalled, she had handed him his walking papers with words more stinging than those: "If I'm going to be alone in life, Wes, it might as well be with myself."

"You're not doing either of us any good by barging in here in the middle of the night, are you," Susan was at now. "If I know anything about it, you were always quite concerned with 'appearances.'"

Wes waved that off. "No one much is up at this hour. I had Monty leave me off at the capitol grounds and came up around the back blocks. Here, come see the new Doozy." With the aimed quickness which had always reminded her of a catapult going off, he launched up on his good leg and was over to the gable.

In spite of herself, curiosity drew her over to the window by him. In the diffused glow of the strings of bulbs on the capitol dome, the butter-yellow Duesenberg could be seen parked down the hill from dozing Highland Street. Despite the night chill this time of year, Wes's bravely outfitted Negro chauffeur, Monty, was caressing the hood of the limousine with a polishing rag. The lanky form leaned into the already burnished surface as if magnetized to the machine. "Monty would sleep in it if I'd let him," Wes was saying.

Susan stood there transfixed. The Williamsons. Their wealth and their fortunes, which were two different things. She closed her eyes for an instant, overcome by the fresh weight of memory. Wes's coming here made her feel piqued, put upon, singled out a time too many, on down the list. There had been another man since him, not married but not worth marrying either. She didn't suppose Wes had shown any more belated wisdom and retrieved chastity than she had. They had gone their old separate anchorless ways. Yet here they were, side by side at a window again as if reviewing life's march bearing down on them. And when she opened her eyelids it was all still there: the penny-colored dome that should have been Wes's by civic right, her reflected outline on the pane of night beside his, the chauffeur stroking the flanks of the costly plaything.

Wes turned from the window, a smile of a more mischievous sort lingering on him as he sized up her reaction. Wondering why she hadn't changed that door lock, she scrupulously created more distance now between herself and him.

He surveyed the room's furnishings again. "I'm glad I wasn't the one to heft all this up those stairs. Know what I think?"

"Not without a Ouija board."

"You're treed, up here. No, let me finish. You've treed yourself. Chased the Susan Duff that was, right up into this upholstered perch." He walked back the length of the room to seat himself on the edge of the bed again, letting drop a phrase at a time as he came. "I see make-work. I see pastimes. I believe I see the unfinished musical masterpiece. I see the man-eating diary. What I don't see is you taking the world on as you always did." When she made no answer, he shifted to the affectionate mock burr he had never been able to master: " 'Tis a waste of a bonny woman."

"It's late, is what it is," she left it at, making a show of checking the clock. "Wes, please. Have your say and take yourself home."

"I have the pupil of a lifetime for you."

Susan laughed uncertainly at the size of that statement. "I don't lack for pupils, they're coming out my ears." Which was not as true as it once would have been.

"This one, I want you to put all your time to, for however long it takes." He lifted a hand, as if taking an oath, to head off the protest she was sure to make. "I'll pay double for everything—your hours, whatever you need to arrange in the way of accompaniment, all the sheet music you can stand, name it. All right then," he said after a moment of gauging how she was taking this, "triple."

"Where does this come from all of a sudden? I have never wanted your—"

"There's no charity to this. You'll earn your keep with this pupil, Susan, don't ever worry about that. It's a voice I'd say is—different. Unformed, maybe you'll say rough as a cob, but hard to resist somehow. It stays on in the ear, is that any kind of musical term? You'd snap this voice up, if you heard it out of the clear blue, I'm sure you would."

His cadences of persuasion tested the walls of the room, as if this familiar floor were a speaking platform over the night-held capital city. Wes himself had a voice the size of an encyclopedia set. Susan knew by heart every gruff note and passionate coax he was capable of, and how effectively the mixture worked. "The copper companies that have looted this state for thirty years think they are immune to fair taxation," she had heard him send crowds into a rising roar as he uncoiled his campaign tag line, "I promise them an epidemic of it!" No other politician in the state had stung back as fiercely at the Ku Klux Klan as it crept west and its flaming crosses began to flare on the bald hills above Catholic towns and railheads bringing immigrants to Montana land: "This cuckoo Klan, they seem to be scared the Pope will descend on them in their beds, else why do they go around wearing their nighties over their heads?" The cause in her own bones, women's right to vote, he had furthered at every chance in the state legislature. "Comets attend the death of kings," his famous words to the 1910 suffrage convention as Halley's fireball swept across the Britain of the newly deceased Edward VII, "perhaps to see whether they truly fit their filigreed caskets. Across the water, there is a government, with complicit silence from its throne on down, that has fought its suffragists with detention, forced feedings, and truncheons. But this country, this state, with its every voice must greet the women who are pointing out true democracy to us." There never had been a hairbreadth of difference between him and her on politics, only every other field of life, and she had been all for his gubernatorial bid and the passions he gave such voice to. In his other great campaign, in the bloody mud of France, the words of Wes were known to have made the difference between life and death. Her head swimming, four years out of practice at dealing with the mesmerizing side of him, she carefully chose her way around his entreaty now:

"If it's one of your daughters, I wouldn't feel right about—"

"Not even close. Fatherly pride isn't anywhere in this. Promise me you'll give a listen."

"I seem to feel the presence of the Williamson disposition to bargain."

He reflected for a moment, as if she had shown him something about himself. Then said only: "I don't consider I've ever lost anything by it. About giving a listen—how can that hurt?"

She had to grant, "For a singing teacher, hearing is believing. All I ever ask is to be amazed."

So I remember, his expression let her know. "Opera, vaudeville," he went right on, "I don't know what we're talking, with this. I honestly don't. But you, New York and Europe and all, you've heard the best and you'll know where this voice can be made to fit. Oh, and when you start the lessons, it'll need to be done at the ranch, not here. It's a shame, but we can't—well, you'll see . . ." He furrowed as he came to the next thought. "I'll work the idea into Whit's skull, but we'd better be ready to make arrangements around him."

Susan scowled, reminding him one more time this was not a woman who could be steered like an ingenue at a tea dance. Wes watched her shake her head no and then some.

"Your old place, then," he knew to regroup. Not for nothing was this prideful woman the daughter of Ninian Duff, he always had to keep in mind. Ninian the Calvinian. The fathoms of bloodlines, always treacherously deep. "You could set up shop there at the homestead, why not? It'd be convenient all around. I'll see that it's outfitted for you, furniture, groceries, bedding, cat and canary if you want."

Scotch Heaven? A Williamson spreading the red carpet there for a Duff? What next, the calendar corrected to come out better? Wary as she was determined to be, all that the Duff place on the North Fork of English Creek held for her flickered up more than a little.

Wes had been counting on the fact that geography has a habit of kissing people in a way they never get over, and he could tell he had said just enough on that score. Now he paused in that spotlit manner, as if to make sure each of his words would register. "I don't ask this lightly, Susan. It isn't some notion that walked up to me in the street. I've thought this over, and then thought that over, and it still comes out the same—I need you to pitch in on this." A tiny stretch of silence he used for emphasis, then: "I'm asking you to do everything you know how for this pupil. The works."

"Wes?" Honest bewilderment broke through in her voice. "Wes, who in this world means that much to you?"

He appeared stunned at hearing it put that way. Sitting there glazed, pale as collector porcelain.

When Wes at last rose from the bed edge, was it her imagination or did he lurch more than a misbehaving knee would account for? She watched him stiffly navigate the length of the room, biting her tongue against calling out to him. Let him march down her stairs and out of her carefully compartmented existence (*Treed!*), let him leave that key in the door, let that be the natural end of it.

But he paused at the gable window and stood there facing out into the night. Over his shoulder he told her: "Monty."

WHITEFACE

· 1914 ·

THE SOUND ALWAYS gave him a bad time, the slobbery breathing at the lip of the barrel. Then the bawl of fury six inches from his ear. *Who said this is easy money?* Panting, he stayed jackknifed in the barrel, chest against his knees and chin tucked down, clutching the handgrips next to his ankles. "Hyah, bull!" he could hear Dolph Kuhn, the pickup man, shouting from somewhere in the arena, but Dolph couldn't ride anywhere close while the animal still was on the prod. A horn tip scraped the metal of the barrel, inches from his other ear; he flinched every time that happened, even though he knew you could go over Niagara in one of these. When the serious butting began and the barrel tipped over and started to roll, the jolt delivered by the bull came as almost a relief; now he could at least concentrate on holding on. "You don't want to let yourself shake loose in there," the wizened rodeo clown up in Calgary who had given him a couple of lessons in this had warned, "or you'll know what a pair of dice feels like." Nor, he had found out the hard way, did you want to keep your eyes open during this or you'd end up dizzy as a cat in a churn. His ears told him enough about it anyway: how the crowd loved to be scared at this stunt, the human ball in the barrel and the bull determined to butt the infuriating object until it presented something to gore.

When the barrel at last seemed to have quit rolling and he opened one eye and cautiously raised his head, he saw the ornery whiteface bull paw the ground one last time, and then its departing rear end, the tail switching slowly back and forth as the critter lost interest. Even so, he waited to hear the whap of lariat on rump as Dolph galloped in to haze the bucking bull out the far end of the arena. "He's on the run, Snowball," Dolph called, "better git yourself out of there."

Monty gulped air and unkinked himself. Somewhat groggy, but he remembered the routine and tossed his hat out first. Reliably the crowd guffawed. When no harm came to the hat, he stuck his head out the end of the barrel like an inquisitive turtle, gawking this way and that. The rhythm of the laughter built, orchestral, mass chortles of anticipation as the audience waited for his next maneuver; he'd been right about this, rodeo-goers could handle the idea of him fooling around. He clambered out, spun around, and peeked back into the barrel, as if the bull might be in there. Thunder of laughter at that, any more and they'd shake the grandstand to pieces. He quit while he was ahead and picked up his dusty hat, bowing to the announcer with the megaphone who was whipping up a nice round of applause for "our artiste of the barrel after that dosie-doe he just did with the gentleman cow." Then back to business, kicking the big barrel along until it was in the vicinity of the bucking chutes again and he was standing ready for the next bull rider who needed his neck saved.

"Artiste" now, am I? Hope they don't pick that up across town. He drew another deep breath and concentrated on the gate where the bull would rampage out. Only one more rider in this go-round, and wouldn't you know, there was a hang-up in the chute. Another recalcitrant whiteface with hay on its horns. He watched the rider scramble up off the bull's back as if it was suddenly too hot a place to sit, while the chute men shoved at the mass of animal. Forced to wait out there centerstage in the arena with only the barrel for company, Monty took the opportunity to mop the back of his neck and under his chin with the red handkerchief. That was another of the jokes, using the red hanky like a matador's cape when he had to draw the bull away from a bucked-off rider. It occurred to him that it was actually pretty funny to be swabbing at himself this way with the hard-used piece of cloth, because at this point of the rodeo he was an irredeemable mess. The bib overalls six sizes too big drooped on him, and the screaming-red long underwear that was the other part of the

costume was darkly wet with sweat. He had fresh wet manure up one pantleg. *Angel Momma ought to see me now. Used to worry about me playing in the mud, she'd have kittens over this.* But that seemed to be how life generally went, any way but straight, at least since she passed on. Keeping watch on the chute situation—the bull had jammed a horn under one of the fence planks and was resisting the profane persuasion of the chute crew—he checked around on himself to make sure his props were at the ready. Out of his hip pocket dangled the head of the rubber chicken that came into use when he and the announcer had to resort to chicken thief jokes, and handy in the bib pocket was the hairwork braid for the other surefire gag where he grabbed a bull's tail and it appeared to come off in his hand.

Weary and filthy as he was, while the action was suspended this way Monty felt almost like he was back at one of the Sunday picnics along Noon Creek, standing around at the edge of the chute crowd like this; something like peace. When he and his mother used to go to those church picnics, they would pause as soon as they were in sight of everybody but just out of hearing. "Well, Montgomery, the two colored people are here," his mother would say solemnly. He would giggle, without entirely knowing why, and Angel Momma would laugh way down in her throat, and then the two of them would take their dark faces amid all the white ones. Well, *that* hadn't changed. The backs of Monty's hands as he comically put up his dukes in challenge to the reluctant bull in the chute were a burnished dark brown that resembled the oiled saddle leather all around him in this rodeo arena, but he was as aware as ever that his color was not repeated on any face within sight.

Including his own. From brow to jaw, and ear to ear, Monty's face was white with theatrical makeup. This of course was the main joke, that he was scared white.

By now Whitney Williamson was parting the sea of riders and hangers-on who were milling around in front of the chutes, on his way to see why three men could not deal with one bull, and Monty straightened up to his full height. It never hurt to be on your toes when the boss was around. That was how he had cozied into this, when word went around the ranch that the Williamson brother who ran the livestock side of things had bought up a string of bucking stock. The very next morning, quick as he was done with the milking chores, Monty stuck his head in the boss's office off the kitchen and mentioned that he'd heard Mister Whit was turning into a rodeo producer and if he happened to be hard up for someone to do that clown job, here stood a person fool enough to try. Whit looked him up and down—young enough yet and built on springs; a bit of a cutup on payday since he was off his mother's apron strings, but it didn't matter to the ranch how a man behaved in town—and saw no particular reason why the Double W choreboy couldn't give it a whirl, on rodeo weekends; somebody had to put on the clown getup.

That had been a dozen rodeos ago and here they were at the last and biggest of them all, in the fairgrounds of the capital of Montana. As was their custom, the Williamsons were using the occasion to play both ends against the middle. Somewhere up there in the shaded side of the stands would be Wesley Williamson with Helena society and the money men from as far away as Boston and New York, while Whit ramrodded the show down here at the level of hooves and horns. The ways of the Williamsons were beyond Monty, the manner in which they divvied up being in charge while leaving the impression it was merely the natural order of things, but it didn't especially matter to him either. Like the other hands on the WW ranch who'd been chosen to try their luck at putting on rodeos, such as Dolph and the stock handlers and the unfortunates trying to pry that bull loose, he was along for the ride, so to speak.

Right about now he could have used a sample of that grandstand shade. He mopped himself some more, taking care not to touch the mask of makeup; he figured he knew at least that much about how a woman felt. It was Mister Whit, who had traveled and knew about these things, who decreed the whiteface cosmetic: "Those minstrel shows, they put on blackening. Be kind of funny if you did the opposite, wouldn't it?" Monty saw the point.

At last there was hope at the chute; the horn was grating out from between the planks after great contortions by all involved. A minute or so more, and he'd be matching wits with a bull again. He dug himself a starting place with the heel of each boot, stretched down and cleared away pebbles of any size, checked once more that the barrel was sited right. Stood ready again.

"Hard to wash all that off, ain't it?"

There is no known cure for what the human voice can carry. Sickened at the insinuating tone, at having to calculate how to deal with this, even out here with the crowd sunny and contented, Monty turned his head not too fast and not too slow to find where the remark had come from.

The telltale expression was on one of the calf ropers lounging around the end of the chutes, he and a pal putting rosin on their lariats. *Explains it some.* Calf ropers didn't have enough on their minds, their event wasn't any harder than tying their shoes. He never heard much from the bull riders; they didn't care what color the man was who let the bull chase him instead of them. With a practiced eye Monty tried to read the frogmouth grins on this pair of lasso twirlers. It always rankled him, a thing like this, from one of the bunkhouse boys or anybody at large. You get so sick of it you're a walking piece of resentment, he could have testified to the world. Again now he banked the anger he didn't dare let flame up. Maybe he was going to be lucky, maybe the show-off one was joshing about the whiteface makeup.

"Oh, I shine up pretty good when I want to," Monty put to him past the greasepaint smile.

"I'm sort of curious about what you use on yourself," the first roper persisted, the other one looking uneasy. "Stove black?"

"LIE," the sound rolled from the depths of Monty's lungs, surprising him as much as the two of them. Both of the ropers were staring at him now, hard.

"Lye soap," Monty sang out, no boom to his voice this time. "Ain't you heard, us boys who've still got the bark on us, we can scrub up good with that and it don't hurt a bit."

The one who'd started this gave him a last narrow look, then grunted and sauntered away. The other roper tagged after him and Monty overheard:

"You maybe ought to let up on him. He's the Williamsons' pet pup."

"Aw, hell, I was only funnin'."

"You find your check in your plate in the morning and a walk to town with your bedroll, you won't think fun."

"Jesus, what's life comin' to."

The megaphone of the announcer heralded readiness in the chute at last, and Monty went back to a bullfighter frame of mind.

This bull erupted sideways from the chute, a side of beef writhing eerily in the air the instant before it struck the ground with all four hooves extended, the rider clinging on but in trouble. *Damn. This one would have to be a twister.* Monty danced from one foot to the other behind the upright barrel, the red handkerchief held ready behind his back. He wasn't to make his move until the whistle blew at the end of the ride or the rider was bucked off. This bull's third jump, the man on his back went flying. Instantly Monty scampered in to draw the animal's attention before it could wheel around and find the figure pancaked into the arena dirt.

The bull turned toward Monty faster than he wanted, and he backed off a step. Just that little half-dance set off titters of anticipation in the crowd. Audiences were the damnedest creatures.

Some bulls stood there in confusion at the sight of the clown, some tamely turned away. This one lowered its head and looked like it meant business. "If you like the look of my tracks so much, I'll make you some more," Monty loudly chanted to the animal for the crowd's benefit, then backpedaled until he had the barrel between him and the danger of the horns. When the bull charged one way, he dodged to the other side of the barrel. Back and forth, beast and man, like drunks trying to navigate past one another in a narrow space. This was another part the crowd ate up.

He knew the time had come to hop into the barrel, the bull was getting good and mad. Hesitated a moment. He'd had enough rides in the barrel for one day. He bolted for the fence at the far side of the arena, sprinting as hard as he could.

The bull blinked once at this turn of events and took off after him.

Running for his life, Monty had the presence of mind to hold the red handkerchief out at arm's length and daintily drop it, as if the bull were a suitor. The crowd howled. The arena fence was proving to be farther than he'd figured, but steadily drawing nearer. According to the bawling, so was the bull. *Best advice I can give you is not to fall,* the Calgary old-timer was cackling in his head.

He aimed for a stout corral post—if you made your jump onto the middle of a section of plank fence and the bull plowed it out from under you, then you were in a hell of a fix—and leaped, grabbing for the post with both arms and pulling his legs up under him. The fence shuddered below him as the bull slammed into it, but he was high and dry, and at that moment full of complete joy at having pulled off the stunt. *What could be better?* the triumphant chorus in the loft of his brain sang all through the rest of him. The bull down there in a fit of snot and slobber and other fluids of rage, himself perched up here a bit out of breath but otherwise cozy, the big Helena crowd yowling in his favor: he'd take this a thousand times in a row.

Dolph rode up to encourage the bull to the exit gate, then reined around to check on the puff-cheeked clown as he slid down off the fence. Hands on his thighs as he spent a minute getting his wind back, Monty admitted: "This is getting to be a long day."

"One more go-round and you can quit teasing the livestock," Dolph commiserated.

There was a break in the action now while the chutes were being reloaded, this time with broncs. Dolph dismounted and Monty swung up into the saddle and slumped there like the end-of-the-trail Indian while Dolph led the horse across the arena, another surefire act. The dried-up little cowboy walked as if his feet hated to touch the ground, which was not an act at all.

When they got over by the chutes Monty slipped smoothly off the horse and Dolph tied the reins to the arena fence.

"Monty?" The pickup man inclined his head in the direction of the bull pen. "You don't want to run too many of them footraces with these bastards."

"I'll have to remember that."

"It makes for quite a show, though," Dolph granted with a chortle, "you lighting out across there with that bull's horns tickling your hip pocket." He sized up the riders and ropers and hangers-on clotted around the chutes. "Now's a good a time as any to pass the hat for our hardworking rodeo clown, don't you think?"

"I been paid," Monty said swiftly. "Mister Whit already—"

Dolph looked as if he hadn't heard right. "What's that have to do with the price of peas in China? You got something against extra money?"

"Not so I ever noticed," Monty stalled. He'd known Dolph longer than he could remember; Dolph himself was a stray who was riding the grub line about the same time the Double W took in Monty's mother as washerwoman. Yet he found he didn't want to tell Dolph, right out, that there had been that run-in with the mouthy roper.

"So how about it?" Dolph persisted. "Halvers?"

Monty glanced again at the men along the chutes. Everybody looked to be in good cheer, beer-induced or otherwise, but you never knew. He drew out deciding until Dolph started giving him a funny look, then nodded. *Go for broke, why not. Last show of the season, any hoodoos in the bunch will have all winter to get over me.* "If you're gonna be the one that does it, Dolphus, sure."

Dolph already had his Stetson in one hand and was fishing into his jeans pocket with his other. "I'm the man what can." He held up a fifty-cent piece as if to fix the specific coin into Monty's memory. "We split halves *after* my four bits is out of the take, got that?"

"You drive a hard bargain," Monty laughed in spite of himself. He watched the skinny sawed-off cowboy gimp away on his collecting round.

"DOLPH!"

Frozen in his tracks, Dolph cast a look back over his shoulder. That voice on Monty; when he wanted to, he sounded like a church organ letting loose. "What?"

"Be sure and trade the chicken feed in at the beer booth for silver dollars, would you?" Monty's tone was shy now.

Dolph snorted. "It all spends, on Clore Street. Don't worry, Snowball, I'll git you dollars."

As Dolph set to work with the hat, Monty stood there loose-jointed and private, the middle of him warming with anticipation of Clore Street. Silver dollars were definitely the ticket. Like in the blues he'd heard the last time he hit town. *Flat to stack and round to roll / Silver dollar, lift my soul.* Not that he had any use for the blues, but good sound cartwheel money, he most certainly did. Tied in the bottom of his side pocket right now was one of those little cloth sacks that Bull Durham tobacco came in, with the ten silver dollars Mister Whit had paid him. If Dolph did well with the chute crowd, as much as another ten might be added to the sack and that was a full Bull bag. Drop one of those on the wood of a bar and you could start to get somewhere in life. In his head he began parceling out the twenty lovely coins across town. The Zanzibar Club: the trick was to hit it early, not so many to buy drinks for. The trainmen came off shift at eight, the porters and brakemen from Chicago and Kansas City piling in to hear the music and have the company of other dark faces here in the white, white West. Things started happening in the Zanzibar then. Those KC boys made him nervous, though, calling him "Sticks" and "Mon*tan*" as though it was his fault he had been born out here instead of on the corner of Twelfth and Vine. And Montgomery Rathbun had as much name as anybody, if the world would ever use it.

So, hoist a few in the Zanzibar before the KC boys hit town, then try to find that sporting girl from last time, the one who took it slow. Couldn't pray for something that fine to happen every time, but it didn't hurt to hope. When a man came to town all stored up, he didn't want a hurrying woman. Then the fantan game, in the Chinese gambling place. He should have half his money left by the time he drifted into the game, and with a stake like that there was every chance he could win back what he spent at the Zanzibar and the cathouse. Head on home to the ranch with a good stake for next time, even.

He watched Dolph passing the hat and saw with relief that the rodeo contestants each were chipping in their four bits, no complaints. Even the loudmouth roper tossed in when Dolph jawed at him. Monty felt like a man whose ship had come in. He hummed a snatch of "Silver Wings and a Golden Harp."

By nightfall the Bull Durham sack was flat empty.

GATES OF THE MOUNTAINS

· 1924 ·

"YOU'RE AWFULLY quiet, Susan."

"Such a place, there is everything in the world to be quiet about." Even her declarative tone was rounded off by the murmur of the Missouri River. "I could pinch myself. Half my life I've spent in Helena, and I've never once been out here."

Wes yanked down on the brim of his hat one more notch. "We could do without this wind." A sharper gust through the canyon buffeted the excursion boat as he spoke. "I hope it doesn't snatch Monty's breath away."

In the sway of the bow, like a bundled statue being borne into a white-walled port, Susan stood braced as she gazed ahead to the Gates of the Mountains. Half the sky of her younger years had been the arching northern palisades of the Rockies, but here the mountains made fists. Precipice after precipice stood guard over these waters, pale limestone cliffs materializing straight up out of the river and lifting forests on their shields of stone and catching on their summits the fresh flags of snow. Every whiff of air held the scent of pine. Off to starboard—at least she still knew right from left—a stand of snow-flecked jackpines on the nearest clifftop filtered what there was of the early-spring sun through the shade of their branches, and she watched this lattice of the seasons until the river left it behind. As the boat puttered deeper into the corridor of channel, Wes kept himself propped against the deck railing near her, resting his leg and evidently his thoughts as well. Her own mind was a maddening merry-go-round, thanks to him. When she insisted on auditioning Monty in private, but someplace spacious to hear how his voice carried, Wes simply commandeered a mountain range.

Williamsons had always owned.

Susan turned her head just enough to study him as he bent to coil a mooring rope that didn't pass muster, seeing in the intent lines of his face the Wes Williamson she had seen the first time ever, eternally tending to details. At the time she was twelve and snippy and inseparable from her father, particularly on trips to town, and they had gone in to the stockyards at Conrad to settle up with the railroad agent on the shipping of their lambs. Commotion bawled out over the prairie from the loading pens. "Ninian Duff! And Ninian's likeness!" the shout came from on high, the ringmaster of cattle himself, old Warren Williamson in the catbird perch above the cutting chute. "Come to see what real livestock looks like?" Susan's father had begun with cattle and advanced to sheep, and along the way contended for every spear of grass with this range potentate and his bony-hipped Double W specimens. From day one Ninian Duff knew when to stand his ground, and now he barked a laugh and shouted back: "Livestock are those, Williamson? Here I thought the flea circus had come to town." Taking their time about it, the two Duffs approached the corral, bearded scarecrow of a man and gangly girl in overalls, and climbed up to inspect the mooing mess. The cattle were being chuted into railroad cars: dogs worked at their heels, dismounted riders stamped around trying to look useful, the stockbuyer slapped the corral boards with a tasseled whip thin as a wand. The herd of brown-red backs was wound tight against the end of the corral, a rivulet of steers banging up the high-walled ramp into the railcar. Down there in the muck hazing his crew as they hazed the cattle was the next of the Williamson breed, Whit, being trained by his father to run the Double W ranch in the next valley over from the Duff homestead.

At her father's side above the milling cattle Susan fiercely took it all in, allotting grudge where she knew it was due—to the grabby

Williamsons, high and low—and something like hunger toward every other face around her. The poor riders, unfit on foot. The stockbuyer, like a big gray jay in his suit of gabardine. The familiar thicket of dark whiskers that marked her father's ever authoritative presence, at the near corner of her vision. Faces, she had decided, were the first letters of stories all around a person. So, she was at the stage of ravenous wondering about anyone within range of her eyes, and lately that included the father whom everybody said she was such a tracing of.

"Ay, Williamson," her father hooted across the corral to Warren as a steer broke back past his swearing son, "any cows ever I had could knit socks with their horns. These seem to be wanting in mentality, not to mention poundage."

Then and there she caught sight of Wes, his expression minted into her memory the way a likeness is stamped onto a fresh coin. He had been half-hidden next to the stockbuyer, flipping through the shipping papers, but her father's gibe brought him immediately hand over hand to the top of the corral, still clutching the paperwork like a crumpled bouquet. She knew him without ever having laid eyes on him before: Whit's brother, the citified member of the family, the one everyone said was the brains of the litter. She kept her gaze glued to him as he poised atop the corral across from her father and her. It had been drilled into Susan, as only recitative Scotch parents could drill, that it was rude to stare. But to really see you had to keep looking. To this day she could bring back that expression on Wes as he studied her father the way he would a wild creature. For her age Susan knew a substantial amount about life. She had grasped almost as soon as he did that her teacher at the South Fork was dreadfully in love with the new schoolma'am over on Noon Creek. She had deduced for herself that the drugstore owner Musgreave's "vacations" to Minneapolis were to dry out from whiskey. She knew with the instinct of a child on a borrowing homestead that her father regarded banker Potter in Gros Ventre as a grabber second only to the Williamsons and that was why they did their banking here in the county seat instead. The Scotch Heaven neighbors, she had down cold—the Speddersons would exert themselves only to avoid work, the Frews were tight as ticks where money was involved, the Erskines would lend you the elbows out of their sleeves, the Barclays kept everything *up* their sleeves—and accepted the principle that each family had some exception that proved the rule. But whatever this look on Wesley Williamson's face represented was beyond her.

They were near enough to Warren Williamson on his cutting-chute throne that he didn't need to shout, but he shouted anyway:

"I'll tell you again, Duff, I want you Scotch Heaven lamb lickers off that Roman Reef range. We've always grazed up in through there."

Her father leveled a stare across the backs of the cattle to the elder Williamson. Then said in his biblical timbre:

"You ought to know by now Scotch Heaven hangs its hat wherever it pleases."

In that exchange of thunders Susan had seen something, and if she had, the young man so intent across the corral surely must have: in the contest of the fathers there at the stockyard, Warren Williamson looked away first.

Aboard the touring boat, the ancient impatience of water moving them steadily into the mountains, she scrutinized Wes as he placed the coil of rope where it belonged. A quarter of a century and then some, on the visage across that corral; the same Wes but more so, if that was conceivable. The boxer's jawline. The philosophical eyes. Jack Dempsey met the jack of spades in that face. After all her trying, in love and its opposite, this was still the greatest of puzzles to her, the different ways of adding up Wes.

He met her gaze for a moment, smiled but kept the silence, then they both turned again to the Gates of the Mountains.

"Have I got it right, that we're out here freezing our tails so's you can sing to us?" the boatman, Harris, was asking Monty.

"This is a new one on me, but that's about the size of it," Monty responded, only half there in conversation but by habit trying to keep his end up, even with this sour looker. He warmed his hands over the boat engine. "Probably the Major didn't order this wind. Throw it in free, did you?"

Harris hunched farther into his mackinaw and steered toward the middle of the river, giving plenty of leeway to the blunt set of cliffs rearing at the next bend.

Exhilarated, apprehensive, and all the rest, Monty took a gulp of the spring air, to clear his thinking as much as he could. *There ain't much I can't do some of, by now. But this?* The most he had been counting on was to-the-point advice from the Major, or possibly a word put in somewhere, or if he really hit it lucky, a nice dab of loan. (*Draw some wages ahead* was always the way you wanted to put that.) So he could have been knocked over with a feather when the Major proclaimed, "I know just the medicine," and produced the music teacher and this dizzying excursion. But then the Major wasn't someone whose thinking a person could always follow.

"Say, how many horses you got going on this pirate ship?" Monty threw out, to get the boatman to talking again. Around somebody like him, best way to be was to listen more than you spoke.

"About a dozen. Who wants to know?" Harris eyed him as if he resented the challenge to the boat's horsepower.

The Duesenberg had ninety. "Just wondering. I been around engines quite a little bit myself." Deciding this was one of those times when there was something to be said for silence after all, Monty clammed up and warmed his hands again in the radiated heat from the cylinder block. Fingers long and tapered but strong from years of milking cows; pinkish palms that had known their share of calluses— these hands had been his ticket to chauffeuring, that time during his recuperation when he took it upon himself to tinker Mister Whit's junked Model T back to life, handling each part of the stripped-down engine until he could have assembled them in bed under the covers. "Handy" was one thing that meant what it said. With all due satisfaction he recalled washing these hands over and over at the end of each day spent in the grease, carefully cleaning under the fingernails with the point of his jackknife blade, to look slick as a whistle when he sat up to the Double W supper table with the hard-used riders and haying crews. Done their job, too, these hands; flagged the Major's attention when he looked around for someone new to be his car man after Frenchy went on one drinking spree too many. Monty kept on rubbing them here for circulation and luck. Now to see what his voicebox could manage.

The hum came without his even inviting it.

You know how you get at the end of the road,
Trying to stand up under life's load.

The memory voice came along with it. *"Can you sing that one by*
yourself, Monty? Momma's momma taught me it, when I was little like you.
Here, I'll help you with it."

Done in and done up and down to a speck.
That's when the right word will lighten your trek.

Whatever that word was, in this life.

Still needing to assure himself this was really happening to him,
he sneaked another look around the boat. The Major and the music
mistress at the bow, taking in the sights. The Swede couple who took
care of the Major's Helena house, huddling under the canvas canopy
bewildered as chickens. Himself and Harris, chauffeurs by land and
water. Six folks total on an excursion craft that would hold, what,
fifty?

The boatman had followed his gaze around the vessel. "Normal
people, I don't take out here this soon in the year," Harris muttered.

Like to meet any of those in this lifetime, normal, Monty's mind raced
on. *But the man has a point. "Normal" wouldn't cut it for a shindig like*
this. Notions jittered in him today like fancywear on a clothesline. It
was boggling: a different life to fit over the one he already had on?
Was there enough of him to change into all that? Let his imagination
tailor it and there was. If he could get trained up for it, maybe he
could show the world something this time around. New York, even.
And right away caught himself letting his hopes run too high; there
was also every chance his bright idea of becoming a real singer was
going to be over the instant he didn't make his mouth work right for
that woman up there in the bow.

To be doing something besides picturing himself in full song
beneath chandeliers that scintillated like the diamonds in the neck-
laces and stickpins of the rapt audience one moment and envisioning
himself pucker-mouthed and mute as a trout in front of this music

woman the next instant, Monty craned out enough to catch a glimpse of the higher reaches of the Big Belt mountains. Gulches to nowhere, slabs of cliff around every corner, round-shouldered summits that didn't amount to that much. Not like the resounding wide-open Two Medicine country he was lifelong used to, with its dune shapes of the Sweetgrass Hills way over east there with the prairie in between as if they were pretty mirages that miraculously never faded, and the mighty reefs of the Rockies pushing up everywhere into the sky to the west. But he had to admit this river was quite a thing, rolling its way mile after mile through rock-solid canyon. And dead-end views or not, the low mountains stacked around the canyon showed nice clean fresh snow on their slopes; good tracking snow. He half wished he was up there hunting, cutting the tracks of a bull elk in one of those open parks near timberline, instead of down here at this. But wishing was what had landed him into this, wasn't it.

Of its own accord his turned-up overcoat collar all at once drooped and let the wind in on him, surprising him the way nearly everything was surprising him today. No reason to be jumpy, he told himself as he turned the unruly collar back up. Yes, there was. White lady variety. They could be worse than the men. Treat you like some sort of moron who sleeps in the sheepdip trough. He sneaked another peek toward the bow of the boat and wondered again about this Miss Duff. Why wasn't she a Mrs. Duff, for starters? She looked lofty, although maybe it was only the altitude temperature that went with her being so ungodly tall for a woman. Whatever way she stacked up, the Major claimed she was the sharpest thing going, where training up a singing voice was involved.

Look at it like resorting to a doctor, one of those specialists; that was the point of view he was going to try to take. It would be a lot easier on the nerves, though, if her skin tone and his weren't as far apart as those white and black Scottie dog magnets he had played with as a boy, one capable of propelling the other across the floorboards simply by being the opposite kind. But that was the sort of principle he would have to put up with to get where he wanted to go, he resolved again.

That's if she even consented to take him on, after this. He could kick himself for the way he'd messed up back at the dock. "How do you do, again, Miss Susan," he'd heard come out of his mouth when she stepped aboard the boat and walked up to him as if examining a bad painting. He had no earthly idea why *again* hopped in there that way. It wasn't as if he was on speaking acquaintance with her— although he had heard enough talk about the Major and her, back a few years before he was driving for the Major—but somehow the fact that he and she both were products of the Two Medicine country seemed like a kind of knowing each other or each other's families or general circumstances of growing up there or some such. His try at conveying that, though, had come out sounding all too much like they were peas from the same pod.

Snooty wasn't quite the word for the way she'd stood there giving him a going over, or at least he hoped it wasn't. *Keen,* that was it, he tried to convince himself. Although maybe *starchy* said it better. Whatever the correct read of her was, she came right back at him with: "You seem to have caught the Major's ear, Mister Rathbun. Such a spot for a debut."

"He's giving me a good help, that's sure." He had not known what more to say about the Major providing all of outdoors as a music hall. Being a Williamson, the Major could do about anything he wanted, couldn't he. So, with that the two of them ran out of the makings of talk and he'd had to stand there like a mooring post while she and the Major went on with chitchat until the boat chugged to life and he headed to the stern in the natural gravitation of things.

What if he got buck fever, in front of her, and couldn't remember the words? Couldn't possibly forget words to something you'd known all your life. *"Sing with Momma while she washes, Montgomery. Ah* ah *AH! That's it, sing with Momma."* Just to make sure, he ran the song through his head again now.

Then what if he sang it word-perfect and she still said she had heard a better voice on a bullfrog?

Nervously he rubbed an eyebrow with the knuckle of his thumb. Nobody around but the clam running the boat and the dumb-cluck couple to watch him make a fool of himself, at least. That hadn't been the case often enough lately, he reflected with overdue wisdom as the boat slowed to an aquatic waddle in the presence of the most imposing cliffs yet. He grimaced, the reminder of his last time in town still so fresh. The dustup over his fantan debt, nothing really hurt except his dignity; but on top of that, the brush-off from Leticia. A man could hardly come to town anymore without getting treated like Job's dog. "Leticia?" those joyboys in the Zanzibar had razzed him unmercifully. "Call out the militia!" This time his wince cut all the way to the heart. He had been stuck on Leticia. She wasn't street baggage, she was a good decent copper-brown woman with a part-interest in a millinery establishment and a sideline in cosmetics. He had sounded her out on marriage, even. And received: "You're a lovely man, Monty, but you are no provider." Quite a lot about life he had learned to laugh off, but when Leticia let him have it with both barrels that way, it registered deep. Off she had gone with that slickback head waiter from the Broadwater Hotel, and that was that.

Maybe it had taken him too long to get himself in gear, maybe he shouldn't have needed yet another dose of Clore Street to teach him. But in any case he had dragged his tail back to the ranch admitting to himself that life as he was practicing it was never going to provide beyond what it already did—the room on the back end of the washhouse, the choreboy's place at the long table three times a day, and wages that were gone before you could clink the dollars together. Which is why he had mustered himself and asked the proper source:

"Major? You know anything about those singers, on stage and that?"

"Pity." Wes was peering critically at the Missouri's volume of water, already running high with the first of spring melt against the shoreless base of the cliffs.

"What is?"

"Oh, nothing. It would've made a wonderful place to put a railroad through."

"You and your railroad notion," Susan made fun of him. "You would levitate it, would you?" Actually, it occurred to her, magic carpets were his stock in trade. Wes had but to say *presto and keep the change* and this steam launch awaited where the Missouri swept into the mountains. Monty and the Doozy presenting themselves at the dock, both looking newly spiffed up. Susan herself had been royally fetched from Highland Street by Wes's household couple, although she had stiffened when she learned the Gustafsons—Mrs. Gus's middle name was Nosey, Gus's was Gloomy—were to be her escorts. In the past she had asked Wes why on earth he kept them on, and he had pondered and then said he supposed it was because they provided all the discomforts of home.

"An outing for the servants, is this to be?" she had jabbed him with, this time around.

"Your old friendship with Mrs. Gustafson must be kept green." Then in his married tone: "It's that usual matter, how things have to look. Please, Susan."

Clasping her scarf to her throat against another incursion of the raw wind, she glanced back along the length of the boat. Mr. and Mrs. Gus sat shivering, dressed too lightly. Susan had little sympathy. Sweden was not exactly a Mediterranean clime, why did the Gustafsons think Montana's latitude would be balmy?

She centered her attention back on the matter of Monty. The taproot of talent is ambition. This man was quite far along in life to be wanting a career; what had he been saving himself for until now? Not to mention far along the palette of pigmentation, compared to the flesh tones of the audiences he seemed to crave. Yet she knew he had already come some way up in life. The dawn-and-dusk chores of the Duff homestead would never leave her, and when she multiplied those by what must be the drudgeries asked of a choreboy on a ranch as huge as the Double W, yes, this Monty person had come considerably up. The emphatic crease of his trousers, the good hat. And he smartly wore a greatcoat, nearly as capacious as that on Wes. She wondered how he and his mother had ever alit with the Williamsons: two shakes of pepper in that salt-white confederacy of riders and masters.

She kept watch on him now as Wes beckoned him from the stern. He had a roomy chest, which gave her hope. Ropy in build, and as yet he had no belly to speak of. Full-lipped, but no more so than the beesting look that was popular on motion-picture women. Glowering brows, but his eyes did not seem to start off with any color grudge; not quite crafty in look, thank goodness, but taking in more than he seemed to, if she knew anything about human nature. No prominent Adam's apple to bob up and down disconcertingly while he sang, she was glad to note. And small ears, tight to his head. Hair that hadn't been fiddled with, no misplaced faith in doses of straightener. Spotless hands and fingernails. In outward appearance, she was forced to admit, so far so good with Montgomery Rathbun, songbird on the edge of the Williamson nest.

"All of a sudden you feel that it's due him?" she had tried to press Wes.

"You might say that."

"Him in particular? I'm only asking."

"Why so suspicious? You make it sound as if I have more motives than Rasputin. Isn't the glimmer of a voice enough for you to go on?"

"Wes, you yourself say that your ear is straight from the tinsmith."

"I knew what I was hearing when I first heard you, didn't I?"

There was a fluster at the center of the boat as Mrs. Gustafson scurried out from under the canopy and announced noon by pointing to the sun. She brought forth the dinner basket: fresh baked bread, headcheese, boiled eggs. A lard can of doughnuts.

"It's a hard-and-fast rule of the profession," Susan headed this off, "that Mister Rathbun must sing with an empty stomach."

"Then we'll listen, in hungry concert," Wes pronounced. He looked around at the cliffs, like opera-house walls grown to five hundred feet: La Scala fashioned out of a fjord. "Will this do?" He seemed to be serious.

Susan smiled ever so slightly. "As good a place as any."

"Harris, can you let us drift?" Wes called to the launch operator. As soon as the engine was shut off, the silence was overpowering. The wind stirred the swags of branches far above them, but evidently was blocked by the oxbow turn of the river.

At Susan's nod, Monty took a position in the center of the boat. She was dismayed to see he stood like a cowboy, hip-sprung, spraddled. But then that's what he was, among a confusing number of other things, she reminded herself.

Here goes nothing from nowhere, he tried to bolster the inside of his head with the chant that breathed luck on a pair of dice, sometimes. As if feeling the need for correction in her look, he grasped the lapels of his coat, thought better of that stance, and let his hands drop to his sides. There they opened and closed. He drew in an audible, open-mouthed breath, but no sound issued forth. Standing as if rooted to the deck, he discovered he was dry-lipped, dry-mouthed, dry-throated, a desert down to the moons of his toenails. *Be there,* he implored his voice. "Excuse me one moment," he half coughed out, went over beneath the canopy and swigged from a glass of the lemonade Mrs. Gustafson had thought to welcome spring with, then returned to his amidship spot.

It dawned on Susan that Wes was making this hard for him, depositing him out here in this magnificence, proffering him his moment in grand style, testing him. Deliberately?

"Ready when you are, Monty," issued from Wes now, not exactly an order but close enough.

Stiff as a cactus, Monty aimed himself at the crowding cliffs and suddenly let out:

> *"Go down, Moses,*
> *Way down in Egypt land—"*

There was a catch of breath, Monty's and everybody else's, then he sang on in a tone as deep as the sound of a bronze bell.

> *"Tell old Pharaoh*
> *To let my people go.*
>
> *When Israel was in Egypt land,*
> *Let my people go.*
> *Oppressed so hard, she could not stand,*
> *Let my people go."*

Wes listened with everything in him, the song taking him back through time. Back nearly as long as he could remember, Angeline Rathbun's spirituals hovered over the white clotheslines behind the ranch house, indeed like angelic sea chanties wafting above a ship under sail. The carry of Monty's voice, though, except when he sang while at his barn chores, had mostly been in evidence at branding time and roundup, when the other riders would encourage him to yell the cattle down out of distant coulees. That, and shouting tag ends of jokes to his interlocutor, the announcer, in his rodeo period. This might mend that, and more. *If he has it in him. If she can't resist seeing if he has it in him.* That skinny compass-needle word, *if.* All the directions it could waver to. But he had given this due thought, in many a long night, and come back to his starting point, the overpowering urge that now was the time if—that, again—the needful was ever to happen. It just might work. *Please.* Listening to Monty now, Wes put his head down and focused on the upside-down steeple of his fingertips meeting, very much as he did when he was in the confessional.

Susan keenly watched Monty's every breath, as the echoes chorused off the cliffwalls.

> *"You'll not get lost in the wilderness,*
> *Let my people go,*
> *With a lighted candle in your breas',*
> *Let my people go.*
>
> *Go down, Moses,*
> *Way down in Egypt land,*
> *Tell old Pharaoh*
> *To let my people go."*

When he finished, the Gustafsons hesitantly beat their mittened hands in applause. The boatman leaned forward in fascination. Wes nodded firm encouragement to Monty. Five faces now turned toward Susan.

"Again, please, Mister Rathbun."

Monty sagged.

"Don't be down in the mouth," Wes consoled at once. "She's known to be hard to please."

"If you could possibly hold off on the man-to-man sympathy," Susan shushed him. "Mister Rathbun? Again?"

"Miss Susan, honest, that's as good as I can do."

She seemed surprised. "Then simply do it the same. I'm sorry, but one time through a song is not being a *singer*. That's merely"—she searched for an uncritical set of words—"whistling with your voicebox. Mister Rathbun, I need to hear certain things again in how you managed that song. I thought that's why we're here." She locked eyes with him, the stare that had conquered a thousand pupils. "Now then."

Wes broke their deadlock. "Harris?" He twirled a finger at the boatman, and the launch coughed to life and turned back upriver to where Monty had aimed his voice at the canyon amphitheater. As soon as the engine was cut, Monty squared away, with his eyes closed this time against the skinning-knife challenge of Susan's, and in slow measure summoned up from wherever he could reach in himself:

"Go down, Moses . . ."

When the last echo expended itself, Wes clapped once, hard, and swung around to Susan. "Well?"

"Well."

"Susan, blast you," Wes was nearly laughing in exasperation, Monty scarcely daring to breathe, "what's the verdict?"

NINIAN'S LAND

· 1924 ·

Scotch Heaven may not have amounted to much as a site, but you cannot beat it as a sight.

—from the diary of Susan Duff

SUSAN SCRUBBED THE floor a second time. The homestead house had stood empty a half dozen years. Almost the same could be said of the valley.

The world was definitely a different habitat on hands and knees. Her kneeling parts ached and her knuckles were red from the harsh washwater as she attacked the uneven pine floorboards with the scrub brush, round two. Cows had been in here; Whit Williamson's drizzling cows, *Wes's* drizzling cows, depending on whichever end of the beasts he held title to in the Double W scheme of things.

Troughs of the past pooled with sudsy water as she slaved away at the old floor. The oblong worn spot in front of the cookstove where her mother had fended, morning, noon, and night, for thirty years. *"Susan, see to Samuel, pretty please. The taties are refusing to boil, the devils."* Over there where the table had sat, the most seriously rubbed groove was the spot where her father's sizable workshoes shuffled. *"A man needs a firm understanding,"* topmost in the tiny horde of jokes he allowed himself. Her father could quarrel with the wind, then turn around and recite from heart the most lilting Bible passage. It picked at her that contradictions were still the fare of this house. Ninian Duff had swept into this pocketed-away valley on the North Fork of English Creek in 1887 with a bemused wife and a daughter inquisitive beyond her three years of life and a ramrod determination to make his chosen acres of American earth a homesteaded Eden, whether or not the given ground had those ingredients. Ninian's land, all this had been called, even the pasture domain up under the mountains that was nowhere on the proving-up papers of the homestead and was now national forest. *And here I am, back at his old haunt. I can hear him now. "Ay, Susan, we couldn't have kept you in Scotch Heaven with heavy fetters, and here you are back because of a notion worth its weight in moonbeams?"* Her scrub brush retaliated with furious vigor on a floorboard. She knew the chapters of her life did not sit well together, she didn't need telling by the echoes here.

In mid-swipe at the next offending floorboard she froze. Motion and furriness where none should be, in the open doorway.

She jerked her head up as the ragged ball of gray settled into cat pose, at ease on its haunches, ready to be waited on.

"You're prompt," Susan addressed it, "wherever you've been mooching previous to now."

The cat licked its chops remindfully.

"Shoo. Scoot now. There's not a drop of milk, canned or by the squirt, on the premises yet. Later." She dipped her fingers in the bucket and flicked washwater at the cat, which flinched, thought matters over, and stalked out.

The vagrant cat dispatched, she made herself simmer down and take stock of what all else needed doing to make the place livable. Except for the want of a door, the house was still in one piece, at least. Windows were filthy, the years of grime and fly life on them, but they would feel washwater before the day was out. The roof seemed sound, although she knew the test of that would arrive with the first cloudburst down out of the Rockies. Other necessities for her stay here— the pump at the well outside that gaping doorway, the cookstove and stovepipe, the outhouse—she had found to be cranky with age but in working order. By nightfall, assuming that Whit Williamson's roustabouts didn't tip over in a coulee with her truckload of promised furniture on the rutted road into here, she would be installed in a reasonably presentable household or keel over in the attempt.

So, about to be all in, one way or another, here she was, intrigued with this familiar old stranger of a place one minute and very nearly terminally exasperated with it the next. It served her right, she knew she would need to admit to the diary, if this interminable day ever produced a night to sit down in.

"Why me, though?" she had tackled Wes after the day at the Gates of the Mountains. "Male music teachers exist, scads of them."

Always one for fine points, Wes could be seen honing his reply before he offered it. "You have edge, and I mean that as a compliment. If Monty is going to be serious about this singing, it'll do him good to see how you bear down on things."

"I can apply 'edge,' as you more or less nicely put it, as well here in Helena as on the North Fork, Wes."

"Helena has its distractions. I don't want Monty's head bothered by anything except toeing the line for you."

She fathomed that there was more to it than that: discretion, for Wes's sake one more weary time, and her own if that mattered anymore, and poor dark Montgomery Rathbun's as well. Everything of Wes's, said and unsaid, could be truer than true and for her this still was a flit out the coop door that happened to have peeped open. The well-furnished solitude of the weeks ahead she could not bring herself to pass up. A chance to catch up and reflect, and, with enough piano time and lined paper, to woo her operetta to completion at last. After all, she pointed out to herself with a rueful twitch of her lips, music is the only lust you can do justice by yourself.

And all the while obligated only to one pupil, the likes of which she had never had in all her teaching, instead of the ceaseless succession of Helena muffets and their impresario mothers. *But the pupil it is? An academy of music here just for him? Never mind the impenetrable head of Wes, have I gone out of mine?* Every kind of doubt applied, despite her best efforts to send them on their way. Absconded to New York meanwhile, Wes had, to spend time in the shallow bosom of his marriage. Susan allowed herself a vixen smile over that, but her mood returned as she had to stoke up the reluctant old stove to heat a bucket of rinse water.

Before the next bout of scrubbing, she stepped outside and took her leisure at the perimeter of the yard, idly whacking cockleburrs and nettles out of her way with a stick. Nearby, the creek ducked past behind its stand of diamond willows, plump at their ends with bud-break. A well-behaved school of white clouds coasted over the highest peaks to the west. Door or no door, Susan conceded, she at least had lucked into the picture-perfect time of the North Fork valley, with wild hay surging in the bottomland along the creek and fresh grass on the buttes and foothills that tilted the valley to the spring sun. On a day such as this when the clear air was a delicate shellac on every detail of each gray-blue pillaring cliff, the mountains castled up even closer than she had remembered over the Duff homestead and the dozen other deserted ones of Scotch Heaven.

Green-stained stick in her hand, Susan stood stock-still for a minute and listened with all her might.

The silence. Eloquent of the space, of the reach of country here along the footings of the Rockies, the cathedral-rise of the continent into the blue stillness of sky, the prairie unrolling from the other horizon like Bedouin tarpaulin.

Her ears took in the solitude while her mind stayed busy with the comings and goings of the dead and the momentarily absent. This place's traffic of presences, of one shade or another. Not that she at all believed in the specter world, but right now she rather wished she was capable of it. Ghosts ought to be interesting company, she reasoned, particularly here. Not gauzy visitors who popped out of walls and gabbed when least expected; she could do without those. But why shouldn't leftover spirits, to call them that, constitute a kind of echo of the soul, lingering tunelike in the air after life was gone? A nocturne, she wouldn't be surprised: ruminative, tending toward melancholy— *after all, the poor things are no longer the freshest notes in the musical arrangement, are they*—yet with a serenade melody that would not leave the mind. Chopin, she decided, pensive a moment herself; Chopin surely would be the court musician of eternity's nightsingers. She wished her piano were here; the opening passage of her favorite of his pieces had found its way into her fingers and wanted out right then.

It took no real prompting to remind herself that she currently had enough concerns dealing with the living. To name the closest to mind—she lopped the head off a thistle with opinionated vigor—Whit Williamson, mastermind of trespassing cows. But bright and early tomorrow the matter would become Montgomery Rathbun, showing up here expecting to trade a chauffeur's polishing rag for the velvet stage curtains of Carnegie Hall. For better or worse, Scotch Heaven would have the human voice back in it tomorrow.

She listened again, as if her life depended on it.

Again, nothing met her ear but the cockleshell ring of silence. Instead, memory hinted behind her eyes everywhere her glance lit. Her mother, plump as a hen, forever there in the front room used for gatherings, trilling one of the songs of the old country with Donald and Jen Erskine or grandly matching installments of poetry with Angus McCaskill. Her father, whiskers down his chest, striding off up the slope to the scattered band of woolies with the fatalistic tread of that first keeper of sheep who ever came to grief, Abel. And Samuel. *Oh God of my father, where in the tune of things is there any explanation of Samuel?*

She squared her shoulders and went back in to where the scrub brush waited.

The sparkplugs lay in two rows on a clean gunnysack rag spread along the runningboard of the Duesenberg, like soldiers formed up on a tan field for the changing of the guard.

Monty fingered the new ones with respect, intrigued as he always was by the notion of bits of fire igniting gasoline in the cylinder heads. He twirled each fresh sparkplug into its place in the rank atop the engine, tightening down just so with a socket wrench. Try as he would, though, to confine himself to what his hands were doing, his mind insisted on going like sixty. *You are stark crazy, a man your age,* ran one line of self-argument about this notion of trying to turn himself into a singer at this stage of life. The other camp just as vigorously pointed out that a man gets in a rut, and the next thing you know, that rut is six feet deep and there's an epitaph over it.

So, try high or lay low. Things seemed to be going his way so far, quite the deal if he did say so himself. Hadn't the music teacher agreed to take him on? Wasn't the Major peeling off the money to cover it? But in each case, he had to wonder exactly why they were giving him a hand up like this. As he'd heard said in the Zanzibar, you could never be sure whether what white folks were passing you was pepper or fly grunt.

Overly picky, his mother would have called that sort of thinking. He extracted the last grimy sparkplug and spun a fresh one in. *There. Firing on all cylinders. That's where I better get myself to.* His engine work finished, he washed up and then applied Bag Balm to his hands to keep them nice, wishing he had something similar for his voice and for that matter the rest of the inside of his head. Tomorrow already he had to start lessons from the woman. Rubbing the balm in and in, he stood there beside the long yellow car for some minutes, looking off to the prairie he had been born to, and around at the Double W ranch buildings that were such home as he had ever had. The air had that spring freshness to it, winter shaken out and packed away in last snowdrifts far up in the Rockies; the mountains this day were blue, as if lightly tinted with clean pine smoke. He loved the Two Medicine country. The question was whether it loved him back. Except when he and Dolph were doing chores together or he and the Major went on a car trip, a lot of his life here was alone, dead-dog alone. Wouldn't get an echo back if he hollered, sometimes.

And the opposite wasn't a whole lot better, as far as he had found. When he was in the company of others—which, short of those rare Saturday nights when he could get to Helena, always meant white others—there were times when he still was as lone as the word could mean. Around whites, in town and so on, he had long since given up furious bewilderment for something like an exasperated wariness. Yet even that wasn't foolproof. He always had to remember that time when he had been in at the Gros Ventre mercantile, treating himself to new leather gloves. Rodeoing had looked like it would pan out then, people coming and going in the store kidded him about the bulls giving him a day off. While he was in the back trying on gloves, the little girl of a Belgian homestead family was skipping around, cutest kid imaginable. No one but him was paying any attention when she came prancing down the store aisle to where he stood, one hand splayed in a glove and the other not. He'd had to freeze in place when she put a tiny finger to the back of his bare hand, rubbed there, and looked to see if the color had come off.

He rubbed that spot now himself, trying to mock away the memory of that breathless moment of hell. Ten or so years ago, that must have been. And here he still was. If he knew anything by now, it was that he'd be here in the Two Medicine country forever, marooned in his own skin, if he flubbed this chance.

Then you might as well get up on your hind legs and sing, Monty-tan-a.

It gave him the jitters all over again, how much his mother's sayings flew in and out of him today. And the jitters kept bumping into his other feelings. All right, he had better admit it: what it came down to was that he was a little afraid at whatever lay ahead starting tomorrow. But then, hadn't he always needed to be a little afraid? This schooling of his voice that the woman was going to do might be a way out of that. And wouldn't that be something.

He petted the Duesenberg for luck.

"There's a holy sight I never thought I'd see again," the voice lilted in from the doorway, "a Duff down on knees."

Susan shot to her feet and raced to him, wet hands grasping him just above his elbows.

"Angus! Hello, you!"

More than a bit surprised to be in her grip, the angular man leaned his head back in order to thoroughly review her. Delight danced in his every feature as he did so. Angus McCaskill had always been as easy to read as a weather vane, even when she had been no more than elbow-high to him.

"Look at you, your eyes out like organ stops," she said fondly.

"It's been ages, Susan Duff."

" 'Ocean's ebb, and ocean's flow / Round and round the seasons go.' There. In Mother's name, I've beat you to the rhyming stuff."

"No fair," Angus protested, his craggy face full of indignant amusement. "I was standing here struck dumb, and you took advantage. Besides, that wasn't Burns, so it only counts when said on Sundays."

Laughing, she released him and drew him into the house with a gesture at the same time. "I was going to come up later. I knew you were still holding school."

"You ought to have stepped in and done a twirl. Let my not-so-model scholars lay eyes on my best pupil ever."

"On a spinster teacher starting to go long in the tooth, you mean."

"Don't. What does that make me?" It was comically said, but she caught a glint of rue. His mustache, which came and went according to private seasons in this otherwise open man during all the time she had been one of his schoolgirls, had turned drastically gray and looked permanent now, and in the lines around his eyes she could read with clarity every one of his decades of fending here. The world and its whirls had shaken this valley empty of all the others, but he was still on the land at the top of the creek as sheepman and as teacher over at the South Fork school, the last burr clinging to the swatch of homesteads called Scotch Heaven. "You couldn't quench Angus McCaskill with the Atlantic Ocean," her father had often said of the nimble spirit of this man, not entirely admiration from a Calvinist.

"And your better half?" Susan inquired, a trifle late with it. "How is Adair?"

"Dair is gallivanting," he responded cheerfully enough. "Varick fetched her down to Indian Head to spoil Alec for a while and keep Beth on her toes. Nothing like a grandson to draw her. And another McCaskill is on the way there, toward the end of summer." He gave out this news the surprised way men do. "We're becoming downright prolific."

Angus stopped. Family talk was a one-way conversation with Susan, the realization caught up with him. "I'm not much of a caretaker for you here, am I," he cast a glance around, away from her. "By now I've worn the legs off three canine generations, dogging Double W cows out of the North Fork, and still they sneak in." Then, giving the rectangle of sunlight where the house stood open to such creatures his consideration: "Mind you, I haven't been asked the whereabouts of your door. But there's one remarkably like it at Rob Barclay's old place."

"Do you suppose it could find its way back here by nightfall?"

Angus gave a grin. "I'll see that it does. You have your work cut out for you, it looks like. I shouldn't be keeping you from it."

"You'll have coffee and a bite if I have to poke it into you," she had him know. "My pantry is the Lizzie, at the moment. I'll be back in two shakes."

He watched her go out to the automobile, striding in the scissor gait of Ninian Duff but bearing herself as if marching to drums strictly her own. The Model T which had caused pandemonium among his pupils that morning when it putt-putted past the school-house, immersed itself up to its runningboard in the creek crossing, and at last crawled up the little-used North Fork road, sat now, black and pert, amid the sun-browned dilapidation of the homestead build-ings. Angus shook his head, frowning, then searched for someplace to sit and settled for leaning against a tilted cupboard.

In no time Susan swooped back into the house bearing an apple box of kitchen basics. "The bite is going to be graham crackers, it appears." She further fished out a blue enamel coffeepot and a pair of tin sheepherder cups. Fussing with the coffee, she asked over her shoulder: "By the way, are you absent a cat?"

"Ah, that would be Fiddle Strings," came Angus's answer, "Dair's footloose mouser. He lives at all the old places, up and down the creek, except our own. If you can hold his affections you're more than welcome to him."

"He'll be company, I suppose, although his manners can stand some—"

"Susan?" He startled her with the gravity of his voice, as if calling on her in school. "You didn't come back to Scotch Heaven to gain a cat."

She looked around at him. "Would you believe, I'm here to teach singing."

"I did hear something of the sort. And to whom."

Susan could not help but give an amused snort. This had not changed. Try to do anything on the sly in the Two Medicine country and Angus McCaskill knew it by nightfall.

"You heard right," she sorted her way through these words, "Wes . . . Wesley Williamson is giving him this chance."

"That's a modest wonder to me," Angus said with equal care. "Generosity from a Williamson."

She tended to the boiling coffee, clattered cups onto the cupboard sideboard between him and her, and set down the box of brown crack-ers with some force before answering. "You know and I know that Whit would kick a blind orphan out of his way. But the Major seems to have Monty Rathbun's interests at heart, don't ask me why. Angus, I've given myself a good talking-to about this, any number of times since I heard the man sing. This all may seem daffy"—she swept a gesture around at the dilapidated room, farthest thing from a proper music parlor—"but the thing worse is not to see what can be done when a voice you'd gladly give your own for comes along. There's something there, when this Monty person stands looking like a hopeless cow chouser and then out pours the majority of a choir."

Angus's expression granted all she had said, but there still was a furrow of concern on him. "Say you brush him up and push him out of where he's always been nestled. Leading where, if you don't mind my asking?"

"Don't I wish I knew. I hear everything you're saying, his color can get in his way that quick. But knocking on stage doors will have to be his own concern, or Wes Williamson's. I don't care if he were made of Limburger, my part in this is to train that voice of his."

"That mightn't be popular with some."

"I've been spat on before," she said levelly.

He knew that look on her. The Susan who was the leader of the girls in the garter snake fights with the boys, the Susan who had brains by the bushel and curiosity by the cubit; the Susan he many a time would have traded places with on the checkerboard of life, truth be told.

"You know my inclination," Angus had ready now. "Teach away. You remember the approach I took with you," he made the old joke of the timid preacher being urged by the deacon to cut loose in his sermons: "'For the Lord's sake, man, fire the popcorn at the porcupine—some of it may stick.'"

They laughed together.

"I've yammered on," he chided himself after a bit. "There's not that much conversation to be made around here, anymore."

"No." This cobwebbed room that had rung with Bible and rhyme. Susan glanced around, then at him. "I noticed on the way up here, the graves are kept."

"Yes, I see to that."

"Angus, it haunts me that they came to Helena to me at just the wrong time."

"People die everywhere, lass, so far as I know." He stepped to the stove and coffeed up again, his back to her. "They went like flies here, too, during the flu." She heard him swallow, on more than a bite of cracker. She knew there was particular loss, Anna Reese by name, his equal at the Noon Creek school and the woman he had waited half his life for, in that slight sound.

Susan had her own tightness of throat to talk past.

"I've been across to Samuel's grave. Twice now."

"Ah. Have you."

His turn to silently bolster her. It was six years on, since his own son Varick had come home from the Great War, and the brother whom Susan had raised like a son had not. Somewhere in his schoolhouse even yet was the homemade telegraph rig that incanted from one end of the room to the other the name of its long-boned inquisitive young maker in Morse code: Samuel Duff, ajump with ideas. Susan had taken the bright lad under her wing for high school in Helena, and right after, seen him climb onto the troop train that never brought him back. Then, their hearts out of them, no sooner had Ninian and Flora lodged themselves in Susan's care than the capricious influenza epidemic doubled back and took them. Angus winced within. The flood of death around Susan, there at the end of the Great War, would have knocked anyone off her feet.

"You've been through the thick of things, I know," he resorted to. "But maybe this is your turn at some of the thin. One pupil, mind you—shall I change the name of Scotch Heaven to Easy Street for you, Miss Duff?"

She made a face at that, as he hoped.

Next task prominently waiting, Angus gave the doorway a pat of promise on his way through as Susan followed him out.

She watched him swing into his saddle and as he departed the yard, she thanked him with the instruction: "Don't you dare be scarce, you and Adair. Ham supper here, as soon I can get the ingredients."

"We'll bring our appetites."

Why this, Wesley bastardly Williamson?

Angus turned that over and over as he went home and hitched his team of workhorses to the wagon he had been using for fixing fence on Breed Butte. By now the wagon ought to know the way up to the Barclay place by itself, he paused only long enough to muse; then climbed on and gave the reins a flip to start the horses.

As the rescue vessel for Susan's door splashed across the North Fork and began lurching its way over the years-old ruts up the slope of the timber-topped butte, Angus swayed on the wagon seat and in the course of his thoughts as well. Great treat that it was to have Susan back in the vicinity, where in the book of reckoning did this open-handedness by the lordly Major come from? A singing school for one, fluffed into Scotch Heaven by Williamson money generous as feathers? A change that was. Angus's mouth soured at the ancient history of contention with old Warren Williamson and his hoofed locusts branded with the Double W. And now the magical Wesley, next thing to a governor, kindly turns the valley into a music parlor? Nothing against the man Rathbun, but since when was a choreboy a logical candidate for the Susan Duff Conservatory of Music?

Arrival at the Barclay homestead silenced all this in Angus. He climbed down into the yard where he and Adair Barclay had exchanged their marriage vows, Scotch Heaven's legion of people three deep around them then. Clapped a hand to his hat to firm it down against the chronic mischief of the wind up here so near the brow of the butte. Walked past the caved-in root cellar where Varick, forest ranger in charge of half the mountains in the Two Medicine country now, had played billy-of-the-hill endless afternoons with his girl cousins. Gingerly approached the house of logs built by himself and Rob, his onetime partner, eventual brother-in-law, and ultimate nemesis. Thirty-five years, gone again in the space of his steps; how was it possible?

McAngus, you're not immune to the calendar, he chided himself. Looking the door over and finding it still fit for service, he went back to the wagon for prybar and clawhammer. Again now the hair on the back of his neck was up a little about the Williamsons. The original of the outfit, old Warren, four or so years ago had gone to his reward—it would take a Dante to know, but Angus figured his was a reasonable guess—on some coast of Hell. But the dirt had barely begun to settle on that well-earned grave when the next in command of what promised to be unending Williamsons, the Major, materialized right here in this yard. Angus thought back through that with care, looking for snares. He had happened to be here on some errand in his ordained role, landlord of the empty. It was soon after Rob's widow, Judith, had loyally sold him the Breed Butte homestead—"Angus, you already made the down payment in sweat"—and with that and the lease Susan had given him on the Duff grazing land, he had been going around feeling fortified about keeping the Double W from buying in on Scotch Heaven. Therefore the appearance of that gorgeous matched gray team and the buckboard with a figure of significance in it coming over the ridgeline had only tweaked his curiosity.

The grays came like winged things, then had halted smartly, as if on target, in the center of the yard. "I merely came over to clarify something, I hope you don't mind," the squire at the reins delivered with a winning expression. Major Williamson was a famous smiler, and Angus didn't doubt he meant most of it, except *merely*. "I understand you put the run on my agent the other day."

"Tsk, Major. I nicely asked him to keep his feet off my soil."

"Does that still go?"

Angus's gaze took in the unnaturally propped leg there on a padded bolster, as if it were an item of cargo that didn't fit with the rest of the imposing person in the buckboard. "Come on down for a stretch if you'd like."

Wrapping the reins in a way that the grays would not get any ideas, the Major descended smoothly enough, considering. Angus watched him alight in fine Western boots but with walker heels; specially made, those, he had no doubt, since the man could no longer put that limb to the stirrup of a saddle. From his end of things, the Major was all manners:

"Angus, if I may?"

That would be an improvement, Angus had come close to saying. In his time the elder Williamson had one boxcar name for all of them over here, *Damnscotchprotestant*.

"We've never been able to deal with—reach a deal with those of you on the North Fork," the Major was saying in a voice with none of his father's rasp. "Wouldn't you agree it's about time for a fresh start?"

"I'd agree it's time the Double W had a fresh dealer, if that's what you are, Major," Angus had set the man straight. "To us over here, your father was every kind of a sonofabitch, and Whit I'd say takes after him."

"You're still here in spite of them, or I wouldn't be standing in this yard with the wind blowing through my every aperture, trying to talk sense to you."

Angus had chuckled. "I'm with you on the wind, at least." They moved into the lee of the house.

"Regrets about Barclay, by the way," the Major had said as though the house reminded him. "I know you and he went back a long way."

Angus's glance followed the other man's to the reservoir, off along the slope to the west, where Rob and his horse had slid on the embankment slick with spring and drowned. A life he had known as well as his own, Rob's, and he still could not make its pluses and minuses come out to a proven sum. The fit recitation cropped out almost without his knowing: "'That blind night waiting, all men darkward go / Unto Inferno, or Paradiso.'"

"Cheyne, is that? 'A tourist, I, on the ring roads of Hell'?"

Angus had to grant that an eyebrow of approval. "Teach him even at Harvard, do they?"

The Major had not seen fit to remark that in Copeland's course on literature of the ages, Copey had delighted in citing Cheyne as the poor man's Dante. With a covering cough, the Major brought matters back down to earth. "Can we talk business?"

"One of us no doubt will."

"Angus, I know you've worked like anything, trying to build an operating ranch over here. But in country like this, it takes a real swath of land to run livestock. Your quarter-sections"—the Major inclined his head around to the quilt-pattern acreages of the Duff place and this one and Angus's own—"are always going to be too small. Homesteads were an Act of Congress, and you know what happens when somebody has congress with you." No chuckle from Angus at that. The Major backed up to the straight and narrow: "Homesteads everywhere are going under. You've seen that yourself."

"I have. That's why I thought to shore mine up."

The Major looked him over as if he were a checkerboard. "Let's try this. Double what my fool of an agent offered. It's a lot for empty country, Angus."

"Imagine. Money raining, and there wasn't even any thunder."

"That still doesn't sound exactly like 'yes.'"

Angus had not been able to resist. Puckish as a Shakespearean, he confided: "Potter in at the bank has kindly offered to take all this off my hands."

That had sharpened the expression on his visitor right up. Angus had no way of knowing how much under it took on an immediate edge, too. If the Major had wanted to spell it out, whenever his father and Potter at the Valley Stockmen's Bank were not trying to outfox each other for some piece of land, the rancher and the banker had done ordinary business together in cordial dislike that went back approximately to their cribs. *That galvanized Yankee in at the bank* was Warren Williamson's offhand scorn for Potter's ineradicable hard-scrabble Missouri family origins. *That slab of cold roast Yankee,* Potter doubtless dripped back in his genial drawl whenever the Boston-degreed patriarch of the Double W, or for that matter the similar Major, got on his business nerves. It made wicked sense for Angus to do his dealing with Potter and let the Williamsons choke on the bone, and the Major too well knew it. He still was trying to muster the barrage of argument to counter that when Angus's face twitched toward a grin.

"Potter has pockets all over him," Angus said dismissively. "I'm not selling this to any of you creatures."

"I hadn't thought I would go home counting that a gain," the Major manfully granted, and made the climb back into his buck-board. To his surprise, Angus held him from going by grasping the near horse's rein. "Potter did have one thing interesting to say. You're buying up homesteads all the way east to the Highwood Mountains, are you?"

"Where they fit into our pasture picture, I am." His tone as much as added: *With both hands.*

"Tell me this, Major. How much ground would you say a man can swallow before he turns into an island?"

No answer given, that day or this. Standing there akimbo, look-ing out over the gentle spill of valley and the meandering creek he and Rob had followed to here like giddy pilgrims all those years ago, Angus put aside the past for the moment, which was as long as he was ever able to. He remained bothered over the open hand of the Major, back down the slope where Susan was strenuously setting up shop. But Susan had always known her own mind, had she ever. Telling himself to confine his prying to the stubborn hinges of the door, Angus set to work opening the house on Breed Butte to the elements.

That night Susan put into her diary:
So much for wishing for ghosts, when they line up in the mind to volunteer.

EARLY sun was sorting the green plaids of spring—blue-green of the timberline on Breed Butte, mossy green of her doddering barn roof, meadow green of the volunteer hay fostered by the creek— when Susan stepped out into the morning and around the corner of the house to gaze north. From growing up here, she could catch sight of a coyote the instant its lope broke the pattern of the grass on the farthest butte. So, she spotted without effort the horseback figure on its way across the benchland from Noon Creek, then could not blink away the duplicate figure next to it.

Eventually the two riders clopped into the yard and swung down, facing her with their reins drooping in their hands.

"Morning, Miss Susan," Monty said in short fashion. She could tell at a glance that he was full of second thoughts over this, about to go back for thirds.

Dolph appeared no more happy to be along than Monty was to have him. The pint-size cowboy reported unwillingly, "Ma'am, the boss says I got to tag along with Monty here, do any chores while you're schooling him up on this singing."

Susan paused over the knot of logic by which, if a woman was at risk from a man, two men were sent.

"You can chink." She indicated gaps between the logs of the house where hard weather had done its work. "The whole place can stand chinking, I'm sure. Mister Rathbun, come on in."

Looking doubly doleful, Dolph moved off in search of buckets and the nearest clay bank as Monty traipsed into the house after her. He was surprised to see it wasn't much of a layout. The kitchen was the center of everything, as was to be expected, but this one appeared to have had a boxcar of peddler's goods emptied into it. All of it made his own room at the back of the Double W washhouse seem a model of order. But through a doorway to the room beyond the kitchen he glimpsed a hulking piano, its white keys like bared teeth.

He kept on looking at every possible thing in the house except the woman standing there like Lady La-De-Dah. All of a sudden he remembered to take off his hat and then had no idea what to do with it.

Susan snagged the unmoored hat, hanging it on her father's peg nearest the door in a way that told Monty there was where it belonged from now on. She wasn't displeased that he didn't sail in here and make himself at home. He had been awkward as a schoolboy there at the Gates of the Mountains dock, too, but for her purposes better that than slick and stuck on himself.

"Let's go on in here." She led the way as if he were the hundredth pupil in this log cubbyhole instead of her first and only.

The piano sitting waiting, Monty edged into the room.

"Ready, I hope?"

"Miss Susan—"

Whatever he had intended to say, he took it back to makings as she watched. Finally he nodded, a sharp inch of inclination and then as quickly gone, and issued only: "I guess I can't count on getting any younger."

I just wish flashed in Susan, right past the ramparts of determination and teacherly creed she had been trying to maintain. In singer's years the man in front of her was a near-eternity older than the pupils who had to prove themselves in her Helena music parlor, and now that he stood here fresh off a horse and in work-worn togs instead of that handsome greatcoat, she was fully faced with the task Wes was letting her in for. And. And of course those considerations paled, so to speak, alongside the fact that among all her pupils ever, there had never been a colored person of whatever age, dress, or capability. Well, she instructed herself, that's why the two of them were here, wasn't it, to drown out *never* with song.

"Don't look so nervous," she passed the mood of instruction toward him. "No one dies of music except in opera. Now then, let's first of all hear how you sound on dry land. That same song, please, and take your time with it."

The flutters in him saw their chance again. Kill this off before it got started. Croak out the spiritual, off-key; cough in the middle; tell her his voicebox had come to the belated realization that it was too old to go to school. *Quit before you even start?* some banshee in his conscience howled back at that. *Why not scoot on home under your momma's bed and play with the cat, while you're at it?*

Feeling like a first-class fool but choosing that over running and hiding, he nodded again and resolutely gathered himself to put what he could into the air.

"One moment, Mister Rathbun. May I?" She strode over to him and pushed his slaunched shoulders back and into straighter alignment, Monty flinching with surprise. "A singer mustn't stand all caved in." Her dress swishing, she stepped back to demonstrate. "High chest. Level head, no, not as if you're gandering around for rain, merely level does the trick. Here, watch again." She looked ready to give the Gettysburg Address, while he felt like he was being turned into one of those hat-store mannequins.

"Go Down, Moses" came out about as it did with the accompaniment of the Missouri, Monty's phrases like one bell after another but no arc of sound in between, his voice punctuating the melody rather than following it. Again Susan was bothered by the labored way he squeezed air in and out of himself, as if his chest were a polka accordion, and she despaired for a moment over the lengthening mental list of items to be worked on.

Yet there was the genuine article somewhere in there, she was back to thinking by the time he was done with the song. When he stood planted (pigeon-toed as only someone who had spent a lifetime in cowboy boots could be, she added to the mental list) and let loose, somehow you ended up hearing more than he seemed to have sung, as if his voice had a shadow made of sound. At the Gates of the Mountains, she had wondered if it was a trick of the canyon echo; here as there she had to try to keep a rein on her sense of excitement at the way his knells of song stayed on for that unaccountable moment, lingering in the ear, the auditorium of the head. That vocal quality was rare and it was the one thing this problem pupil had going for him.

"Spirituals suit your voice nicely," she said to be saying something uncritical. "Your mother always sang those at her work, the Major told me."

"She did. She came from church people." He hesitated. "Although it was hard, out here."

"No doubt."

The slap of wet clay against a furrow of logs startled them both. Dolph had chosen to start chinking outside the exact room where they were. The pair of them tried to keep straight faces at being chaperoned with mud and trowel.

"Let's get ourselves under way," she did away with that distraction and set right to work on what was nagging at her the most, the drag of his breathing as he sang. "The first of many first things"—the quick toss of her head was meant to take the edge off that, and didn't quite—"is that you must learn to properly draw air into yourself."

Disappointment clouded him over. He hadn't come here to take his nose for a walk.

"This all counts more than you may think," Susan came close to a coax a lot sooner than she wanted to. "You can't expect to sing your way to the top of the world without your wind under you, now can you." *Suppose not*, Monty's manner came around to, and he presented himself for whatever she had in store. She drilled into him that he was going to have to breathe from deep down, bulge his middle so his diaphragm would let air all the way into the lower region of his lungs. "It's like cleaning out the bottom of a closet so the rest of your things will hang right." He gave it try after try, and his intake still was the worst part of his vocal wardrobe.

"Don't worry, there are exercises. Mister Rathbun, you're not to let yourself be perturbed about whatever you think I'm inflicting on you. Are we agreed? Now then, pretend you are smelling a rose."

He gave a minimum sniff.

"A nine-year-old girl can do a better job of it than that." She looked stern until he inhaled lustily. "That's not bad," she commended. "Now put your fist in front of your mouth as if holding a bugle."

How does she know these things? His sudden little amused expression took Susan by surprise. He had a good contained grin. She felt silly. What had she expected, a minstrel show gawp?

"Mister Rathbun? What is it?"

"I have me a bugle. I do. Played it all the time when I was a bit of a thing."

"Angeline, the boy is driving us mad with that bugle."

"I'll have him put it up, Mister Warren. It was his father's."

"Then you know very well what I'm asking of you, don't you," Susan swept on. "Put your clenched hand up, no, against your lips. As if with a bugle, for heaven's sake. Now smell the rose, but put the air back out through your fist. *Deep* breath, now blow out, make it sound like a tea kettle. Again—in, out. Until I tell you to stop. Again. Once more. Take your hand down, keep that same rhythm of breathing. There. Feel the muscles work? Down there in your flanks?"

His flanks felt as if they were an unwilling topic of conversation. "Some, I guess." He wondered how much of this Dolph was hearing, outside.

"That's what you must practice," she decreed. "At home, in the mirror. Do it a dozen times first thing each morning and again over the noonhour and again at night, and I guarantee, I can tell whether or not you have been doing them." Monty considered himself notified. "Next let's acquaint you with the notes."

Apprehensively he listened while she demonstrated how to sing the scale. Her voice was smooth, each note up the ladder a tease of song; how was he ever going to get there? She would hold pitch, he would frown in concentration and then sic his voice onto hers. After considerable of this she called a break, with tea and honey for his throat and enough advice from her to make his head swim. Then back to traversing the notes. It took many tries, but finally she granted that he had approximated the scale.

By the time they called it a day, he felt as if he had gone fifteen rounds. Heading for his way out, he made his manners and said he would see her tomorrow.

"You will not," Susan informed him with a slight smile. "Three lessons a week are as much as a voice can stand. Every other day and Sunday off. But practice the breathing exercise in between, don't forget." He stood there at the door looking as if he had been swatted with the calendar, but she couldn't help that. "Wait, let me give you my list for some more provisions. And tell Whit Williamson for me that I am going to need a milk cow."

Monty fiddled with his hat while she kept jotting down foodstuffs. The adjusted ciphering of musical career that he was doing in his head was not coming out well at all. "Miss Susan? How long you figure I'm going to need to take lessons?"

"Oh, forever," she said absently, still writing her grocery list.

"How—how's that work?" His dismay was the purest note he had hit all day, causing her head to snap up. "I can't be coming here until they lay me away!"

"No, no. I only meant that every singer needs refresher lessons, all through life. As to how long these sessions need to go on—we'll just have to see." Her face gave away nothing, but the provisions list she handed to him looked long enough to endure a siege.

Monty turned at the door. "Mind if I ask? These lessons forever—who gives you yours?"

"I administer them myself. I take my own medicine, Mister Rathbun, don't worry."

Nights run slow here, rationed out by the wick. Why hadn't I remembered?

She moved the lamp some more until it almost touched the open diary, annoyed at how spoiled the electricity of Helena had made her. There was no great reason why a person couldn't write and read by courtesy of kerosene. Compose an operetta.

"Fiddle Strings, will you quit." The cat tickled its moppy fur back and forth across her ankles, purring without shame or letup. "You're a tyrant, you are," she addressed downward. Rather than go out in the dark to the springhouse for milk from the pail, she resorted to the can of condensed milk she used on coffee, cutting off the top to get the last teaspoon into the cat pan. The cat looked a trifle critical, but lapped it up.

She fed the fire next, last of the night's chores except for the load of good intentions she had brought here with her. Piqued by Monty's question, she nightly put her voice through its paces before she ever sat down to the diary and the waiting noteless sheets of score. Good thing, too, because if she held off on her vocal exercises until she accomplished what she wanted on the page these nights, she would be in direct competition with Angus McCaskill's rooster as it summoned the dawn up there at the head of the valley.

Having given herself enough of a scolding, she resumed at the table again. *Prairie Tide* lay there side by side with the diary; inert, the weight of ten years on it. How could this be, that the mud-road cavalcade for the vote refused to shape itself to music for her, after she had been the one to pour forth its soul in song? She could see, fresh as this moment, the famous trio of flivvers, dubbed the *Niña,* the *Pinta,* and the *Susan B.,* grinding from town to town along the length of the Yellowstone River and then looping north to the wide plains of the High Line and the even newer counties and sprigs of towns there along the immigrant seedbed of the Great Northern Railroad. Blindfold her and spin her dizzy and she could still perform the evening of favorites that drew the homestead families to the scattered one-room schoolhouses and the fledgling motion-picture emporiums, so that on the heels of her rousing songs the speakers could have at those audiences on behalf of the statewide suffrage referendum. "Our ambassadress to the shanties," she was deemed by Jeannette Rankin, high-born and connected and said by everyone to be Congress-bound as soon as Montana women wielded the vote. Susan, her father's daughter in quickness to take umbrage, had swallowed that from Jeannette because there was a flavor of truth to it; as the carloads of the crusade trundled past isolated gulches where kerosene lamps glowed yellow, puddles of light such as she had come from, she felt singled out by some circular law of the draw.

Of course even then she had known that the performance of a lifetime would not go uncriticized. The costs, back in Helena. "Miss Duff, I must know—are you one of those suffs? My child does not need a singing teacher who believes in disrupting the home."

"Then she will never have the historic privilege, Mrs. Moberley, of a teacher who believes the female of the species has the right to be distinguished from the lower animals by possession of the ballot. Are we not persons?"

In the end, all had been worth it. The overshoe counties, the prairie tide of settlers, carried the day in the so close referendum on suffrage. It was a famous victory, and lacked only its snatches of tune. The

moment Wes proposed Scotch Heaven to her in this charitable enterprise of his, to call it that, Susan saw the interlude here as her chance
to remedy that lack. Here she had solitude, that Cheshire countenance
of creation: find the face of what you wanted to do and lock on to it
without blink or hesitation, wasn't that the prescription? Here she was
even paid ("All right then, triple," the most welcome words Wes had
spoken to her in those four years) to sit and stew over music. (Unbid-
den, the schoolyard song chanted in her: *A diller, a dollar / a high-collar
scholar.* Why on earth should that take up room in her head, and not
some passage fit for an operetta? Maybe there was her answer, have
Angus's tots compose the lyrics that seemed beyond her.) Here she had
but a single student—although he frequently seemed like more—
standing in the way of the time and strength and patience that ought
to set that pageant of mud and glory to music. And tonight again she
couldn't capture any of it, the flivver journey of 1914 as scattered as
the Milky Way.

"Trunk songs," she delivered the verdict on this work of hers to the
noncommittal cat. What little she had composed so far was only
worth being closed away under a firm lid, in there to ferment with the
mothballs. With *Prairie Tide* swept away one more time, she went
back to the diary and today's other frustrating musical chapter.

*I am so down I can hardly write. Monty works hard at these lessons, but
there is no reservoir of breath in him. It's as if the man has no diaphragm! He
chops along from note to note. This morning I braced him as to whether he was
doing his exercises when he is out of my sight. "Religiously," he had me know.
I must hope that did not mean only on Sundays.*

The next day came blowy, perfect bad weather for staying in and facing unwritten music, and she was trying to get under way when a
voice outside resounded like the language of kings:

"Susan! I've brought you a person of importance!"

Angus's hail drew her to the window. He rode past to his schoolhouse every morning about now, but the bundled-up figure perched
on the saddlehorse next to his, those formerly auburn pincurls peep-
ing out from beneath a severe scarf—*Adair, at this early hour?*

She was more wrenlike than ever, Susan saw during the doorway effusions, the years carving her down to delicacy. Most un-Scottish, for a woman born not a pathlength away from her hewn husband, but then Adair had always been the other side of category.

"Come in, hang your hat on the floor," Susan fell back on the habit of the house.

"Not I, thank you just the same," came back from Angus at once. "I have to go put roundish thoughts into squarish heads."

"And you wouldn't have it any other way," Susan told him, Adair chipping in with "You'd mope like a spent rose without that old school of yours."

"Leave it to Scotch women to shed a ray over the affairs of men," he jested. "If one of you doesn't tell me what I'm about, the other one will."

It took two to set the likes of him straight, they assured him, and off he went to his schoolday. Susan turned and groped at the cupboard.

"Adair? I have coffee on, but beyond that, I'm afraid it's graham—"

Adair produced a dishtowel bundle. "I brought you a loaf."

The bread was still warm from the oven. Susan sent her a look. A woman who had baked bread before breakfast? And then ridden down here in the dew hours to spend, what, the day? From girl on, when Susan had sung at the wedding of Angus and Adair where even to a knock-kneed schoolmaid it had been obvious how Angus's eyes searched past his bride of convenience to Anna Reese, Susan had tried to fathom what this person's view of things must be. But there seemed no knowing, no way in past those deflecting gray eyes with their odd guardpost of freckles directly beneath each. In the time after Adair's second stillbirth when the women of the other home-steads would visit in and always find a deck of cards laid out in columns in front of this woman, Susan's mother would come home shaking her head and say, "Adair and solitaire," not a commending rhyme. Now Adair was fixedly saying, "It's so fresh, it may be hard to cut."

"No, no. It'll be a treat."

Susan mauled off two large floppy underdone slices and the two women silently buttered and ate. They brushed their hands of that, and took up one of those dutiful conversations about the how of things, how was the Rathbun man doing, how were the further generations of McCaskills coming along. Susan was delving desperately—she was relieved out of all proportion when a gust rattled the kitchen windowpane as if wanting to come in out of its own weather and join them, and the two women were able to say almost in chorus that today's was a thieving wind, it had stolen through snow somewhere—when Adair came out with:

"Susan, I'll not keep you from yourself."

With a start—*written all over me, is it*—Susan began to say something patently insincere about company other than herself probably being good for her once in a while. The other woman interjected:

"I only came to ask a bit of a favor. I would like lessons."

Serves me right, Susan let herself have, suddenly longing for the procession of sugarplums with ringlets through her Helena music parlor. "Adair, really, I'm just here to tutor this one pupil."

"Every other day, according to when I see him and his wetnurse riding across the bench."

"That's so. But—"

"That leaves the other days."

Susan gave up any pretense of politeness. "What brings this on?"

"I'm not asking you to make me into a fine singer or famous or anything of the sort." *I'm spared that, at least,* Susan thought with relief. "It would be something to do with myself, is all." Adair spoke this as if from a slight mocking distance away from herself. She floated a glance to Susan. "A person can sing to herself and not be thought soft in the head, can't she."

Susan blinked a couple of times. "It's a help, I suppose. Music is delirium on purpose." She wrinkled her nose. "Who came up with that? Chopin? Puccini? Madame Schumann-Heink? Me?" In the bit of time this had bought, she made up her mind to the songless soul across the table. "Adair, I always need to know—what manner of music do you have in mind for yourself?"

"Songs with the old country in them," Adair stated. "Your mother's songs would do me."

Susan that night thought long and hard about the populace of solitude. About the dots of humankind, connected and not, strung through the weathered valleys and across the girth of prairie like con-stellations reflected on the ground. The Adairs, the Anguses—and those between them even when no longer there—of the flivver trip: the women hungry for any other women to talk to, even dressed-up ones from Helena; the men half-bemused and half-alarmed that they would be hearing these suffrage arguments from their wives and daughters forever after. Then episodes began to come back to her, the elongated memory shadows from the dots. The syrup sandwiches that were all the supper that could be mustered by the host family fresh from their emigrant railcar near Ingomar. The proud Pledge of Alle-giance in Danish by the Frisian colony gathered civically in their church in their fledgling town of Dagmar. The way smoke would fall to the ground before a storm, the smell of the weather riding out to the road to meet them as the *Niña,* the *Pinta,* and the *Susan B.* chugged into view of yet another isolated homestead chimney.

"Out of my way, star boarder," she directed the drowsy cat. She fetched the sheets of composition paper to the table and spread them there in the wash of light.

By midnight she had unraveled two lines for every one she had written, and endured her way through another one of those spasms of hopelessness when not even the prepositions seemed to fit into her sentences, but she had a few lyrics and something hummable to show for the night.

H OW come the Major is so generous on this singing of yours, and not on my trick riding?"

"Dolph, the only riding trick you know is to climb on the side of your horse a person is supposed to, and you've got a fifty-fifty chance on that."

"What the hell you talking about?" Dolph sputtered. "I can do the saddle stand, and the Comanche tuck, and, and—" Monty's effort to hold in laughter registering on him, he grinned sheepishly. "Tune up your tonsils, then. But you end up back at rodeoing instead of con-certizing, I'll ride circles around you any day."

"Fair enough," Monty said soberly.

"Here, I'll barn the horses, you git in there and take your medicine from her," Dolph rattled on as they dismounted in the now familiar yard. "Ask her for me what she's doing with all the milk from that damn cow, feeding an orphanage?"

As he approached the house Monty could hear her in there plinking the piano in a testing way, *da dum, da dum da da.* Knowing she was just waiting her turn at him, he knocked and already had the door handle in his grip and his hat ready to flip onto the peg by the time she called the customary "Come on in, Mister Rathbun."

She didn't migrate into the kitchen to swoop him in as usual, though, only poked the top part of her around the inner doorway like the front end of a clipper ship. "Here's an idea. Come see."

Monty sensed something arduous ahead. But when he stepped in to where she had taken up her station, the only thing new was that her windup Victrola had been moved to front and center, its morning-glory horn expectantly aimed their way.

"Today I have something I want you to hear, Mister Rathbun—do you suppose it would be all right if I call you Monty? It would save some on the world's supply of breath that I'm eternally after you about."

His short-measure nod. He still was trying to come up with an educated guess as to what this was about. Stand around and listen today, after standing around chasing through the scale those other days? *Am I ever going to get to just sing?*

Vigorously she cranked the phonograph and set the needle onto the record. Out poured a profound bass sound as if the foundations of Heaven were shifting; Chaliapin in *Boris Godunov.* Monty appeared ready to take to the hills.

"Whoops, not that one," Susan said with a chuckle. She grabbed the intended record from the imposing stack on the sideboard. More whirls of the phonograph handle, and a voice soared high and clear:

> *"Let us break bread together on our knees,*
> *Let us break bread together on our knees.*
> *When I fall down on my knees*
> *With my face to the rising sun,*
> *Oh Lord, have mercy on me."*

She cut the song off there with a practiced pass of her hand over the Victrola and looked at Monty to judge his reaction. He felt dry-mouthed as he managed to say, "It's nice." He hoped to everything that it was Roland Hayes. If there was more than one spiritual singer like that in the world, he had might as well go back to polishing car fenders right now.

She divulged that the voice was Hayes's as if it should be obvious even to the snoozing cat over there, and talked on a bit about the full-ness of that voice, the technical polish on a natural purple tone. "Now we're going to pick up the trick from him."

Another spirited winding of the Victrola, but this time she hov-ered over it, putting her finger lightly against the edge of the turntable as it spun. Slowed down that way, the voice on the record became a stately warble.

"There," Susan said cagily, Monty still listening with the despera-tion of a man trying to decipher pig Latin. "Hear what he's doing, inside the words? I'll play it again. Here, this part."

This time he could catch it all:

"Leht uss brayke brehd toogehthur . . ."

"Our Mister Hayes e-nun-ci-ates," he could hear every pore of every letter the way she said it, "doesn't he. He's shaping the words, there in the vowels for instance—each word carries into the next and brings the melody right along with it. Now then. I'd like you to copy him at it until you catch the knack." Wind wind wind, went her hand on the Victrola handle.

"Sing along with that machine while you make it logey, that's what you want done?"

"Only if you're not shy to be around a voice that knows what it's doing."

She had him by his pride now. Keyed up, he stepped over there and put his voice over Hayes's as she slowed the record. They tried it again and again and again. It was a lot harder than a person would think. He could keep in tandem with Hayes for a line or two, enun-ciating for all he was worth, but his air would not hold through the whole verse. Finally Susan looked over at the clock and although it was not yet time for the tea-and-honey break, she declared it to be. She covered her concern—*What is there to try next?*—with kitchen clatter and determined conversation, Monty pitching in a word here and there when utterly necessary.

Turnabout came when they were down to their last sips. Out of nowhere, Monty inquired: "Miss Susan, excuse my asking, but you're on your own, aren't you? Far as family goes, I mean?"

"A raft of shirttail relatives over toward Glasgow, but we don't keep in touch. I don't have anyone left other than that, why?"

He was slow to answer. "It fits with the sort of thing I been thinking about, is all."

"And what's that when it's at home?"

He settled his cup into its saucer. "Been wondering if it does something to us. People who are in their own company pretty much, I mean. We get to trying things to keep ourselves busy, nobody around to say us nay. Don't get me wrong, it's a quality I wouldn't trade and probably you neither. But maybe sometimes it makes us bite off more than we can chew, you think?"

Susan studied him before answering. He was quick-witted, she had caught on to, although he stood around in front of that capacity until he absolutely had to let it show. Today's Victrola venture hadn't been a cure for the internal shortcomings of his vocal ability, and he was right to be skeptical of it. As she was right to be persistent.

"I think it's better to bite big than to be bitten," she stated, rising out of her chair. "Let's get back at it."

The rest of the morning they slogged on, Susan applying rudiments as if they were poultices and Monty the leery patient. At last, weary of working at getting air into the man, Susan went to the piano. "All right, we can both stand a change. Let's try 'Moses' once with accompaniment and see what happens."

He hung back to the other side of the room.

She took her hands off the keys. "What is it now?"

"I haven't ever sang with a piana."

She made sure her expression gave nothing away, but the mental list had unscrolled. Good grief, in so many ways he still was at the level of her elementary pupils.

"Surely you're not afraid of a musical instrument."

"Afraid, who said that? But . . . how do I go about it?"

The piano music startled Dolph where he was puttying the weath-ered sash of a kitchen window. Monty's voice thundered out some-times atop the notes and sometimes not, the song lifting uncertainly over the valley.

A LETTER for you, Mister Williamson."

Here? "Popular, am I. Thank you, Jenkins." Wes plucked the envelope from the deskman's hand and went on in past the oil portraits of one titan of learning after another, their own expressions carefully fixed in the obligation unto eternity to present the face of Harvard to heathen New York. Not until he reached the quiet library, deepest recess of the club, did he hurriedly slit open the envelope with his penknife.

Her handwriting leapt to him, from love letters now consigned to ashes.

> Dear Wes—
>
> I thought you were due some accounting of our pupil, and it seemed best to send it to your lunch lair.
>
> You will be pleased to hear we have made some strides, or rather, I have pushed and Monty has progressed in some steps. Some, I emphasize; less so in others. His vocal range is improving, although of course not yet as much as it ultimately must. His tone remains his strongest point. In presentation, he no longer stands as if he were made of warped barrel staves. All in all, after these first weeks, I can say Monty is in better possession of his voice. But his voice is not yet in possession of him, which is the breakthrough for a true singer.
>
> You are missing quite the contest. He is a striver. Amenable, to a point, and stubborn as a stump beyond that. (He will not hear of using a music stand, insisting it flusters him to have that in his face. Besides, he indignantly tells me, his memory is good enough for a few songs.)

Unfortunately he seems invincibly convinced that the lungs installed in him at birth are adequate, but I am determined to build him up, there in the solar plexus and below. The flag of this expedition you have set us upon, Wes, reads not "Excelsior!" but "Exercises!"

I must talk to you when you venture to our neck of the woods again. I presume that may be soon? It is the buzz of the countryside (I'm told) that you have bought the Two Medicine & Teton Railroad. The TM&T added to the Double W—at this rate, you will possess the entire lower end of the alphabet.

I will leave you with a scene of how our days go, Monty's and mine. Yesterday when I demonstrated a note in the uppermost range that I wanted him to practice, he balked.

"Can't reach that high one," says he.

"Monty, lacking proof that you can't, assume that you can," say I.

"Just can't," he is adamant. "Sorry."

Such a look as I gave him. Then sprang to my feet and dragged a straightbacked chair in from the kitchen and climbed up on it. "This," I intoned down to him, "is a high note." I then sang a perfectly normal lower C. "All others are within reach without a chair."

It has been a lovely spring here in the Two, but is now turning dry.

Sincerely, Susan

Wes assessed the unexpected flow of words from her. Soon, yes, but not soon enough he would be back out there, over Merrinell's fretful protest and the plaints of his daughters, who had their incipient debutante hearts set on a European summer. Some more rounds of pacifying, another spate of promising, and he would be able to head west in relatively clear conscience.

He checked the clock ticking discreetly in the corner of the library. He was late for his lunch with Phil Sherman, but Phil was always late himself, entangled one sinuous way or another. He winced, catching himself being envious of his oldest friend. A bachelor who was also a theatrical producer evidently had innumerable affairs to tend to, some more fair-haired than others. "Surely you remember your Mendeleyev from chem, Wes," Phil had said after Wes spotted him at the latest war orphans' benefit with a chorus girl as leggy as a racehorse. "Chorine is the element I've added to the Periodic Table."

That would do for some people, Wes supposed. Unfolding Susan's letter again, he ran his eyes down it as if it were a balance sheet. The lowdown on Monty's vocal status could be more heartening and could be less. It was her remark about buying his way through the alphabet that nettled him. *Susan, Susan, you don't have to pour it on.* She was supposing that he had set his sights on the TM&T—"the Empty," he knew people called it, not that he cared—only because it ran from Valier, the Double W's handiest shipping point these days, to the mainline at Conrad; another cattle baron grab, another annex to the House of Williamson. True as far as it went, but motives seldom know pure boundaries. *What if I were to tell you, Susan, that this is more like an old military maneuver—shaking the blanket to get rid of the cooties.*

He rubbed his temples with a shielding hand, trying to rid his head of the tensions of last night. In the ever-flowering wilderness of progress, a person now did not even have to leave his favorite chair to visit the battleground of politics. (Election years were always going to be the hardest, he knew. When a spell like last night's came, he missed participation in politics as if a basic sense had been ripped from him, touch or smell or speech.) He had sat up until the bitter end listening to radio voices describe the Democratic nominating convention tying itself in knots over the Klan. The Smith and McAdoo factions would go back to endless balloting again today, deadlocked over a simple resolution against the bigotry which everyone knew went under the initials KKK. The Republicans hadn't really been any better, standing by that mute fool Coolidge, successor to that incoherent fool Harding. Very much, Wes wished he had Susan in front of him instead of her all too representative letter. She could joke all she wanted, but in times like these he was the one who had to face what the Two Medicine & Teton was likely to carry other than cattle. Word had it that railway workers were the web on which the Klan was spreading itself through Montana, the skunkholes called Klaverns by all reports in forty counties by now. *The sneaking bastards.* He wasn't having that in the Two Medicine country. He would need to clean and gut the little railroad, fire every one of them, and have the sheriff kick them to the county line if that's what it took.

Like the mills of the gods, the drivewheels of faith sometimes could grind exceeding fine, and Wes took what satisfaction there was in that. He tucked the letter away. Wouldn't Phil Sherman relish this railway venture, a homely little set of tracks as an excursion for exquisite banter. "But this is perfect for a Galahad like you, Wes," he could all but recite the conversation to come at lunch, "a chance to operate a railroad as something other than organized robbery of the public." "Yes, Phil, and I'll maintain it by passing the hat here in the club." (But he thought he would not make the case, even to Phil, about the railroad as necessary angle-iron against the Ku Kluxers; as a Catholic cautiously let in to Phil's natural Gold Coast set at Harvard, Wes had learned considerably more than was in the curriculum.) The two of them would spar from there—the East tended to be a sparring match; the West always was a wrestle—and he knew it was time, past time, to go on up now for asparagus and epigrams.

Yet he still could not bring himself to move from the spot in the library, pinned there by too much memory. He did not often let himself be like this, but the mood had come today as sudden and inescapable as the flip of a card out of the deck. The jack of spades, another of Susan's teasing tags for him whenever she caught him trying to see around himself to both sides of his life; but at moments like this, he figured he amounted to nothing more than the jack of clubs. A little over four years ago, the evening in Helena, at the Montana Club. He had sat in a deep leather chair very much like this one, gazing in perplexity at the man from the other wing of the party, a bald timeserver known for doing exceptionally little in the legislature except carrying out the mining cartel's bidding. "Pull out? You can count on precisely the opposite. When I'm governor I'll make this state so hot for you, you and the copper boys will need to go around in furnace pants."

"Wes, Wes," the politico chided. He put down beside Wes's brandy glass a newspaper clipping.

> Miss Susan Duff, Helena's renowned alto, will give a
> recital this evening at the Missoula Atheneum for the
> benefit of the Over There memorial in France, where so
> many of Montana's men at arms lie. . . .

That was followed with the receipt for the Missoula hotel room
where she joined him for the night. Under Wes's staring eyes, the
man crumpled the two pieces of paper and flipped them into the fireplace. "Naturally, there's more where that came from."

Most of a continent and a career away from that now, Wes smiled
wanly to himself. At himself. That damned henchman had spoken
more truth than he knew. There still was a multiplicity, written down
and not, where that came from.

OVER THERE

· 1919 ·

"HALLO, AMIS!" The not combative how-do-you-do had wafted across the few hundred yards of battered ground between the Germans' trench and his men as they were digging in. *"Woher kommt Ihr?"*

"Aus Montana, Fritz," a buck private fresh off a potato farm in the Gallatin Valley cupped his hands and shouted back. *"Wir sind Rocky Mountain buckaroos."*

"Aus dem wilden Westen? Habt Ihr 'six-shooters' wie Old Shatterhand und Winnetou?"

"Nein, nein! Fur Euch Hunnen genügt ein!"

At the time Wes laughed helplessly. If only the conduct of war did match up with Karl May's dashing pages of prairie shoot-'em-ups as imagined from the woods along the Rhine, and if only one bullet per Hun were enough.

The enemy's attentiveness to newcomers in the stale flat-footed killing match that was the Western Front was understandable: Montanans were the mould for reinvented soldiers, American Expeditionary Force–style—hunters from the time they were boys on ranches and homesteads, well acquainted with shovel calluses and dirty chores and rough quarters. Most of all, not worn down as the Europeans and British were by the routine of trench life, which was mud and rats and boredom interspersed by the warning whizzes of every caliber of weapon known to man. Wes remembered thinking that Company C handled better that day, their first in the frontlines, than they ever did on the grumblesome troopship or in the poker-wild disembarkation camp, and that sort of thought had told him he was thoroughly an officer once more. At the time, of course, only newly commissioned as an old captain, not yet a young major; but back in command comfortably enough. "Sergeant, instruct Private Imhoff to limit his conversations with the other side," he had issued the order to keep matters rolling his way, before jauntily setting off to inspect the remainder of the position. Not twenty minutes later, a salvo screamed in on the Montana battalion. He and Lieutenant Olsen had to make themselves thin together behind a shared snag of a tree, shrapnel whining sharp as a singing saw.

A year and a half ago? Was that really all?

To keep warm, Wes paced back and forth on the fresh wood of the parapet the French government had installed for visitors to the battlefield, of whom he was privileged to be the first. *Luck of the draw, if you count mortality tables as any kind of luck.* Forcing that thought back into its den, he made himself concentrate on the now quiet spectacle in front of him, the vast empty butcherworks that had been his second war in one lifetime. Cuba, the fabled rough riding there, had been just that—a short dangerous jilt-jolt canter and over with—compared to the herd gait of death here. From habit he traced the lineaments of even this dread landscape with the care of a geographer. Somehow still lethal now that they were ghostly, the trenches gashed for miles in both directions through the once rustic valley like vicious whims of an earthquake; somehow worse because they were man-made.

Perhaps because it was the one piece of contested earth anywhere around that vaguely held its original shape, Wes made it known he would like to go up onto the hill. The French military attaché was solicitous about whether Monsieur Williamson would wish to walk that far, which meant whether he could. Wes glanced at the officer's own mark of the war, a monocle worn derisively over an unseeing left eye—glass the fitting companion for glass, *n'est-ce pas?*—and said he would be all right. Then he set off up Dead Man's Hill with the Frenchman.

Actually he was surprised that the only thing he could not manage so far, this first time back, was the weather. November, peeled raw by the wind. Naturally the French had wanted this to coincide with the anniversary of the Armistice. No reason for the weather not to be coldly seasonal too, and toward Verdun he could see clouds building from the ground up. Gauzy gray heaps common to low country, nothing like the flat-bottomed floes shaved white by coming over the Rockies. Wes had a moment of wondering what Karl May did about prairie sky.

He and the escort climbed with odd austere care, the dark maroon topcoat and the blue dress uniform the only advancing spots of color in the dun landscape. The rise of ground was so pitted with shell hole upon shell hole there was barely room to walk in single file between, and to Wes's irritation the escort periodically steadied him with a hand to his elbow. Fresh earth was turned wherever the French graves registration teams had been about their business of exhuming and removing bodies to the memorial cemetery. Across about a hundred and sixty acres, Wes estimated—a quarter section, back home—lay the litter of old rifles, helmets, ruptured canteens, even scraps of uniforms and bone bits.

Beforehand he had set himself a mental exercise of trying to anticipate what would be most uncomfortable about this journey back to where he had made his name and countless others faded onto tombstones; but of all things it seemed to be simply the stillness, lack of any of the signature commotions common to entrenched armies, that was getting under his skin. Nowhere he had ever been was so gruesomely silent, nor so hard on the ears.

The French officer kept to himself whatever thoughts he had about the formidable American insistent upon the view from the top; merely more of the battlefield. Nevertheless, Wes needed to see back through time in more ways than one. *But Lord, to spell it out in bones:* he swallowed on that as if trying to get rid of an overpowering taste. From the first day he and his company of men marched in here, he had recognized the Western Front for what it was: history's most gargantuan stockyard. Trenches and bunkers and sentry posts rather than chutes and corrals and cutting gates, but the herd-handling system, the organizing principle, was shockingly the same as the Middle Ages abattoir he and Phil Sherman had traced out of its famed ruins near Aylesbury, as a lark, in their wander summer after Harvard. First and foremost, the cattle pens—except that here, the constructed containments had been insanely built in unending quantity, across half a thousand miles from the ocean to the Alps. Then the commodity on the hoof to fill the expectant channels, in this instance a million soldiers on each side, and when those were consumed, another million and another. Feed them, water them, care for them as best you could, these penned droves: then hope against hope that their weight, the avoirdupois of armaments and guts, would tip the scales. Whether it did or didn't, adjacent to the slaughter yards waited the next sites in the process: the trade yards (replacement depots and hospitals), the tanyards and the boneyards (cemeteries and ossuaries such as this hill). Modern continental war this may have been, here, but in grotesque recourse to the invention of organized slaying it was also fundamentally medieval—a four-year market in the alive, the dead, and the in-between.

Wes pivoted away. This was not a situation where he could say he was satisfied, but he had certainly seen enough, again. "Ready when you are, Captain."

They picked their way back down the hill. Then he climbed into the staff car beside the French captain to go into St. Mihiel and meet the others of the delegation.

Come all the way to the heart of France, and the first notable sight that meets you has to be Wesley Williamson grandly hoisting a glass of champagne? Susan snorted to herself at life's nearsighted ticketing. Quickly covering her reaction—"Merely the bouquets, *pardon,*" she made the requisite face to her concerned escort—she squared her shoulders and strode on into the gauntlet of introductions in the St. Mihiel municipal chambers that appeared to have been dipped in national concoctions of red, white, and blue.

She stayed close by the stammering Missoula haberdasher who was state chairman of their committee for the memorial project; his red-eyed wife, with two sons in the cemetery which all but surrounded this town, was worse than no help in this situation. Gently pummeled with hospitality as they were, Susan let her stage sense steer her through. Back when her voice was still regarded as finding its promise rather than having reached its limits, she had performed throughout Europe—cities a cut below Paris and Vienna and Berlin, true, but a swath of Europe nonetheless—but never at an occasion so bedecked as this. Franco-American tricolors aside, everyone there knew this gathering was intrinsically auspicious, coinciding as it did with the imminent date on the calendar which would put the worst of wars one full year into the gentling distance of the past, into calculable history. Here at St. Mihiel, where America's doughboys and France's *Poilus* had fought together and broken the German salient, their countries would erect for all the world to see a monument of that hardest alloy to attain, peace. If her given part in that was to hold herself high enough tonight for the French to sight along, she could stiffen herself to it.

Yet under this sense of mission Susan, for all her common allegiance with the other Americans who had been sent, was there to represent the postage-stamp trust territory populated entirely by herself and Samuel. The colossal memorial statue, to rise out of the field of white crosses marching in place, she had not bothered to have an opinion about, and could not believe Samuel would have. But the archive proposed by the French, to hold forever the letters and diaries of the killed soldiers—their stories in whatever scrawled moments, adding up to the last chapter of a sacrificed generation—she would have skated the Atlantic to see done. Tucked in her luggage back at the clammy stonewalled pension was the packet of Samuel's letters, the most costly of donations.

Dear Susan—Funny place this world, where they put a fellow on a troop train at [censored] *and he gets off a ship at* [censored]. *Where's any progress in that?* She had seen him and the other recruits off at the Great Northern depot at Havre, therefore he had alit at Le Havre, the first of the pushpins she deployed on the wall map of Europe newly put up in the music parlor. Without him, the house seemed howlingly empty. Four crammed years, his high school years when his rambunctious intelligence broke the boundaries of the homestead as her voice once had done, he had been both the man of the place and its kaleidoscope of boy. It was with an eye to Samuel's future, and the music academy for wherewithal, that she had taken the great step of buying the house on Highland Street.

Sister dearest—They do have wind here. Reminds me a bit of a constant chinook, but more of a washelli. Samuel, with his love of code and collector's passion for language. She went to his notebooks, found the one with his lexicon of wind names, across the airy face of the earth: *chinook, williwaw, datoo, mistral . . . washelli,* a coastal Indian word for "west wind." She took another pushpin from her supply and, eyes all but closed, thrust it into the map on the Western Front.

Susan, ma chérie—"Solve this, Solomon," as Mr. McCaskill would say: *With my size 11½s, I am now a runner. My lord and master hands me orders, I twist and dart and squirm through—there is no flat-out running in these slits in the ground crowded with thousands of us, it is more like carnival dodge 'em—and deliver the message, wait for the reply, then struggle back to HQ.* There were three letters after that, brimming with the intrigued jottings of a big-shouldered bright man somehow singled out to trot slips of paper through Europe's artificial canyons of men and earth; and then instead of the mail one day, the apologetic adjutant from the armory across town was at her door, sent specially.

With duty in France now up to her, Susan managed to put aside emotion except to keep tensely dabbing in, sotto voce, the correction "Mademoiselle" on the endlessly effusive welcomes from the endless officials. Not to take away anything from the grief of others, but she considered the loss of an only brother worse than widowhood would have been. A bereft wife could remarry.

The rest of it, this initial evening, was a matter of maintaining a measured smile and accepting apologies for the inclemency of climate within the confines of France. She played the role of weatherproof visitor to the hilt until inevitably her little group was brought face-to-face with the famous Major Williamson, whom they surely knew? Oh, they did not?

"Sad circumstances to meet in, Mr. Averill, Mrs. Averill," the distinctive voice undiluted in the several years since she had heard him speak at the suffrage convention—he was the state senator from Pondera County, as a Williamson or one of their bootlickers customarily was—and the commanding mien that even then had his listeners whispering *higher office* was similarly undiminished, quite the contrary. Wesley Williamson looked like he always had a cushion under him about six inches higher than anybody else's.

As amused as the occasion would allow, Susan watched him turn in her direction and read her family resemblance with surprise and probably worse; you could not be the daughter of Ninian Duff and pass for anyone else. Uneasy though he plainly was, he spared her any pat remark about resemblance or coincidence and seemed to step back in himself in unexpected apology. He must be here, she realized, as the representative of the veterans, which was to say the survivors, the lucky ones. But how does one qualify for such luck? *The Lord called Samuel,* her father had put a trembling finger to the Bible passage so many times the page bore a smudge, *and he answered, Here am I;* she herself would no longer go near a God who summoned by way of the epidemic of madness called war.

But that was neither here nor there, the concern of the moment was to come up with enough manners to obscure those grudges, older than themselves, that met at fencelines back in the Two Medicine country. Fortunately the occasion was running over with politeness, so she and he could simply extend a hand to each other and apply enough as needed. For public consumption one or the other of them murmured something to the effect that their families long had been acquainted—each would later tease the other for being so slick at watering it down that way—and that was the extent of it.

Curious, Susan checked to either side of him in the crowd, but the high-and-mighty Wesley Williamson seemed to be unaccompanied. Somewhere he had a wife to tend to, rumored to be high society, doubtless taking in Mont-Saint-Michel or Lourdes while he dirtied his hands with this obligation. Momentarily Susan was distracted by a freshly bubbling glass someone placed in her hand. By now the mingled Montanans had become the object of ceaseless toasts. Tonight and tomorrow belonged to them. Missing no chance to underscore the cost in lives caused by the foe across the Rhine, the French had expressed the wish to honor before the great gathering of memorial delegations from all of the United States those from the state that, per capita, had bled most grievously in the war.

When the honoring sips and accolades to the bravery of *les soldats du Montana* were done, naturally Wesley Williamson was gestured up onto the bunting-draped rotunda by their hosts. Susan had to stifle the little something at the back of her throat again when, a sudden study in concentration, he disposed of his champagne glass to the monocled military aide as if to the nearest waiter.

Exactly as she remembered, his speech-making voice sounded sandy, unvarnished, and the more appealing for that. He spoke not in thunderous phrases, but as if concerned to find the right words, the path to their ears. He did not pander to this audience with bits of college French or frontlines *franglais* and while it was not clear how much of his well-carpentered tribute to the fallen of all nations was understood, Susan noted that the French men of government, in their various sashes and decorations, angled their heads in connoisseurial appraisal. Was there anyplace in the world, she wondered ruefully, that didn't eat out of a Williamson hand?

The haberdasher followed in the speaking order and stuttered out how honored, deeply honored, they were to be there.

Her turn. Susan stepped forward and in a voice clear as mint delivered the fiscal report—the amount pledged from bereaved Montanans toward the Great War memorial over here—to somber applause. Then onward to the banquet, and no backward glances until the morrow.

"In the style of Saint-Gaudens, is all I am saying. I have in mind 'Grief,' a statue which a family I've known—"

"The Adamses, you must mean, Major? In memory of the sad case of Henry's wife, Clover, isn't it?"

"You have seen it then, Miss Duff?"

"Of course. It is indulgently weepy to the point of lugubrious."

The French members of the advisory committee on the design of the memorial were managing to appear appreciative of spirited debate rather than appalled at the American war hero and the American woman going at one another as though they wore spurs on their tongues. The haberdasher from Missoula doodled circles in the margin of his agenda sheet, looking at neither Wes nor Susan.

"And you aren't one for weeping?"

"Oh come, Major. Tears have their time and place. But we can't bawl our way through life or we'd end up drowning in them, wouldn't we. Saint-Gaudens is irredeemably that way. And Clover Adams, I'm sorry to have to point out, took her own life. The tragedy we're trying to commemorate is of a different order altogether. A grief incalculably more vast, if you will pardon my saying so. The memorial here should speak to the soul and the mind rather than the tear ducts."

"You're a hard critic."

"I take it you have never had your career tremble on the words of a music reviewer."

To his credit, she had to grant, Wesley Williamson laughed.

On the day that was to culminate in the closing ceremony, Susan would have been nervous if she had let herself. But, dressed in her aqua green best and with enough on under it to compensate for the cobblestone chill of the town square, she sat like a picture of poise through the speeches that began at mid-morning in both languages, or in instances when the French tried to incorporate English or the Americans made forays into French, pulverized fractions of the two. Then through the rainbow swirls of folk-dances. Then through a rather carousel-like version of Sousa marches by the French military band.

Nerves were one thing, brain cells were another. Yesterday's tour of the cemetery had set matters off. All during it and up to the present moment, she found herself thinking back to the homestead and the dead pile—the heap outside the lambing shed where the dead ones were thrown. Some of the lambs when they ended up there still were yellow with birth fluids. Pink tongues poking out of others. Stick legs, ribs showing. Eyeless; magpies lost no time. Similarly Samuel was plowed under the lifeless mass of crosses here, torn who knew how by a barrage somewhere in the labyrinth of trenches. The sickening aptness, rising to mind the way an insistent nightmare would, she had not been able to get rid of in the past twenty-four hours. She closed her eyes a moment, against everything that crept back. Breathwork came to her rescue, the cadence she made herself feel in the rise and fall of her trained diaphragm muscles, the calm of air supporting her from inside. She had never fainted in her life, and did not intend to start now.

To distract herself further she directed her gaze—very much as if she were taking all this in for the sake of writing it down for Samuel— to this homely old town's black iron lampposts, so ornamented atop that they seemed to be wearing ponderous crowns, and to the ambling patterns of its spotless policemen, making their rounds at the edge of the crowd like, well, like gendarmes sampling from one pâtisserie to the next. Almost before she knew it, she was being beckoned up to the platform by the beaming mayor of St. Mihiel.

This had not been her own idea at all. After someone had put it in the mayor's ear that she was a singer—Susan strongly suspected Vandiver, national director of the Over There committee and indiscriminately given to expressions of headlong amity—His Honor had come importuning in person for his most favorite of American songs, could she not possibly oblige? Resigned to doing what she could with the tumpty-tum tiresomeness of *"Over there! Over there! Send the word, send the word, over there! That the Yanks are coming . . ."* as she had at endless Liberty Bond rallies, when she heard the mayor's actual request she burst out laughing, she couldn't help it. So much for George M. Cohan.

Now, presenting the song as precisely as if it were a set of linked *pensées,* each haunting line in dance with itself to the last downcurl of its comma, she stood onstage and, a capella, delivered:

> *"As I walked out in the streets of Laredo,*
> *As I walked out in Laredo one day,*
> *I spied a dear cowboy wrapped up in white linen,*
> *Wrapped up in white linen as cold as the clay.*
> *'I see by your outfit that you are a cowboy'*—"

She had been up half the night polishing this presentation, but it was paying off. When her voice was in good working order like this, the audience became a kind of pantomime accompaniment, she had never seen it fail: heads nodding, feet patting out rhythm. This crowd, pensive to start with, had begun to sway, American shoulders and French shoulders touching as they wove the air in unison, and verse by ode-like verse Susan gave the song her alto all, to the immemorial last lines:

> *"We beat the drum slowly and played the fife lowly,*
> *And bitterly wept as we bore him along;*
> *For we all loved our comrade, so brave, young, and handsome,*
> *We all loved our comrade although he'd done wrong."*

The applause thundered off the stone buildings of the town square. She bowed her head the sufficient number of times in acknowledgment and deftly made her exit. Schoolchildren followed on to the platform, shyly waving handkerchief-sized flags. The band pranced into action again.

At ease and pleased enough with her performance, Susan relaxed into her seat. Spectator now, she could watch as a contingent of military braid thickened in the nearby archway leading in to the square. Some of the American military leaders in the cluster she could match to their newspaper pictures, others not. Her attention was taken by what must have been a staff officer who detached from the group and made his way along her row of dignitaries to the far end where Wesley Williamson sat, obviously sent to fetch him. So Susan witnessed it: Wes rising and following, the surprise impromptu ceremony at the archway obviously keyed to this place where Major Williamson had saved the day, the medal being pinned to the lapel of his highly unmilitary topcoat by an officer whom she realized with a start was Pershing himself. The tidy cookie duster mustache, the tannic personality that could be felt from here, the dour nickname "Black Jack" that was all but stenciled on his tunic: the supreme general chatted in rapid-fire fashion, Wes showing commendable at-attention poise during the medal ceremony but appearing more and more startled to be held in conversation by Pershing.

At last they shook hands, and the American commander was bustled around to the speaking stand. John J. Pershing exhibited a marching stride even in mounting the steps. Standing at exact midstage, he threw a salute to all of France and recalled the famous AEF slogan of 1917, "Lafayette, we are here"; no one had expected him to do other. A few minutes of crisp tribute, and the storied general was gone in a flurry of aides, on to the more elaborate ceremony at Verdun.

Clergy took their turn at the podium, Susan not listening now, lost in herself until the minute the mayor sprang onto the speaking stand and held up a hand, turning all eyes to the town clock.

Within a matter of moments, up in its mechanism some venerable laborious sledge struck a sounding iron repeatedly, one short of a dozen. Once again, the eleventh hour of the eleventh day of the eleventh month, when the guns had stopped.

After a minute of silence, a single bell pealed and then doves were released, tornado of peace into the autumn sky of gray. Anyone not already crying dissolved under the band's first notes of the *Marseillaise.*

When it was over, the crowd had trouble making itself leave. Handshakes, embraces, kisses upon cheeks. Promises to keep in touch. Wes shouldered his way along the dignitary row past the awe and clinging congratulations. Now or never. He caught up with her at the archway. "You're staying a few days, Averill tells me."

Eye to eye they were about the same height and so this was risky, but Susan could not resist the almost imperceptible downward glance learned from her years of reading musical scores without seeming to. His lapel, though, showed only its finely stitched self. Why on earth had he already taken the medal off? "Don't worry, Major, I promise not to take advantage of your absence and drive the ghost of poor old Saint-Gaudens any farther into the ground. I'll be at sessions having to do with the archive."

"Actually, I'm staying too. There's a reporter from the Paris *Herald* who wants to do a walk-through of the battlefield with me. I merely thought—should we have dinner together?"

"Thank you very much, no. Funny tummy," she evaded with not the greatest grace and resented having to do so. "You and Mrs. Williamson will have to excuse me."

"My wife is never—she's not well enough to travel."

Susan pinned a look on him that should have squashed him but didn't appear to in the least. "This doesn't seem right, is all," he was saying as if working at a puzzle. "I said dinner because I thought you might want to talk."

"Whatever about?"

Now he faced her with an expression so radically mixed she blinked trying to take it in. "You don't know, then." It came out quizzical, but what else was she hearing in his words, something as callow as relief or as profound as absolution? "Sam was my runner."

SAND MAP

· 1924 ·

A SATURDAY, whistling day for Dolph, who had a night in town ahead of him, and just another spent set of music-drill hours for Monty, the pair of them were riding back to the ranch when a dozen cows came out of the North Fork brush at a trot, and behind them an angular rider and a thoroughly employed stockdog.

Dolph's puckered rendition of "Pretty Redwing" evaporated. Monty knew the approaching man only to nod to; the broad rise of land between the Double W's Noon Creek watershed and the forks of English Creek was a divide in more ways than one.

"The very lads I'm looking for," Angus sang out. "I have some well-traveled livestock for you." He whistled low to the dog. "Heel them, Bobby."

With the border collie industriously coursing behind them as close as the tassels of their tails, the cattle raced past the paused pair of riders.

"Helping the wayfarers on their way a bit," Angus informed Dolph and Monty, pulling up his horse next to theirs. Keeping watch judiciously on the cows' galloping exodus, he called the dog off. "No charge, though, for setting them into motion for you," he told the two in a tone of extreme generosity.

Dolph unhappily studied the jangled bunch of cattle hightailing off up the ridge in the exact opposite direction from the town of Gros

Ventre and his night's recreation. "We ain't exactly riding for cows just now, are we, Monty."

"But you are drawing wages from the Double W, and the brand on these specimens looks very much like one W followed by another," Angus's voice had shoulder in it now. "Either you take them, or I sic Bob here"—the short-tailed dog keenly looked up when his name was mentioned—"onto them until they're halfway to Canada."

Dolph rubbed his saddlehorn with the palm of his hand as if wishing for a sudden change of luck, then sent a sigh toward Monty. "I guess we better throw them in the west pasture at the wood gate."

"Suits me."

Before they could spur their horses forward, Angus had the rest of his say. "And tell the Williamsons for me my mysteriously frail north fence is about to have new posts and nice fresh barbwire. They'll be wasting their time encouraging their bastardly cows in that direction."

"Mister, they don't want to hear that sort of thing from me," Dolph protested.

Monty was decidedly staying out of this.

"Maybe it doesn't hurt to have it generally heard, then," Angus said, keeping his gaze on the veteran Double W cowhand. "You're lucky it's me who caught up with you and not the incarnation of Ninian Duff."

"That old scissorbill." Dolph saw the expression this brought on Angus and amended: "Excuse my French. But he was always putting the jump on me whensoever I'd ride anywhere close to the North Fork. Acted like he had this whole country in his pocket."

"Man, he did. The one Warren Williamson was always trying to pick."

"Have it your way," Dolph muttered. "C'mon, Monty, those cows are making miles on us."

Angus inched his horse closer to Monty's. "A minute of your time?"

Now what? One bossy teacher isn't enough for one day? But sure as the world, if he didn't bend an ear to whatever this unbudging man had on his mind, there would be some later price to pay. "I'll catch right up," he told Dolph. The wizened rider looked even more put upon, but trotted off alone.

"I don't mean to detain you," Angus said, doing precisely that so far as Monty could see. Elongated as he was even sitting in the saddle, the graying teacher seemed to study Monty's face from way, way up. "How's the songster life agreeing with you by now?"

"Sort of seesaw, one time to the next." Monty resented having to hedge, to someone who happened to pop out of the brush and glom on to him. *What am I all of a sudden, everybody's flypaper?*

"Brave of you, to undergo tonsil exercises when you wouldn't have to."

Monty continued to meet Angus's gaze, although it was not easy. Those agate eyes were too wise for comfort. He knew what they were taking in, a scuffed-up colored cowboy who had arrived at the middle of life but nowhere near its center. He felt the old weariness of having to deal with what he was when every face around him was pearl-handled. Why prolong the malady?

"Tell you the truth, I'm about to bunch it. It's just not working out."

"Are you not getting along with Susan Duff?"

"It's not that, so much."

Angus waited him out.

"I'm maybe not cut out for this," Monty finally said.

The two men tested the taste of that for a moment. Surprise to Monty, Angus shook his head as if he wasn't having any whatsoever. "If she says you have the goods, she's not wrong. Monty, if I may call you that"—people had always called him whatever the hell they pleased—"when it comes to the human voice, Susan knows more in her little finger than you and I and Wesley Williamson combined. If she's had at you this long and is still giving you a chance, man, you're daft not to hang on to it for dear life."

Monty absorbed this, staying wary.

Angus looked off up the creek. "She's been a while gone from here." He turned to Monty again. "I wouldn't want to see her come back only to be disappointed." Preparatory to going, he snapped his fingers above the dog, which crouched and sprang high against the leather of his chaps, and was scooped to its nestling place between lap and saddlehorn for the ride home.

"Mister?" Monty did the detaining now. "'Curious' is a habit I never been able to break."

"Say on."

"You make it pretty plain there's some things you don't like about the way the Williamsons operate."

"Just everything about them."

"I take their dollar, same as Dolph there does." Monty trailed an indicative hand down to the WW brand on the pinto flank of his horse, Angus eyeing the dark set of fingers against the snowy patch of horsehair. "And, can I put it this way, you don't know me from a coal bucket."

"But I've known Susan Duff since she was watch-pocket high," Angus replied. "If she's for you, I'm never against you. Tuck that away in case it's needed, all right?" He rode back into the cloaking brush of the North Fork, and Monty spurred away up the slope of the bench-land.

Atop, he pitched in with Dolph to round up the last of the spooked cows. When they had the cattle under control and headed for the west pasture, Dolph beelined over and let his horse fall into step with Monty's.

"What was that about? You going back to kiddygarden, next?"

"He's known Miss Susan forever. Felt he had to put me through the wringer a little on her account."

"Probably stuck on her himself. Scared we'll beat his time with her." When that didn't bring a rise out of Monty, Dolph cleared his throat. "She's not so bad a looker."

"I wouldn't know."

"I bet. What would you do, though, if you was to git the chance?"

"Do?"

"Don't dummy up on me here, I'm real interested," Dolph pressed on despite the sharp glance from Monty. "Say she sort of gave you the eye. Answer me that now, just what would you do?"

In no way did Monty like this territory of talk. Dolph and the other Double W hands could trot into Gros Ventre any Saturday night and have their needs taken care of by a bottle-blonde whore upstairs at Wingo's speakeasy, while that was out of the question for him. Clore Street or nothing, for him, and that sort of trip to Helena wasn't anywhere in the picture until the Major had enough of New York, and why did Dolph have to start yapping about this anyway?

"Dolph, the woman is teaching me singing, is all. That's as far as it can go."

"Aw, I was only trying to be sociable, Snowball. Excuse me all to hell if I tromped on your toes."

I DON'T *quite know what to make of this,* Susan resorted to the diary immediately after supper a few nights later, *but somehow we got off onto Wes today. It was mainly Monty's instigation, and it threw me for a loop. We had reached our daily stage of tea and honey—I administer it as a kind of soothing syrup when we hit a certain level of frustration—when he looked at me over the lip of his cup and asked:*

"*If the Major ever gets back here, you think he'll figure he's getting his money's worth on me?*"

I answered to the effect that Major Williamson can afford any price we could ever cost him. Monty's expression told me he was not remotely satisfied with that, so I added that really, he needn't worry, the Major had no short-age of either funds or hope for this musical endeavor of ours.

He wagged his head as if considering that and after a moment said:

"*Well, he is a praying man, even if he can't get down on his prayer bones anymore.*"

His skeptical tone surprised me, given his mother's life of gospel. ("Angel Momma" is long dead but still ticking, from the way he cites her.) Without thinking I said:

"*For him it seems to have worked.*"

He wanted to know how I meant. Monty is more than bright enough to realize that Wes and I did not find each other in baskets in the bulrushes, and so I went so far as to say:

"*The Major once told me he felt the cupped hand of God around him, in the war.*"

By now Monty has seen, any number of times, Samuel's picture on my makeshift desk. I may be imagining, but I think sometimes I catch him study-ing it. This time, he did me the cold kindness of not looking in that direction when he said: "I guess maybe in any sort of situation, there's soldiers and then there's officers."

T HAT woman was going to drive him to desperation.

Breathe, breathe, breathe. You would think she was a lifeguard pumping away on a drowner.

Monty eased the Duesenberg across the cattle guard at the main gate of the Double W, grimacing as the bumps made the elegant car bounce and groan. The county road on in from the ranch was no bargain either, with ruts fried into it by the abrupt turnaround of weather. He wished the Major would go back in the legislature long enough to do something about these christly awful roads that he was always having to baby the car along on.

Even this day off from her tasted bad, thanks to her. "Breath capacity, I hate to keep bringing it up," she had brought it up, last thing yesterday. "Yours is lazy. That's not your fault, it comes with chasing around the countryside with the Major and otherwise never exercising."

"I'm exercising now, seems like," he had pointed out.

"It doesn't come out in your singing yet. You must keep at it and at it."

Her and her *at-it*-tude. All he wanted was to sing. No, that wasn't quite all. He wanted to sing as free and easy as Angel Momma had, and have the world sit up and listen, and make enough money at it that one wrong turn of a card or stray shimmy of the dice wouldn't leave him flat busted, and for that matter not have to shine up another man's car and then right away be called on to drive it over these dustbaths called Montana roads. (It went without saying that he was always going to have a general desire for a Leticia Number Two, which he had not had much time to have on his mind lately until damn Dolph touched it off the other day.) Granted, turning yourself into something took work: he knew that in every fiber of his being, he had put himself through plenty back there in rodeo clowning. But these dipsy-doodle nose and gut exercises she kept after him about—it was like she was trying to turn him into one of those carnival freaks who could tie parts of themselves in knots. " 'Smell the rose, blow the bugle,' " he mimicked.

Even the way he talked, she had started giving a going-over. The other day when she was soft-soaping another exercise prescription by claiming it had probably let her hang on an extra year in New York back when she was trying to make it as a singer there, he had chimed in without thinking: "I been there myself, one time with the rodeo, and that New York ain't to be sneezed at, for tough."

"'Have been,'" she instantly repaired that, "and 'isn't' wouldn't hurt, either. Any good habit like that will help with your singing, I guarantee."

She had laid that on him mildly enough, for her, but it produced a spat. He huffed up and let her know that the Noon Creek schoolhouse was not shabby and that his last couple of years there, the seventh and eighth grades, were under Mrs. Reese, a stickler for words if there ever was one. "Then you had better get back to stickling," she came out with next. "It doesn't take that much."

"I do that, I'll hear about it from the boys in the bunkhouse."

"So? Your singing has to count for more than your hearing."

That was like her, to have the first word and the last and the majority in between. Yet there she was, still persevering on him when she any number of times could have said "That's it" and folded the whole deal.

He frowned, then had to half laugh, at all this arguing with himself. It hardly even did a person any use to get a good mad on against her. Last thing she had said to him in yesterday's go-round was: "If it makes you happy to be cranky, you go right ahead."

He was Johnny-on-the-spot at the Valier depot. Swaying under its pushing finger of smoke, the locomotive of the Two Medicine & Teton Railway teetered across a final coulee on a trestle that had seen better days and came laboring across the last mile or so of prairie into the scant town. Monty was as ready as he could be when the private coach drew to a halt exactly even with the waiting car. "How you doing, Major?"

"I expected you to set that to music."

"Not just yet." Monty contrived not to notice that the train porter wanted him to take the Major's luggage off his hands, instead holding the trunk of the car open for the man to heft suitcases in. Enough bags that it looked as if the Major was here to stay for a while, so at least there might be some stretches of driving when he wouldn't have to be huffing and puffing trying to please the unpleasable over there on the North Fork. Seeking some topic of conversation other than that, Monty asked: "How do you like your railroad?"

"At least it's wide enough."

Monty shook his head as if that was a good one. When he tenderly shut the trunk of the Duesenberg, he turned around to find the Major still standing there looking him over.

"You can't keep me in suspense, you know," Wes prompted as if the report was considerably overdue. "How are you and Miss Duff coming on your musical education?"

"Scuffling along. She probably can fill you in on me better than I can." Monty ducked into the driver's seat, and after a moment, Wes climbed into the rear seat. But before starting the car, Monty mustered the request he had worked on all the way from the ranch. "Major? On that. Ask you a favor, can I?"

"It depends on the caliber of the favor, doesn't it."

"Keep Dolph at the ranch, when I go for my lessons? Dolph is the sort, anything that comes into his head runs out his mouth."

"Am I hearing right, Monty? Here I thought the two of you were fast friends, all this time."

"Something like that, I guess. Doesn't mean he hasn't got a tongue on him like a longbox wagon."

"That's as may be. Whit insists you have somebody along with you over there."

"Then how about somebody right there handy?" Monty had in reserve. "School's let out, I was thinking that what's-his-name teacher—Mister McCaskill?—maybe he could be around to do it." This was an original approach, Wes had to admit; he hadn't expected Monty to already be finicking over the exact composition of his entourage. He would need to ask Susan if artistic temperament was the first thing she taught.

Head still turned to implore, his erstwhile chauffeur kept on: "Couldn't we work it out some way, he be the audience or whatever when I'm at my lessons, and I pitch in on his chores?"

Only at times such as this did Wes long to be back in the military, when he could snap out an order and watch everybody involved fall

all over themselves following it without any quibble. "Damn it, Monty, this is Whit's department," he confined himself to. And he knew Whit wouldn't speak to Angus McCaskill if he met him in Hell in charge of the ice concession. Still, if it would smooth Monty's feathers any, maybe someone else from the ranch crew could go in Dolph's place. "Oh, all right, I'll take the matter up with Whit. But I don't promise anything. Now, does this car still have a motor?"

Monty wheeled away from the depot, creeping the car over the pot-holed byways that passed for back streets here in Valier. At the inter-section where the three-story hotel anchored the young town, he was actually looking forward to the road back to the ranch when he heard the backseat command:

"The other direction."

Mystified, he slowly turned the Duesenberg onto the road out to the eastward prairie. *The man just came from this way.*

Taking a pleasure in this that he knew he shouldn't, Wes let him drive a mile or so, shoulders skewed questioningly, before saying:

"I should have warned you to bring your baby pictures. We're going to Fort Assinniboine for the day."

"Fort Skin-and-Bone?" Monty blurted. "I thought there's not much there anymore."

"Enough to buy," Wes replied mildly. It was true that the aban-doned fort persisted in burning down, from vandals or lightning fires or spontaneous friction with the prairie it so incongruously reared out of. But there had been so much of it, when it was built as a Pre-sidio of the north to make sure the plains tribes did not rise from defeat, that rambling buildings still stood and the land that had pastured hundreds of cavalry horses still grew grass.

Monty glanced at him by way of the rearview mirror. "The Dou-ble W need its own fort now? You gonna take on Canada?"

"Very funny." Wes didn't smile. "The whole military reservation is being auctioned, the buildings come with. They'll do for a line camp." He was a bit miffed at the turn the topic had taken. The need, and Monty and every other bunkhouse prognosticator doubtless per-fectly well knew it, was for a ranch to set up for Whit's son, Wendell, whenever he flailed his way out of Stanford. The Eastern Front, Whit had called the quiltwork of prairie they had their eye on, until Wes's reaction cured him of it. Wes now gave due regard to the human question box serving as his driver, and in turn wanted to know: "Remember it when, do you?"

Remembering had already taken Monty over. In his farthest reach of mind the Tenth Cavalry wheeled on the vast parade ground at Fort Assinniboine. The big, big horses, clatter of everything on the men and animals, the band tootling on horseback, too. Here and there a white officer, but all the blue riders, faces on them like his mother's and his. *"See him, Montgomery? See your papa? Can you salute him like a little man?"*

"Only barely," he finally answered the Major. Those first three or four years of life might as well have happened in Bible times, so far removed were they from growing up under the crisscross of clothes-lines at the Double W. Distance was the only reliable arithmetic he knew for Fort Assinniboine. The road unrolling straight ahead of the car, Monty calculated the time to the Marias River and a similar stretch after that to Big Sandy Creek, and then they would begin trending north. "The fort, it's a ways."

"This will give you and the Doozy some exercise," Wes replied, settling as comfortably as he could and reaching for his attaché case.

"That's a thing I never did get a good understanding of." Monty checked quickly over his shoulder, getting this in before the Major drifted too far into his thicket of paper. "How my folks ended up at the ranch from all the way over there?"

As neutrally as he could, Wes gazed back at the dark face that was the remaining result of that other. "As far as I know, your father rode in out of the blue. There was a job on the place for someone like him, he was quite something on horseback. And of course, for your mother when he fetched the two of you."

"Been different if I could remember much about the man," Monty chanced slightly farther. "It sort of keeps the curiosity going."

"Montgomery, sit down here by me. You know you're my treasure. More so now." Her face so twisted, it hurt him, too. *"Your papa—Mister Warren tells me he quit the country on us. Him and another. I don't quite know what they got up to. But the mister, he tells me we better not look for him back."*

"It would have been different, yes." Wes, older, all too well remembered Mose Rathbun. The same dark brow on Monty, maybe some of the same slant of shoulders from a life on horseback. If Monty was lucky, all resemblance stopped there. Mose's ilk, in denatured white form, Wes had met up with again and again in the AEF: lifer sergeants, old stripers, who thought the chevrons on their arms meant they could get away with anything. He'd had to bust some of them so far down in rank they slunk around saluting civilians, but Mose Rathbun had never been his to command, thank the Lord. Soldiers not in the manuals became the pencilings of fate.

"Major? Something I did?"

"Why, is there something on your conscience?"

"Not any more than usual."

"Then concentrate on the road for a change, will you."

That put a stopper in Monty, and Wes tried to find his way into the maze of papers in his lap. In them lay the route to bring bald-faced cattle to the dun hills of the Fort Assinniboine country, a fresh new Williamson brand seared on their left hips. But this other business, the Rathbuns and their wander into nagging orbit around his own father and now Whit and him, kept slipping in between the lines.

"Damn it," he murmured. Then notched up more civilly: "Monty, I take it back."

What now? was registered in the pair of eyes that met Wes's in the car mirror.

"These papers can wait a bit. How's that voice of yours?"

"In operating order, I guess."

"Then why don't we have a sample." Wes swished his sheaf of papers down onto the seat next to him as if the matter was decided. "What type of thing are you and Miss Susan working up?"

"You've pretty much heard them, one time or another," Monty hedged.

"Try me on a fresh one then."

"Uhm, lot of songs in the world, Major."

"The kind your mother would have sung."

For once Monty was glad of all Miss Susan's bellyaching at him about posture, what with the man making him sing while he had to sit here like a lump. He squared himself up behind the steering wheel, pouter-pigeoned his chest for all available capacity, lifted his chin to a goodly elevation, and here came as safe a song as he could think of:

> *"Look there, my son, my sleepyhead one,*
> *the moon followed you home.*
> *It's yours to keep, while you sleep.*
> *Show it your dream and it won't roam*
> *Until the night is done. . . ."*

"Very moving," Wes stated when the last verse was finished, leaving Monty in doubt as to whether it was high praise or he was merely acknowledging that the song had propelled them a little way along the day's long road. Back into his documents went the Major, and Monty once more settled into chauffeurdom.

Both men were accustomed to Montana's long-legged miles. But this journey on a day that had grown sultry, the car turning into a roaster even with the windows open, seemed to go on and on, methodically, doggedly, hypnotically. Gradually the tawny hills gave way to homestead farms, spotted onto flats of land rimmed by benchland. On the section-line roads across the prairie they met no other travelers, black-locomotived Great Northern trains passing them by distantly to the north the only other moving things in the blaze of afternoon. Wes caught himself drowsing, snapped awake and checked on Monty; he was peering ahead over the steering wheel the same as ever.

"Hateful weather," Monty eventually offered above the steady purr of the Duesenberg. Wes entirely agreed.

Time upon time now, the big car topped a rise and the two men were gazing down at another lustreless expanse. There had been a distressed air to farms all along the way, the houses and outbuildings brown howls of dry wood, the cropland even more stricken. Coat and tie off in vain sacrifice to the heat, Wes put his papers aside to keep them from getting sticky and simply stared out at the fatigued fields. To every horizon, the earth had been plowed and anemic grain was trying to grow, but its stalks would barely tickle a person's ankles. This turn of weather, he could tell, would furl up even more of the homesteaders, those who were still left. He had been reluctant to see it on his route from the East, but the puddled settlements on the great prairie were drying up, too. Banks were evaporating, entire towns would go next. It was incredible, the reversal of the wave of settlers that had made Montana and the Dakotas the coming places, before the war. *Buy,* he knew he was going to hear out of Whit the minute he set foot on the ranch, *get out there and buy them out.* That had been the Williamson way, it had built the Double W ever since their father had come into the Two Medicine country on the fading hoofprints of the buffalo and swamped the prairie with cattle.

This drought, though, good God, how many summers of this were there going to be? Wes felt himself turning into hot salt soup in the stifling car. "What do you think," he solicited Monty's opinion as though the day might be more readable from the front seat, "might this bring rain?"

"Got me. The air does feel sort of funny."

Even though the road ran straight as a rail for a dozen miles ahead, Monty never shifted his eyes from it. Wes, gandering, was the one who puzzled at the smudged sky to the west. The banked horizon of hills was dimming away into the sky's haze. He knew it had to be cloud, but the formation was strangely edgeless, almost more a tint than anything else. "Does weather always have that much trouble making up its mind out here, I wonder?"

Monty sneaked a look, then jerked his foot off the accelerator and all but stood on the clutch and brake pedals until the car slewed to a halt. He put his head out the window and studied the mass of murk to be sure.

"Dust," he said as if afraid of the word. "We better get ourselves there before it does."

The butter-bright car sped on the dimming road for the next five minutes, ten, fifteen, with Monty pursed and restless over the steering wheel while Wes tried to watch both the road and the phenomenon approaching from the west, the earth rising in wrath. A half-light, yellow-green, descended, perceptibly darkening as if a shadow-dye from the dust storm was flowing ahead into it. Wind began buffeting the car, the steering gone woozy in Monty's clenched hands. Wes registered, to the instant, the full arrival of the dust, the prairie flooding by him in the air, a dirt-sea surging up into the next element.

Abruptly a cascade of antelope, blazewhite at throat and rump, fled across the road, flickers of Africa in the dust eclipse.

Monty braked and veered, swearing, and just managed to miss the last leaping animal. "Your headlamps!" Wes ordered in a shout and Monty already had darted a hand to the button on the dashboard. In the headlight beams, dust blew across the surface of the road like a ground blizzard of brown snow.

Before Monty could see it coming, a rolling washtub met the Due-senberg's radiator grille and bounced away. They were in past the parade ground before they could discern any of the buildings of Fort Assinniboine.

Monty managed to steer in close to an abandoned barracks that sat broadside between them and the dust storm, the building's turret dim over them like a castlement in the fog of some terrible era. The dust fury kept on without letup. The pair of men could hear it sting-ing wherever it could find wood, scouring off the paint of buildings around them. And they watched astounded as on the pathway between this barracks and the next, not mere dirt but gravel, actual small stones, blew into long thin drifts. Tumbleweeds spun tirelessly across the parade ground, and every so often a stovepipe flew by.

Held in confinement by the groundstorm, each man went into himself as he sat waiting it out in the increasingly grimy sanctuary of the car. Wes's mind was doing its best to reinforce itself with sound principles for investment here, the airborne nature of Fort Assinni-boine at the moment notwithstanding. But Monty's thoughts were speculative. Hidden somewhere out there was everyplace a sergeant of colored cavalry had courted a hymn-singing laundress, and the exact room in the married men's quarters where they had done their busi-ness of conceiving and he had squalled his way onto this earth. But for the life of him he could not pull back anything substantial from his first handful of years here. What he best remembered, as if he could reach down at this instant and touch its magical cool skin, was the fire escape at the post hospital. It must have been the latest thing, a chute like a metal tunnel that even a mite of a boy could climb up inside, barefoot, and then slide ecstatically down. He wasn't to go climbing the ones of the other big buildings, the post headquarters and like that, but the hospital's was the best one anyway. Up he would go, then the glorious seat-of-the-britches ride down, shooting out the end, and there would be his mother in the white field of wash. But that, and nothing beyond dimness about the parade-ground figure whose seed deposited him into this Jericho of the prairie. That and his mother's drumbeat of verdict: *"I tried so, with that man. And for him to pick up on us with never a word."*

At last Wes roused and peered out into the lessening hurricane of murk. "I think we better give it a try, now."

Monty crept the car through the ghostly fort until Wes leaned over the seat and pointed. An aftergust of the storm caught them before they could make a run for it to the building where other vehicles were haphazardly parked and lights glowed wanly in the first-floor windows. The brown blown grit could be heard doing no favors to the glossy finish on the Duesenberg, and they could feel the dust collecting on them as deep as their teeth, the air about thick enough to chew. Wes tied his handkerchief over his face like a bandanna, and at a motion from him, Monty quickly followed suit. They struggled against the wind to the door of the building. When they clambered in, the small crowd of bankers and ranchers and the bowler-hatted auctioneer looked around in alarm at the masked invaders. Wes yanked his bandanna down, and Monty rapidly followed suit. As they swatted dust off themselves, Wes said to those assembled: "The Fort Assinniboine land, gentlemen—we had better hope it's not blowing by for good out there."

I T'S GOING to be the ruin of a good choreboy."

"Whit, he has a rare voice. You've said so yourself any number of times." Still feeling sanded raw by the dust blizzard of the day before, Wes was in no particular mood for debate, but that had never stopped his brother.

"Calling cows is one thing," Whit stated. "Putting on a bib and tucker and squalling out 'Doo Dah' is another."

Wes plumped up a neglected cushion of the chair on the visitor side of the desk—his brother made a point of doing the same on his rare New York visits—and settled in. "For Lord's sake, man, you had him sing for the Archbishop."

"That was here. Under our own roof."

"Monty deserves this chance to get out on his own. He's not ours to do with as we please, forever and ever, amen."

"Next thing to it. Monty still wouldn't have a pot to put under his bed if we didn't keep giving him a job."

"Giving him?" Wes grated the words out. "You know better than that."

Whit ran a hand across his forehead. "Aaah. There's the woman, too."

"Susan Duff came into this of her own free will. She can take it."

"So you've already proved once."

"I told you at the time she's no concern of yours," Wes abruptly was giving this private speech his all. Whit eyed his brother there on the far side of the scarred old desk. Was his case of petticoat fever coming back? No, there had been more to the Duff woman than that. Which must have made it even worse for Wes. There were times, though, when he wondered whether Wes was secretly glad to have been cut out of the governor's race, even the hell of a way it was done. Not glad, that would be too much to say. But relieved, maybe? Absolved somehow? Whit still couldn't tell. Wes was too complicated for him.

"What she gets out of this is her damnedest pupil ever. Are you listening, Whit? I'm seeing to it myself that she's taken care of, on the money end. I don't tell you how to run the cattle—"

"Good thing, too. When it comes to cows, you don't know which end eats."

"—and I'd appreciate it if you didn't volunteer your every thought about this."

"Have it your way. But this haywire notion of Monty's that Dolph all of a sudden isn't good enough to tag along with him—does he want tea and crumpets, too? I'm not pulling Dolph off this and putting someone else to it, no way in hell. There's no sense in creating hard feelings among the crew." Whit settled deeper into the ancient office chair on his side of the desk. "Could we talk some business about where we're going to put cows, you think?"

* * *

Word always raced around the ranch when the Major, natural inspector-general of corral-sitters and dawdlers, set foot out of the big house, but for once it failed to reach Monty and Dolph before he did. Splattered just short of polka dots, they halted amid their task of whitewashing the harness room and looked around at him.

"Caught you at it," Wes said sternly enough to maintain his reputation. "Working. Are you trying to ruin the reputation of the whole crew?"

The two told him that choreboys always had more to do than they knew what to do with, which for both of them had an element of truth in it, and stood waiting to see what he wanted, brushes dripping.

Conveyance to the North Fork, he informed them.

Where's this come from? Monty's thoughts lined up in alarm. *Why don't he just go over there with us tomorrow when we do?* Very slowly he wiped his hands. "Take me a little while to get cleaned up enough to bring the car around."

Wes waved that off. "Let's keep life simple. Hitch up the grays for me, I'll go cross-country." Everybody on the Double W knew singular from plural, particularly when uttered by a Williamson, and Monty and Dolph apprehensively slid away into the main barn to fetch the horses.

They watched the Major drive the buckboard up to the big house, hating to admit to themselves that he handled the reins as spiffily as either of them could. Minutes later, team and well-kept wagon went back past them at rattling velocity and kept on at a smart pace until starting up the incline of the benchland.

"So what do you suppose?" Dolph was intrigued. "He's heading over there to git your report card from her?"

"Or maybe yours," said Monty.

Once atop the broad bench of land, Wes spanked the reins across the rumps of the horses, setting them into a prancy trot again, and anxiously studied the sky to the west for indication of how the weather was going to behave. Indeterminate, as usual in the Two Medicine country. He put the weather question aside as best he could and concentrated on handling fine horses again, the leather feel of the reins tethering him to the moment. A kind of pleasure he had almost forgotten took him over, the team of grays fresh and wanting exercise and snappy at the ends of the reins, the bolster beneath his knee with almost the feel of a saddle, although he knew that was stretching imagination some. The commanding officer who came up out of the cavalry had singled him out even in France, that incredible time, to remark on how lucky Wes was to have grown up in such glorious horse country for a soldier. Wes ruminated on that now, the assumption that where you were born fitted you to the country. As sure as anything, before his wound he would have cantered across this benchland on a saddlehorse as if under a satin guidon. But he didn't mind at all having been dealt out of Indian fighting by chance of birthdate. San Juan Hill and the St. Mihiel salient had been enough wars to hold him. Those and Montana politics.

So, he concluded contentedly, take the saddlehorse part out of the equation and it still was glorious country on a day such as this. Up here on the level divide between the creek valleys the scope of earth opened, the Rockies suddenly enlarging with the skyline expanse of cliff and reef and cuts of crag chipped like the faces of arrowheads, and the sun-browned prairie boundless in the other direction. As ever to Wes's eye and mind, the sweep of it all curved away through the profound distances of the Two Medicine country to where geography turned into history. This reach of earth drew its name from the canyoned river thirty miles to the north where the Blackfeet tribe in legendary times twice built their medicine lodge for sacred ceremonies; but in more ways than that, Wes knew to the innermost timber of his being, this had been a land of two medicines, two sets of the most potent beliefs a people could hold. The struggle for the prairie could be said to have begun here, when Meriwether Lewis and his exploring party bloodied the Blackfeet in a parley that turned into shooting, in 1806, on the banks of the Two Medicine River. Evidently inheritors by nature, one of the creeds of the Williamsons which they did not even need to discuss out loud was that if they had not put together a cattle empire on swaths of land here for the taking after the eventual diminishing of the Indians and the buffalo, someone else would have. It played through Wes's mind now that he was on his way to take his medicine from Susan, who had once told him that when it came to owning chunks of the Two Medicine country, he and his father and Whit behaved like Saint Bernards in a windowbox.

Long thoughts ended abruptly as he reached the edge of the benchland and had to wagoneer the still-spirited team down the slope and across rough meadow to the ford of the North Fork. He eased the team and wagon into the clear creek. Pulling into the yard with the wheels still shedding water, he whoaed the horses vigorously enough to announce himself, but no one appeared. Women's voices in duet carried from the house. Wes had to smile. Susan would not interrupt a song no matter what. He stayed in the buckboard, listening, the ears of the matched horses up sharp in curiosity.

When the singing concluded, the door of the house opened with alacrity. "If it isn't Major Williamson," Susan announced for the benefit of the interested. He saw her shoot a look past him for Monty and Dolph.

A smaller figure joined Susan at the doorway. Wes climbed down from the wagon and made himself sociable:

"Mrs. McCaskill, isn't it? Don't break up your songfest on my account. You sounded like a set of larks."

"No, it's time I wasn't here." Adair too seemed to search the air around him, more than addressing him with her eyes.

"Please, don't let me run you off."

Adair looked squarely at him now, as did Susan beside her. Uncomfortably Wes amended: "I didn't know I would be interrupting anything, I only came over to make sure everything is squared away. With the music enterprise and all."

"I dasn't take too much advantage of Susan," Adair said, leaving the impression there might not be enough to go around. She plucked out a pocket purse and paid some coins into Susan's hand. "If I don't go home and get at things, we'll have to eat sin for supper. And probably borrow the salt and bread from you for that, even."

Susan gave a hoot at the old saying. "Careful, or you'll set off that sin-eater you're married to. He'll be rhyming *sin* and *thin* at you until the words wear out."

"Wouldn't he, though."

Wes let all this pass as if he had wandered into a conversation between Frenchwomen. Adair mounted her horse in climbing fashion as Wes held it by the bridle, then her small solo form went from sight around the bend of the chattering creek.

He assembled himself again for what he had come for. "Here I am, as summoned."

"'Summoned,' that will be the day. Won't New York fall down, without you there to support it? We thought you had forgotten your way back to Montana." The tingle of the song still seemed to be all over Susan. She spun to go back in the house, but he made no move to follow. "Wes? You could step in. Homesteads don't bite."

"Actually, I was hoping we could make an outing of it—I haven't been up under the Reefs in ages." He stayed rooted in the yard, appearing abashed. "More fool, me. I'd forgotten that even up here there would be the matter of the neighbors."

For her part, Susan looked highly amused. "Neighbor, singular. You haven't that much to worry about, here. Adair McCaskill holds to herself, in every way I can think of."

"Well, then." Wes drew himself up. "If this won't set tongues off, near and far—I brought fried spring chicken and hard-boiled eggs and fresh biscuits and chokecherry jam and a jar of Mrs. Gustafson's dreaded pickles and a bottle of Chenin Blanc."

"A picnic! Who would have thought the soldier man had jam in him."

"Susan, damn it—if you don't want to go, just say so."

"Don't be so touchy, of course I want to go. What's left for me to provide? Ah. A representation of strawberries. There's a patch of wild ones along the creek bank. Let me change, and pick those, and I'm at your service, Major."

Their route took them west on the uneven scrape of road, hedged with tall bromegrass. After the climb out of the creek valley they were up onto the shoulder of Breed Butte, the buildings of the abandoned Scotch Heaven homesteads here and there below them like wagons in a looping circle, left to fall apart. Wes clucked encouragement to the horses when he wasn't regaling Susan with everything he had stored up for this. She listened eagerly to his account of what was on in New

York, even to his dodgy report of subscription evenings—"*con*scription is more like it"—at Carnegie Hall with Merrinell's circle, and all the good dirt about politics in Coolidge climes. When this ran out they found enthusiastic things to say about the day's weather, the sun holding the Two Medicine wind at bay for once. To look at, the two of them might still have been lovers unencumbered by discovery.

But Susan was careful not to promote touching against each other in the sway of the buckboard over the thin-tracked road, and they both looked relieved when the wagon reached timberline. They agreed on an open grassy circlet that gave an opening of view there near the top of a foothills ridge, where the rimrock of Roman Reef capped the entire sky west of them. Finding a spot with a welcoming smattering of wildflowers, they spread a serviceable tarp. Cork came out of bottle, mutual faces were made in scorn of Prohibition, and they sipped at the wine and the day.

"You were right," Susan gave him his due. "It's best to be up here, before the summer gets everything again."

Wes smiled absently. "Even a tossed coin comes down right half the time."

Turning his head, he searched along the base of the towering reef to a particular swatch of timber with an open park many times the size of the grass pocket they were in. "That's where my father took Roosevelt after elk, that time," he said as if refreshing his knowledge from a guidebook. He and Whit along as youngsters who would be heirs to such behavior someday, watching in awe and envy as the men sat around the campfire drinking whiskey chilled with fistfuls of snow. Theodore Roosevelt full of bounce as he emerged from his tent the next morning and woke the entire camp with his yelp to their father, "Perfectly bully country, Warrie!"

Wes grew aware Susan was watching him with her studying expression. "What?"

She merely shook her head and put her eyes to the same use again behind a sip of wine.

Caught by the day and the chance to see it all from up here, he scanned out eastward over the dun grasslands and fields. To him it resembled a sand map, in the vastest headquarters, but instead of the croupier sticks of staff colonels and toy troop movements, the contest for land was deployed on that miniature of earth. He could have recited it to the nearest dollar to Susan, if she wouldn't have batted him off the ridge. There below them the west pasture of the Double W broke off, like a salient that had been blunted by the boundary of the Two Medicine National Forest. Wes could even pick out the wood gate, called so because the Double W used it as access to timber for firewood and corral poles and buckrake teeth. Over the shoulder of Breed Butte from there lay the North Fork of English Creek, the old Duff and Erskine and other homestead pastures where Angus McCaskill's band of freshly sheared sheep were as visible as peeled eggs. Beyond the last barb of McCaskill's wire fence the rangeland was the Double W's, all the way to the irrigated farms around the fledgling town of Valier and the blue eye of lake there which seemed to be returning Wes's appraisal. Once more he was helpless against too much memory. In the boom before the war he'd had to talk like a good fellow to convince Whit to yield that Valier land to the Minneapolis grain concern and their irrigation engineers—*Cattle are no good to us unless there are stomachs around for them to find their way to.* He had been ahead of things then, guessing with terrible rightness that the dry-land farming that was bringing needed people to Montana would someday go drier yet. Irrigation, roads, towns that amounted to more than wooden tents, progress paid for by taxing the extractors; he had seen the shape of what could be. On what proved to be the sand of a political career.

Susan brought him back to himself. "Wes. On most picnics, there's food."

"Let's dig in, then."

The wicker picnic basket disgorged. They passed its ingredients back and forth, forgoing conversation for flavor, until Wes no longer could stand not to ask.

"All right, I give. What's a sin-eater?"

"If you were lucky enough to be a *Low*lander instead of one of those ridge-runners in plaid skirts," Susan responded with mock severity, "you wouldn't have to ask such a silly question."

The ins and outs of the Scotland-born were beyond him; Williamsons had been this side of the ocean since hiking their kilts after the Battle of Culloden. "Deprived as I am, you could take pity on me."

"I'm to instruct you in sin-eating, am I. Very well then, it's, mm, a kind of wake. To relieve the dead of earthly sins, I suppose you'd say. I wasn't all that old when Gram Erskine passed away and I saw it done, right there." She inclined her head toward the Erskine homestead, next up the North Fork from the Duff place. Wes felt the stir of his father's voice in him: *"That Erskine is another one—in cahoots with Ninian Duff."*

Susan was saying, "Scotch Heaven's first death, she must have been. So, they were all still full of the old country," pronouncing it *auld countrrry,* "and nothing doing but they had to have a sin-eater. They take and put a piece of bread and a salver of salt—oh, it's easier to show you. Assume for the moment I'm not among the living." She took one of the biscuits and the salt shaker in either hand, lay back on the tarp, and carefully positioned them atop her chest, where her clavicles met her breastbone. With eyes shut and held breath, she made a perfectly still body there on the shroudlike canvas. Wes watched, fixed as if hypnotized, as one hand ever so slowly came up out of the grass holding a single shooting star and joined the other hand in folded repose beneath her breasts, the tiny flower in mischievous droop there.

"You're spoofing and you know it," he burst out. "That damned posie—"

"You caught on, but a wee wilted bouquet is a nice dramatic touch, isn't it," she sat up and tossed the tiny flower at him as biscuit and salt cascaded off her to the tarp. "The rest of it, though, I swear to you is done just that way. I remember being surprised my father wasn't the one to do it for Gram," she glanced again to where the Erskine place was in slow descent into kindling. "Anything civic and grim usually fell to him. But maybe he was too much artillery for the occasion. 'Ay, Gram, as ye were better than ye were bonny, it is beyond our imagining that ye could have been up to anything, in your younger time over across the water. But on the odd chance that ye strayed from the beaten path into yon bushes of sin, we'll relieve ye of that indiscretion now.'"

Her uncanny mimicry of her father sent Wes's blood a bit chill. Susan sobered out of her role, but her lips twitched at the complicated remembrance. "The Erkines asked Angus McCaskill to be the sin-eater instead. He always had the knack, at any of that old ritual. There he stood, right by the corpse, I can see him yet. Eating of the bread and salt, to lift the sins off the poor old deceased."

Wes seemed to be in one of his deeper mullings. After a long moment he said: "A penitent for all concerned, it sounds like."

"If you have to be Latinate about it."

Stung, he scowled across the carpet-width of tarp at her.

Tell her, it all screamed in him. *See how she likes knowing. Let her try all the bread and salt in the world, then judge the lot of us.*

"Leave it to me to take the shine off a picnic," Susan apologized, torn by the abrupt twist in his expression. Someone who had been patted by presidents and supreme generals, and she was having him on as if she were a devilish schoolgirl. She never would see why he let a stuffy church stand in the way of all else available in a life such as his, but—"Wes, really, I'm sorry I got so wound up."

Wes sat up. "Water under old bridges, some in Rome and some not." His face found its mask of command. "Wasn't I promised strawberries?"

They ate the thimbles of flavor, then Wes, seeing the afternoon go, brought out the name of Monty and it was Susan's turn at serious.

"That's what I need to talk to you about. I have to know, how long are you willing to put into this? He has quite a way to go."

"How do you mean?" Wes propped on his side facing her directly, the better to take issue. "Training in anything worth doing takes some while, why should singing be different? I thought you told me once there were songs it had taken you all your life to learn."

"Monty picks up most things, he'll outwork the clock," Susan granted. "With any other pupil, I'd be thrilled silly by now at what comes out of him at times." She stopped to gather the exact words. "But there's something holding him back, he cannot seem to get his wind built up. I've tried everything on him but a tire pump. His breath capacity simply isn't there. Without it, he'll never be more than a kind of human hurdy-gurdy."

Wes had to laugh. "All the lungpower he puts into conversations when he's ostensibly driving me, I'd have thought Monty has as much breath in him as anybody."

"He needs half again as much as mortals with tin ears," she took a bit of the point off with a smile.

The expression on Wes she could no longer read. He retrieved the crumpled shooting star from the surface of the tarp, sniffed it as a bullfighter might a rose, and tossed it back to her. "As long as it takes, Susan."

She hoped they were talking about the same thing. "Very well, then. We'll battle on, Monty and I."

"That's what I bargained for. Oh, speaking of, I need to borrow our prize student back around the end of this week. Helena business, a couple of days should be enough."

"Make him practice his breathing while he's in your tender care."

"What am I, the assistant choirmaster now? Here we go, there's a drop of wine apiece left. Mustn't let it go to waste." He sat up to perform the pouring. They toasted out of habit, then Wes put his glass out of harm's way and turned half toward her. "I did recognize that song when I pulled in, I'll have you know. Not bad, for me."

"It's only an old ditty."

"It didn't sound so, in Edinburgh."

His words came out lightly enough, but Susan froze, locking a look onto him over her tilted wineglass.

WES. I don't know, this may be something run-of-the-mill to you. But I have it bad."

"Catching, isn't it."

Restraint had gone out the mullioned windows of one French hotel after another, then Amsterdam's, that of Brussels, one or two in London, and now the casements of the misnamed sleeper train to Edinburgh. Something in the water in St. Mihiel, they naturally joked; how else account for such a sudden onset of the malady of love? After the first curious but cautious dinner together, then a second and third as if they were plenipotentiaries returning to a truce table, it had them. Now here they were, two weeks into a romance as full of sway and pulsation as this galloping train compartment. She was a woman grown, whose heart had been lent more than once before and retrieved with no great fuss. He had the world, what need had he of an elongated spinster lover? Ridiculous for the two of them to be bumping around Europe in a fog of love. And proving irresistible.

"How much longer can you fib by cable?"

He said nothing, then caressed her cheek with an odd shy stroke. They still were getting used to touching each other. When he managed to speak, his words were soft with regret. "Until Monday. I have to be aboard the *Aquitania* or they'll be sending a search party for me."

She knew nothing to do about that except acknowledge it, brisk as a whisk broom. "At least we have somewhere that a weekend amounts to about three days, a Scottish Sunday is so slow."

At the railway station they raced to a black taxi with *Mackay* primly lettered on its door in gold, and were trundled up the hill to the Royal Mile. Restless with the thrill of their affair, both of them wanted to walk and walk, go arm-in-arm through this sky island of stony grace, stroll unafflicted under the exclamatory church steeples jabbing home their points to the clouds over the city. They gawked at sites thick with the soot of history, lunched, kissed behind a kiosk, sampled bookdealers' wares, took tea, and at last worked their way up to the Castle, various in its stone textures—all dark, but subtly different, like some natural palimpsest of the centuries. Susan felt as if she had stepped into someone else's life. But at last she had to admit: "My feet are about worn off. Where are we putting up?"

With the sorcerer's aplomb she had come to know, Wes gently pulled her into the doorway of the building just outside the Castle gate. "Here."

They bumped and laughed their way up the corkscrew wind of the stairs, to the top-floor flat. "The agent said it should be"—he triumphantly plucked a key from the top of the doorjamb—"here!" In they went, breathless. Every window threw them a view of another essence of Edinburgh. Down in the Princes Street Gardens, the flower clock told time in autumn blossoms of heather. Regularities of roofline chimney pots thrust up as if each street was a soberly engineered steamship. On the Castle side of things, the room offered a pert ironwork balcony which looked onto the stone-laid parade ground.

"It's an enchantment, Wes. We had better treat it as such." She went to him and they ardently invented each other all over again, starting at the lips.

After, they lay in bed facing each other, lazy and replete, not needing to say anything. They burst out laughing together when a whistle shrilled and bagpipes began to drone under the window as if mocking their dormant state. *Hiiiyuhhh!* came a rouseful shout from practically beneath their bedsprings. "That'll be a sergeant-major, sounding the tattoo," Wes identified as if by rote. "Come on, let's get ourselves decent and see this."

By the time they reached the balcony, the Castle parade ground had been turned into a vast drumskin, the slow-step of the kilted marching contingent seeming to be echoed in the bass thuds and staccato rustles of the drum corps. "I suppose you ordered this up, too," Susan put to Wes as she hooked her elbow in his in reckless dance-like fashion, maybe some innate Lowlander defense against ferocious Highlands music. "That would take tall ordering," Wes answered in a voice husky enough that it caused her to peer at him. "They're from the Black Watch. 'The Ladies from Hell,' the Germans called them. They were two or three down the line from us, when we took St. Mihiel." Now, with the pump of a dozen elbows at once, the piper corps resumed its determination to make the wind work, earn its supper by inhuman humming. Flaunting their plaids to gray rational Edinburgh, the Black Watch honor guard marched confidently to music like no other.

Wes held Susan close as life itself while they watched the spectacle. He could not help but wonder what accompanied the skirl of tunes through her mind. His own thoughts spiraled, but back and back to the same place to ponder from. If Susan had not been avid to know all she could of Samuel's service unto death, and if he himself had not been equally conscience-bound to make her know that only the war's worst havoc, in the form of the desperate barrage with which the Germans tried to head off the St. Mihiel assault, had been able to kill Private Sam Duff, the two of them would not be on this balcony with arms twined around one another. How in God's name—and it was a question Wes was addressing to the higher order of things more than nightly—could love be sired by war this way? He kept feeling that some eternal apology was owed to Samuel Duff. Men by the hundreds in the Montana battalion, enough for almost any soldier to be anonymous to any officer if fate would let him keep his head down: but not that one. While Wes stood seemingly entranced by the ceremonial soldiers below the balcony, the trench scene populous with his own men kept insisting its way back into him.

"You're in for it now, Sammy."

"Whooey, listen to them over there—'*Mein Gott, Mein Gott!*'"

"Too good a shot, old kid!"

Not liking the way that hullabaloo sounded, he had come out of the HQ dugout to tend to the matter himself. The sergeant spun around to him and reported:

"It's Bucky, sir. Sam Duff bagged him. He dropped out of that tree over there like a ton of bricks."

By then the battalion had made something like a mascot of the camouflaged German sniper possessed of buck fever, or instructions to merely pester the Amis but not make them mad, or perhaps some personal indisposition to chalk up kills of time-serving trench inhabitants no more careless than himself. More than a week before, the men had assured Wes the sniper they had inherited with this sector couldn't hit a bull in the ass with a shovel. Wes had taken time to make sure, but the bee buzz that flew harmlessly high over helmets maybe half a dozen times a day backed up their assessment. In one of the infinite manipulations that constituted the conduct of war, Captain-soon-to-be-Major Williamson accepted this ineffectual sniper as a token from his German counterpart across the way. Oblique considerations of this sort had invisibly grown in these armies mired together in years of blood and mud. The shouting back and forth, the enlisted men's common language of jocular calumny. Patrols that didn't go out of their way to pick a fight. Reluctance by either commander to call in salvoes, with shells that fell short, shells that were overshot. It sporadically tore apart into savagery and blind killing during the offensives—Wes knew more than his share about that, too—but there existed a morbid mutual etiquette of the trenches.

Heart sinking, he singled out the big-boned young soldier in the mob crowded on the duckboards. "Duff, come with me," he said with enough bite in it for the others to take notice and led the way into the HQ dugout, Samuel ducking his head to follow through the doorway. Wes waved off the lieutenant and went on into the backmost area, where there was an actual scavenged door. "In here, Private."

This was going to take a while. Wes dropped into one of the prized

chairs that had found their way here from some wrecked French farm-
house. Alone there, difference in rank notwithstanding, the two men
looked each other over with utter frankness. They were a long way
from the Two Medicine country. They were a long way from anything
as simple as rangeland feuds.

"Oh, at ease, Sam, before you solidify."

The young soldier shifted his weight enough to comply. Wes studied the lean ungiving face, wondering what blade of fate had created
the Duff family line. As much curiosity as rank in his tone, he
couched the reprimand:

"I thought I passed word for everybody to lay off that miserable
sniper."

"I didn't hear the straight skinny on that, sir." That last word
obviously came hard to him. "I just this morning got back from the
field hospital."

"You're a wicked shot, Private Duff."

"That's the way I was brought up, on the homestead. Sir."

Samuel's gaze gave nothing. Wes knew better than to try to wait
him out, the young man's version of soldiering—which was to say his
springsteel approach to life—would never be amended by anything
either of them could say. Sitting there, Wes felt the weight of command push at him from another of those oblique vectors. Trained as
he was to both politics and war, there were times when he could sense
the force of the future moving over him like wind-kited clouds; here
standing opposite him, he could tell, was a certainty on the casualty
list that would arrive to his desk after the next patrol or the one after
that. Soldier Samuel Duff was too fearless for his own good. Then and
there, compelled by something he did not want to put a name to, Wes
had called in the lieutenant and ordered that Private Duff be taken off
combat duty and assigned as HQ runner.

And put him in the eventual path of a barrage? Or granted Samuel
a few more vital days or weeks before the slaughter market herded
him in?

Wes became aware he was gripping the wrought-iron railing hard
enough to cramp his hand. There on the balcony, the long figure of
Susan lithe and warm against his side, he retreated again from the
past. He had told her everything he could bring back about Samuel,

except the sniper episode and its aftermath, consequence, call it whatever. How do you tot up the incalculable? The parade ground was drawing a curfew for him, he was glad to see. The pipers were winding down, the drums muffled, as the honor guard slow-marched away in the dusk toward a portal of the Castle. Gratefully renewing his clasp on Susan, Wes realized she had been deep in her own drift of mind. To help bring her out, he pinched his nose closed and made a try at the drone of Edinburgh accent they had been hearing all day: "And where ha' ye been, Miss Duff, while the laddies were makin' their march?"

"You asked. My father marched here."

Wes nearly fell off the balcony in surprise.

"He never did! Ninian Duff, on parade at Edinburgh Castle?!"

Susan failed to see amusement in it. "Wes, you're a famous soldier. But you're not the only soldier there ever was."

"No, no, not that." Wes covered as best he could: "All I meant was—kilts on your father?"

She had to laugh at that.

But Wes could not leave it alone. As they went inside, he said as if it was merely curiosity getting the best of him: "Humor an old soldier on this, can you? Outfits like the Black Watch, regulars probably since Waterloo, ordinarily have the honor of marching here. What on earth deposited your father onto this parade ground?"

"Some shire regiments' whoop-te-do, I don't know any more. He and the others from Fife carried the day, you may be sure." Susan paused. When she looked around at him, her assessment came with that alarming Duff frankness. "Now one for you. Why does every man who has meant most to me have to be a soldier?"

Wes would not go near that.

Interruption saved him, footsteps on the stairs bringing victuals enough—Wes never was one to underdo—to suffocate all their appetites but one. Back to the basics of laughing and love, they rollicked through that evening as though it might be the only one they would ever have. Before long they revisited the bed, where kissing led to teasing—she had to disprove his speculation that her exuberant new floor-length French nightdress copied the dimensions of a Breton woolsack; he in turn had to abandon brocaded pajamas that she claimed made him look like a misplaced bullfighter. By the time proper night had found Edinburgh, they were drenched in each other.

Eventually the fireplace had to be fed. Susan said it was her turn and Wes lay watching and making her laugh with his preaching of admiration for her, high and low. "The shins of the father are not visited upon the daughter."

"You." She returned to bed with a flounce, but there was something serious to be asked. "How soon will you be in Helena?"

"It'll have to be after New Year's."

"That's a scandalous length of time." No sooner was that out than she regretted her choice of word.

"The best I can do. Susan, you have to know—there's going to be a lot of that."

"I didn't exactly think I had title to you all of a sudden."

I . . . you . . . sudden. All this was a field of thought that his imagination at its most wild could not have led him to, back when he had been safely loveless, with only a war to worry about. But here Susan Duff indisputably was, next to him in their mutual state of altogether. A woman a man could make love to six directions from true north and she would slyly keep track of the compass for next time. And each time, after lovemaking, he knew that everything outside of that was stacked against them. An incurably married man (doubly wedded, actually, given what could only be called his inbred necessity for a faith; he regarded the church much as he had the army, cumbersome but the only thing on the particular job), politically on the rise, fortune's palmlines clear as a map on him—and this woman who stood out a mile, as Duffs always did. Again now he traced tentative loving fingertips over the features of her face up to that distinctively Scotch high forehead, vault for a canny brain; her expression told him she knew the odds as fully as he did, and he despaired. Throughout these past two weeks he had tried to break through rationality—it was surprisingly like the coldness of combat bravery, a pane in him that covered as if with frost and that he could not see beyond—and make himself give up everything for her. Pull a Robert Louis Stevenson, flee off with her to the South Seas, why not. And vegetate happily ever after; that was why not. Grasping this, knowing it in himself as deep as the fissure in the heart where the soul pools up, he even so could not let go of the anguished wish to be otherwise than he was. He hated being incapable in any capacity, especially the one—call it flight—needed to leave behind all the others in his life. Now the mustered words came out of him haltingly:

"I'm not much at this, you know."

By now Susan had learned that like all heroes, Wes had a side to him that didn't always come into daylight. She could have told anyone interested that he liked to fool people by going around as if he were the pluperfect example of a stuffed shirt; until the shirt came off him.

"No, I didn't know that at all," she issued back to him. "Here I was hoping for a cross between Sergeant York and a sultan who knows his way around a harem. Why, Major, you're blushing. All over, I do believe."

"You're a handful."

"What, me? 'Jaunty as a feather, faithful as the heather.'" There was another of those cloud-bringing words, *faith*.

Wes shifted his lower part carefully on the bed. To preserve the night, he said:

"The martial music about did me in. Could I talk you into singing something for the occasion? Us, that is?"

"Ah. All this is a plot to coax me, is it." Susan gave him a mock discerning look, like an abbess who knew very well what Chaucer was up to. Then laid a solemn finger on his lips, as if marking her place, and was up and searching for her nightdress. More or less sufficiently attired, she strode back, performance already perking in her, came to the foot of the bed and folded her hands in professional ease on the bedstead there. She gathered herself, with the slight lift of her chest that drew breath in, and softly delivered:

> "*The evening brings all home, 'tis said*
> *Those who stray, and those who roam,*
> *The evening brings all home.*
>
> *In the restless light of day,*
> *We abandon ourselves to quest.*

When the blushing sun kisses the west,
We awake and find our way.

The evening brings all home, 'tis said
From islands far, and Heaven's dome.
The evening, the evening,
The evening brings all home."

THERE on the picnic tarp, Wes immediate and intent across from her, Susan knew better than to remember a golden blush over that time. The two of them had been no perfect fit, from the start they had known which parts were ill-suited for the other. It can grow musty in the loft of the mind; Wes, when he wasn't activated by politics, tended toward an attic-headed collecting habit: rare books, manuscripts, scraps of language that pleased him, property. Herself, she had constantly had to wonder, another possession in among those? In turn, Wes understood of her that she was of brusque blood, given to directness when that wasn't the route that had come to be expected, as a Roman road will fly like a spear from the past through the modern swerving muddle. Not a match, a Williamson and a Duff, that either of them would ever have dreamed of. Yet they had coupled as naturally as wild creatures, until they were found out.

"Susan? Something?"

"Yes. We should be getting back."

CATCHING BREATH

· 1924 ·

THE SUNDAY MORNING of the Helena trip, Wes walked the few blocks home from early Mass at the cathedral pondering how he had ever thought he was in any way fit to govern half a million people, given his record lately on a number he could count on his thumbs. He tried to put the mood away, box it in the admission that the lives of others are not something you can catechize. But no sooner was he into the house than Mrs. Gustafson came swooping on behalf of his breakfast with a glint of intrigue that would have done credit to a stiletto, and it was only a matter of time. After her third hovering pass with the coffeepot, he told her: "All right, tell him I want to see him."

Monty gingerly stepped into the breakfast room.

"Let me hear your side of this." The Major, as if he had a wayward boot recruit in front of him.

"Things got a little out of hand, is all."

"A little? I have to bail you out of jail and haul Doc Walker away from his breakfast to wrap you like a mummy and that doesn't amount to anything?"

"Major, I got more than I bargained for." This was tricky ground, Monty knew, but it had to be negotiated. Saturday night had to belong to a wage hand, not a lot else in life did. "Knocked up, locked up, and doctored up, like they say—I didn't go looking for any of those."

"How are your ribs?"

"Tenderized." He winced with the word. They would have to go after his ribs. Those Chicago brakemen had some sort of instinct, when it came to working a person over. Ten years ago, he'd have taken any of them on, the entire Zanzibar if it came to that. But that was ten years of the general wear and tear of living. Deep down he knew he had been lucky last night's brawl had been only fists. Clore Street wasn't a gun place so much, but you could easily get cut there. At least he hadn't run into somebody who would have worked those ribs over with a clasp knife. "Honest, Major, it don't amount to anything. I can be on the job right this minute, I can drive."

"What was it this time? Fantan again?"

"No, sir," indignation ringing through. Pause. "Wrong spots on my ponies." He could still see the fatal dots on the dice that wiped him out of the craps game. "Had them loaded, is what I think, and slipped them in on me despite how I was watching. I called this bruiser on it, and next thing I know, him and another ugly case were giving me what Paddy gave the drum."

Wes still eyed him, standing there stubborn as a government mule. From long experience he knew you couldn't take the spree out of a man, but you could shunt the man out of a spree. He would make sure there was no more Helena for Monty for a good long time. As to the here and now, what harm had been done, other than to Monty's epidermis?

"This stays between us, you hear? It's not to reach the ranch, and particularly not the North Fork."

THE North Fork was murmuring a diminished tune now that spring runoff was past, and Susan could hear the first splashes of the pair of saddlehorses finding their footing as they forded the creek these mornings. Readying herself, she kept track of the scuff of hooves coming up from the creek crossing, then heard tones of voice that sent her out into the yard.

"Makes no difference to me what you do," Monty was saying crossly to Dolph.

"Snowball, I still bet you there are fish in there big enough to hal-ter, now that the water is down." Dolph dismounted and came over to her at just short of a trot. "Ma'am? I'm pretty much caught up on the chores except milking and the woodpile and little stuff like that. Would you mind if I was to go fishing awhile? I'd be right down there at the creek, first hole or two."

"I would very much like for you to go fishing, Dolph, especially if you guarantee a batch for my supper."

"The fish doesn't live that can resist me, ma'am." Whistling, he headed off to dig worms for bait.

Monty was a case of another sort today, she saw at a glance. His trip into Helena with Wes did not seem to have refreshed him. His eyes were not exactly bloodshot, but they were not the picture of milk-like calm either.

He hugged his elbows warily, aware that she was looking him over as if she were candling an egg.

"Ready?" she asked in a tone that was pretty close to an opposite verdict.

She put him through the same songs as before. As the last note waned prematurely, she did not even have to say the obvious.

He ventured: "Can't I stick to songs that don't take that much breath?"

"Only if you want a career of singing Mother Goose ditties," she snapped and stormed across the room. "One thing singing is, is processed air. Breath made wonderful, into a kind of painting that the ear can see. Yours is still daubs."

She swung around and stood gazing at him as if he were put together wrong. "Monty, I can't understand this," she expressed the obvious, her voice wound tight. He watched her warily. She could crank out indignation like a jay when she got going, but he had never seen her like this. "This runs against human nature," she let him know in no uncertain terms, "that your breathing isn't working up the way it should. I saw Jack Johnson in his prime. He had a chest like an ox"—elbows flung back, she dramatically held her hands wide either side of her own not inconsiderable chest—"he could have sung Caruso off the stage in *Pagliacci*!"

"I'm no kind of a Jack Johnson!"

"That's not the point, you're not any approximation of a living breathing singer and by now there's no reason you shouldn't be!" She flung out a hand as if to indicate him to himself. "You don't have that many years on you. And you haven't led as dissipated a life as some, I wouldn't think." He looked askance at her, but she seemed to intend that as a compliment. Susan dropped silent for about a breath and a half, then said as if draining the last words out of herself: "I have tried until I'm sick of myself at it, you seem to give it all that's in you, and we get nowhere on this. I have to tell you, I don't know why but we're up against it."

Monty shifted around, trying to decide. She would wear him down to a dishrag, with these everlasting exercises, if he didn't own up to it.

"There was this bull."

One moment your feet are under you, dancing zigzag in the arena dirt, the scarred steel barrel all the barrier you've ever needed between you and the horns, then you take the least little step wrong and stumble, maybe on a hank of a rider's grip rope, maybe on a heel-size rock brought up by the frost since last year's rodeo here, maybe just on the blunt edge of the law of averages. The crowd responds with glee, thinking you are teasing, pretending to go down on a knee in prayer in front of the bull. The noise reverses to a gasp as the bull piles in on you, butting, hooking. Over by the chutes they all yell at the bull and someone dashes out and bats it across the face with a pair of chaps, keeping the animal off you until Dolph can wedge his horse between. Whit Williamson charges down on you, whey-faced. "Snowball! It get you?" You can't quite catch your breath to answer. Somebody knows enough to keep them from moving you until the doctor waddles from the grandstand with a black bag in his hand.

The hell with it, he tried to maintain to himself after the story spilled out of him. *If this's all she wrote, then that's how it has to be.* Telling her lifted the teeter-totter off him, the ceaseless back-and-forth in himself about whether the goring was a mere excuse or an everlasting pinch his body was in. But at the same time it emptied him, left him voiceless inside as well as out. Dully he looked back at the fierce face throwing questions at him.

"How deep did the horn go?" Susan demanded for what was probably the third time.

"Collapsed my lung."

"Aha!" Apparently sympathetic as an ice pick, she pressed him: "And when exactly was this?"

The terror of that time flooded back. White sheets, unnaturally so, and while he was flat on his back like death warmed over, the real thing kept trundling by, its spore maybe in every labored breath he took. Lying out there in the arena dirt after getting gored was nothing compared to weeks in that Helena hospital with corpses being wheeled past almost hourly. Remembering, he gritted all the way to his wisdom teeth before managing to get the words out:

"Same year as all the flu."

For a moment Susan seemed stopped in her tracks. Then she asked in steely fashion: "Why on earth wasn't I let in on this?"

"Wasn't any way to, was there," he burst out. "What was I supposed to say, 'Oh, by the way, I'm a one-lunger'? The minute you figure I'm some sort of cripple in the chest, you'd drop me like a bad habit."

"That's not so!"

Isn't it? everything in his stance asked.

Susan thought furiously. All this time she had been trying to build up diaphragm strength in this man but if the muscles in there were mangled beyond repair—she glanced in despair for her copy of Hargreave's *Illustrated Musical Corpus,* snugly on its shelf in the music parlor of the house in Helena, then rounded on the living subject.

"Take off your shirt, please."

Monty looked everywhere around, then straight at her. "I can't do that. It wouldn't be right."

"There are only the two of us here," she said.

"That's why it wouldn't be right."

Red spots appeared on her cheeks. "Monty, for heaven's sake. I need to see your ribcage, is all. If you're going to be bashful about it, it's merely a matter of pulling your shirttail out and yanking it up to about here," she pointed a finger to the base of her breast.

He shook his head, eyes cutting to the nearest window. You never knew.

"Very well. I'll fetch Dolph up from the creek to—"

His "No!" filled the corners of the room. The last thing in Creation he wanted was to have the whole Double W bunkhouse in on this.

"Please." He angled half away from her, but his plea was painfully direct. "If this counts so much, I can come back tonight, on my own. Get Mister Angus here, can't you? His missus, too, if she'll come."

"Honestly, Monty." The rosettes were not entirely gone from her face. "If that's what you want, I can fetch them."

Angus contemplative, Adair indeterminate, and Susan grim, the three of them gathered on straightback chairs.

Susan leaned to the lamp and turned up its wick as far as it would go, casting more light to where Monty was standing tense as a stag.

"I'm still sorry about the need for this," she said delicately to him, knowing he was on simmer, "but I don't see any way around it. Now then. Please show us."

He stayed still, gazing across the circle of light to the jury of their eyes. Even the cat came out from between ankles and leveled him a green gaze, its pupils like black darts. Monty felt like the biggest fool there was. Why had he bothered to come back over here on his own? It wasn't as if he was able to trust white people, even these toned-down ones. Yet how could he get anywhere in this lopsided world without them, most especially her, sitting there as if she held all the secrets.

Hating the moment, all it brought back—*Memory is what we forget with, Monty,* his mother's baffling prescription whenever he pestered her too much about then instead of now—slowly he tugged the tail of his shirt out of his pants, unbuttoned, and pulled the cloth up. He looked at it with the rest of them. There on the right side of his ribcage, centered on the dark bronze skin, the puckered scar where the horn went in was the size of a large tire patch.

Susan arose and came over. As if with her head down into an anatomy text, she traced spread fingers back and forth above the wrecked skin, careful not to touch him.

"Missed your sausage works," Angus contributed. "There was a bit of luck."

"Mister Angus," Monty set him straight, "there's been too many times when if it wasn't for bad luck, I wouldn't have any luck at all."

Nodding to herself, Susan still was examining him. "Wait. Those scraped places—those are still healing."

"Those were something else."

"Such as?"

"Little difference of opinion."

"At the level of your chest?"

Monty wadded his shirttail in his fist, then let out a weary sigh. "Couple of people jumped me, when I was in town."

Susan's face said she knew which town and which part of town.

"Poor old body." Adair's murmur surprised them all. "It's all a person can do to rub along in this world, isn't it."

Not sure whether that was specific sympathy or ready-to-wear epitaph, Monty attended to the matter of his bare skin. He looked straight at the one who had put him through this. "Miss Susan? Are you happy now?"

Susan managed to meet his eyes. "Monty, hear me out. As much damage as we can see there, I can tend to." He closed his shirt, dubious. "I promise you," she insisted, "I see now how to build up your breath. A lot was learned from the lung cases in the war, there's an entire literature on it. But there isn't one thing easy about it. You'll need to work at it until you're blue in the face."

He stared at her. Angus and Adair, their heads to one side in owlish fascination, kept mum.

"Monty, I only meant—"

He allowed himself the smallest of grins. "That could be quite some while."

A IR was at a premium. How had he ever outrun all those bulls but one?

Breed Butte loomed over him, he was barely halfway up its slope but pretty far toward done in. He gasped, trying to make more breath gust into him than was whooshing out. Both directions, it burned between the back of his nose and the bottom of his chest. The rest of his laboring body simply wanted to call it quits. His feet, in the shoes for this that were the Major's latest contribution, felt heavy as buckets of water.

Riding a dozen yards behind him, leading his horse behind hers, she called out: "A bit faster if you can stand it. The day is hotting up in a hurry."

Susan was having him run on the shank of midday, after his voice exercises but before the blaze of noon bore down on them. "It's merely roadwork of the sort Dempsey and Gibbons put themselves through all the time," she told him at the onset, sheer reasonableness. "And at the end, you don't have to do battle with either of them."

No, only with her. Monty concentrated on the ground in front of him, picking out a stunted jackpine ahead alongside the baked set of wheeltracks and forcing himself to keep in motion that far, then taking aim on the weathered gatepost beyond that and closing his mind to anything but making it to that stout pillar of wood.

Water was the reward when he jolted into the yard of the old Barclay place at the brow of the butte and could at last pull to a halt. Susan swung down out of her saddle and proffered the canvas waterbag to him. She watched critically as he swished water in his mouth, spat it out, then took a few moderate gulps from the bag. They did not speak much, Monty generally too winded and Susan absorbed in putting him through his pulmonary paces. The Barclay homestead here was the halfway mark on the course she'd picked out, the steep half as he could have told anybody. The next leg was the old sheep trail angling west under the shoulder of the butte, across the dry cracked reservoir, and gradually down the long incline of the valleyside to the road, where she permitted him a cooling-down horseback ride home to the Duff place. In Susan's mind it was a perfectly logical circuit, uphill at first and then coasting downhill. To Monty it was like running up one side of a Nile pyramid and down the other.

Barely visible back at their starting point, Dolph was hammering battens over the cracks in the barn walls, and Monty imagined that even at this distance he every so often could see him gawking up here and shaking his head in disgust over these jackrabbit games.

"Ready?" she asked promptly as a metronome.

"Not so you could notice, but let's go," he said as usual, and set off onto the sheep trail at a lope. His gait improved with every long stride on the more level trail and by the time he was jouncing down the welcome incline toward the creek, you could see hints of the limber rodeo clown.

Susan would not exactly have said she was happy to be out here running him ragged, but there was undeniable pleasure in being on horseback again. She rode astraddle, in her comfortable old velveteen divided skirt, and sat as natural on a steed as only someone brought up on the back of one from the age of three could. The first day Wes came across the butte in his buckboard to take a bemused look at this new regimen, she galloped down on him as if he were the buffalo and she the huntress. Whirling to a stop, she lit into him. "Why didn't you tell me I'm dealing with damaged goods?"

"That's a bit strong, isn't it? Maybe Monty is somewhat beaten up around the edges, but—"

"His goring? That's more than edges."

"His what? When?"

"He told me it was during the—it was in 1918."

"Susan, I was overseas, wasn't I. All I ever heard from Whit about ranch doings in those scraps of letters from him were the sky-high prices of hay. I knew Monty had been laid up somehow from rodeoing. But he never told me he had caught a horn, I swear to you."

She had looked at him as if she could not believe it. But neither could she doubt it. His brother's habit of paying no more attention to other members of the human race than if they were the Williamson family furniture seemed to irk Wes, she was glad to see. Meanwhile Monty, standing at a distance, panting, had his mind solely on the swimming bath he would take in the creek when this sweaty jaunt was over, the water as warm as fresh milk.

Weeks went this way, then a month, but time of this sort cannot be so easily summed. For there came a particular day when Monty did not plow to a stop and seize the reins of his horse from Susan when he reached the road but instead loped on for another quarter of a mile, the ease of it leading him on and on in astonishment at himself, until he finally spun around to her with the realization he had run years off himself.

I MUST *take care to put this down with every exactness,* she wrote of their turning point. *Angus would have the poetry appropriate to it,* Adair *its cockeyed essence,* Wes *would chalk it up to the wily ways of God and the reward of duty. I have only my pair of astonished witnesses, my ears.*

It already had been a day to mark on the wall. Monty's vocal exercises had gone well—this in itself is like saying the earth took a turn around the moon—and his performance of the practice repertoire grows stronger as he does; it is the sort of leaping progress that a teacher always hungers for. He just then had ripped through "Moses" without evident effort (at last!) and I was about to call it good for the day when he announced: "I have me something of my own I want to sing."

I was surprised, to say the least. What could I say but, "Be my guest." Looking very determined he took his position in the middle of the room, studied off into nowhere—the next habit I need to cure him of—then clapped his hands a couple of times and out it came. I render it here on the page in as close a manner as possible to the way he sang it, for the lines were distributed in the air like poetry:

> *"Does the hawk know its shadow?*
> *Does the stone roll alone?*
> *Does the eye of the rainbow*
> *Ever weep like our own?*
>   *I am vexed,*
>   *I am hexed,*
>   *I kneel at all Your thrones.*
>   *One of so many*
>   *Just another praying Jones."*

That was the first verse of several confounding ones. The song sounded as old as the hills and yet unknown as the next heartbeat. Monty's is a propitious voice for such a song. In his new bottom range, he can put such resonance into the "ohs" of "stone," "own," "alone," "thrones," and that ending-line surpriser "Jones" that it makes one wonder, How could one throat hold that?

When he had finished I remember that I rested my chin on my fist until I could trust my words. Finally I managed: "I know most gospel songs. Why have I never heard the likes of that?"

Monty shrugged as if to say my musical education, or lack of, was no doing of his. "Just a spirit song I learned when I was little."

When he saw that the phrase threw me, he said: "What I always heard songs like that called. The spirit moves a person, I guess you'd have to say, and next thing they know, these words show up out of them."

"Why did you sing it now?"

He puzzled at that a moment himself. "It runs through my head sometimes, and this once I wanted to try out my new air on it, is all."

I hardly dared ask. "Are there more where that one came from?"

"Oh, some."

"Then let's have them." I at once got out music sheets, Monty as surprised as if I had produced a rabbit from a hat. By then Dolph was stomping around out in the yard, both their horses saddled and waiting, but I didn't care. I took down several—"Mouthful of Stars," "End of the Road," "The Moon Followed You Home," "Unless I Be Made To," all of them music up from the bones—as fast as I could write while Monty chanted or half-sang them, before I could stand it no longer: "How did you come by these songs, exactly?"

He looked as discomfited as if I had asked him where the wind keeps its nest. "You won't laugh?"

"Of course not."

"Promise not to think it's loco?"

"Monty, I will not think anything, I will not laugh"—at this point I probably could have been heard a mile up and down the creek—"but I will take the broom to you in about half a minute if you don't tell me where on earth such songs came from."

He said, word for word:

"Angel Momma and the holy rollers."

SPIRIT

· 1892 ·

THE CONGREGATION was short on ecstasy, and Jones was having to bide time by dinning Deuteronomy into them.

"Give ear, O ye heavens, and I will speak! And hear, O earth, the words of my mouth!"

Sister Satterlie, usually the first to quiver with the possession of the spirit, was barely even swaying. Jones himself was trying his bottom-dollar best to will the outbreak, but you could never hurry the Lord. The jolt of exaltation would happen when it happened, that was the weekly history of it all the way back to their knotholed church in the mountains beyond Gatlinburg. Their Appalachian faces hung out from under Stetsons and catalogue bonnets these Sundays, but they kept to their strenuous religion here in the foothills of the Rockies, where the whole passel of them had been shipped in as tie-cutters for the Great Northern Railway. Third- and fourth-generation sawyers back in the Smokies, the men were proud to call themselves timber beasts and the women had long practice in making do at gulch logging camps such as the one up Noon Creek from here. They were God's patch pocket on this land where the ways of the world had sent them. Looking out over the small assembly, Jones as their lay preacher duly cherished every one of them, but he did wish somebody would feel the call and start thrashing or declaiming in tongues; he didn't have all Sunday up here at the portable pulpit.

"My doctrine shall drop as the rain! My speech shall distill as the dew, and the small rain upon the tender herb, and the showers upon the—who's out there?"

Every head in the room turned. "I feel the presence beyond the door," Jones boomed. He had seen movement through the window. "Who comes calling at this holy house?"

The door peeped open, then swung wide to reveal a Negro woman, lank as a carpet-beater. Down where her dress billowed, a wide-eyed seven-year-old clasped on to her. When Jones peered at the boy, the dirtiest face in the world was looking back at him. Jones was prepared to take umbrage on behalf of the Sabbath, but realized the smears on the small dark face came from exuberant eating of berries. If childish joy didn't qualify as wearing your Sunday best, Jones didn't know what did.

The woman gestured apologetically. "I don't want to bother, in no way. We been chokecherrying," she indicated the lard can half full of wine-colored berries the boy was shyly holding. "But I couldn't help but hear. Voices like your ones—I don't know what got into me."

"We're having church," Jones hardly had to point out.

"People I work for," the woman hurried the words, "I heard them say folks like you fought on the side of the North like they did."

"The sunrise side of Tennessee did not follow Jeff Davis to perdition," Jones stated with pride. No one in this room was ever going to forget the Confederate Army's clamp on their small-holding plantation-scorning corner of the South. The oldest of the congregation, Brother Cruikshank, had fought in blue at the battle of Stone's River and had the scar of a wound to prove it.

"My husband," the high-tan woman was saying, "he was a soldier, out here."

"That so? Auntie, who do you be?"

Angeline Rathbun identified herself while the boy peeked around at all the hawknosed faces. He wanted to tell the people about picking the chokecherries and where all he and Angel Momma had been along the creek, but it wasn't nice to interrupt grownups.

"Service in the uniform of our country, that's all well and good," the lay preacher allowed. "But if you'd excuse us now, we have the Lord's business to tend to yet."

"Mister? Couldn't I sing with you? Just sing? I could"—she swallowed—"wait outside between songs, if you'd want."

Jones gave her fresh regard. The congregation had visibly perked up. The spirit making itself known, was this? Jones waited on his own words, wetting his lips. Then heard himself poke the question out: "Just what sort of singing do you know?"

"By your leave?" Angeline moved a step farther into the room. She clapped her hands a few times to set a beat for herself, then began to carol in a voice dexterous as fine fiddling:

> *"Take a mouthful of stars,*
> *Set your ladder 'gainst a cloud.*
> *Go hammer up Heaven,*
> *Oh hammer up Heaven,*
> *Fixin' up Heaven,*
> *Slickin' up Heaven,*
> *Silver nails of Heaven,*
> *Driven nails of Heaven,*
> *Heaven, strong roof of my soul!"*

Jones took a fresh grip on the pulpit. "We make our own singing, but this's a new one on us. Yours sounds like our spirit music," he mulled, "yet it don't quite, either. Am I right, brethren?" The congregation murmured affirmation. Jones felt a tingle. "Where'd you ever pick that up from, Mrs. Rathbun?"

"Slave days, when I was a bit of a thing like him here. In the war times. Every day before sun-up, what we called in Kentucky 'cain see'—"

"We call it that to this day," Jones could not help but put in. "'Cain see' to 'cain't see,' that's our working day in the woods."

"—my momma and me had to take the mistress's white saddle-horse up in the woods and mind him there."

"Nothing goes over the Devil's back that don't buckle under his belly," Jones chanted in contrary praise of those forced to shoulder the work of the world.

"The mistress was afraid the War Department was gonna see that horse and take him for the army," Angeline ventured on. "My momma, she'd pass the time remembering songs, maybe make some up. Got me to doing it with her. Then when night come, she and me led that horse home in the dark—"

"In the dark," Jones crooned experimentally, "Satan's satin dark."

"Yes sir. And the mistress would go out and ride that white horse with a black blanket over him. And Momma and me still had to wait, to all hours. So then we'd sing those songs we put together. Play we was a whole church, like your one here."

"Why are you not singing them this Sabbath, somewhere with your own people?"

"Mister, we're it," Angeline Rathbun smiled forlornly down at her fidgety son. "No other colored, not in all this county."

Jones brooded there in front of everybody, the congregants as still as the prayer-worn benches under them.

"She brings mighty fine singing, brothers and sisters," he felt moved to put the matter to the general will. "What say you?"

"She been sent!" Sister Satterlie shouted, with a lurch that gladdened Jones's heart. "The Lord ever is mysterious in His ways!"

Brother Cruikshank climbed to his feet and testified: "I for one see no reason our congregation cain't have a colored auxiliary."

Jones turned back to Angeline. "You may stay," he spoke for them all. "We will together sing the songs of one tongue, Our Maker's. But there's another consideration." He pointed a not unkind finger.

"The boy here, he'll be fine," Angeline vouched. "He has a voice, too. Don't you, Montgomery."

SUMMER NIGHTS

· 1924 ·

"OL' SNOWBALL, he thinks the world's wagging its tail at him."

Dolph's elbow slipped off the edge of the table for the second time in as many minutes. Irritably he anchored it there again, determined not to let go of his Saturday night spree just when the whiskey was getting good.

"They're that way," the man across the table from him ground out. He topped up Dolph's glass again and then his own, and sat back. The two of them were by themselves in the back corner of the speakeasy, their conversation oiled by the bottle of prime stuff bootlegged in from Canada that the man sorely needed some company on.

"Monty ain't a bad sort, far as that goes." Dolph wanted this made clear. "But he's latching on to too much of a good thing, if you was to ask me."

"He actually goes back to her at night? What manner of woman is she?"

Didn't Dolph wish he knew. Perpetually parched for women, cowboys tended to believe there must be winks of ecstasy waiting for them somewhere, if only the circumstances ever would line up right. But tonight's perfunctory prostitute whom he had sprawled himself on in one of the rooms overhead was more like a blink. And the Duff woman, she seemed blind to her own kind. Dolph had to shake his head. Whenever a man met confusion in this life, it almost always wore a dress. How was it in any way fair for Monty to be the object of her eye?

"Like I was telling you, I suspicioned that something more than do-re-mi was going on. So I sort of checked up on it." The day he caught the string of fish, he came whistling back up to the house to find the two of them looking like they were ready to jump out of their skins. That evening he had sauntered over from the bunkhouse to Monty's room to try to find out what was what; no Monty. "Middle of the night, here he comes scooting back." Dolph walked his fingers along the table to show so. He fought through the haze in his head to see again the pinto saddlehorse coming down the benchland from the North Fork, pale hide in the moonlight. "Puts his horse away real quiet. Goes to bed." Dolph widened his eyes in wonder. "Second time that night, I guess."

"And during these . . . music lessons?"

"I'm right there, ain't I? They can't git up to anything then, me around keeping my eye on them."

The man clucked one last time at the goings-on Dolph was forced to put up with and said he had to call it a night. He clapped Dolph on the shoulder. "See you in the funny papers."

The town of Gros Ventre, nippy even on a midsummer night such as this, lay tucked under its double blankets of darkness and leaf canopy. The man walked home with great care, taking to the deserted street rather than trust himself on the undulations of the board sidewalks forced up by the roots of the big cottonwoods. It had been a night's work, lubricating that mutt of a cowboy. But even a common cowhand knew an abomination when he saw one, give him credit for that.

He tromped on through the dark, filled with a consuming urge to shout to the whole town about the Williamsons and what they spawned. But that wouldn't do. Late as it was, and quiet, he confined himself to humming fiercely the hymn of him and his kind:

> *"Klansman, Klansman, of the Ku Klux Klan,*
> *Protestant, gentile, native-born man,*
> *Hooded, knighted, robed, and true,*
> *Royal sons of the Red, White, and Blue."*

NIGHTFALL wrote itself across the hills of Helena, the rowdy downtown gulch as ever the first to be shadowed and street-lit, then the slow summer darkness gently inking out the superior slope-sitting neighborhoods around their punctuations of lamplight. Throughout the evening Wes glanced out now and then as if to compare the progress of the dark to his own. His desk was a ranch in the making—the Deuce W, incipient in the piles of title abstracts and livestock tallies and crop records and tax rolls of three counties its clusters of acreage would dapple like a prairie archipelago. A separate stack of paperwork high enough to be teetery held foreclosed mortgages, walked away from in the dusty exodus of the landed settlers these past half dozen years and lately bought from the banks by the Williamson agents for pennies on the dollar. Wes was sifting it all as if he were a monk among Alexandrine scrolls. Dyed into the documents, beneath the legalistic curlicues where it took a kind of second sight to go, rested actions of the past that changed everything caught in their path. The shaping hand of a senator on the generous contours of the Fort Assinniboine military reserve, there in the act of congressional appropriation that had created the great and needless fort. The decisive signatures of a handful of sodbusters, who had thrown in together to buy more tractor than buffalo grass could withstand. Receipts that remorselessly followed the decline in rainfall, depositions that attested to the economic laws of gravity even in virgin land as flat and beckoning as a trampoline. If you were trained for this, and he by nature and imperative was, it was all discernible, under the ink. He paused a long while over a contested bill of sale for a pitiful herd of workhorses, depleted by half by the blizzard of 1906, which was signed by his own father.

Hallway noises roused him out of the watermark whispers of the papers.

"Busy, I tell you."

"Only take a minute, Mrs. Gus, don't get yourself in an uproar." The predictable barely restrained knock on the door.

"If it's who I think it is," Wes emitted like the warning blast of a foghorn, "come in and have your story ready."

It took a few moments for the doorknob to turn. Then Monty

stepped in, ranch clothes on him but Saturday-night readiness in his expression. "Major, bother you just one minute, can I?"

"How did you get to town?"

"Bummed a ride with the brand inspector. This way, see, I can take the driving off Gus's hands when you head back to the ranch."

Wes's ire stalled momentarily in the face of this tactic. It was perfect fact that Gustafson took the wheel of an automobile with the glumness of a lumberjack unfairly sentenced to pushing a baby buggy. "Wasn't that thoughtful of you," he at last responded to the all-too-ready volunteer sticking close to the shelter of the door. "And other than that, what's on your mind this hour of night?"

As if he doesn't know? Going to be like that, is it. Monty might have been philosophical about this if he had time. But this was never any too much fun, dealing with a boss who wasn't in a mood to be dealt with, and he drew himself up some to stand his ground. "Mister Whit didn't have his checkbook on him, there at the stockyards. Say, he told me to tell you—let me get it exactly: he hopes your writing hand is in good shape come Monday, because there's one hell of a bunch of new cows going to need a ranch under them."

Wes let his brother's words pass without comment. Monty's next ones he waited for as if ready to lay down the law.

"I know it pesters you, something like this," Monty came out with it. "But tonight being what it is, I need to go out for a little while."

"Can't you ever—"

"Don't even have to draw a whole month's pay," Monty hastened this in, "but just about."

"—steer clear of that?" With difficulty Wes kept control of his face, but his voice sharpened to a stab. "Monty, you have to think about these things now. What is it going to take, some drunken gandydancer beating your brains out in an alley? Hear me on at least this, can't you? Clore Street isn't the best place to be, anymore."

Monty rammed his hands into his back pockets to hide his clench of dismay. As if he hadn't turned himself inside out thinking about this. As if someone who could take that district of paper there on his desk and Monday morning turn it into a ranch that stretched out of sight over the bend of the earth, as if anybody that mighty knew anything about the tight corners of a colored Saturday night in Helena.

Three months ago, as Monty too well understood about himself, in this situation he would have turned turtle, pulled his neck back in and stood planted there allowing as how the Major no doubt knew best. But the Major and her, wasn't that what they were supposed to be at in all this, to help him shore himself up into something more substantial than a choreboy standing on one foot and then the other? Change his chances in this life, from squat to sky-high? And that took some doing like tonight's, if he could only zip across town and get it done. There was no way around it. He couldn't hope for the Major to give him his blessing on anything like this, but a bit of room to operate, out on his own, ought not be too much to ask by now. For about the hundredth time in one day, he assessed his chances with the man on the far side of that big desk. If things had really changed, his best hold with the Major was man-to-man.

"Got to go do it," he said as if sentenced to it. "I'm not gonna gamble this time. I'm not. Honest." As usual, that word called into question any preceding truth, and it was taking all of Wes's effort not to turn that protestation against games of chance on its head with a sarcastic *I'll bet.*

"See, if I don't show my face there, before I start out as a singer," the rest of it was tumbling out of Monty, "I'm written off. Major? They'll think I turned uppity. Say I caught that skin condition: white-itis."

"And that would be too bad."

"It'd be attached to my name. And you never get rid of that."

For whatever reason, Monty could see, that hit home. The mighty Major for a moment looked like a boy accused. He of the family that had employed Rathbuns back to almost time beyond memory seemed to stare as if he had never seen such a stranger. Then his face set. The anthracite eyes of a snowman could not have been colder. With rough motions he shoved out of his chair and stalked to the dark green safe in the corner of his office, half knelt, twirled the combination as fast as fingers could move, and in an instant came up with a money caddy that held silver dollars as if they were bleached-out poker chips. He grabbed out a full stack, then a judicious half of another, plunking them side by side on the parquet table by the window. "You might as well take the works."

My whole pile? All of a man's wages usually showed up in a boss's hand only when the words *You're fired!* or *I quit!* flew through the air. But the lord of pay, there by the safe, so far hadn't decreed the one and Monty had no intention of uttering the other. He hesitated, then went and scooped up the tall-standing coins. "I'll stay a stranger to trouble this time, honest."

Wes still didn't say anything. He sat back down to his desk, eyes into the familiar field of paper, as the door closed behind Monty.

It was not that many blocks to where Clore Street elbowed a gravelly hillside for enough room to cavort, but it was to the city limits of the world known by white Helenans. Among other parts, Clore Street immediately took a nighttime visitor by the ear and nose. "Night bite!" the swooping chant of the street vendor echoed every minute or so among the hard-used few blocks of buildings, brazier smoke and smells of cooking wafting from his cart of savouries. "Baloney cold, molly hot! Night bite here!" Supperless, Monty stopped long enough to devour what was advertised as a tamale. Laughter and protestations between women and men could be heard from second-story rooms overhead, and between that and the cart-man's Tabasco a considerable warmth began to spread in his middle.

Fortified in at least that much of himself, he quickstepped on up Clore to the destination that announced Saturday night with a good-time wall of noise. In the Zanzibar Club, which had taken on the Pro-hibition guise of a social card parlor that happened to have a bar still in place along one entire side of the room, the permanently bored bar-keep greeted him with the usual:

"Look what the cat dragged in. Where you been keeping yourself, Sticks?"

"Home on the range," one of the nearby regulars furnished, "where the steers and the roping dopes play—that's still the stomping grounds of Wrangler Rathbun, ain't it?"

"Funny as a bunion, Hawkins," Monty said levelly. Ranch hand that he was accused of being and indubitably was, he stood akimbo a minute at the head of the bar looking over the situation before putting his shoulder to it. Pretty much the usual Saturday-night bunch of jokers, from all appearances. He could pick out the railroaders down the bar by their starched shirts with suitcase folds. Here nearer the door but leaving a newcomer enough space to get his buying hand into action, the customary batch of opportunity drinkers consisted of Hawkins, who had a mouth on him like a terrier but didn't mean much by it, and the more questionable pair of Loomises, unrelated except in an approach to life that counted on deuces being wild. The one from Petaluma in California was known as Petaloomis, and the one who claimed no fixed previous address was called Nowhere Loomis. Thirst cases that they were, the threesome sat with the patience of long practice while the barkeep did his part: "What do you know for sure?"

"Not a helluva lot," Monty went along with the ritual, resting his elbows onto the bar and pattycaking the wood as if he had all the leisure in the world.

The barkeep began drifting in his direction, drying a glass as if wringing its neck. "Keeping busy?"

Here was the opening. "And then some. Been taking singing lessons."

"You guffing me?" the barkeep kept on mechanically. "You ain't? What sort of music you studying on? Blues? Hymns? Hers?"

"Easiest thing to call them is spirituals."

"Singer of spirit-you-alls?" The barkeep chortled. "You been holding out on us, Sticks."

"Don't remember you ever asking, Jacob."

"So we going to see you famous around town, your mug on every lamp pole?"

"Don't say I didn't warn you," Monty said with seeming serenity.

The barkeep chortled again, his eyes moving off to check various customers' levels of liquid. "What does an about to be famous person drink?"

"Canuck beer, same as ever. Give the Sunday school here a round, while you're at it." He took out a pocket change purse, leather still new to the touch, and reached in for a couple of silver dollars. Carefully he laid them out on the bar and pushed them one by one toward the bartender as if making checker moves.

Naturally his every word had been snapped up by the Clore Street telegraph of Hawkins, Loomis, and Loomis, so that was taken care of. He skated his beer bottle down the bar to join them and start fending with their boisterous questions about where had this singing racket come from and where he figured he was going with it. A bottle lasted no time, in the heat of such conversation. He throttled back on the next beer, telling himself, *Nursey does it. Can't keep my guard up if I don't keep my bottle hand down.*

It was proving to be one of those nights, tough sledding over and over the same ground. "I'm still feeling deprived of this heavenly voice," Petaloomis ragged him for about the sixth time with Nowhere's sly backing, "can't we have a taste? Come on, give us a little render."

"Aw, no, don't," Hawkins put in. "He'd set off every howling dog from here to Butte."

Monty's hand clamped hard as it could around the beer bottle as matters reached this point. Who would have ever thought being sociable was such exhausting work? The gibe from Hawkins was at least open teasing; the urging expressions on the Loomises were about as sincere as crepe paper bowties. *God damn it. Why can't they ever say, like she does, "You're getting there."*

He slammed what was left of his beer to safety an arm's length away, Hawkins and the Loomises too startled to clear away from him in time. Turning his back to the bar, he boosted his rump onto it, then clambered to his feet on the slick polished wood. The three faces directly below gaped up at him like big baby birds', all the other heads were turning. It strongly occurred to him he had better give proof of ownership for the attention he was drawing, awful fast. He put out one foot and scooted Petaloomis's beerglass off the bar with a ringing crash. "What the goddamn hell you doing?" the barkeep shouted, charging toward him. Only to retreat with equal rapidity as Monty's workshoe booted another stein into the runway behind the bar, where it shattered like shrapnel.

"Run me a tab on glassware, Jacob. You all wanted singing, I'll give you some."

As careful with his footing as if he were up there on ice skates, Monty took his stance. Remembered the litany, every lilted word of command, every push at his posture. Shoulders level and back, head up but not snootily so. Breathe, all the way down until the flanks registered it. He felt as if he had as many parts as a beehive, honeycomb after honeycomb to be minded, but he was doing his absolute best to tend them all. Every moment of it, he could hear that voice from the

North Fork as though she stood at his shoulder. *"Lacking proof that you can't, assume that you can."* Talk about taking her at her word: this escapade had better be a high note, higher than any ever delivered from a mere chair, or he was going to have to battle his way out of here, ragmouth by ragmouth. Whatever the outcome, amid all else going on in him he burned with the sudden absurd wish, deep in him as the gather of his breath, that she could see him at this.

"My friends down at this end of the bar have requested a spiritual," he told the eyeballing crowd since he had to be telling them something, "and I can't stop it from getting on those of you at the far end either." Pouring forth for all he was worth, he gave them the song that his mind had been rehearsing ever since he knew he had to do this, his bold voice stilling the restless bay of faces around him.

> *". . . one more soul down to bone,*
> *Just another praying Jones."*

When he was done, for perhaps five seconds the only sound was the barkeeper nervously treading on broken glass. Overall, the Zanzibar Club was not quite sure whether to encourage this sort of thing. Then a goodly number clapped and called out, while others shrugged and let it go as one more Saturday-night hijink. A few laughed harshly. Monty noticed, though, that the sharp operators—the tiger riders at the card tables; the hooch merchants; for that matter, both Loomises—were not among those laughing.

"Give us another," Nowhere's voice of insinuation floated up to him, "so we'll know that wasn't a fluke."

Perfectly ready to oblige, Monty smiled, cleared his throat, and from his Adam's apple on up, went blank. No such thing as another song seemed to exist anywhere in his frantically upended mind; right then, he could not even have done "Praying Jones" over again, even though it wasn't much longer ago than an echo. Dread filled him to overflowing as he sensed this bunch watching for him to go into a stumble, the way the rodeo crowd had been when he hit the ground in front of that bull. In a panic, he assumed what he hoped was an appropriately haughty expression and told the lesser Loomis: "Nothing doing. From here on, you can pay good money to hear me."

His expression still fixed, he hopped down. He retrieved his beer, took a single solid swig, and dug out enough silver to cover the breakage. The bar crowd turned back to the business of drinking now that he was down here mortal again.

The Loomises glanced at each other. "Wasn't that fine," Petaloomis provided, Nowhere nodding at his every word. "Now we got another situation calling for your talents. Serious shortage, over there at the game. We need a man."

"Not this one, you don't. What I need is my beauty sleep."

That was no way to be, they protested. They had listened, civil as anything, and now he was too good for a sociable game with friends?

Now this part. His heart was thudding harder than it had when he was up there singing. "I'll watch, little while."

The clocks of Danzer's Time-Repair Shop, on the next street back from Clore, were ticking toward dawn when he finally trudged back to the Major's place. Manor among manors, the darkened brick mansion sat coolly apart from its couple of streets of peaked and turreted neighbors. Big Helena houses like these usually carried some story about the original owner finding gold flecks in the mud on his boots out at Confederate Gulch or right downtown in Last Chance Gulch. It must be nice, the thought made its way to Monty through his weariness, to have the means to whatever you wanted volunteer itself to you up out of the ground. By the evidence of the big silent houses, a person could then afford sleep. He himself wasn't the only bedless case at this ridiculous hour, but close; one lone putt-putting jitney of starched waiters heading for the breakfast shift at the Broadwater Hotel seemed to be Helena's total traffic besides his dragging feet. As he fumbled for the latch on the Major's front gate he felt done in, drained dry inside but the shirt-drenching sweat of his hours beside the gambling table clammy on his back.

Wes lay dozing on the divan in his office, a pillow under his bothersome leg. The open and close of the back door brought him awake. "Monty?"

The footsteps in the hallway halted, then slowly approached the office. To the figure draped in the doorway, Wes asked as tiredly as if he had never slept: "How bad this time?"

The answering voice was exhausted but even. "I'm in one piece. No battle royal, for a change."

After a moment of getting his bearings Monty stepped in, and in the dim light he crossed the room. Wes heard the clink of dollars on the top of the safe.

"Stayed out of games of chance, too. Could you hang on to the rest of these wages for me? Good night, Major."

Angus walked Susan to the car with a lantern, handing it to her to hold while he gallantly cranked the black-as-night vehicle. "There, the steed is onto its legs," he proclaimed as the Model T's engine coughed to life. "Have a care there at High Centerville by Allan Frew's gate, mind you."

"Don't worry, all Fords are part goat," Susan said loyally from behind the wheel. "Angus, thank you again. Go back in there and tickle that wife of yours in the ribs for me. I haven't had better deer steak since—"

"—the last time you were here, Saturday night."

"The singing and the cards, smartypants, they came out different this time though, didn't they. You have to admit Adair and I cleaned your clock at both."

"I don't suppose you'd believe I held back out of modesty? I didn't think so. Good night and best of dreams, Susan." He held the lantern hoisted until she navigated out of the yard, then retraced his steps back inside to Adair.

Susan sang her way home from their place. Reliable night; how it always welcomed a song for company. The moon itself seemed to keep coming back for more, poking a plump encouraging ear from behind the blowing chintz of clouds every so often.

> *"Had we never loved so kindly,*
> *Had we never loved so blindly—"*

The old trouper of a song lent well to alto persuasions, if she did have to say so herself. Angus was right yet again: that rascal Burns knew how to pour the words. During the evening's spates of songs that Wes inescapably would have called heather-and-thither, the look on Adair's usually sheltered face became a girl's at Christmas.

> *"Never met, or never parted,*
> *We'd not sing now so broken-hearted . . ."*

"Bravissimo, Robbie," she accorded the plowman poet, absent from the evening by a mere hundred and some years, as she steered around the stretch of deep ruts Angus had warned her about. A jackrabbit jigged in agitation in the thin corridor of her headlights, then found a sagebrush avenue back to its universe and vanished.

Her mind itself was on the move, this night. Scotch Heaven could do that to a person, most especially on a proper night of summer like this, with the darkened buttes stationed up so close to the stars that sky and earth seemed one perfect geography, the willowed creek every now and then dappling in the car lights companionably to show the road the way. And the day had been of the same inspirational flavor. (She made a mental note to capture that phrase in the diary.) This morning Monty and Dolph had ridden up in improved moods—men and their Saturday nights—and the day's session had gone like a dream: she would gladly give her all to pupils for the next two hundred years straight if each lesson could go like that. And she would have bet a considered sum that Monty had been bolstered by the day's progress as well. Only rough edges remained to be taken off, the main one his tendency to lose himself in what he was singing at any given moment with no strategy beyond the song's last syllable. (Presentation, she made a further mental note, was another; bless him, he still tended to introduce a song as if he were addressing a chicken-thief joke to the back row of a rodeo grandstand.) "You can't just pop out with one song," she had explained. "A careful program, a repertoire, is needed and you must have it in mind as clear as a list at all times." At that, he tilted his head and looked ready to say something. But all that came was one of his inchlong nods, and on they went in fashioning the creekside spirit songs into some sort of order. Now to her own somewhat surprised ears she heard herself experimenting with one of those.

*"This old pig-iron world
Keeps trying to put its mark on me—"*

She didn't carry it very far, merely tasting the song with her voice, curious how it clung. Monty's inherited trove all carried that immemorial pungency, made up of his mother's washboard life and the misery-whip labors and testifyings of those itinerant sawyers, as if each song had been aged in a kind of smokehouse. Steeped in sing-to-get-by as Burns's were in peasant prance of rhyme. "People are gonna like those old things, you think?" Monty had guardedly asked her. People were going to have to grow used to having their ears in love with the words and music of Montgomery Rathbun, if she knew beans about it.

A pang came with that knowledge. Monty's time under her tutelage was now down to a matter of mere weeks rather than the infinity when they started at this. Her calendar of herself was going to have to change again as surely as that moon would find a next phase. But to an unexpected degree—she had been a teacher more than long enough to know that every pupil took wing—she found in this case she was resenting that, resisting it even. There was something beguiling about Monty, even when he was in his worst snits about the exercises. The storm before the calm, she had come to think of those heavy-browed moods. By now she was convinced he had the mental substance to go with that extravagant gift of voice, and while she was having teacherly longings she let them carry all the way to the wish that she could pick out the stage for him to debut on, the acoustics where the spirit songs could so wonderfully linger. No, though, pretty soon Monty's career was going to have to be up to Monty, and she and Wes would only watch from the wallpaper. To herself as the Model T made the turn into the gateway of the homestead almost of its own accord, Susan smiled one of the harder smiles: she and Wes had taught each other all there was to know about losing an object of the heart. Or had they.

As her car trundled into the yard, she did away with the headlights to begin to accustom her eyes to the dark between the Lizzie's usual spot and the house. The thin clouds actually helped, sharing out what the moon had to offer without stark shadowpatches of black, and as she went humming her way up the brief path she could even dimly make out that someone had hung a sack on her door. More than likely the latest unsought generosity sent over by Wes, a gunnysack of the past week's newspapers and, who knew, another helping of picnic makings?

She would have to remember to tease him about his Williamson bag of surprises, she was telling herself as she stepped to the gray shelter of the doorway and reached her hand to the hanging shape, and touched not burlap but cat fur.

The realization struck her like a hot spatter. Jerking her hand away from the blood and hair, by instinct she stifled outcry with a gagging swallow, not giving whoever might be out there the satisfaction of hearing her scream. She backed away one step, then reached around for the doorknob from the side of the doorway and waited to a count of ten. Breathing with greatest care now, she pushed open the door with the cat nailed to it, and hurriedly stepped over its puddle of blood on the threshhold.

She sensed, as much as saw, that the kitchen had been disrupted. In moments she managed to feel her way to the silverware drawer and had the butcher knife in her hand. Every ounce of her knew she had to get back to Angus and Adair's at once, but she also had a furious need to know how much had been done here. She felt along the wall by the stove to the matchbox holder. In the flare of the first match, she saw that the kitchen table had been kicked over. Carefully lighting another, she sighted in on the spare lamp on the sideboard and brought it to flaring life. Corners; the kitchen suddenly seemed to have many. No one but shadows there, though, and she was drawn, lamp high and knife clutched as tight as her fist could go, to the doorway to the next room.

Then she saw the white paint across the music room wall, using the worst words about her and Monty.

His door erupted open, bringing him blinking out of a jumble of bedclothes and dreams. He swung his feet onto the cold floor, meaner chill whiffing in from the doorway but, further confusing him, a flicker of flames candled somewhere out there above and behind the figure bulking over him. Then his hearing picked up the gunfire, quite a way off, the kind when a hunting party gets into a herd of something.

"Stay put." The Major wasn't there much longer than his words. "The men are around the place."

As if in a trance Monty shed his nightshirt and put his clothes on, his eyes never leaving the window looking south where the distant flames branded a cross onto the night.

"Reynolds didn't sound in any hot hurry to get here, when I telephoned him," Whit conferred with Wes as soon as they had the ranch crew deployed in a fireline on the ridge. They would wait for daylight before going to see what the toll in cattle was from all the shooting the nightriders did in the vicinity of the east pasture.

"So, on top of it we have to shop for a new sheriff."

"Looks like. Firebug bastards," Whit let out, one more in a litany, whapping a patch of smoldering grass with a wet gunnysack. "They could've set the whole country going, dry as it is."

"We're lucky they only had guts enough to play with matches around us, this time." The moon was fully out now, too late; Wes slid his rifle under the seat of the buckboard, then climbed in and took up the reins. But before turning the grays toward the house, he scanned again the terrain that made it so easy for the Ku Kluxers to sneak onto the Double W and then race off east to wherever they hid in their everyday lives. In whatever crevices of themselves; in whatever hideous kinks of the soul that caused people like them to despise him and his simply for the church they were born to, Monty simply for the complexion he was born to, Susan simply for the habit of adherence she was born to. A cold poise took Wes over as he considered the nightscape of earth out there and the dips of life where such creatures might go to cover. Then, like a man coming to, he brought himself back to the trace of themselves the Klan had left behind. He sat fixed into attention a few moments more, staring down at the pattern of char and embers where the sizable wooden timbers had fallen. As much to himself as to his ash-smudged brother, he murmured: "What are they thinking of? They burn it, the cross."

"I wouldn't say they're absolute bundles of brains," Whit responded. "What we have to worry about is what kind of push they put on us next."

"If I have to fill Hell with them, Whit, I will."

"Suits me. But there's our musical auxiliary they're after, too."

"Don't rub it in."

"I never would, Wes."

"I'm not supposed to let nobody by."

"Would you care to tell that to either or both of the almighty Williamsons, with whose blessing I'm here?"

"If I get my ass chewed—"

"—it will grow back, plumper than ever. Man, will you look out over that field for incendiary lunatics and let me be about my business?"

Listening so intensely he could about hear the angry disturbance of the air as the visitor tromped past the cowboy sentry, Monty was ready for the call at his door. "Hello in there," Angus's voice sounded as if he had trooped here from one of the ends of the earth. "Can you stand a boarder, for whatever's left of the night?"

As quick as Angus was in and the door held their words in the room, Monty feverishly put the question "They're at her, too?"

"Trying, in their miserable way."

"She all right?"

Even in the murk of the lampless room, Angus could discern the anguish of the man. "So mad she can't spit, but other than that, I'd say Susan is in working order. Don't worry your head on that score, she and my better half are up here at the house, probably in a canopy bed."

Wearily Angus told the rest of it, the Model T flying back into their yard after he and Adair had gone to sleep, Susan with a butcher knife on the seat beside her, then the ungodly drive cross-country over the benchland. "Susan at the wheel gives no quarter to badger holes," Angus reflected, rubbing the base of his spine. He squinted around in the gloom hoping for accommodations to be offered, but the perfectly still figure across the room kept on staring out the window toward the bluff where the last glow of the fire was vanishing under the stomp of Double W boots.

Angus sidled across the room toward him, bumping furniture as he came. When he gauged that he was near enough, he reached with one hand and gripped Monty's forearm to ensure full attention.

"Monty. Odds are that the commotion is over for now. To get at any of us those dunces would have to come through the Major, on his own ground, and I don't think anybody who hides under a sheet wants to do that."

Monty swore with a force that jarred Angus. Then swung away from the window so they were face-to-face, his words so heated that the taller man flinched backward an inch or two and let his hand drop. "How the hell come they're out after her and me? It was nothing but singing lessons!"

In response Angus's burr was measured but carried everything he had. "Why are there maggots like that in the world, you're asking? It's been a long time since I thought I was bright enough to figure that out. But I do know we've all lived through the night, and that gives us another start against the likes of them."

"People who could have been left off the face of the earth," Monty gave vent to. Like a shot he broke past Angus and halfway across the room, but then spun around toward him again. "Can't even give the sonsabitches what for," his voice was low and seething. "I have me a thirty-ought-six and used up my last shells on a coyote yesterday, can you beat that?" He made a furious swipe with his hand as if to bat away the door and get at the sentry on the other side of it. "Tony won't give me any, either. Major's orders, he says."

Angus already had his own indictment in on the Major this night. Once Adair and Susan were headed upstairs to whatever refuge a Williamson bedroom constituted, he had steered the Major aside for a few words. "If you let anything happen to Susan or Monty out of this, I'll deliver you to Hell personally."

"I know the way by myself," the damn man had answered as if that was another thing they taught at Harvard.

But importing that to Monty's presence wouldn't help the situation any. Instead Angus suggested: "Let's let some daylight on the issue and see how this stacks up then, all right?"

Sounding a great deal more distant than he was, Monty spoke back: "You putting up here till morning—you don't have to, you know."

Angus sighed. "If I have to snuggle with a Williamson or with you, it might as well be you. Probably you at least can carry a tune when you snore."

It came to Monty then that setting foot on this ranch had put this man behind enemy lines. Ordinarily, Angus McCaskill would rather have eaten dirt than come to the Double W for anything. And all the Major or Whit or their father before them ever wanted to see of a North Fork homesteader was the back of him, quitting the country. The Klan couldn't have kicked everybody more cockeyed tonight if it had tried. *And her, why'd they have to get after her? How'd they even know to?* Not that there was any sorting this out, but he reluctantly gave in to the fact that daylight was a better time to try. The man here was right, all you could do was stand the gaff and see who else ended up with you. "All right then," he told Angus heavily, "let's get you installed. I'm gonna make a light. Just as soon catch a bullet as live like a mole."

"It's at least a philosophy," Angus concurred, "but I'm going to be a rude guest and bring down the shade."

With the green blind firmly down, he turned as Monty lit a bed-side reading lamp. Everything that could be done with the sparse room had been, he saw; cloth ceiling carpet-tacked to the rafters, beaverboard put over the walls and painted a resounding aqua green. There was far too much furniture, belongings of all kinds, for the size of the room but not, Angus realized, for a man's full life lived in its confines. Picture calendars, the freest art there is, rioted on every wall. Across the exact center of the ceiling stretched a wire where a cloth curtain could be drawn to divide the room in half; on one side of that was a mussed bed and on the other was one neatly made up with a quilt of many colors atop.

Monty went across and untucked the covers, then made an awk-ward take-it gesture. He said gruffly, "My mother's bed."

"I'm honored."

As played out as he had ever felt, Angus deposited himself on the edge of the bed and took his shoes off. Then looked up; Monty still stood at the curtain line, hesitating.

"Mister Angus?" he finally brought out. "I've always done my level damnedest to watch my step, here on the place and out in town. But tonight tells me there's people who think I've stuck my foot in it and I'm not even sure what *it* is. Can't even be in the same room with a white lady, while there's Dolph riding herd on us right outside? I better get myself woke up about where all this comes from." He eyed the graying temples of the man seated on the bed. "You been in the Two country practically forever, haven't you, about like me? Both of us, longer than Montana itself has been around?"

"A dead heat, in my case," Angus reflected back. "I lit in Helena the day of statehood. But you're pretty much right, I was on the North Fork by the spring of ninety, why? And if you don't pull up a chair, I'm going to keel over from exhaustion watching you."

Monty sat, but like a coiled spring. "These hoodoos, tonight, what brought them on? Butte and places like that, I know they have trouble with them, but I'm pretty low to the ground from a couple of hundred miles off, aren't I? All I even know about the bastards is what my mother would tell me when I'd complain about some half-ass thing some white person did to her or me. 'This is a flea bite, compared,' she'd always say. Then she'd get going on how the Klan clucks would light their cross on fire to get themselves stirred up, hang some colored person if they happened to feel like it, cut down the tree and paint the stump red as a reminder. She saw all that, when she was only a bit of a girl. But that was back in the South, all those years ago. And now here's this." He wiped his temple with the palm of his hand as if trying to move elements of this around in there. "You hit here in early ninety, you said? You must have just missed my old man, wherever the hell he took himself off to."

Angus stirred. "When was that?"

"What I remember is"—Monty scanned his mother's side of the room as though it might help—"we didn't make it to the statehood celebration in town. I was all excited that my mother was gonna sing for the people, Mister Warren had arrangements already made—the Rathbuns were gonna strut their stuff every which way that day. But right before, there went my father."

"Come here to me, Monty. Momma is sorry as anything we can't be going to town, but I'd just cry in front of everybody if we did. They'll need to put Montana on the map without us."

"What I'm driving at," Monty persisted, "things don't always reach ears like ours then. Yours maybe are a better shade for that." Monty jerked his head toward the window that had framed the cross as it blazed. "Was there anything like *these*"—he spat the bitter word—"around here then?"

Angus took his time putting an answer together. When he had the past assembled as best he could, he set in. "I was fresh from the old country, and Two Medicine life all was a startlement at the time, mind you. Sit in town there trying to have a restful drink and you'd probably have to dodge a traveling fistfight over whether aces chase faces or vice versa. There was a shooting or two in Gros Ventre before I came, cowboy life as it is in the books, but things had already tamed down from that. And that was the extent of it, I'm sure as anything. These ninnies weren't kiyiing around here then, Monty, if that's any help."

"Maybe not just like this." To Angus, Monty looked as bleak as any human could. "Story's always been, my old man pulled out on my mother and me. Now I'm wondering."

Life marched in long review in Adair's nights, and thanks to Susan Duff, this was one of the more restless processions of thoughts her mind had ever set out on.

Not all that many hours ago the familiar dark of her bedroom wall had been lit with a pale frieze of shadowvines, the climbing rose at the window sketched into motion by the headlamps of the approaching automobile; only trouble took to the road at that time of night, and with held breath she had watched the trellis design grow and grow into the room before she undertook to shake Angus out of sleep. And now here in a Williamson guest bed as large as a barge, she lay open-eyed nearest the wall while the deep sleeper in the lump of covers at the outside of the bed was Susan.

It had astounded Adair these thirty years how life reacted to Susan. She was like a hot poker into cider. A savor came from her which, whether it was to your exact taste or not, boilingly changed the flavor of a situation. Adair lay there bringing back that most distant day when she and Angus were wed and all at once a great unforgettable goose of a schoolgirl with the majestic neck she had not yet grown into and those sinewy Duff shoulders stood up tall and in the finest voice gave the one gift that, even then, Adair knew would last:

> *"Adair Barclay, she was there,*
> *Gathering a lad with red hair . . .*
> *Angus McCaskill, he was there,*
> *Paired with a lass named Adair . . .*
> *Feel love's music everywhere,*
> *Fill your heart, fill the air,*
> *Dancing at the rascal fair."*

She tensed now as Susan stirred, hoping she had not unwittingly hummed her awake. But Susan simply gave a bit of a dreamer's groan. Angus so often did the same. Down through the years sleeplessness had given Adair more than enough experience at sorting sounds in the dark. Sentrylike she lay there, her thoughts obstinately marching back over how it was that here they were, Susan and poor wishbone Monty, Angus and herself, under Williamson roofs while outside one or another of those high-and-mighties—she was pretty sure it must be the Major—every so often could be heard making the rounds of the guards put in place against those who tormented the night.

The morning came haggard, with waterless clouds in the way of the sun, and the burnt patch on the slope above the Double W ranch house emerging to Wes on his dawn round of inspection as incontrovertible as a tender new scar. By the time he was an hour into this day, he had kowtowed to the McCaskills with the loan of a buckboard to go home in and accompanying apologies for the night in harm's way, held Whit back from several precipitant actions, had it out on the telephone with the nonfunctioning sheriff, and now was faced with Susan.

"I don't think I heard that," she was telling him with the type of enunciation he wished she would save for waist-high pupils. "Call it quits?" Her gaze cut back and forth from one burly Williamson brother to the other, Wes the office master untanned as fine stationery, Whit on the permanent brink of sunburn. At the moment the pair were anvils for her words to strike blue sparks from. "Nothing of the sort. You're surely not going to let Klan imbeciles make mincemeat of all our work, what's the good of that?"

"She can't be back over there on the North Fork by herself," Whit spoke as if she were not in the room. "Monty can't be scooting over there for any more lessons anyway. Some loony up a coulee with a thirty-ought-six—" He stopped, at the expression on Wes.

Susan gave up on Whit with a glance that told him so, and set out to surround Wes. "This is new of you, Major. Since when do Monty and I have no say in this?"

Wes had never thought of himself as someone trouble follows around, but if Susan was any evidence, that seemed open to question right about now. "Last night you escaped a whipping or worse," he tried to keep it crisp. "Lord only knows what they would do to Monty if they get the chance."

"And you're going to put it to him that he has to take off out of here."

"I didn't say that."

"You were about to. He's not yours to ball up and toss somewhere!" By now her words were practically molten. "Can't you see, you're taking away exactly the chance you wanted to give him. Monty and I still have work to do, and it can't be done if you simply throw him to the wind."

"Susan, please. You're going to have to turn loose of him sometime."

"When he's good and ready, of course I will. Wes, you wouldn't send a soldier out when he was only partway through his training, you know you wouldn't, and how can you think this is any different?"

The rap at the door forestalled what he was about to say.

Monty stepped in with the look of a man holding himself together by the knots in his middle. He stood his distance from all three of them, but his head inclined a smallest notch in Susan's direction. The remorse in that she answered with her own. She was dismayed to see he was wearing town clothes.

No one even went near *Good morning*. Monty's voice found its footing before anyone else's could. "I guess, Major, I'm going to have to draw all those wages after all."

"Monty, maybe—"

"Wait, Wes." Susan brushed at his words as if erasing a black-board. "Please, there's something Monty and I have to go over first. A minute alone, may we?"

Williamson etiquette came to rest on Whit. Wordlessly he gestured them to the office.

After the two of them were out of the room, Whit turned to his brother. "Going to lose some of the crew. Saw it in their faces at breakfast."

Wes nodded. "Any others we want off the place?"

"I can think of a couple or three."

"The ones we stick with, jack up their wages a bit. That never hurts loyalty."

"Didn't mean to lay you open to trouble." Staying standing, Monty put his hands on the back of a chair and kneaded the leather. "I never thought, with the Major and all—"

"Shush about that."

The chair leather still was receiving a going-over. "No, I've got to make you know. Whosever bright idea, I wouldn't have opened my mouth on that boat if I'd known this was coming."

"Don't let me hear anything of the sort from you, now or ever." Anger spots as round as dollars had come to her cheeks. He cocked a look at her. *Ever? Where does that come into the picture?* "Your music," she was saying as if to drum it in, "is worth whatever the Knightynights hiding under their stupid sheets try to put any of us through. Never mind shaking your head, I know what I'm talking about when it comes to a voice like yours. Climb over them with it, you have to— Monty, it's the only way for you to leave them behind. Up in life is the best distance to be from those who want at you." For all she knew she was the first person from Scotch Heaven ever to be in the Double W's inmost lair, but she gestured to the office and its furnishings and its shelves of the royal maroon ledgers of the Williamsons as if showing him around. "You don't have to ask very far around here to discover that."

Monty could not hold it all in any longer.

"'Climb,' that's right in there with 'breathe' and 'enunciate,' is it?"
He accidentally kicked a leg of the desk, startling her, as he set off
around the room. What could only be called grief for all the hours
they had put in and now lost coarsened his voice. "But how's that supposed to happen if I get grabbed on to as quick as somebody decides
they don't like the look of me? Look at us here, all I wanted was to
sing and all you did was to try and get it out of me—"

"We'll only know 'all' when we hear it from you onstage."

"—and we're treated like a pair of sneaks. Whoever those were last
night, some of them had to know me a long time, from town and
around. I've lived here all my life that counts any. Never drew a second look when I sloped along doing the chores or driving the Major
around. Why's it any different when I try to make something of
myself? If I was yay-high"—he put a spread hand at the height of a
seven-year-old—"and you were giving me lessons, everybody'd think
it was just cute. Or if you were—" His words ran to a halt.

"—dried up as a prune?" Susan provided.

"—a lady older than what you are, there wouldn't be no problem
either, would there." He drew a breath. "But there is."

"Those, last night." She hammered the point for him again.
"They're in no way entitled to decide your life or mine either."

"Doesn't seem to stop them from trying. Last night gave me the
definite impression that if I don't watch my every step, I'll end up
leading St. Pete's choir. And in your case, they don't just have it in for
cats."

Impatiently she waved that away. Monty wished she had done anything but that. He had stepped in here as primed as he could be for
goodbye, and here she was ready to take on the Klan to both of their
last drops. He let it burst:

"All right, you can stand there and say you're not going to let
them put the run on you. It's different for you. You're—"

"—white and female and possessed of a singing voice about half
the quality of yours."

"Will you stop!"

"I don't say we can go on as if not a thing happened. But idiots of
the world aside, sooner or later you'll still have to get back to work if
you're going to live up to your voice."

He furrowed up, which she took as a favorable sign. "What on?"

"Presentation, stagecraft, adjustment to audience," she immediately ticked off on as many fingers and stopped as if running out of capacity.

He studied her for the long part of a minute, then shook his head.

"Then what's your next stop?" she asked tiredly.

"Really trying to figure that out, I am. Where am I supposed to go?" He circled the room as his sentences came out like stones being slung. "Down South, where they maybe won't even take time to light up a cross before they fling a rope around my neck? Talk the Major into some la-de-dah job at his New York place and still never amount to anything? Quit the whole country? As I savvy it, those old tickets from Africa were one-way."

Susan let it all roll out of him. He came to rest across the room from her, facing away.

"Monty. Monty?" she said until he would look in her direction. "Just so you know. I had a rope around my neck once."

"You don't mean the business end of a rope."

"Oh, don't I? A lasso. With a noose at its end. All right, a loop, but it very nearly came to the same."

Is she making this up? flashed into his mind. Just as rapidly followed by: *Be the first time. She has about as much guff in her as that inkwell.* His mouth dry, finally he managed to say: "Probably shouldn't be, but I'm here listening."

He watched her try a smile that did not quite catch hold. "It was in Havre, rodeo time. That's always risky, isn't it." Then she rushed on. "During the campaign for the vote, this of course was. We won over the mayor's wife to our side, and so three or four of us who could ride were allowed into the parade. Little knowing." Bit by bit she had been pulling this out of herself, onto the score sheets of the operetta. "Banners across us, of course, with slogans sewn on. I remember mine was, 'Eve was his equal, why can't she vote?'" She gestured as if the next was inevitable. "A cowboy bunch down by the depot took it into their heads that it would be fun to rope the suffs. They were drunk, stupid, hateful—some of all, I suppose. The one who threw in my direction didn't get it all the way on to me." She drew a hand across the top of her chest. "The loop settled there, and then my horse spooked. It yanked up tight on my neck, the fool was too drunk to let go. It hurt like anything, and I couldn't breathe until someone jumped in and caught the horse." Her hand traced the slender column of her throat, then dropped.

He stared over at her. "Lucky you're still on this earth."

"There was a week when I wasn't so sure. I couldn't sing, Monty. Could barely even croak, and didn't dare do much of that. I had to write out anything I wanted to say. You can imagine—"

He could. The flaming words on paper if this woman could not speak, let alone sing.

Godamighty, no limit to the things they do to us when they get the least little chance. All at once he put his face in his hands. Susan started across the room to him, but did not know what she would do when she reached there. A grown man she had driven to tears; she hadn't wanted this. But when she tentatively lifted Monty's hands away from his face the worked-leather cheeks were dry, his expression set. He spoke as if into the teeth of a grit-filled wind:

"Say we keep on. How would we? Where, even?"

"That's the Major's department."

MEDICINE LINE

· 1924 ·

WAS HE LOSING his marbles, Monty wondered every little while, or did this constitute the exact last place on earth he could have expected to be plunked down in and told to set up housekeeping? And the music that came with it wasn't helping any.

> *"Jake and Roany was a-chousin' along*
> *And Jake was a-singin' what he called a song—*
> *Oh-da-lay-de-oh-da-lay-de-ooo . . ."*

"Now there's homegrown music for you," the announcer's voice crackled out of the radio set with professional enthusiasm. *Not in my book,* Monty grumbled to himself as he made his bed, the only chore he could find left to do. *Call that a yodel?* "That was the Medicine Line's own Prairie Troubadour, Andy Olswanger, singing a traditional cowboy song," the announcer rattled on, "right here in our studio. Well done, Andy! Say, friends, we here at station CINE, the voice of Medicine Hat and the province of Alberta"—a gulp of distance, then the sound wavered in strong again—"bringing you the finest listening that radio has to offer, from the Medicine Line to the High Line, all across these splendid wide open spaces where two nations meet in—"

Bunch of open spaces between their ears, Monty fumed as he stepped over and pinched off any more yowling from either the yodeler or the announcer. *Putting that on the air.* Yet, it had only been last night, late, when the radio set swept voices in from anywhere, that he had come across Roland Hayes singing from Minneapolis. He had nearly shouted across to Miss Susan to come over and hear, but that was complicated, even here.

As he had been doing all morning, he told himself to set his face for it. Complication was not going to leave either of them alone for a while now. Glancing around the strange room, he did not feel beckoned by any of the well-intentioned motley furniture and sank himself down on the freshly made bed. His mind ticked on their situation as steadily as the unhelpful clock beside him. The Major had better be on the mark about this crazy hidey-hole, or the clucks would come night-riding again, ready to scorch the life out of more than grass this time. *Flock of bastards them anyway.* Lying there trying to be calm as he could, the thought of the Klan pack kept setting off reactions like a string of firecrackers in him. What he wouldn't give to take on those Klan buzzards, one to one, he didn't care whether with rifle, jackknife, tire iron, name it. On the immediate other hand, what he wouldn't give to be a thousand miles from here about now. Somewhere that he wouldn't stick out like this from rubbing up too close to white people.

But her, cooped up here with him. These Klan hoodoos had her on their bent little minds, too, and she was about as white as they come. So maybe that wasn't the cure either. Tired of trying to calculate it all, right now he would settle for the most temporary of medicine; he half-hurt all over from his desperation to get back into the swing of singing.

Once again he checked the three-legged clock on the apple box that was his new bedside stand. He could scarcely believe it, but it was still twenty minutes yet before his lesson could happen, under her decree that it took two hours for breakfast to settle. Privately he figured she was underestimating the staying power of Mrs. Gustafson's stiff hotcakes, but he wasn't going to broach anything that produced more waiting.

Too restless to stay on his back, he rolled onto his feet and prowled back over to the window. The windowglass was the old wavy kind. The sprawling parade ground, the tired old barracks across the way, the windbreak of skimpy dried-up cottonwoods that had never quite died and never quite flourished here, all had a waver to them, as if flowing in place; as if the air still held the slightly turbulent rhythm of parading cavalry.

The afternoon before, they came to Fort Assinniboine in a cavalcade of horsepower and dust, with Monty driving Wes in the Duesenberg, Susan in her Tin Lizzie, and three clattering Double W trucks of furniture and provisions. Out on the paintless verandah of what had been the commandant's quarters stood the Gustafsons, Vikings of the prairie, awaiting them.

"Sit tight," Wes instructed Monty, "while I get our marching orders." Ignoring how stiff his game leg was from the long car ride, he pegged his way to Susan's car and told her the same. A man none of them knew had come out of the guardhouse on the far side of the expanse between Officers' Row and the barracks. Pulling on his suitcoat and walking carefully around the patches of cheatgrass that infested the parade ground, he advanced to them. Not looking forward to meeting him, let alone spending the time ahead under the eyes of him and his, Susan scanned around at the gaunt files of empty reddish-brown buildings, as sudden up out of the prairie as ruins scoured free by a shift in desert dunes.

"What, Wes, no sense owning a fort if you can't put it to use?" her astonishment had spoken for her when he singled out this as the refuge for her and Monty and his voice-in-training.

"Something new in the history of amortization," he'd admitted with a trace of amusement inadvertently showing on him. Sober-faced again in an instant, he'd looked as if there was more he wanted to tell her than what she heard in his eventual words: "It's remote, up there. It wouldn't hurt for the two of you to be out of sight for a while."

"Why not good and far out of sight?" she had demanded to know, unsure as ever why he wanted to play his cards this way or even what game they were now in. "Let's think about this. If I had to I could quit Montana until we're done, and you know after the other night Monty would, that quick."

"Not until"—Susan had caught the hesitation there in him again—"we settle some scores. If we don't, neither of you will ever be rid of these pests. Susan, something like this is supposed to be up my alley. Trust me on it, can't you?" Which would have been easier if she hadn't recognized the public-speaking pirouette he then performed with his tone of voice: "Besides, you'll all but be out of the country. The Medicine Line"—the old Indian phrase for the boundary with Canada and the prospect of sanctuary there, she knew as well as he— "is just about in sight from the fort."

"That's guff, Wes. It's not like you to count on the Mounties riding to the rescue, rooty toot toot."

Unexpectedly he had smiled again, but with grim lines in parentheses around it this time. "We'll have some troops of our own. You'll see."

The main one of these was finishing his roundabout trek to them now, looking apologetic for the time it had taken him to negotiate the weedy parade ground. Susan saw that except for the way his eyebrows were steadily up like little hoisted battle flags, he seemed mild enough, the kind who wouldn't say boo to a goose. She understood perfectly well, though, that what she had caught a glimpse of while he was shrugging into that suitcoat was a shoulder holster.

"Bailey," Wes met the man and introduced him to Susan with that single grated word. "As you know, Miss Duff and I have had a taste of how well you do your work."

"I'm in the business I'm in, Major." To Susan's hot stare, he seemed impervious as anyone could be who ferreted out trysts in hotels for a living.

"Why else would I want you?" Wes observed dryly. His gaze was fixed past the private investigator to the weather-worn guardhouse where the small fleet of cars with Butte license plates was parked. "All your men solid?"

"They know their stuff. Busted enough miners' heads for Pinkerton, in their day." Bailey put the next with surprising delicacy. "They're all Catholics, just to make sure they remember what side they're on in this."

"In that case, come meet our other interested party." With Susan next to him but willfully silent, Wes led on to the sun-catching Duesenberg where Monty had been taking this all in by rearview mirror and applied ear.

Act like you know what you're doing, fool, he counseled himself and climbed out trying to look as if a private eye was assigned to him every day. Bailey went along, and from the grave way he shook hands with him Monty might have been footing the bill instead of Wes. Wes liked that. "Give us a look around," he instructed Bailey moderately enough.

"Rattlers," Bailey reminded everybody even though his cautious tread already had, and without a further word, the man led the three of them back over toward the guardhouse. Along that side of the parade ground, brick barracks stood lined up for what seemed half a mile, a number of them gutted by fire, the surviving ones looking rundown and rough to the hand from pockmarks made by decades of blowing grit. Monty chuffed a rill of dust with one foot; it more than likely was left over from the dust storm, and he wondered how long it would be until the next one. Out here like this where the tallest thing to break the wind was sagebrush, the buildings of the fort were like morsels on an immense platter for the weather to pick at. Even on a comparatively benign day such as this, restless squadrons of soft-edged little clouds dragged disconcerting shadows across the prairie anywhere he looked.

He reluctantly resigned himself to a climate only rattlesnakes could prosper in. His eyes joined the others in trying to take in the mass of deserted habitations over these arid acres. Ranked across from the ramshackle barrracks and seeming to squint toward them in disgusted inspection stood prim old house after house of officers' quarters with randomly broken windows and shutters half gone. And down the middle the wind blew, the parade ground its permanent right-of-way.

Bailey gestured to the barracks building closest to them as though shooing it out of their way. He murmured, "My fellows picked this one for theirselves, because of," indicating upward. A three-story tower, its parapet crowned with castle-style battlements, buttressed the near end of the building. Susan, Monty, Wes, all three goggled at this. Rapunzel could have let down her golden hair perfectly in character with the odd medieval aspect, except for the mat of buffalo grass beneath. Bailey whistled through his teeth, and a lookout carrying a rifle peered down at them through one of the battlement notches. "That's Ned," said Bailey, and left it at that.

Susan drew in her breath, as if she had stepped by mistake onto the stage of some fantastic opera.

Wes fell into logistical conversation with Bailey while the four of them trooped off toward further batches of buildings. Monty thus far had no sense of recaptured past such as the visit during the dust storm had whirled up for him here, his mood too heavy for memory to make any headway. Behind the backs of the other two, Susan and he exchanged a look as castaways might have. They had compared, and in the session of argument each of them had with the Major against being made to hole up here, the Major could not have been more highly reassuring: "You're just going to the other ranch." Some ranch; you could lose track of cows for a week just in the jumble of these buildings. Although right now, both of them saw, a couple of the hands were down at the road putting up the set of gateposts where the freshly done Deuce W sign would hang. The Williamsons never wasted any time in putting their brand on anything.

A wrangling corral, holding a restless new saddle string of mares and geldings, loomed into their path now, and beyond it, a tumble-down blacksmith shop for horseshoeing and enough stables for a major racetrack. Susan was impatient to scoot on past these, but the men were not.

"Barns aren't in any too bad a shape," Monty at length was moved to remark to the Major, one connoisseur to another.

"That was the cavalry for you," Wes assessed, "the horses lived better than the troopers."

Susan was not growing any more patient. "Wes, you said a fort." Directly ahead there was another tower, and doubtless another Ned, in a further contingent of barracks and other buildings beyond the stables. "This is like a military city."

"They went at it a bit strong," he could only agree. "Maybe the War Department thought it was making up for lost time. Custer would be cleaning spittoons at West Point right now, if all this had been wangled in here before the Little Big Horn."

"But what were they thinking of, building all this that late?" Susan persisted as if the prairie deserved an explanation for all this intrusion on it. She ran a hand through her hair, which the wind was fashioning into knots. "I was only little at the time, but even as early as we lit in this country, my father said the Indians long since had no more fight left in them than a dog's breakfast."

"Your father would," Wes said, lightly enough to take any sting out of it. "But he more or less had the right of it. The tribes here were already on the reservation," he gestured off to their route here where they had passed any number of small Indian ranches that looked as if they were all corral. "I hate to say so, but this wasn't the most popular post that ever existed. It had more than its share of deserters. The saying was, you could always count on one thing on the menu at Fort Assinniboine: 'Desert.' So," Wes summed, "fetching back their own troops, and there'd have been some chasing of Blackfeet horse raiders once in a blue moon, and of course handing runaway Crees back over to Canada"—he glanced in Monty's direction—"in between parading. Garrison duty was the only way this was put to use, really."

Monty had been listening thoughtfully. The Major seemed to know a remarkable lot about the soldiering that went on here. What did they call that, osmosis?

"Wes, Monty," Susan called over from where she was peering into a higher-standing boxy building a little apart in this next cluster of structures. "Look at this, will you."

They joined her at the doorway, Bailey trailing. Inside was a shambles, but it perceptibly had been an auditorium. The quite sizable stage, complete with bandmaster's podium, lay under a snowlike coating of dust from fallen plaster. The seating area was full of trash and broken seats. Up in the backstage rafters a community of pigeons lifted off in panic. The men protected their hats with their hands as the flock exited over them.

"You're not seeing it," Susan pointed the matter up for them. "Here's just what we want."

Her version of exactitude brought a wince from Monty—he was putting his neck on the line for *this*?—and a considerable scan from Wes to make sure she was serious, before he dubiously turned back to the maze of awry seats and general mess. "Susan, it's pretty badly out of commission."

"What it is is a *stage*," she overrode that, "with an actual prosce-*ni*um, and there can't not be acoustics." She sailed on into the audience section as though dilapidated auditoriums were her first love.

"We need a few of these seats in working order, is all. Here . . . over here . . . and back there. The rest can be, well, imaginary audience."

The three men edged in after her, twenty years or so of seeping dust and the droppings of those pigeons meeting them. Wrinkling his nose, Wes estimated: "This would take days on end to kick into shape."

"By tomorrow will do fine," Susan answered absently. "My, how the regimental band must have lifted the roof off in here." She put her head back and sang out as a test: "A capital ship for an ocean trip / was the Walloping Window-Blind." When the sound of the downward-tripping range of that seemed to satisfy her, she tried its higher end: "No wind that blew dismayed her crew / nor troubled the captain's mind." The return on that too met her standards. "Quite nice. Monty, see there, even a balcony. We'll have you projecting your voice like Caruso before you know it."

"I shouldn't wonder," he managed to give that.

Wes backed out of the squalor in surrender. "Oh, very well, have your auditorium. As quick as they have the trucks unloaded, I'll put everyone at this. Bailey?"

"Mine won't like it, but I'll have the ones who aren't on watch pitch in."

They moved off back toward the housing. Susan stopped by where things were being unfreighted off the trucks and made sure that the radio set offered by Wes would go to Monty's quarters—he would need whatever company he could get, here—and she would take the Victrola. Then she girded for the face-off with Mrs. Gustafson over territorial rights within the commandant's quarters. Similarly trying to square himself up against whatever was to come, Monty went with Wes over to the Duesenberg to get his suitcase and bedroll out. Once his things were on the ground, he looked around as if trying to remember which way to head in the multitude of ghost-buildings. Over there stood the empty-windowed post hospital and the laundry-works tucked behind it, but he could pick out nothing of the tyke, him, who had the run of the place. *Gone downhill since I was three, that's some life.*

"I'll leave you to it," Wes was saying to him, already occupied elsewhere from the sound of it. "Gus is driving me back to the Double W."

Seeing the expression that drew, he tacked on: "Don't be that way. You're in another calling now."

"That better be the case," Monty muttered, spit-rubbing a dab of dust off the door panel of the automobile.

"Oh, and these." Wes reached into the backseat and presented him a plump bundle wrapped in butcher paper and twine.

"What's this then?"

"Tailoring," Wes spoke as if the brown-paper bundle could not be anything else. "Susan's orders. You didn't think you were going to make your Fort Assinniboine debut dressed like a ranch hand, did you?"

The clock finally having to confess to the appointed hour, Monty hustled out of his quarters dressed in concert gear, drawing deep practice breaths as he went. The mid-morning light here where there was nothing any higher than those stunted cottonwoods to break it was already hard on the eyes as he gingerly navigated his way to the auditorium. He felt more than medium ridiculous at having to try to keep the cheatgrass out of these silk socks, but he had decided that if any of Bailey's bruisers snickered, they were welcome to do so until they choked on it. He wasn't the one sitting on his tail day and night up in the drafty second stories of Fort Skin-and-Bone guarding them.

When he stepped into the capacious horseshoe-shaped room, which was cleaner than it was yesterday but still not clean, naturally she was already up there in possession of the stage. Ensconced at the piano, she was writing furiously on a sheaf of paper held in her lap. Looking things over, he did have to grant that the piano, by whatever method it had been manhandled into here, added surprising serenity to the scene of harum-scarum seats and lath walls with bare ribs showing. But everything else within the confines of the gaping performance space seemed in what barely passed for working order, and he had a growing feeling this included him.

Susan halted her scribbling to herself to take in his appearance. The tie was not quite flying level beneath his chin but at least it was proportionately tied, and the tails of the tuxedo draped as suavely as any ambassador's. His boilerplate white shirt would have wakened the blind, and from the way he held his wrists out from him as if they were newly precious, she would have bet that Wes had thrown in a pair of those mother-of-pearl cufflinks he so favored.

"My. If clothes make the man, you've certainly been overhauled."

"Miss Susan, I feel like I have doilies plastered all over me, all right? Now do you suppose we could get going?"

Acting to himself as if this amounted to just another chore, he went up on the stage, which creaked as he came. To his surprise, she did not launch into whatever point of a lesson that happened to be at the front of her mind, and instead patted a weathered chair next to her piano bench. He scraped it back—every sound in here seemed to live on and on—and sat, on edge in more senses than one.

"Monty." He could tell she had deliberated this, and his attention sharpened accordingly. "Do you know why I nagged so for this next dose of lessons?"

He could not help but grin this off, all they had been through beyond any other summary. "So you could have the pleasure of hearing me breathe like a tea kettle?"

"There's that," she laughed the way she only rarely did during lessons, low and earthy, the kind of laugh that he happened to like to hear from a woman. "When we started at this, I had no intention whatsoever of taking things this far," he heard out of her now. "Tune you up, so to speak, and that would be that." She delivered him a look as if he was solely at fault for this next. "Then you had to go and get worthwhile. Don't bother to puff up, there are still any number of kinks to be worked out of your hide. But the way your voice has come along would knock over any teacher, and I'd be a traitor to the profession if I didn't give you whatever seasoning I can for actual performing. That's why I wanted us to practice, even here, in full getup from now on." No wonder she seemed so primped and pressed, he realized; she had on an aqua-green gown long enough to pass muster at a fancy ball. Now that he looked, she was even in womanly war paint; face powder, touch of rouge, something done to the lips. Her hair fixed a way he hadn't seen it before. If the imaginary audience grew tired of his performing rig, it could feast attention on the accompanist.

Those cobwebs of thought she swept right through. "What we're going to do are called runthroughs. Done right"—she gave every appearance of being in charge of that nationwide—"these will help to put you at ease no matter what happens when you're actually performing."

Help put him at ease, none of her *I guarantee*? And what was *no matter what*? Monty discovered a longing for the old days when she only drilled the daylights out of him about breathing.

Shifting on the chair, he sounded out his doubts: "Something like that really have to be in the cards, here? I guess I figured I'd pick those kinds of things up when I have to stand out there and behave myself in front of a bunch of people."

"You're going to need a flying start." From her warning tone, any sugar for the day was over. "In your, you know what I mean, situation, you must be better than good from day one. Knock their ears back from the moment you open your mouth, you absolutely must. And you start at that"—before he knew it, she had him upright and being steered toward the back of the stage—"by knowing every pore of the theater."

For what seemed an hour, she trooped him back and forth through the whole enterprise, the considerably mystifying workings of backstage, the angles of getting on and off the stage without becoming encumbered in the curtain, the exact unarguable line of sight necessary between accompanist and singer, the carefully considered plank of the stage that should be his mark to sing from and that she chalked an unmissable X on, protocol after protocol that he tucked into so many corners of his head that he began to wonder if he would run out of space. Each time he thought they were done, Susan would rattle off some more. This auditorium turned her into something like a schoolma'am administering a spelling bee, it seemed to him, but with all the words as tricky to remember as those French ones in the newspapers during the war: Ypres, Passchendaele, Douaumont, so on and so on.

Eventually she swung around to him, the edge of her gown flipping just short of his ankles, and informed him, "Then when you've instilled all that in yourself, you can relax and let your performance take its course." She stood out there at centerstage—on the exact plank she had chalked for him, he noticed, without ever so much as having glanced down—looking lit from within. With all the reassurance in the world in her voice, she confided: "There are only two rules of being onstage, doubtless since Shakespeare: remember your lines, and don't bump into the furniture." He managed a laugh, which echoed back at him from the wing of the stage as if from a big empty rainbarrel.

Susan straightened his tie, then went over and fluffed herself into place at the piano. "Let's give it a try. Don't worry, I'll provide the audience when needed as we go along. Today let's just hear how you sound in a room this size. 'Mouthful of Stars,' first? It has nice range to it."

Toeing the mark there at centerstage, Monty fought the flutters that had accompanied him all morning. Try as he had, the thoughts dogged him at every step toward this mournful relic of an auditorium, then in every square foot she checker-moved him through. In the feel of this fort, its blind grip into the prairie, he sensed how it was that the Rathbun family began to flake apart, back there in his first years. The spectral rubble of this place somehow held them yet, maybe invisible to see but outlined as if by firelight in his imagination: Sergeant Mose Rathbun, rough-hided veteran of the Tenth Cavalry, sent trotting here to fight Indians who no longer needed fighting; Angel Momma, imported to do the linens. And in here would have been the one gathering place outside of duty, back when this fort was manned. The regimental band—Miss Susan had said as much—would have held forth in here, every-so-often concerts of rowdy-dow marches. But that was the kind of tumpty-tump his mother had hated—*"They might as well beat it out with a spoon on a washtub, parade theirselves to that."* This must have been where what Sunday services there were got held, too. His father the absconder, sitting here listening to hymns of faith? Somehow he could not picture that either—*"Your daddy wasn't ever what might be called churched."* Even here, desperate temple of music it was supposed to be, he saw how those lives sundered. Other imaginings rose to him like fever vapors from a swamp. The lordly white officers, probably not a one of them a patch on the Major or they wouldn't have been shelved out here, they'd have filled the front rows like a streak of calcimine, wouldn't they. And in back of them, the uncomfortably unhorsed cavalry troopers in Chinese-checker rows where every marble was black.

All of them, swept west like so much dust, to this fort which constituted a military wild goose chase, it and everything it came in touch with an epidemic of failing, failing—

"I said," Susan's voice notified him this was time two and that was about enough, "we'll start again. Ready now?"

Monty jerked a glance to her that would have to do for an apology, and made himself concentrate on getting his breath ready. After a few moments he nodded, and the start of the low croon of "Mouthful of Stars" issued from the piano.

But the auditorium would not let him issue sound of his own. He stood there as if in the grip of a slow strangler. He could not account for it but he could not break out of it either: the gaunt wooden canyon out there, empty yet not, simply swallowed him, held him in dazed suspension like some Jonah on the verge of going down in a great gulp. In turn, nothing of any more substance than a gasp showed any sign of ever making its way up out of his own throat. It was worse than when he had gone blank up there in front of the Zanzibar denizens.

"No, I am not ready this time either," he choked out an answer to her question before it came. "Just give me a minute and I'll try to get that way." He retreated to the side of the stage, feeling her eyes on him. He dropped onto the chair there, his arms onto his knees and his head out past his toes. If he was going to throw up, he didn't want it to be on these clothes. The prompter's chair, she had said this was, when she was showing him it all. Then how about some promptitude with these songs, any damn one of them, that he had supposedly known ever since ears were fastened on his head?

Good grief, is even an audience that isn't there going to bother him? He isn't afraid of his shadow in any other way, why this? Susan clasped her hands in her lap to keep from flinging something at the musical fates. "I'll tell you what," she brightly offered, to give him a cloak of time to reassemble himself if he possibly could, "let me play a piece. Just to put some music into this room—it hasn't had any for a good long while."

Monty sat back, passed a hand over his face, and made an effort to look like someone who belonged in the vicinity of an auditorium. Then, just like that, music filled the place, solid to the roof. The fancy brand of melody, for sure—her fingers racing all over the piano keys—but everything new that kept coming into it tiptoed back to meet the main tune. Then off a wonderful trickle of music would go again, eventually to shy back to the melody. It had its melancholy side, but the piece stayed full of exalted tricks like that, and as many of them as his ear could catch, Monty followed with stone-still attentiveness. He couldn't not. This was music that savvied the way into the darkness of mood he had come down with, but lulled it into thinking better of itself. Showed the mood how to console itself, so to speak. Curative music, all the way. Mesmerized, he watched her fingers in their minute acrobatics along the keyboard, *forth and back,* as the Major would have said. How did she know to pull off a stunt like this?

When the last elegant notes had faded up into the rafters like setting stars, he shook his head to indicate he couldn't come up with what such music deserved. "What's something like that called?"

"Chopin. Nocturne in F sharp." She was tingling from the playing. It had been a long time between auditoriums. Abruptly she announced, "Here's mine," and began fondling from the keys the opening bars of *Prairie Tide.*

This music too rose and rose, finding its way as if riding a breeze, then taking delicate steps back down, raindrops would they be? A beat, a beat, another beat, and the piece took on storm next. But glided at the end into harmony so perfectly lovely it seemed to settle the air of the room.

He was thunderstruck. When she had finished, the best he could do was whisper, "You're up there with him," meaning Chopin.

Susan frowned, hiding pleasure. "Nowhere close. That's the overture, then it gallops off to be sung to, like so." She demonstrated, the music bounding out of the piano now, but still as sure of itself as anything he had ever heard.

The clatter of a chair going over backward cut that off.

Monty was up, but leaden on his feet. "And you're putting in all this work on me? What for?! Holy God, woman—Miss Susan, I mean. You've got yourself to try and pitch to the top of the heap!"

This had turned around more than she intended. "Monty, no. There's every difference. As the old fiddler of Ecclefechan said when he heard a Stradivarius being played, 'Ay, mon, there's knackiness and then there's geniusness.'" But she saw he would not be joked off from this. With all the firmness she could muster she told him: "I had my run at it. Yours now."

And if yours played out, where does that leave mine? He stayed planted there studying her with something between revelation and despair.

A Bailey agent had popped in through the doorway from his post outside. "Everything hunky-dory?"

"Rehearsals are like this," Susan took care of him, and after he backed on out, she lost no time in turning teacher.

"Now then. This matter, Monty, of you here"—she was briskly over by him, and with a twirl like a top, aimed herself around to the audience area—"and those out there. They will try your air."

Monty lost the meaning of the saying in the fierce roll of *r*'s. Susan indicated out to the farthest reaches of the auditorium as though it was full of something besides howling emptiness. "They'll snatch the breath right out of you, they'll wreck your concentration, and even if they're sitting out there sucking cough drops with the best will in the world, they can stop you cold if you let them. And every audience is different. One night there will be little dibdabs of applause," she patted two fingers into the palm of her hand, an exaggerated prissy expression on her. "And the next, they will beat their mitts until they hurt," she clapped her hands above her head like an overwrought aficionado at a bullfight. Her tone softened substantially. "It's odd. A singer needs people to come hear, and they seem to need the music. But they're a—I don't want to say a threat, but they're a force to be reckoned with."

Monty hugged his sides as he listened. He could not quite feel the horn scar through the fancy coat and shirt, but he knew vividly its exact place beneath his palming hand. *It about got me killed, remember,* his response simmered just under the surface, *trying to reckon with people that way at the rodeo.*

He found he had to tell her all of it. "The time that horn went in me. Not just everybody in the crowd was bothered to see a colored person get it that way. I heard some things while I was laying there."

"Then you know what I'm talking about," she instantly flipped that on its side. "That's why you have to get as good as there is at what you do." She rammed past him, gown crackling like a comet's tail, and swooshed down onto the piano bench. As fast as she could make them go, her hands wove the ravishing music of the nocturne again. It took only a matter of seconds to transform the auditorium into a glorious chamber of sound once more, and she broke off to peer pointedly over the top of the piano at Monty. "Chopin was one of the silliest men in Europe in person," she told him as if there was going to be a test on this. "But nobody called him a moonstruck Polack after music like that."

Maybe that works okay for Chopin. But . . . Soberly he swung his head, in an indicating scan of the auditorium's populace of seats, as though an invisible multitude were out there crouched and waiting. "It still sort of shuts me down, sometimes."

Susan fixed him with a stare that ignored that and told him he had better declare war along with her. "If you don't dominate the audience, the audience will dominate you. You have to overcome them," the words drumming out of her like separate sentences.

He realized she was not even remotely talking rodeo, on this. The stumble that sent him under the horns, she didn't put that up there anywhere close with letting himself be crippled in his throat. So she knew even when she didn't know firsthand. She had might as well have been in the Zanzibar that night when every word left him, when those faces all at once focusing hungrily up at him had dried the voicebox right out of him. Still bunched to himself by his arms the way he had been, he stood looking down at the X chalked on the stage, the spot where something all too similar happened here.

All Susan could do was to hope he would not turn away.

Finally he gave one of his quick waterdipper nods and brought out:

"There is this about it—I could stand to have songs written out and on one of those, those music stands. Even the spirit ones I know by heart. Just sort of in case."

"A sound idea. I'll tend to that, and then we'll get started, all right?"

The bottle of good Canadian whiskey stood right there handy on the desk, but if the Klan chieftain was not going to reach for it another

time, his second-in-command certainly wasn't. He already was nervous about this nighthawk session, just the pair of them here, not the
entire Klavern. Funny kind of way to operate, it still seemed to him.
He had to accept his superior's reasoning that it was up to the high
ones like them to single out nighthawks, recruits who if they proved
themselves could be inducted as Knights, but somehow it was a lot
easier to go through with things when you had the hood and robe on.
This wasn't the secret meeting place, either; sure, it was after hours,
but even so, he flinched at sitting around smack in the middle of town
like this. No telling who might—

He jumped some when his leader spoke up. "You fellows played
hell with cows easily enough. Too bad you missed the woman that
night."

"Would have been best of all if we could've caught both her and
the licorice at her place," the other said as if cheated. "We'd have
dragged the pair of them behind the horses together until you
couldn't tell one from the other, you can damn well bet."

"It didn't turn out quite that way, did it. The Big Horn County
boys are one up on us now, you know." They both knew, all right.
Across the state at Crow Agency the other night, the sole Negro in
town had been killed and his cabin set afire with his body in it.

"Not our fault the sneaking pair of them quit the country."

"I don't grant that they have. Our lookouts who work the trains at
Havre and the Falls haven't seen them. Even trying it by car, he'd
stick out. They're tucked somewhere, I'd say." He studied his fellow
Klansman as if wishing for better material. "How do we stand—do
we have anybody on the ranch?"

"This Williamson bunch is no cinch," the other man complained.
"They cut loose the couple of boys out there I had in mind."

The leader resorted to the whiskey bottle now, pouring them each
a strong splash. "One of them kind of a runty sort, gimps a little when
he walks?"

"No, that don't fit any of our likelies."

"All right then," the leader said in relief. "Spread the word to the
Klavern that we're going to lay low for now. Let me see if I can
nighthawk us a certain somebody when he gets enough of this"—he
flicked a finger against the bottle—"in him on Saturday night."

* * *

Monty popped awake. By reflex his near hand reached out and made sure the rifle was there. Every bedtime he propped the 30.06 against the apple-box bedstand. And every morning he got up and slid it and the couple of boxes of ammunition—thoughtful parting gift slipped to him by Angus McCaskill—out of sight behind the woodbox, as nicely hidden as when he'd brought them here in his bedroll. The Major maybe didn't want him doing anything crazy against the Klan, but it wasn't the Major's skin that was on the line with those maniacs, either. Just now he'd been dreaming about them again. One of those jumbled dreams, there was a rodeo arena in it, and Dolph standing up on top of the saddle showing off while his horse moseyed around and he himself was the announcer but could never find the megaphone and so had to keep cupping his hands and shouting to the crowd at the top of his lungs, and while he was trying to do that the clump of white hoods and sheets down around chute number one kept opening and closing the chute gate, like they were getting ready for an event. He touched the cold metal of the rifle barrel again for reassurance and rolled over to drift back to sleep, dream or no dream. Dreams were one thing and a loaded 30.06 was another; if any of the hoodoo bunch came after him—her, too—here at the fort, he would show those nightriding bastards this wasn't eeny meeny miney mo.

In Susan's room, a light still burned and the nocturne repeated softly on the Victrola.

Wes noticed nights now, more than at any time since those he had spent with Susan.

Ordinarily, dark amounted to a change of clothes. Dressing up, in New York, because with Merrinell's situation it seemed proper to meet her for the evening meal looking as lustrous as possible. Out here, fashion ran the other direction, downward with the sun; even alone here at the ranch, as now, he did not feel right until the day's tailored suit was hung away. After supper both he and Whit liked to be in fresh comfortable britches and old corduroy shirts soft as chamois. It was a habit caught from their father, and as he dressed into it this evening, Wes wondered as he sometimes did whether he and Whit would end up like their father and Teddy Roosevelt, chesty men with years and weight piling up under the fronts of their shirts as they sat back talking ranching, on into the prairie night.

If, Wes amended the thought, *they don't burn down us and this house first.*

They. He took those phantoms downstairs with him now, much as he once shared room in his mind with the German officer who commanded opposite him in the trenches. The adversary always held a certain fascination, particularly with the polish of darkness. Still thinking on this, he steered himself toward the office off the kitchen.

With the office door shut behind him, he paused as if taking a reckoning on the familiar old room of maroon ledgers and manly furniture, as steeped in itself as a cigar humidor. At some point tonight he had to make himself settle there at the desk for a good long while. His lips twitched at the thought that while he may have avoided his father's exact footsteps in life, the familiar indentations of the seat of the pants awaited significantly as ever in the aged leather cushion of the desk chair. Warren Williamson after each day of roaring around the ranch at a pace where you could have played cards on his shirttail—Whit had taken naturally enough to that headlong role, thank God—had then settled in here nightly at the constant arithmetical puzzle of adding acres to cattle and vice versa. *Too bad the old boy didn't have these nights to occupy him.* Wes well knew that the legerdemain that now needed to be performed at that desk was beyond anything his father had ever tried to conjure. The WW Cattle and Land Company had more than its fair share of money, and Wes himself had married another substantial helping, but doubling the ranch holdings the way he and Whit and the eventual Wendell were attempting would have put a dent in Midas. Coming in here tonight, Wes felt oddly like an officer reporting for duty after a furlough—particularly odd to think of the grapple with the Ku Klux Klan as amounting to that—once again. Assembling the Deuce W was turning out to be like fitting together jigsaw puzzle pieces made of layers of paper, and the next of those layers had to be currency. *We'll tap a duke or a lord,* his father airily said in the early years when overseas investors had faith that cattle on the endless open range of America were a bonanza. Those days were gone, and now it was banks, banks, banks. There were rounds of nameplated loansmen to be made, and before then financial figures to be put in trim like a troupe of acrobats.

Not yet ready to nest at the desk, Wes crossed to the outsize mahogany breakfront which Whit, like their father before him, regarded as the height of furniture manufacture. There he poured himself a decent but not overwhelming amount of brandy and, still following the motion of his mind, circled on over by the big west window. It had never bothered him to nip at people's heels, so he had no glimmer of doubt that the thoroughly notified ranch foreman had men on watch every minute since the nightriders slung up that cross and brazenly set it and half a pasture ablaze. In any event, damned if Major Wesley Williamson, possessor of enough combat medals to clank when he walked, was ever going to hesitate to stand at his own window, whatever white-sheeted pack might be skulking out there.

He knew he wouldn't be playing to an audience of himself and imaginary Klansmen like this if Whit were around. But Whit was in Great Falls for a cattle auction, although about now he would be with a woman in one of the upstairs rooms along First Avenue South. Wes felt more alone at the thought of that. Maybe he who owns the land owns all the way up to the sky, but that didn't increase the companionability of a night such as this. *"If I'm going to be alone in life, it might as well be with myself."* That's a strong prescription, Susan.

He did justice to the brandy and sent a chiding look around this room that had known nothing but males for all these years. Not that the rest of the ranch house was any better—something like a hunting lodge with a stockmen's club thrown in. Antlers penetrated from every wall, any furniture that conceivably could be enveloped in cowhide was. Whit's one concession to decoration in here was a Charlie Russell painting of riders with a square butte in the background while the foreground was, of course, all cattle. Unfortunately, Wes mused, the female half of the human race did not seem to share his father and Whit's opinion that decor ought to begin on the hoof. His brother's young wife from Memphis had lasted here barely a year. Merrinell had been here a total of once. Not for the first time, Wes pondered whether the place was a deliberate no-woman's-land that the Williamson men had strewn in self-defense, like concertina rolls of barbed wire between the Western Front trenches, or whether women of a certain social cut simply couldn't be bothered to try and civilize the Double W.

Well, one had had her say here lately. He thought again of Susan holding forth with that ferocity of hers, that night last week. "Wes, you're going to be the ruin of us all," she'd let out in exasperation when he suggested she break off Monty's lessons. (It had not helped that Whit for an instant looked as if he sided with her in that general sentiment.) He glanced around obliquely as though her presence might have somehow lingered in a corner of the room. He would have given considerable to know what magic she worked on Monty, in here. Enough that they now were all on war footing, surplus fort included, with the damnable Klan.

Knowing he had to get at the work waiting on the desk, Wes even so stayed a while more at the window and the questions out there in the dark it framed. The adversary, the unknown, the other side of the spinning coin of fate. What faces fit onto the Klansmen? Who was the main push behind them? Because he was all too sure it was somebody sharp. Some one man or at most two, spurring the others—the usual bigots and misfits powered by hate—into this. Someone who had been sent in, perhaps. On that possibility, Bailey was giving the railroad workforce another scouring, but Wes would be surprised if that turned up the answer. *This doesn't have the marks of some out-of-sorts gandydancer.* Beyond that avenue, there was town after town to sift and the Two Medicine country abounded in distances. It all took time. What most bothered Wes in the meanwhile was that these Klansmen were not surfacing. Elsewhere they were showing off in the open, a couple of hundred gathering on Gore Hill at Great Falls the other night to burn a cross. Those "peaceable assemblies" provided a chance for the Baileys of the world to ferret out identities, and when the time was right, those Klan members would get a rude cure. But these. Crucify a cat, kill off some cows, hurl a dead skunk onto the hood of the Duesenberg as someone had done the other night—the Two Medicine brand of Klan picked away just nastily enough to worry a person. So that he had to notice the night, even a quiet one such as this. It reminded him of the too innocent stillness before a barrage.

T HIS was the morning Monty was able to give the auditorium what for, showing it no mercy, the free and easy force of his voice all but making its walls bend outward, each syllable-scrap of song plucked up off the music stand, no trouble, and sent with perfect dispatch to the farthest seat of the balcony where Mrs. Gustafson stoically sat.

He was putting his voice around a triumphant chorus when, with a yawn like a box canyon, Mrs. Gustafson rose to her feet and walked out, bumping every seat as she withdrew.

Thrown by this, Monty stared out from the stage. "Where's she going? We aren't but half done with the runthrough yet."

Susan sent him over that look that said the spelling-bee was in session.

"You put her up to that," he sputtered.

"Of course I did. Mrs. Gustafson has just played the part of the audience you weren't holding with 'Unless I Be Made To.' Now then, what do you do? We went over this only yesterday." She pattered the toes of her shoes against the hard floor of the stage to suggest the sound of a stampede toward the exits. "Quick, quick. The audience isn't getting any—"

"—less restless, I know, I know." He still was peering huffily at the balcony doorway where Mrs. Gustafson had steamed out of sight, but Susan was pleased to see him get hold of himself and begin to grapple. "Fit in 'Praying Jones' next," he calculated promptly enough. "It's livelier."

"Good." She still sat there with her hands in her lap instead of on the piano keys. "And?"

"Cue-the-poor-confused-accompanist-of-a-change-in-the-program," he recited as if at gunpoint. He cleared his throat and all but trilled the code phrase, "We shift now to a different hue of the musical rainbow," then dumped in the new song title and barely had time to think *Rodeos were nothing compared to trying to keep up with her* before Susan's fingers came down on the keys.

* * *

"I'm telling you, I don't know where they got them hid out. The Major is a bearcat on something like this, he wasn't a big officer in the war for nothing. Off he goes, somewhere, sure—but the rest of us on the place don't know zero."

Trying not to sound exasperated, the man across the back table repeated what he had been saying the two previous Saturday nights. "We can't take you into the Order just like that, not until you prove out. Can't you find some way to give us some help on this?"

Dolph preparatorily rubbed across his lips with the back of his hand. "Speaking of proof."

The man tipped the bottle of 80-proof whiskey once more toward the waiting glass.

Another day in a diary page, another session of music made (well, hammered at) in this old flat Gibraltar. Here we sit in confinement, Monty and I, and for that matter Mr. and Mrs. Gus and Bailey and his no-names, while the Klan chameleons can openly go about their daylight lives.

I lay awake on such things: is he one, I think back over someone I once saw be so terribly mean to a horse; or the slyboots woman in town we always called "the common carrier" because of her chronic gossip, would she press the sheets for her husband to wear and pat him out the door to hunt us down? Whoever they are, I live for the moment when Wes can get his foot on the throat of this bunch.

She whapped the diary shut with good-night finality, but held on to her pen as if she never went unarmed. Her clock had been banished beneath clothing in the deepest drawer until bedtime—she agreed with Monty that the tick-tock here was crazily more loud than elsewhere—so she leaned sideways far enough toward the window to check the progress of the moon. High in the sky; if this long night had a meridian, the moonlight should be close to shining down on the morning side of it by now. And she still was not one bit sleepy. She sighed, and chuckled at herself because she knew she was not much the sighing type. "Get a grip of yourself, lass," she mocked in the burr that had been burnished by her Scotch Heaven stay. Drawing out a sheet of stationery, oddly fresh in this barn of a room where gloom hung in the corners, and an envelope, she put ink right back to work.

Angus and Adair, hello you two—

I am promised this will reach you by favor of Major Williamson. How odd to be resorting to this method, as if we were all back in the era of passing billets doux (or as Samuel expressed it when he would have to collect his trenchmates' love letters and deliver them to the continually shocked censoring officer, billets coo) from hand to hand. But the Major has cautioned us against trusting our whereabouts even to the post offices.

We are biding as well as can be expected. Our surroundings are the opposite of plush, but Monty and I have been afforded all the accoutrements needed to continue with his lessons. Adair, I can hear Angus now: "The caliber of money the Williamsons have, they <u>ought</u> to be aiming high." Ought or not, the Major seems set as can be on providing Monty the polish he needs to stand forth as a singer, and I am oddly flattered to be the applying utensil. A voice such as his comes along about as often as the dawn of time.

Refining that voice, confining it to the magic spot on the stage where someone gifted takes sudden root as a true singer—that is another story, which the two of us work on until we are sick of the sight of each other. Not really. Since that dreadful night it has hit me like a slap, what Monty is up against in life. I thought I knew—no, I imagined I knew, if that will pass your classroom inspection, Angus— what it must be like to be in his situation. Something akin to the unwanted singling-out a woman is sometimes subjected to when men have the full run of things, that was my imagining. But that notion was stupidly pale, in all senses. What Monty is doomed to if Klan thinking (to flatter it with that) has its way is a kind of imprisonment forever painted right on him. His only key out of that, so far as I can see, is his voice.

But this is overmuch for a note that was merely meant

to say I miss you like mad. Who knew, when the rules (?) of chance deposited me back into Scotch Heaven, that you two would so take me into your lives that I now regard myself as an honorary McCaskill.

> With all the affection there is,
>
> Susan

Susan, rascal you—

Adair and I were heart glad to hear from you. Wherever you be, take every care. The hooded ones no doubt will eventually trip over their own monstrous trappings, but until then—

Scotch Heaven of course is lame and wheezy without you. I see to your place, and will batten it for winter if it comes to that. Beyond the whistle of the days going past, we have little news. The summer tutorials I am giving as ever lack toot. Varick and Beth are still awaiting their addition, any moon now. The hay is at last up, the sheep will soon come down.

I must break off—Petey Hahn has forgotten the head of the discourse and is leading his report on the episode of the Trojan Horse off into the personality of his own pony, Bloater. Do tell Monty for us that we listen with cocked ear for when he will make a gladsome noise in the world.

> Fondness from Adair, too.
>
> Angus

MONTY did his running on the worn wagontrack around the parade ground, in the cool of the evenings. Loping there, on the long oval that moved him counterclockwise past the troopers' barracks, then the married men's quarters, then the hospital and its washhouse again, he circled to the slapping of his footsteps like thinnest echoes of the cavalry paradings that had coursed across here. He waited until after a good enough session in the auditorium and they were on their way across the blowy parade ground for lunch, to try her on this. "Know what? I miss being on a horse, any."

Susan stopped short, the better to weigh the dimensions of the oblong field—untrotted on for so many years—hemming around the two of them. "It would be about like being on a merry-go-round, but let's see."

When she went to Bailey, he instantaneously said: "I'll need to ride with you."

"Whatever for? We know you'd all hemorrhage if we set a hoof outside the fort. We just want to canter around the parade ground."

"So my men don't see you and him alone together any more than they already do."

"What a remarkably hateful line of work you are in."

"Miss Duff, my business right now is to try and save your skin. Not to mention *his* skin."

The next day when the worst of the noon heat was past, Monty whistled as he saddled up for the three of them. Once they were on the parade ground, Bailey rode between Monty and Susan like an extra shadow of one of their horses, until she spoke up.

"Mr. Bailey, as much as we appreciate your company, there are matters I must talk to my client about in confidence. Secrets of the singing trade, shall we say. It would be worth it to us to put you in for a bonus with the Major."

"Miss Duff, I go deaf when I have to. If you have things to say to each other that you don't want the light of day on, I can ride ahead a ways and you can talk soft." He spurred to a short distance in front of them as if his horse was too frisky for theirs.

Susan and Monty kept their voices at a murmur.

"You worked that pretty slick."

"Loyal to the last dollar, our Mr. Bailey. Well? There was something out here you wanted to go over with me, you said."

"Promise not to think I'm ready for the bughouse?"

"Monty, please don't start that. I'm already putting up with riding circles in a weedpatch."

"All right then. You know how sometimes a person pretends? I'm at that, an awful lot."

"Would I know a case of it if I saw one?"

"Not if I have brains enough to grease a skillet with. The bruisers already think I'm the oddest thing going." She watched as he tugged his hat down to a sharper angle, for more shade against the sun or the speculating eyes of Bailey's men. Barely moving his lips, he went on: "I don't mean pretending like an actor or some such would do. Just in my head. Trying to figure out how things were to my people here."

Susan encouraged him by not trying to herd him with questions. Monty rode alongside her in the easy slouching way a cowboy could go all day, hands resting on the saddlehorn and the reins idly held, but he wasted no time in indicating toward the old hospital and the wash-house in back of it.

"You take, over there. Put my mind to it and I can about tell you how any of Angel Momma's days went. From the night before, actually—she'd butcherknife some pine shavings off, leave them on the oven door so they'd be dry and nice to start the fire in the morning. Did that all her life." He squinted in concentration, as if to see this next more clearly. "Quick as breakfast was off the stove, on went her irons. Then had to carry her own water, for the washing. She was swimming in laundry and ironing here, and me to handle, besides. And all the time having to prop her clotheslines"—the memory was one of those that stood out like a tinted picture in an album, of himself darting around beneath the poles she used as though he was loose at a circus—"so the wind didn't take them to Wyoming. All that, she must have been one hard-put woman, wouldn't you say?"

"'Man's work is from sun to sun / Woman's work is never done,'" Susan responded rat-a-tat-tat. She patted under her horse's mane to steady the animal as a charge of hot wind came from nowhere and a tumbleweed skittered by. What Monty had depicted sent her thoughts in a loop, out across this prairie to the ruts into homestead after homestead, the suffrage campaign's flivvers quivering to a halt in front of yet another shanty where the blue-gray scab of ground in what passed for a yard told of washings done with water hard as lique-fied mica. "I'd say your mother was very much of her time, out here, in being worked to death, yes. Go on."

Monty took a minute in piecing together the next. "Then there's my father, here," his words rushed when they came, almost as if he and she were riding up on Sergeant Mose Rathbun in horseback prance ahead of them instead of the blue-serge back of Bailey. "He was away soldiering so much of the time, it's harder to put myself in his place than hers back then. But I've been having a pretty good go at it." He slid his eyes her direction to gauge her attention, and she nodded, a single keen echo of his own usual manner of acknowledgment, for him to keep on. Glancing away toward the gapped wall of long barracks along this side of the parade ground, he began in a low ripple of voice:

"The Tenth Cavalry most of its time was never anywhere but down in the desert, Arizona, New Mexico some. They fought Comanches and Apaches and whatnot—I pestered this out of the Major once. Then all this gets built, some outfit is needed to man it, and the Tenth lights in here, four or five years before my mother does. Middle of a blizzard, naturally. Summer here isn't any too wonderful either, is it." The hot wind found them again, making them duck their heads to fend it off with the slant of their hats. Monty checked from under his hand clasping his hatbrim: no dust storm riding this wind, at least. As soon as the elements would not whisk his words away, he went on with his spoken thoughts.

"So there had to have been hard going for my father, too." Susan watching, the handclasp on the saddlehorn was a fan of fingers lifted one by one now as he named off. "No way up, sergeant was as high as somebody like him could ever go. No war to really fight. No other colored anywhere around, except his troopers." He laughed softly. "Angel Momma always told that she was barely off the steamboat at Fort Benton before here's this Sergeant Mose Rathbun making eyes at her. But that's after he's already been at Fort Skin-and-Bone those years. And that's kind of interesting to me."

"You had better spell that out for me."

"All kinds of reasons to skip off out of here, and he never did," came the reply. "Didn't desert. Upped and re-upped. When the last enlistment they'd let him have was over with he had a good discharge—my mother hung on to that one piece of paper of his, that and the bugle. So, something here held him, even before my mother and me came along." Anxiously: "Miss Susan? You still with me?"

He was badly aware how far beyond common sense he was venturing. But he had no one to go to with this but her. If they were bound together in this godforsaken place like a pair of people in a three-legged race, what better time to take this on? *You're good and smart,* he put across mutely but he hoped legibly; either those eyes that doled it out only as she pleased were registering every line of him or expertly hiding how well they kept their distance, he couldn't tell which. *You had a soldier in your family, too. Music aside this once, can't you give me some help on me and mine?*

"I'm here listening, aren't I," Susan provided and no more.

Spurring his horse lightly on the near side, Monty made the mount shy around in a well-reined pirouette. Startled, Susan watched man and horse turn into a tableau that needed only the sound of bugles behind it.

Bailey glanced back at the brief fusillade of hooves, then away again.

With the horse under perfect control but edgy about the sudden authority on its back, Monty held the high-headed parademaster pose just enough to be sure it registered on Susan. He sidled the horse back toward hers, his voice coming lower and quicker than before.

"Maybe it was something like this parade ground. Could be this was his auditorium, you think? It took something to run soldiers—we know that from the Major and his decorations, don't we. I can pretty much see my father out here, bossy as you can imagine"—this drew him a deep look from Susan—"to make his troops look sharp. I don't have much memory of it, but from what I do, the Tenth liked to put on a show. I'd bet anything their inspections and parades were pure spit-and-polish. And he had to have been front and center at all that."

She did not say *While a white officer stood right over the top of him on everything he did?* Nor its corollary *Until he had to go out on his own and leaked away into the landscape at the first opportunity?* Monty's family pangs peeled her heart. But they also worried her sick. It didn't matter one spark to her what was behind his father's evaporation unless it ran in the family, and she had natural resistance to that prospect. Or unless—worse yet—Monty let himself be eaten away at by example: that whenever a man of the color passed down to him by Mose Rathbun stepped across a certain line, the world was always going to be too much for him.

"So here he is," Monty said in a near-whisper as if the conjured sergeant again was about to gallop up and inspect the shine on their buttons. "Parading when he can, hanging tough when he can't, and in either case he never cuts and runs from here. But over at the Double W, he didn't last hardly any time at all. Doesn't that sound sort of funny to you?" Susan knew a question that did not need answering when she heard one.

The fingers on the saddlehorn already were enumerating again. "A better wage and all; whole lot easier place for Angel Momma and likely him too; rider all his life with a chance to shine at a riding job—and he couldn't hack it? Why was that?"

Monty paused to consider. "Angel Momma didn't give him the benefit of any doubt," he at last said in an outbreath. "Got himself in some kind of scrape, she'd always tell me, and that was enough for her. Nobody else at the Double W would ever say scat about him, because of her, I suppose. But when you think about it, here's a man fought Indians all his life—what's it take to spook him out of the Two Medicine country, if that's what happened? I can't see the Williamsons catching him at something either, and kicking him out and hiding it from Angel Momma. No," he shook his head decisively, "old Mister Warren would have given him one hell of a talking-to, excuse me, and fobbed him into some job in Helena, packed us off along with him so breaking up the family wouldn't be on the Double W's conscience, that's more their way." He pondered off to the perimeter of prairie beyond the far end of the parade ground. "Lately I had to wonder if something like this Klan bunch got him. But Mister Angus would have picked up on anything like that, if it'd happened. If anybody would ever level with me, he would."

Susan knew it was her turn to try. "Just hearing all this, I would have to line up with your mother. Some kind of scrape."

"Which puts him back to being a quitter."

"Monty, this can be argued flat as well as round. I don't see why he couldn't have been a worthwhile trooper—"

"Striper. He was an old-hand sergeant, that's what the Major says they were called."

"That, then. I don't see why a man can't serve as a good soldier," this did not come out of her easily, Samuel's stubbed-off service life to be gotten past, "and be whatever else he is, besides. What your father was faced with here, obviously a lot—if it makes you think better of him, I find nothing wrong with that. I wouldn't say it necessarily wipes out your mother's rendition of him after that. People are the full alphabet, none of us is just the ink teardrop on the *i."* She watched for any accepting of this in him, but he had gone to that expression where you couldn't tell much. "You did want my opinion."

"Knew I'd get it, too. How about we race Bailey to the stables?"

Against the evidence, Wes hoped Whit had only had a bad night's sleep. Chances of that diminished with every step as Whit came hot-footing for the house. By now he had all but flown across the yard from the Double W foreman's quarters, and Wes with alert dread turned from the office window to await him.

"They hit us again last night, more dead cows," Whit came in say-ing, breathing heavily. "Somebody got into them up in the Marias pasture and cut the throats of fifteen." He looked at his brother as if pointing out arithmetic on a blackboard to him. "That took a pretty fair number of men, to work over that many cows. Wes, this isn't pattycake with this Klan bunch. And don't tell me the war wasn't either."

"I never would, Whit." Wes whipped his coat on. "I'm going to the fort to see what Bailey has come up with."

"Godamighty, Mrs. Gus, you ever hear of an invention called the cough drop?!"

Mrs. Gustafson's phlegm spasm ceased and she beamed tri-umphantly up at him from front row center.

"I see the picture," Monty said with resignation. He turned and faced the music, Susan sitting expectantly at the piano and wearing her surely-you-can-spell-Passchendaele expression. "Sorry I let it throw me off. I know, don't let anything short of Kingdom Come take my mind off the music."

"Once again, this is the place to get mistakes out of your system."

"I'd like to run out of those, at some soon point."

"Oho! The first perfect singer there ever was?"

He quit gripping the music stand as if he wanted to shake it and walked over to her, holding the sheaf of songs as a pretext. In a businesslike murmur that would not carry clearly out to the seats, he said: "Need to ask you about something. Just us if we could."

Susan eyed him. She had been expecting this, but that did not make it the least bit welcome.

"Mrs. Gus," she reluctantly called out, "thank you the world. That will be all until I give you a holler." When the broad stern of Mrs. Gustafson receded up the aisle and out the door and the curiously depopulated auditorium was theirs, Susan sighted back onto Monty. "It doesn't look like music on your mind."

He shook his head, meaning she was right. They both knew it was going to be that kind of discussion. "I'm still not getting any younger at this," Monty set out. He surprised her with a commiserating smile, as if sympathizing that she didn't have a twelve-year-old prodigy here beside the piano to put her stamp on. "Look at that another way," he went on, "if I'm finally old enough to have some sense I better ask myself if we haven't given this our best shot. We plug along on these runthroughs, some of them aren't that bad, and others we wouldn't either one of us wish on anybody, would we. And maybe this's about the way it's going to be. Maybe this's as good as there is in me, you think?" He watched her long enough to see how she was taking this, then looked off as if something beyond the walls had caught his attention. "Besides, I don't know how much more I can take of Fort Skin-and-Bone."

That makes two of us. Aloud, Susan armored herself with the teacher's creed. "You're nearly there. True, there were some times this morning that we could have done without. That's part of the profession, though, learning to take the rough with the smooth." But then she halted, up against the actuality of what their time together on this old trouper of a stage amounted to for her. Monty saw her grasping for words, a shortage he had never expected she would come down with.

"Pretend you're not hearing me say this," she managed, "but I'd give anything if you could see yourself from in me. This auditorium has been the making of you. I've sat here putting you through a dozen predicaments a day, Monty, and while you still stew over them a bit much—we'll work on that—you've come miles in your performance." Still grappling, Susan husked out as if it were a stage direction: "It has been a wonder to see. Bear that in mind, but not enough to pop your hatband, all right? Now then. We'll run through the rest of the morning without the aid of Mrs. Gus, what do you say."

"Christmas come early, that sounds like to me." All at once under the scrapes on his patience and the wear on his equilibrium, he had the oddest damned feeling he was someday going to miss all this, the time on this monster of a stage with her.

"Ready then?" Susan fixed a gaze on him that told him he had better be, and down came her fingers on the accustomed keys white and black.

Fort Assinniboine shimmered in the noon heat, as if the brick buildings were bake ovens, when the Duesenberg nosed onto the long approach road. *What next,* Wes mulled as he began to come out of the fitful waking doze the miles had induced, *Beau Geste on the ramparts in a kepi?*

But when the car at last drew to a halt beside the Saharan expanse of the parade ground, on watch in the nearest tower per usual was a sunburned-looking agent, and coming out the door of the guardhouse Bailey himself, looking as spruce as a man in a dark suit could in such heat.

Telling Gus to go and reacquaint with the Mrs., Wes stepped over into the shade for the civilities with Bailey.

"No luck at the railroad," the investigator met him with. "But we're working on—" Wes's sharply raised hand cut him off. The two men stood motionless, listening. From across the fort, the soar of a voice lingered in the air like a long lovely alpine call, then followed the faint steps of a piano down, down, down to poignant silence. Throughout this, Bailey watched Wes with care, wishing he could know everything under that expression. Finally he said, "They'll be at it a while yet. Major, I—"

"Boss!" Thunder from an open sky, the sentry's roar clapped down on them. "I see something!"

Bailey ran hell-bent for the tower. Grabbing from the car the Zeiss field glasses that were a prize of war, Wes went lurching after him. The interior of the tower was like the tight twist inside a lighthouse, a narrow iron spiral staircase winding and winding to the portal of blue above. The binoculars thumping against his chest, Wes pulled himself up the clammy guardrailings by his hands two lunging steps at a time.

"Over by that coulee." The sentry pointed south to a distant break in the tan sameness of prairie. "Some kind of white shapes, hard to make out."

Bailey had his own binoculars on the forms. "What the hell—? Major, can yours pull that in?"

"Yes." He let the field glasses drop on the strap around his neck. "Antelope rumps."

Neither Wes nor Bailey said anything during their clanking descent.

At the base of the tower, Bailey glanced around and put this in a low voice: "Miss Duff and Rathbun—I think you ought to know. They have plenty to say to each other. Just to each other, sir."

"I imagine." Wes looked impatiently at the shorter man. Bailey shrugged. "Now that we know we're not going to be attacked by antelope," Wes rapped out, "let's talk over our chances against the Ku Klux Klan."

"Are you crazy? Why'd you come in here?"

"Can't I have business, like anybody else? You ought to be gladder than that to have me show up."

"In broad daylight? Step over here where the whole world can't see you, at least."

"Figured you'd want to know, I come across a way to git the goods. On Snowball and her both. Hadn't ought to take too long now."

"Why didn't you say so? Well?"

"Thing is, I'm tired of this nighthawk stuff. I want to be in for real."

"I've told you and told you, we can't induct you until—"

"Who's all this 'we,' anyhow? Seems to me you pretty much run things."

"If you really can find out where the pair of them are, I can stretch matters and make you a provisional. Wait until Saturday night and I'll bring your—"

"'Wait' ain't generally the way to git anywhere."

"All right, all right. You have your dues on you?"

A happy nod from the little cowhand.

"Then show up at my place at noon. Come around the back. And for heaven's sake, make yourself scarce around here."

Feeling spent to dime size after that morning's runthrough of music and her as well, Monty came into his room ready to plop down on his bed. It was inhabited.

"Major. Didn't expect to bump into you until chow time."

"I thought I'd come see how performance is with you," came the reply from the figure sitting as if carved to fit the edge of an army bed. "Mind if I take the load off like this?"

Monty proffered the premises with a gesture and seized a rickety chair from by the table, straddling it so he could rest the top part of him on the chairback. With the Major, you never knew how long a siege you were in for.

Wes examined the room as though he had been thrust back through military history to, say, the interior of the Trojan Horse, but was smiling a little. "How do you like the accommodations?"

Truth to tell, the big high-ceilinged room that Monty had chosen because it faced out onto the full sweep of the parade ground practically whistled when the wind blew. But then, all of Fort Assinniboine seemed to be drafty. "This'll do."

The smile Wes could not keep off his face was oddly sly by now. "You're in officers' quarters, you know. Quicker than any of my promotions."

Monty gave that a dry laugh. "Ought to be some reward in this singing business, don't you think?"

"Speaking of. How's the auditorium working out for you?"

Monty skewed his head as if considering. Where to even start, on that? "I'd have thought I knew how to walk out on a stage, but she's—Miss Susan's been showing me tricks of the trade. I'll tell you, she's got them."

Wes perched in wait, but that seemed to be all that was forthcoming. Monty showing some independence probably was all to the good. Still, he needed a sounding on morale here, how long he and Bailey had. "Those loonies in their bedsheets—are they still making you nervous, with Bailey's bunch on the job?"

"I was born nervous, in that respect."

Wes started to say more, then swiveled one way and then the other in mystification. "I keep hearing something."

Monty leaned toward the woodbox, found a chunk he could heft nicely in one hand, and tossed it against the base of the far wall. "Mice eating the wallpaper paste." The smorgasbord of gnawing stopped. "You were telling me about the bedsheeters."

"Monty, we're working on them."

"Figured you were." Monty looked off out the window toward the barracks across the way, where every empty room was a hiding place for a cluck with a rifle. *Working on them, the man says. How fast, though? A bullet wins any kind of a race.* This next had been forming in his mind since that night of the burning cross, but even so he took extra time now to frame it just so. "Major? Do I savvy it right, that they don't have any love lost for you either?"

"A mackerel snapper like me?"

Shock showed in Monty's eyes. Since when did a Williamson use those kinds of words about himself?

Not looking up, Wes industriously kneaded his knee. "I've been after them," he said as if it was a satisfying memory, "back when I was in politics." His voice took a sudden turn that Monty was not familiar with. "The damned mongrels. Who do they think they are," it shot out of him in bursts, "to tell me what church I dare kneel in? Or to take after you like a pack of bloodhounds just because they feel like it? Wholesale haters, is all they are. Scum who need to take out their own shortcomings on others. They're going to catch it for this, Monty. We're going to get a handle on them, don't worry."

The tone of the words, however, did not undo what had been on Monty's mind.

Onto his feet now, a passage in one motion from soldier to land-holder, Wes was back to sounding merely brisk. "I'm going to have to eat and run, although that's not easy after Mrs. Gus's food, is it. Coming?"

"You go ahead, I need to change out of this rig and wash up."

Shedding the little tie and then the tailored coat, Monty watched out the window as the Major went down Officers' Row in that gait that wouldn't admit to being a limp but carried a wound. From this angle Monty couldn't quite see to the verandah of the commandant's house, but he knew Susan would be out there, keeping a safe distance from Mrs. Gus's kitchen. He hoped she would light into the Major about why the pair of them at Fort Assinniboine kept hearing the Klan was being worked on when what they'd like to hear was some heads rolling, out from under those hoods.

Stripped down enough to scrub up, Monty still was in a storm of thought as he stepped over to the washbasin. The water he dippered from the galvanized bucket was tepid when he wished it was bracingly cold, but he doused himself with it like a man diving deep. That the Major had old tangles with the Kluxers was not exactly news, but the blood-boiling contempt was. He had been like a man suddenly off his rocker when he got going on the Klan that way. *And he doesn't even have a skin reason.* But was contempt enough to do the trick? Why wasn't the man tooth-and-nail into some session with Bailey about wiping out the sonofabitching Klan? Church was something strong, no question, but strong enough to stir up the clucks and the Williamsons like bobcats in a gunnysack? *And me—and her—just being used as catnip for the Klan?*

That couldn't be right. Monty looked the question to his dripping face in the mirror. *Could it?* If this was about church, it was going to be beyond him. Even Angel Momma, praying woman that she was, had joined in with the holy rollers for singing's sake, you couldn't say she caught the religion. The one time, as a boy, he had tried some hopping around when the rollers started their bodily commotions, as soon as he and Angel Momma were home at the washhouse she spanked the daylights out of him. "Those folks can let fly if that's what they feel, but you aren't going to, just to be doing it," she had whaled the lesson into him. In his life since he hadn't seen any reason to church himself to any one or the other: whatever was in charge of things of this world—more or less in charge, he had come to think—that's what the spirituals and her spirit songs represented to him. But Catholics, Protestants—could those kinds of people in this part of the country where you could ride half a day without seeing a steeple, could they go at each other like his father and the Indians whenever they got the chance? Had the Major, maybe the Williamsons back to time immemorial, had to wait this ungodly long for a crack at the other side? Toweling his face furiously, he wished again he had Angus McCaskill around to talk to, he was strong on the past.

FENCELINE in decline waits for no man. The pair of dun work-horses switched their tails in idle resignation as Angus wrapped the reins around a wagonbrace, barely taut so he could talk the team ahead from the ground, and climbed down to his work.

He took another squint at the mountains as if hoping the sun was going to fool him and go down early for a change, but nothing doing. This time of year, there would be a good couple of hours yet for him to finish off this damnable fencing. The only thing working after supper had to say for itself was that it was out of the worst heat of the day. "What's this old weather going to do?" Adair had asked, quite on schedule with the question, as they sat up to the table. Drought having been written across the forehead of every day since sometime last spring, he hadn't known what to say except, "Blaze on, I suppose."

Tools of the earthgouging trade arrayed in the back of the wagonbed like a crusader's cudgels, he readied, if that was the word, to take on his rocky north line one more time. The dog Bob, with the older wisdom of his species, scooched in under the wagon and took a position there with his head pillowed atop his crossed paws.

"Have the decency not to snore," Angus admonished the snug dog.

He honestly could have stood more company out of Bob, particularly this day-end. Susan's leaving was like air going out of a lamp chamber, a leak of life he and Adair felt with each visitorless dusk. Not only that, but the valley somehow seemed voluminously empty without Monty and that odd bodkin Dolph riding in of a morning. Scotch Heaven truly was on thin times, he reflected, when the only caller to be looked forward to was the paradoxical postman Wesley Williamson.

Taking his time about putting his barbwire-scarred gloves on and assigning his reluctant thoughts, Angus contemplated boundaries and their needs. He had fought this ground countless times, a shale shoulder of Breed Butte that repulsed fenceposts, heaving them out with frost and pinching off their strands of wire with contemptuous rust. All summer he had pecked away at repair up here, choring on this stubborn sidehill an afternoon or evening at a time when not haying or shearing or otherwise carrying the homestead on his back, and to say the truth, he found it supremely tempting to let this last sagging stretch go until next spring. But the jog of fence here was where his land butted against the range of the Double W, and while he had never grasped how, the Williamsons and their invasive cattle could always sense any tingle of opportunity at a fenceline, much like that monitoring that occurred from the verges of a spiderweb.

Angus puckered in exasperation at this situation of perpetually losing ground by holding on to ground. He had to say for the old grabber Warren Williamson that Scotch Heaven at least had known where it stood with him; and Whit had pretty much filled his shoes since they came empty. Major Wesley Williamson, though—a piece of work of another sort he was proving to be, that dazzler.

He went to take his mood out on the first posthole. Feet splayed substantially wide of the target—"Ay, Angus," Ninian Duff had pointed out to him all those years ago when he was a greenling at this, "you don't want to have to count your toes after a day of fencing"— he hefted the crowbar and in a double-handed thrust jabbed the point of it downward with full force and conviction. A chip of earth about half the size of his palm flaked away. He took a half-comical gander at the crowbar to make sure he was using the chisel end rather than its blunt top. This invincibly dry summer had left the ground harder than ever. And while he never would have said he might be getting a trifle old for this sort of thing, the crowbar had definitely put on weight over the winter. Excuses never counted for much in this life, though, as far as he had found; and hard labor generally led him to hard thinking. So, knowing he would have to go some to finish with this by dark, he hoisted the digging implement again with a grunt.

From posthole to posthole as he broke ground, shoveled, set fresh-peeled posts and tamped them in, Angus bothered the question. It had only been twenty-four hours now since he had contrived to bring telling shape to the story, but it felt like the majority of a lifetime. He went back over and over it like an apprentice minstrel, still disturbed, still shy of what he knew he ought to do. Maybe better not to have ever known for sure; but Monty Rathbun was not the only one with curiosity for a habit. Besides, after enough time suspicion gets to be even worse company than Double W cows.

Ceasing crowbar rhythm for a moment, Angus ran a finger around the inside leather of his hat, wiping the sweat out. It had taken the wearing of his other hat, his snappy dove-gray town Stetson to the county superintendent's yearly summoning of all the teachers at Valier yesterday, to funnel all this into his head. Just as soon as he could decently take leave of the teacherly gathering, he had beelined across town to the irrigation project headquarters. In luck, he found the ditch rider, Toussaint Rennie, just unsaddling from his rounds of inspecting canals.

"Angus. You have on your clothes for marrying or burying."

"It's one of those rare times I need to be presentable, is all. Have time for a gab, do you, Toussaint?"

Part Cree, part Canadian French, part seed of the loins of the Lewis and Clark expedition, part in-law to the Blackfeet by his contentious marriage to one, part roving ditch rider and more than a little coyote when it came to sniffing out what people had been up to, Toussaint as a one-man League of Nations possessed a memory as deep as anyone's in the Two Medicine country, and Angus had shopped there countless times before for delight and intrigue. This time, one of those would have to do, and it was not delight.

He could have taken and shaken himself for not seeing it before. But who knew how three-sided a picture this was? He'd had to alibi to Toussaint like a good fellow as to his interest in matters practically back to Genesis, in terms of the earliest days of landtaking here. But there it at last was, clicking into place like the orbiting shards of a kaleidoscope. All it took had been to fit Toussaint's canny gossip about a long-ago shenanigan or two up there in Cree and Blackfeet territory onto that oldest rumor, distant but so echoing now, within his own compass of memory at this end of the Two Medicine country. Stopping again to blow, Angus rested his hands atop the crowbar and his chin on his hands. Still thinking full-tilt, he stared up the slope of Breed Butte to the falling-down homestead there and the now doorless house where he and Rob Barclay batched together when they first came. No more than six months old, that lingering indistinct whisper must have been, when the two of them rode in here in search of the land America promised. Straight from Scotland, Rob and he were the youngest young men there ever were, but between them they possessed brain enough to recognize something that probably was not wise nor healthy to pursue. Which did not lessen Angus's discomfort now that the old haunt of an incident was in apparent pursuit of him.

Hawk weather, like now, that first Scotch Heaven season of theirs had been, and Angus for another half-minute watched as an evening lift of breeze carried a windhover above him, around and around. The reddish tailfeathers of the sleek bird caught some last sun in the upward twirl of its flight. Under such seasonal spirals all of Scotch Heaven had lived, when it lived. He had to wonder: did Wesley Williamson, coveting this valley in the glandular way that ran in his family, ever even bother to enumerate its inhabitants in memory, or were they just ciphers of acreage to him? Sharp-pointed Ninian Duff and genial Donald Erskine and Rob and himself counted as specific burrs, no doubt, for they had bothersomely tenanted the North Fork before the Double W managed to get its head turned in this direction. But the Frew cousins, George and Allan, hard to reason with as anvils and as sturdy. The feckless Speddersons, short-lived here but loyally selling off to their neighbors instead of the bank in town or the land hoggery on Noon Creek. The populous Findlaters; old sad bachelor Tom Mortenson. The wives, most of them formidable, who went the limits of their lives on these homesteads, and the cavalcade of children on horseback who descended on the schoolhouse down there at the forks of English Creek and madly recited their way through the schoolyears under the tutelage of Angus McCaskill. Scotch Heaven empty country? No country that has ever had human eyes pass over it is empty of memory. *What about it, Major—when you orchestrate this way, how many of us are words to your tune?* Maybe the man himself no longer knew. Not even a contortionist, Angus thought tiredly, could see all sides of himself at once.

Never mind that. Just make up his own mind whether or not to speak up. He could not believe that the cat's cradle of Susan, Monty, and the manipulating Major would hold together if he were to sidle up to the right one and murmur, "I hate more than anything to say this. But for the welfare of all concerned, you ought to know . . ." Could even do it by note delivered by the silky hand of Wesley Williamson his very self, a notion that brought Angus a fleeting grin. But he sobered back to the question: spell out or leave lay. It was one thing to let bygones be gone, allow the long silence over this to keep its seal; but hellishly another to hold your tongue when some inflamed dunce hiding under a hood but able to peep through a rifle sight could yet get Susan and Monty in reach.

Despite the nearness of dusk, the sweat still rolled from him. He slammed the crowbar into the making of the next posthole. A piece of Adair's dried-fruit pie and a sip of coffee would be uncommonly welcome before bed. He hadn't said anything so far, needing to think, but tonight would need to be a war council with her. Adair couldn't read the weather, she had not much more notion of the ins and outs of the Two Medicine country than when she was deposited into it thirty-five years ago, but she knew more than he wanted to admit about the wear of living with silences.

Angus glanced west. Nearly to the corner-post now, one post in between to go. He clucked the horses to attention, and they dutifully paced forward with the workwagon until he called "Whoa." He felt more tired than he should, but it was worth a bit more strain if he could put this fenceline away for another year and rewardfully head home to—

The spasm hit him dead-center in his chest, and he knew. Clutching himself there, he tried for all he was worth to catch his breath. His arms felt afire. All the wonder he had ever had about this tipping point of life coming out of him in gasps, he lurched his way to a cut-bank. The dog came and nosed at him urgently. Angus hunched there, holding hard to himself, but slipping and slipping in his wrestle with the last pain ever.

MONTY was the first to hear the Duesenberg pull in, the next evening.

Looking not at all like a man who again tonight was cleaning out the Gustafsons and Susan at poker in the parlor, he had just ruefully flicked in his next ante from his heap of winnings. Kitchen matches. Where was this run of luck back on those silver-dollar paydays when he could have really put it to use? On the other hand, the Zanzibar Club's poker habitues generally had not placed as much faith in a pair of treys as the Gustafsons tended to, or for that matter shown Susan's abiding sense of conviction that she could fill an inside straight on a two-card draw. At the moment, she was vowing what she would do to him if she ever got him in a game of rummy.

He and Gustafson peered at each other in confusion at the sound of the big car. After driving the Major to the Double W the day before, Gus had hitched right back with the camptending truck. Major's orders; one more sign to Monty that there was still nothing but delay ahead on the Klan front.

All four of them around the table heard the click of a rifle being cocked by whatever bruiser was on duty on the verandah. Then Bailey's call into the dark: "Major? Is he one of yours?"

"It's all right. He drove me, is all."

Bailey and a couple of hastily summoned operatives came in first like sweepers before a processional. Looking compelled, Wes stepped in, Dolph immediately behind him as if in tow.

"Monty, kiddo. And ma'am." These salutations hung there, until Dolph managed a further blurt. "How you faring?" Eyeing around, he seemed to be in awe of the contingent it took to tend Monty and Susan here, when he had managed it single-handed on the North Fork.

For all Monty knew, Dolph's only transgression was his bad case of mouth when they'd had to ride across there together. When his yap wasn't open, he'd do. "Just ducky, Dolphus," Monty gave him back generously enough, "how about yourself?" Susan only sent him a distracted nod, focusing on Wes and whatever had put him on the road this late in the day.

Wes's eyes stayed steady on hers.

"You'd want to know—Angus McCaskill passed away. I'm sorry, honestly."

Frozen there in her chair, she looked the question to him.

"He was fixing fence," Wes told her as much as there was, "his heart gave out."

Monty sat there helplessly next to her, hands doubled to fists under the table so they couldn't touch to hers in sympathy in front of all these. After a moment Susan broke through the awkward pall they had all retreated into:

"The funeral is when?"

"She's not going."

"Hold off a minute, Bailey. He's right, though, Susan, it's not the best idea."

"Don't even try," she halted that from Wes. "I'll make my good-bye to Angus if I have to crawl to get there."

It took none of the accumulated detective powers in the room to know that she would do just that. Wes seemed to be shuffling mental papers and not finding the precise one he was looking for. Bailey appeared ulcerous. He began, "We're still not—"

On the instant, Monty decided. "Miss Susan, I hate to butt in, but if you're going to be away—suppose we could work in that night run-through you promised, first? Tonight, yet? The evening's still a pup."

The faces in the room were a silent ring around him after that came out. Even to himself his words had sounded as cold as if chipped out with an ice pick. But right now he figured that was what it took. Susan looked as if she wanted to hit him, but while he watched, silently willing her, her expression came around to consideration. "Maybe we had better," she said in a tone no warmer than his had been. "It would get that out of the way, wouldn't it. We'll need the auditorium lit." She tore her eyes from Monty to seek out Gustafson.

After a moment Wes stormily seconded her look. "I get the coal oil lamps going," Gustafson vouched and left the room.

"Excuse me, all," Monty said hastily and went out behind him.

Wes's brow still held thunder. Susan's words came before he could say anything. "Leave us to this. Monty is at a point where this means quite something to him."

"It must." Mustering himself, Wes looked around to where the fresh arrival to their midst was standing there looking fidgety. "Dolph, I know you're new at this. Just hold on here, while Bailey finds you a bunk."

Wes waited up for her. The fort had quieted. The moon was at its most tentative—the crescent of its new phase, thin as thin can be, mingling with the almost-circle of the darkened waning one like an escape of light from a shuttered portal—and delineating only the outlines of buildings, their details staying hidden. With only the general night for company this way, he thought back over everything.

"You went on late," he called out when he at long last heard the screendoor slap closed behind her.

"Sorry. What we're at takes time, too." Susan sounded done in. She came through the scarcely lit hallway out to where he was, surprised him with a touch on the shoulder, and navigated from that to the wicker chair next to his.

"I hope he was in good voice, at least?"

"He's always that, it's the rest of him that takes the work."

They were on the big screened-in rear porch of the commandant's house. A brick wall enclosed an oddly prim garden area back there which the Fort Assinniboine seasons probably had always rendered more theoretical than botanical, but it did provide a place to talk in private. This night itself seemed a kind of seclusion. The soft dark gentled everything except the sound of the graveyard shift of sentries as they called out now to the coffee caddy making his middle-of-the-night round with a hot pot in a bucket of coals. Wes listened, checking the arithmetic, until the shouts matched the number of towers. "Quite a collection of people Monty has in his entourage now," he mused. "Even me."

"You brought it on yourself, remember."

"You know what road they say is paved with good intentions." He could sense her attention rouse at that. To head off what she might ask, he hurried out his own loop of question: "Monty out of sorts, that way—how close are you to done with him?"

Susan seemed to consider this from numerous sides, until finally replying: "He's nearly there. I'd say another week of practice and he'll have everything down pat."

"Do you think that could be made two weeks?"

"What then? Does Bailey count on the Klan flying south with the swallows?"

"Susan, he—we're doing our damnedest." He rubbed a hand along the wicker corrugations of the chair arm, whetting what he wanted to say next. "I know you're bothered by a lot tonight. I wish it didn't have to be so."

"It's ghastly to me, Angus gone," she said, dry grief in her voice. "From girl on, I looked to him. For everything from the ways of words to justice in our fights at recess. But do you know what's odd? I spent all those years in his classroom, I can tell you the exact part in his hair and every mood of his mustache, yet when I think of him it's at the schoolhouse dances. He and Adair could shine together at that, at least, and at every dance the time would come when people would make him step out on his own." A remembering laugh unsteady in its sound, which increased Wes's ache for her. "He wasn't the inflated breed of Scot," she tried to lighten this with a mock chiding, "like you Highlanders. But somewhere he picked up the Highland Fling." Wes could just see her profile as she looked up into the night, gave a hum to find her note, then softly sang:

> *"I saw the new moon, late yester e'en*
> *with the old moon in her arm—"*

She ended the chorus with a croon that swept upward like the flung hand of he who danced to it: *"Hiiiyuhhh!"* The drums and pipes of Edinburgh came to Wes's ears, the similar cry of the Black Watch drillmaster drifting up to that balcony that had held the two of them. The medley of it all, the coarse beat of time mixed with the magical lilt of Susan's voice then and now, overpowered him. "I didn't mean to carry on like this," Susan's strained speaking voice broke that memory. "I realize you and Angus had your differences."

"We were born to them, let's just say, Susan."

"This is a night I'm not made for," she concluded as if regarding herself from a distance. Across it, across the years stretching back to those other nights, her hand found his. "Keep me company? As before?"

For a moment he thought he had imagined those words. But this was Susan, imagination could not begin to keep up with her. They rose, not exactly steadying each other but needing to feel their way together, and went to the bedchamber where, in the courses of other lives, commandant and lady had lain together under a mingled moon.

Does what we were at give off some spoor he picks up? Or has he had enough experience of bedsprings that it amounts to an instinct?

Breakfast was in every conceivable stage, knives and forks still in action among those of them left at the table when the morning shift of tower guards scraped their plates into the scrap bucket and tromped out, while over at the stove Mrs. Gustafson was forcefully dolloping hotcake batter onto the griddle in anticipation of the grave-yard shift coming in hungry.

Susan met Bailey's eyes again across the table, over their coffee cups. She was as sure as in any performance she had ever given that she showed no outward sign of last night, and Wes was managing what she thought was a perfectly passable impersonation of himself as the fated officer who had drawn the duty of the morning. But Bailey knew. All the way since the infamous Missoula hotel room? she wondered. Did he read forward into people's lives, that clear-as-glass gaze of his more certain than any crystal ball, that they would again and again be caught at what they had done before? *We'll see.*

Bailey settled his cup to the table and turned back to Wes. "With the funeral on Friday, that doesn't give us enough time to get our ducks in a row, Major. The number-one thing I don't like about this is it splits our force. We can maybe—*maybe*—keep her safe if we put half our men around her there at the graveyard. That leaves us thin here. What would help like everything would be for Rathbun to lay low, keep in his room in case of any snoopers. No prancing around the parade ground on a pony, just for instance."

At this, Dolph looked up from spearing a bite of hotcake into the yolk of his fried egg, wagging his head chidingly in the direction of Monty's place at the table. Susan again wondered about the inner workings of someone like him, human equivalent of a shirttail on Wes or Whit, whichever one on any given day tucked him toward a back pocket of ranch life as needed: milk this, saddle up that, which this time happened to be a Duesenberg. Perhaps the little man simply saw all this as something he could tell endlessly in the bunkhouse. Certainly he had been sopping in everything that was said since he alit here, far and away more attentive than he had ever been to chores for her. She tried to set aside her irk at his witnessing this; there was enough else strumming away on her nerves.

Now Wes glanced at the empty plate waiting for Monty. "I know he's entitled to sleep in after singing half the night, but he ought to be in on this." Bailey left the table, stepped out and said something to one of the guards coming off shift, and was already laying out the plan by the time he sat back down. "McCaskill would have belonged to the Woolgrowers' Association, I figure we can put three of the boys in the crowd as a delegation from the Helena office of that. Myself and one of the others, anybody asks, we can say we're stockbuyers he dealt with—"

"Only if you say it in gabardine, Mr. Bailey," Susan informed him.

"I'm afraid she's right," Wes said impassively enough. "You can't show up there looking like you're dressed for a Butte wake."

Grimacing, Bailey jotted into a notebook a shopping trip to the haberdashery in Havre. "All right. So. The five of us can cover the funeral, just. Now to get her back here in one piece, we'll need to make like she's heading to Helena, then swing off—"

"It's Rathbun!" The guard who had been sent to fetch Monty half tumbled into the room, his footing out from under him in more ways than one. "He lit out of here! Bedroll's gone!"

"How?" Bailey looked swiftly at Susan.

"Goddamned if I know," the guard said as the others from his shift scrambled to their feet and crowded around him. "I was in the tower but could hear them both in the auditorium there, her playing and talking away and every so often he'd let out with a song—"

"Or somebody would play a recording of Roland Hayes, would she, Susan?" This came from Wes, and was not impassive at all.

Bailey's agonized forehead made her take pity. "Oh, if it makes that much difference to you. Once we were in the auditorium, all

Monty needed to do was to go up to the balcony and slide down the fire chute."

"He'll be horseback, with plenty of head start. The whole damn prairie he can choose from." The way Bailey spoke it, Monty had gone to ground and pulled the hole in after him. "Major, how many people am I supposed to protect who won't let themselves be protected?"

"He knows what he's doing," Susan told them as if she did too. Hard as it was, she faced Wes directly. In front of the others, he had to hold in the arrowstorm of questions, the sudden entire nightful of them. She alone saw in his shaken expression the deeps of their time together it came from; motives off the map left a person that way. "Wes, if we take care of our end of things"—the sweep of her words was not lost on Bailey either—"Monty can handle his. You'll see."

Gruff as she had ever heard him, Wes said back: "Try to be reasonable, Susan. We'd know better about that if you'd tell us where he's gone."

"You'll have to take it on faith."

It became the frieze of Fort Assinniboine ever after for those of them in that room, the faces spaced around that table then. Susan had been in front of skeptical audiences before, but these were ready to pucker with it. Bailey could be seen to be revising her, for better or worse she probably would never know. In back of him, the men on shift when Monty ghosted away into the night looked as if the same case of distemper had swept through them all. Dolph appeared to be in tattler's heaven. Wes had the look of a man whose hand had been forced. Still bleakly turned toward Susan, he intoned to Bailey: "Ready or not, now we have to."

You have the day for it at least, Angus.

Scrubbed by yesterday's local rain, a piece of weather the rest of the Two Medicine country would have paid hard cash for, the valley of English Creek and the beveled benchlands around it showed a surprise blush of green. Beyond and more than a mile up, the reefs of the Rockies were standing rinsed in the sun, blue and purple in their cliffs. Along with her sense of loss Susan felt the distinct touch of the day, the vast old clockless surroundings playing tag with memory.

"You could eat the air here," her father liked to proclaim on such rare fine mornings. "We'll need to," her mother would have ready, "if you don't butcher one of your darling creatures."

With one of the Neds beside her and others of Bailey's crew drifting nervously nearby, Susan had detached from the other earlycomers toward the rows of markers. The graveyard here on the hill overlooking Gros Ventre held more people than she knew down there in the town anymore. She visited for several minutes among the stones and their epitaphs. The names, the names. They filled the years of her younger self. Now, with Angus, every family of the Scotch Heaven homesteads was incised, a member or two or all, in this knoll. She stepped last to the graves of her parents; stood there held by the thought of how much the world had turned over in the handful of years since their deaths.

At her back she heard the slick whisk of gabardine pantlegs approaching. Bailey was gray-sheened as a dove from head to toe, his dandy new Stetson and boots matching the cut of everything but his eyes. "The family's arriving," he said as if introducing himself. "So's half the county, it looks like. It would help if you would take yourself over there"—he was gazing around at the Two Medicine country's sculpted perimeter of buttes and peaks and benchlands but only, she knew, as far as a rifle could carry—"and blend in with the others. What do you say?"

"I'll be where Adair wants me," she told him. "Give them a minute to sort themselves out and then I'll come."

Bailey sucked his teeth as she stood there, tallest woman for miles around, sticking out perfectly for any Klan gunsight.

"Mister Bailey? I do hope you know, there's movement down there in the brush every once in a while."

He rapidly checked on the brushy line of the creek as if to make sure it hadn't crept closer to the cemetery. Then turned and sized her up again, and this time it had nothing to do with her height. She either had extreme guts or pure lack of common sense.

"Double W riders working the brush, is what you're seeing," he told her, hoping that was a hundred percent true. "The Major had Whit take his best brushpoppers and sift through in there, just in case."

"It's nice they're being put to use on something besides cows," Susan commended.

"What would be really nice," Bailey put his professional best into this, "would be to know whether Rathbun is anywhere in the neighborhood. Just for instance, do we have to worry about the Klan siccing itself on two of you here today in these lovely surroundings, would you say? He's not going to pull some stunt like popping up here to sing a hymn over this gentleman, is he? Miss Duff? Is he?"

She calculated for some moments more and decided she could safely say: "I'm the one whose singing you will have to put up with. Monty will be here in spirit only."

"That's something, at least." No less gloomy than before, Bailey cast another put-upon look around the general scenery. Sighing, he signaled with a tug at his earlobe and as quickly as the nearest of his men tagged onto Susan in the rotation of protection, he himself trudged off to keep an eye on the crowd. In his considerable experience, trouble could happen so damn many ways. You never knew.

Susan watched him move off, to have someplace to keep her eyes occupied instead of trying to stare through clumps of brush. So far she seemed to be up to this role, but the curtain was not very far up yet, was it. She marked in herself that she did not feel anything resembling brave about being here; stubbornness would have to do. The inescapable question rose in her again: terminally stubborn, if it came to that? Her Duff blood was answer enough. If so, so. She was not going to let lunatics who tromped around at night with their heads in pillowcases have their way. If this was what it took to bring the Klan out where they could be got at and propel the Baileys and the Williamsons of the universe at them, she could play the lure.

She waited a bit longer, tensed as if taking on music she did not thoroughly know. The day seemed to rest its weight on this exact plot of ground, on her. The air was still, the canopy of cottonwood leaves motionless as a pale-green roof of domes over the town, down at the base of the knoll. Somewhere there, Wes at his business, surprisingly coldblooded about matters of that sort over this one. He had dodged like a Nijinsky when she wanted him to attend Angus's funeral. Dealings to be done, he intimated; it would do no good for him to be on hand, he protested, Bailey had set everything possible into place. Under her unquitting stare, he put it at its simplest:

"I'm not wanted there."

Susan levied that back at him. "You know, don't you, I'm probably not either, with the exception of the McCaskills."

Wes had digested that in silence. The past couple of days of tension between them—held off from one another by the forcefield of unsayable motives but in the pull of what each still needed the other for—showed on him as if a mask had slipped. She knew it was all he had in him to tell her when he said at last: "Some dealings won't wait."

Speaking of. Susan bolstered herself and crossed the cemetery to the graveside. By now people were pouring in. Maybe it was just as well for Wes's vanity that he hadn't come, this was a crowd befitting a governor. This entire end of the county had passed through Angus's South Fork classroom, and she catalogued faces by family resemblance. Some, such as the wrinkled bard Toussaint Rennie, gave her a nod of recognition. A good many carefully gave her nothing.

When she reached the McCaskills, Varick as the new head of the family shook her hand and thanked her for coming. Beside him, Beth was resoundingly pregnant. The boy Alec was too old to cry but too young to stand still in the family grouping. Then Adair, eyes glistening, turned from the Bible-holding minister—*Oh, Angus, surely they'll balance that off with a helping of Burns*—and clasped her.

"You sang in his schoolyard, you sang at our wedding," Adair spoke as tranced as if telling a fortune. "I knew you wouldn't stop short now."

Delicately as possible, Susan hurried out the necessary as the minister began to thumb into his Bible: "Dair, is there a particular hymn? Or do you want me to pick—"

"A ballad, I'd like," Adair's voice held no doubt. "He was something of one himself, wasn't he." Susan blinked her way from hymnal considerations to far different ones. What unpredictable bits and pieces we are made of, Adair was causing her to know anew. "Do a bit of old rhyme for Angus," Adair was saying, "do this one," with sudden softness humming the air of the old song that went:

> *"World enough, world enough*
> *Did I search till there was thee.*
> *And at last, oh at last,*

> *The discovery of your charms*
> *Is world enough for me."*

After the bit of hum Adair braced back from Susan, dabbed away the tears which had joined the freckles beneath each eye, and looked off as if for the missing. "Fickle old wind. Angus would laugh, this is the one day it didn't come by to pay him its respects."

The town looked as if it could use a customer, any make of customer, this morning. Wes checked his watch, although he could have told the time by looking at the street: the customary point of day when funerals were held in the Two Medicine country, late enough after morning chores to dress up and make the trip to town, time left for work in the afternoon. He felt some relief now that he could mentally put matters into operative categories, thinking back over the war council he'd had with Whit and the handpicked Double W squad before tending to this other. Patting his pocket to make sure of the day's documents, he climbed out of his backseat workspace in the Duesenberg, parked as discreetly as something like it could be behind the Sedgwick House hotel, and walked on up the empty main street of Gros Ventre. Still making his calculations but careful of the off-angle set of steps into the Valley Stockmen's Bank, he went in. He could see Potter riffling papers of his own, and he headed on back.

"Well, Major," the banker said cordially, looking up over his desk. "Business first thing in the morning?"

"That's why daylight was invented, George."

"With me, the only crack of dawn is my sacroiliac as I roll over in bed." Wes was sure his father had heard the same ritual joke from Potter in one financial go-round or another in this same room. "But that's how the Double W gets the jump on the rest of us, hmm? Have a seat, and what can I do you for?"

Through the open door of the banker's office Wes glanced out to where the tellers were going about business as usual. He asked idly, "Why didn't you close for the funeral?"

* * *

Holding her head high, standing tall there at the brow of ground in front of them all, Susan sang the closing verse as if it could reach over horizons.

> *"Long enough, long enough*
> *Were my heart and I at sea.*
> *Now at last, oh at last,*
> *The circle of your arms*
> *Is world enough for me."*

She took a step back from the graveside, and the stiffly dressed crowd watched somberly as Varick sprinkled a handful of earth slow as salt into the grave.

"Whose? McCaskill's?" Potter had the air of genial sharing that he employed on everything from foreclosure notices to remarks about the weather. "We can't shut down every time there's one less homesteader."

Wes stepped over and closed the office door. He said as though it had only now occurred to him: "Do you realize there's only one letter's difference between *skulk* and *skunk?*"

"You lost me there, Major." The banker rocked forward in his chair, staying attentively tilted.

"I'll bet." Wes reached into the breast pocket of his suit and brought out the documentation. *Realm of Pondera County, Invisible Empire, Knights of the Ku Klux Klan,* each of the membership-and-dues cards in the packet was headed. Each was about the size of a schoolchild's report card and was thorough down to height, weight, color of eyes and hair, and date of oath. They were alphabetical, and he riffled rapidly to the *P*'s. He flipped a card across the desk.

Potter's glance rebounded instantly from the card with his name on it to Wes's confronting eyes. "Where did you get those?"

"Don't make me tired. At your house, where else." Wes watched him as he would something that crawled. "Not me personally, of course, but someone who knows how to deal with firebugs and cow killers and would-be assassins."

"You Williamsons always think you're good at running a bluff." Potter's mettle as a hater was fully in his voice by now, but so was last-ditch cunning. "I would imagine you're a clubman yourself, Major—you must know there's no law against belonging to a fraternal organization."

"Maybe not, but then there's trespass at our place, breaking and entering at Susan Duff's, malicious destruction of property, reckless endangerment—"

"You want to get giddy citing laws, try the one against miscegenation. That woman and that horse cock you keep around."

Wes in that instant wished bayoneting was legal without a congressional declaration of war. He looked at Potter as he would a gob of spit on a dinner plate. "Even if there was anything to it, you yellow-belly," the words snapped out of him in pellets of cold rage, "there's no witness." Dolph, for safekeeping, by now would be halfway to Chicago on the cattle train, his conscience long since repaired—"Major, I better tell you, there's some bastards in town trying to git me in on their funny stuff"—and his wages handsomely upped for stringing the Klan along while the Williamsons readied their fist. His Klan card, Wes would tuck away for him as a souvenir and reminder, but the one on the desk stayed pointing at the pale-faced banker like a deadly warrant. "And don't count on any others of that skulking bunch you head up. They're busy being reasoned with."

Potter glanced involuntarily at the clock behind Wes. "That includes that henchman of yours," Wes took extreme satisfaction in letting him know, "the one you sent off into the brush with a hunting rifle. It's not hunting season anymore, Potter, particularly that kind." Caught and hogtied and ready for delivery to the sheriff, the Klan's second-in-command was in for the rare privilege of having a Duesenberg serve as his paddywagon. The rest of the bunch were having the run put on them. Whit and his men right now were going name to name from those cards through this town. The remainder of Bailey's force was doing the same in Valier; the rejuvenated sheriff and muscular deputies were spreading the gospel of persuasion in the county-seat town of Conrad. Across the state at this hour, Wes's old political allies were hitting the Klan with what he knew would be varying effectiveness, but some of it was sounding effective enough;

the sheriff at Butte had put out a public declaration that any Klan members caught lingering would be shot like wolves.

The specimen across the desk from Wes made another try at dodging. "I have standing in this town, you're dreaming if you think you can turn people—"

"Potter," Wes said as if instructing the clumsiest member of the awkward squad, "half the banks in this state have gone under in the past couple of years. I'd only need to lift a finger to push yours over that edge. And the bank examiners would pretty quickly find out if any depositors' funds went to pay for white sheets and rednecks and Klan rifles and ammunition, wouldn't they."

The man sat very still, trying to see beyond the corner Wes had him in. He moistened his lips enough to speak. "Maybe I got swept up in this more than I should have."

"Fine. You get to tell that to whatever hooded fools are above you. Now I suggest you close this bank for that funeral, even if the decency is a little late. Then go home and pack a bag, and get out of the state. I'm sure you can find a rock to live under, somewhere else."

The crowd began to disperse from the cemetery, back to common day. "This mother of mine," Varick was saying to Susan at his first chance to do so without being overheard, "has her own idea of one last thing you could do for Dad. I think it asks a hell of a lot of you, frankly. But I said I'd try it out on you."

"Anything," said Susan.

"Let me go get Fritz Hahn," Varick said with a ghost of Angus's smile. "He's head of the South Fork school board."

THE convoy of cars, Susan's dust-caked Tin Lizzie in the middle like a ragamuffin caught up in a royal parade, pulled into Highland Street as Helena's dusk was turning to evening.

Bulked into the passenger seat, Wes had ridden with her so they could talk. Words had been abundant on the trip from Gros Ventre, understandings less so. "You feel you have to?" he had pressed her when she told him she had agreed to take on the South Fork teaching job for the year. "Have to, and want to," was her double-barreled response to that. "For once they go together." Eight grades: she knew that she would be running up and down the stairsteps of lessons like the keeper of a mental lighthouse in the months ahead, but she could always come back to the mark of the presence she was standing in for. While she could never be Angus, she would have no shortage of notions about how he would have done things.

Wes wondered wearily whether the two of them were always going to be like people on passing trains, her chronically in the West and him chronically due back East, coinciding once in a while in the middle of nowhere as in their Fort Assinniboine night together and then the distance doubling between them, over and over, from the split second the engines of their lives flashed past each other again. *Silly*, a word he wasn't used to using on himself, came to mind along with such thinking; he hadn't been in mental sweats of this sort since Harvard mixers. But there Susan sat in the driver's seat, set on her own course until school let out next spring. "All right," he'd finally said in a tone to the contrary, "step in Angus's schoolmaster slippers if you must," and in return she'd given him a look that seemed to say they might try each other on again after that.

At the moment, though, he could not let her vanish into that house taking Monty's whereabouts with her.

"I give, one more time. Where is he, up Houdini's sleeve? Susan, I'm begging you. Bailey and I can't swear we nailed every last Klan thug, Monty may still need whatever protection we can give him. And what if he's out there laid up on the prairie somewhere—a horse can break a leg in a gopher hole, any number of things can happen riding alone—"

He broke off, at the slight sidelong grin on her. Until that moment he had never counted cunning among Susan's many talents. She said simply, "Come in."

As they got out and Wes looked uncertainly toward the other cars where Bailey and his crew awaited orders, she told him: "We won't need Mister Bailey's services."

He handled Bailey as diplomatically as circumstances allowed, then went over to the Duesenberg and told Gus and the Mrs. to go and open up his house, he would be along later. Susan had waited for him at the front door and let him do the honors with the key.

They stepped in to apparent emptiness. Wes did not know whether to feel vindicated or crestfallen. Helena had been searched these past days, the one Negro policeman on the force shaking Clore Street by the heels, Bailey's men casing other parts of the city, and Monty had not turned up. Nor did he now. Susan, however, was everywhere at once in her downstairs, opening a window to let fresh air in, putting a shoulder to the music parlor doors, asking Wes what time it was as she set the grandfather clock and wound it back to life. Catching sight of herself in the hallway mirror, she abruptly stopped everything else she was doing. Wes looked on, the apprehensively fascinated way men do at women tending to themselves, as she plucked out hairpins unerringly. Her hair flowed to her shoulders.

"Come up." She was already on her way to the stairs.

Wes swallowed hard. *Have mercy for once, Lord.* If she was hiding Monty in her own bedroom and word of it ever got out—

The long loft room was so full of belongings it took him several moments to be certain none of them was alive and breathing. Susan was making her way through them on some course known only to her, trailing fingertips over some, the cupped palm of her hand on corners of others as she passed. With Wes watching as if trying to learn the secret of the ritual, she bypassed her desk to a cabinet along the wall. A crackling noise took over the room. She tinkered with the radio set until the static quit.

Monty watched the clock.

He squared himself up, attentive now on the figure almost shoulder to shoulder with him. Somebody else made a pointing motion, which after the workings-over Susan had given him in the auditorium he would never have to think twice to recognize as a cue.

"Now for your listening pleasure here on station CINE, our latest troubadour of the Medicine Line, Montgomery Rathbun." The announcer looked at him sidelong but kept his mouth aimed at the almighty microphone on its spear of stand between them. "Welcome to 'Evening Encore.' For those of you not fortunate enough to have been introduced to him through his music earlier today, Mister Rathbun's background is an unusual strand in our prairie background. Your father was a member of the colored cavalry down in the States—the buffalo soldiers, as they were called, I believe?"

"He was," Monty said easily into his hemisphere of the mike. The first time, he had worried he would need this written out, along with the music, but talking on the radio was proving to be a snap; an invisible audience was just right. "Sergeant in the Tenth Cavalry, right across the line at Fort Assinniboine. He was in charge of troopers, my mother was in charge of laundry, and I seem to be the result."

"And a lucky outcome it was for music-lovers," the announcer orated from inches away. "For those of you who do not know the Fort Assinniboine story and the part it played in our Medicine Line past"—here he resorted to a script of what these radio people called canned history, for what Monty knew would be the next two minutes.

Making sure of his music sheets, in that noiseless way they'd shown him so the rustle of paper wouldn't make ten thousand listeners think their radio sets were on fire, Monty drew everything of the past half week into him for the effort to come. That feverish after-dark conference with her as soon as they were by themselves in the auditorium, in absolute agreement that they had to get the Major and Bailey into gear somehow. He had left her in loud conversation with herself and the Victrola version of a night's singing, thrown her a wave from the balcony, and gone down the fire chute. Led the saddlehorse out of the fort with the blanket over it. Reins in one hand, the 30.06 in his other; take some of the bastards with him, he would, if he met up with any of the Klan out there in the dark. The long ride north to here, couple of hard days' worth; it had been like riding in the roundup again, except he couldn't remember ever being so saddle-weary during even the longest loops out after cattle. By the time he was across the border—the section-line roads he had been following ran out at Canada, the only way he could tell—and sorted out the town of Medicine Hat to find the radio station, he was feeling hard-used. A hot meal and a scrub-up at the hotel, then presenting himself in full singing rig to the station manager exactly the way she had said to do. The man had been intrigued enough to try him out on a few songs in the back room, and then excited enough to sign him on, a full week to start.

All that was lacking was her. He wished like everything she was over there governing the keys for this. Wherever the station had dragged up this accompanist, the woman plowed around on the piano like she was doing Sunday school. But he would make up for it. *Oho! The first perfect singer there ever was?* As perfect as he could make it, on this.

The announcer was finishing his scripted patter. "And now, out of that historical heritage, here is Montgomery Rathbun to sing the ballad of the Tenth Cavalry."

Monty took the cue, and out into the air, out over the Medicine Line and the weedy parade ground of the old fort and the time-browned washhouse of the Double W and the silent homesteads of Scotch Heaven, his voice began to travel.

> *"Forty miles a day*
> *on beans and hay.*
> *Scenery all the way*
> *on cavalry pay.*

> *When I was young and in my prime,*
> *I dabbed my X on the Medicine Line.*
> *Suited up blue, and since that time,*
> *Boots and saddle have suited me fine.*

> *Forty miles a day*
> *on beans and hay. . . ."*

As the piano accompaniment went into a romp that made Susan wince, she said: "Even I'll admit, Monty is full of surprises. I thought I knew all his songs, but I've never heard this."

> *"Buffalo soldiers, that's our lot.*
> *Midnight sons of the Medicine Line.*
> *Prairie life is all we've got,*
> *I'll stand your guard if you stand mine.*

> *Forty miles a day*
> *on beans and hay. . . ."*

It had taken him any number of nights, with a stub of pencil always within reach on the apple-box bedstand, to bring all the verses back. A dab at a time all the way back in memory to the parades, the band rattling out the turbulent tune that his father practically horseback-danced to, man and mount in flourish there at the head of the rank of blue coats. Other bits remembered from the drifts of song from the barracks nearest where he and Angel Momma and his father lived, when the troopers would pass the night with songs he knew his boy ears were not supposed to be hearing, but always ending up with this one. The chorus—even his father would bellow that out if he was in a good enough mood, slapping the sides of his belly in rhythm like beans and hay were battling it out in there. When Monty eventually had it all down and softly crooned it in his quarters at night—he had intended to surprise her with it, whenever their finale in the auditorium would have been—the old song seemed to bring him the feel of the dark displaced men who had been stationed there at the farthest north edge of the American prairie, singing to keep their spirits up.

On oldest maps, a cloud maestro blows benediction to those who travel the edges of the world. Now Monty similarly gathered breath and all else into the last of the song:

> *"Sergeant Mose and old Black Jack,*
> *They make you toe the mark on the Medicine Line.*
> *Trot you to Hell, gallop you back,*
> *Seat of your britches take on quite a shine.*
>
> *Forty miles a day*
> *on beans and hay. . . ."*

"It's a rouser," Susan appraised, patting hand into palm in contemplative applause. "A bit off the spiritual side, but he can make good use of it in his program as— Wes, do you feel all right?"

"Just my knee taking a fit."

He had risen from his perch on the bed and gone over to the window alcove as Monty's next song was enthusiastically introduced. Stood there full-front to the night so Susan could not read his face. He did not want to know himself what was written there. *Susan may think the Scotch know something about sin-eating, but*—Mose Rathbun resuscitated by Monty's balladry. *Lord, what next?* The scene that no longer would stay put away suffused Wes. The Tenth Cavalry parade song had set it all off again, like a phosphorus recon flare freezing into light that particular pounded ground of memory. The day of the medal from Pershing. Small talk from lordly Black Jack himself, surprisingly companionable with his entourage restless around him, strung along the edge of the St. Mihiel town square. Did Major Williamson by any chance know the Medicine Line country there in Montana? "I know it quite well, sir. Some of our range runs nearly to Canada." Coincidence, said the general. Had an interesting piece of service at a Medicine Line fort himself in cavalry days; there was nothing like the Montana prairie as horse country, was there, except of course in the instance of that vapid gloryhound Custer. Anyway, Fort Assinniboine: known as the Presidio of the north then, but was that before your time, Major? Wes, startled: "I was not aware you had served there, sir." Most decidedly; colored troops on station there at the time, but it was a truth of war that soldiers were all the same shade in the reddest part, wasn't it. Had a bit of adventure out of his first command there at least; escort duty along the Two Medicine Trail, over west of the fort, to put a band of Crees back into Canada. Queer sort of chore, the great man went on now as Wes had listened with everything in him. Like trying to carry water in a basket; the Crees would leak away into the brush of every creek his Troop D forded with them. Pershing laughed the dryest laugh Wes had ever heard; he had about worn the stripes off his ruffian of a sergeant siccing him after them.

STRIPER

· 1888 ·

"SERGEANT, CLOSE UP their ranks again. They don't need to smear themselves across the entire prairie, this isn't one of their buffalo hunts."

"Yes, sir. Good as done." Drawing on his long experience at the pretense that all orders from a white officer were created equal, Mose Rathbun spun his mount from beside Lieutenant Pershing and spurred off to pass the word to his men as they endeavored to herd Indians. The line of march of the captured Crees, to call it that, had funneled nice as anything through the single street of Gros Ventre, but out here north of town the Indians were dribbling off again. The few good wagons with Little Bear and other chiefs were drifting out of line, already almost side by side across the grassland, and behind them kinked the long train of limping buggies and scraggly travois and even a few groaning Red River carts, with the spotted herd of horses fanned out behind. From past episodes of rounding up Crees, Sergeant Rathbun figured that the Indians gravitated out that way so as not to eat each other's dust, but this new lieutenant could be a stickler when he wanted to. Pershing in fact reminded him of the bristles on a grooming brush, with that brisk cookie-duster mustache and his parade-ground way of sitting in the saddle even out here on the march. *Not gonna cost me my honorable if I have anything to do with it, though.* This was the big roundup, Little Bear's band, and Mose Rathbun's last before his retirement discharge at month's end, and he was trotting along through it with a short-timer's determination not to get out on skin ice with his commanding officer.

"Tinsley, Goggins, all you," Mose called to his corporals and his troopers, "poke them up in here, or old Black Jack's going to have you cleaning the stables until you're gummers." He stood in his stirrups and made a bunching motion to the trudging mob of Crees, not that he expected it to do any good. "Ride herd on those women and young ones, too," he warned his men, "next creek we hit. They'll light off out of here on their own, quick as anything."

The greenhorn of his complement of men had the misfortune to catch his eye. "Bovard!" Mose bellowed. "Shove them together there, or I'll curry your head with a quirt." From everything Private Bovard had heard, it would not be the first such occurrence. He threw the heavy-shouldered sergeant a flustered salute and began swatting the nearest Indian pack ponies with the ends of his reins.

Mose knew he was going heavy on his troopers. But it paid. Their blue field uniforms were never more crisp, every buckle and button on them gleamed with polish, they wore their campaign hats cocked just so. The men naturally groused about it but by making them snap to, he pointed them up in the estimation of the white officers like Pershing. Call it a personal conceit, but here on his last time around he most definitely did not want any man of his written up for sloppy behavior. And the entire troop was doing him proud so far; they looked like saddle soldiers ought to look, if he did say so himself. Give those play-pretty Mounties something to see, when Troop D handed these godforsaken Crees back to them yet another time.

Trotting back along the column to keep everybody on their toes, the sergeant impassively scanned the miserable parade of Indians for broken-down wagons or any other contrivances of delay that the Crees seemed to be so good at. Truth be told, he still rather would have been fighting this blanket bunch than shooing them back across the Medicine Line like a flock of chickens. Days of the prairie campaigns seemed to be over for good, though, to his regret. It was sad, sort of, for tribes like the Crees as well as the cavalry, in his estimation; having to trudge along in each other's dust like this instead of scrapping it out in a whirl of horses and whooping. War was hell but peace was boring; what was a man to do? His sympathy for the Crees stopped about there, though. Canada and the U.S. had been flinging these vagabond Indians back and forth across the border like a game of Auntie-I-over ever since the Riel Rebellion, up north there. Louis Riel had found himself on the wrong end of Her Majesty's rope and the Crees had found themselves on the losing side and without a homeland. The sergeant knew the iron rules of fate when he saw them, and he had seen them more than enough. Down here, if the South had won the big war, the Tenth Cavalry as a frontier regiment of freed black men would never have come into being and Mose Rathbun right this minute would be in some hopeless procession himself, with a hoe on his slave shoulder.

By now he had busied himself all he could in putting the troop on its toes, and the line of march had accordioned into a better semblance of order. Still restless, wanting to stir his blood more than escort duty allowed for, he rode rapidly back up the column to where Pershing was conferring with Lieutenant Hardeman of Troop C, which had drawn the candy end of this assignment, lackadaisically strung out around the Indians who were herding the tribe's horses. Two West Point shavetails in one spot; Mose made sure his salute practically sang through the air. "They're bunched better, sir. Permission to reconnoiter on ahead to that next creek? Corporal Tinsley can see to the men, be good for him."

Pershing cast a cold eye over the long winding procession and reluctantly decided to call it tidy enough. "Very well, Sergeant," he granted. "While you're at it, find out if that provisioner is making any progress on our rations for this bunch. Tell him the company commanders said we could all stand some slow elk on the plate for a change."

Mose galloped off ahead of the column, toward the next flat-topped ridge to the north. *Black Jack's handling me with a loose rein, that's interesting.* Couldn't always be sure with this lieutenant. That had actually been pretty funny from him, picking up the troopers' lingo for opportune beef the way he did; but he was a stiff looker for good reason. Mose gave thought again to the day of departure from where they had been holding the Crees, when Pershing went on foot through the entire camp of crying women and wailing babies and sullen braves, patient as paint while he tried to sort out the pandemonium. In the hubbub none of the soldiers noticed one of the Cree men, said to be wanted for something in Canada, emerge from his tent with a rifle, sit down, pull the barrel end to himself, and jam his big toe against the trigger. Blooey, and the slug tore on through him and just missed Pershing about a dozen feet behind him. When Mose and his men came rushing over, the lieutenant said, as if to himself, "That very nearly canceled out West Point."

Mose laughed harshly at the memory. It took a fairly hard hide to shrug off a close call like that. Pershing was not an easy one to figure, but he seemed inclined to give a man room to operate, and that was all Mose ever asked.

As the sergeant topped the ridge now, the first sight that met him was the snowcapped line of the Rockies, on a march of their own, extending on and on into what had to be Canada. He pulled up and simply stared. By damn, you could see from here to Judgment Day in this bench country. With a practiced eye he studied the lay of the land, the swales of grass in the creek basin to the west and the dark droplets that had to be cattle, no more buffalo in these parts. He spotted the provisioner's supply wagons down ahead there where a road led off to ranch buildings quite a ways in the distance; a place with some real size from the looks of it. The saddlehorses and little cluster of people by the wagons must mean the cattleman and the provisioner were in the midst of dickering over the price for slaughter-beef. What he had to put his main attention to, however, was the thick ribbon of willows and cottonwoods that wound out of the ranch and across the prairie ahead. *Another damned one of those already,* a grimace coming with the thought. At each of these creek crossings, Indians who had been taking prairie squats all their natural lives suddenly were overcome with the need to go modestly in the brush. *And when they go, they keep on going;* the grim humor of it did little to lighten Mose's disposition where brushy creeks were involved.

He put his pony into a prancy trot as he headed down to the wagons. Never hurt to show people like these that a real rider was heading their way. When he reined up in front of them, the provisioner paid him all the attention he could have asked for, and as far as that went, so did the blocky man wearing specs who stood next to the provisioner, and the pair of highly interested boys next to the man they resembled down to their well-made boots. Mose noticed the older one, maybe eleven, watching him more gravely than the grownups were, while the younger brother simply looked like he was itching to get his hands on Mose's horse. The little misters of that ranch, he would have bet his month's pay.

Greetings were exchanged, and to Mose's total surprise here came a white mitt of a hand up to shake his. "How do, Sergeant," the voice that arrived with it was as chesty as the rest of the cattleman, "I'm Warren Williamson. It's a pleasure to see a man who knows how to sit on a horse. I wish more of my lazy crew did. Phil Sheridan always drilled it into my old outfit—put some spiff into your riding even when you're only on review to yourself." He indicated to the youngsters hanging back, trying to stay out of adult range but not miss anything. "These are my boys, Wes and Whit—I only get a crack at them when they're not in boarding school, but they're picking up on their riding. They know they'd better."

Mose guardedly took in the unexpected conversationalist down there by his stirrups. Every once in a while he came across a white man of this sort, slightly better disposed toward him than most because they had both straddled a cavalry saddle. Williamson's eyeglasses rode high on one ear, maybe giving him a cockeyed view of the world. On the other hand, the man evidently owned this spread where cattle were grazing halfway to the horizon, and that must have taken some fairly clever sighting in on. Forthcoming as the man was, Mose figured there was no harm in a bit of conversation.

"I have me one of my own," he nodded in the direction of the boys, "little stinker back at the post. Keep a fellow hopping, don't they." He gave the young gentlemen a solemn salute, his dark brows mischievously pulled down in a parade-ground glower; then provided a broad smile to lighten things back up. The younger one grinned back, the older one still studied him.

"That lieutenant of yours," the provisioner was heard from now, "is he gonna march these right on up through Blackfeet country or take the branch over to the Whoop-up Trail to keep from mixing Indians with Indians? Makes a couple days' difference in figuring out how much beef Mister Williamson here gets to hold me up for."

Rather needlessly, it seemed to Mose, he had to admit that the commanding officer did not spell out his every intention to him. The provisioner nodded in disgust as if he'd expected that, and muttered that he'd better find out the lieutenant's thinking for himself. "I'll try talk him into the long way. Help out my wallet and yours too, Mister Williamson, if we can put that much more beef into these so-called wards of the government."

"I don't care about that," the ranch owner retorted, ice in his voice all of a sudden. Both boys went quite still. "Just so the cavalry operates the way it's supposed to and clears them out of this country so they don't get to build their shacks and pony corrals in every damn coulee anymore. Good riddance." There was a great deal more boss in his gaze than there had been when he looked over at Mose now. "Sergeant, how long before the column will be at the creek crossing?"

"Close onto noon, I'd say, sir"—it never hurt to add that, Mose had found, even to a civilian.

"Gives me time to get these boys home and working on their suitcases for stagecoach time," the rancher said crisply. "Don't pull such a long face, Whit, the rest of us didn't rate any Easter break." The men laughed at that. "I'll fetch up with you there at the creek," Williamson told the provisioner, simultaneously nodding an offhand goodbye in Mose's direction. "Wouldn't miss seeing this parade."

"Sergeant! I want that man's name!"

Bovard. Mose knew it before he could even swing around in his saddle and put the best face on the situation for the lieutenant. He and several half-drenched troopers were trying to use lariats to tow out a grievously overloaded wagon which had bogged in the axle-deep water, and he had posted Bovard on the south bank meanwhile to push the Crees farther downstream where the creek crossing wasn't so jammed up; that should have been simple enough. But Mose had to look twice to even spot the beset young trooper in the mess of people and Indian ponies and what-all crammed on the bank now. Amid it all, Cree women and kids and apparently even their dogs were setting up a fuss about not being allowed to take a squat in the bushes. Mose swore under his breath. Either in spite of Bovard or because of him, the whole procession had tangled to a halt there next to the brush. And here came Pershing like his stirrups were on fire.

The lieutenant's shout had come from the far bank where the beef dickering was still going on, but to Mose's dismay the officer and his horse were amphibious now, Pershing parting the water in uncaring sprays in order to corner him there in mid-stream. "Have you gone blind, Sergeant? They're taking to the brush again. After them."

Mose was burning with indignation that this had to happen here, in front of that rancher and the provisioner and the rest of the troop and for that matter the damnable Indians. "Yes, sir, right away. I'll detach Tinsley and send him—"

"By now you ought to know an order when you hear one, Sergeant. Am I going to have to put you on report along with that fool trooper of yours? Gather up that squad and chase those runaways down yourself, grasp that? I want the point made to these Indians they can't just take to the brush and expect to get away with it."

"Yes, sir. We'll fetch them, sir."

Strenuously ordering his other soldiers to take up the slack at the creek crossing, Pershing watched the sergeant and the corporal and seven troopers, dark as shadows under their jaunty hats, peel away from the column and fan out west along the creek. The sergeant was jawing hard at them, he was glad to see. Old stripers like Rathbun could grow lackadaisical because of those comfortable chevrons, and that's why you had to light a fire under them every so often. By now the lieutenant knew that this particular one was not averse to fiddling with a duty roster or a supply consignment if there was a bit of side money to be made from it, but he also had been a decorated platoon leader piling into the Comanches on the Rio Grande before John J. Pershing was even a plebe at West Point. Skin or otherwise, the lieutenant had nothing against Rathbun and nothing for him: it was merely a matter of rank. All he cared was that the man made sure to do his job on horseback.

The Crees did not have much head start, Mose was sure, but in the brushy bottomland it did not take much. He was mightily upset at the turn things were taking. All of a sudden even the time of year was against him, the cottonwoods and willows leafed out fully so that he and his men could hardly see an inch into the thicket.

He deployed Tinsley and half the squad to the opposite side of the creek, and took the rest to scour the near side. Everybody assiduously crashed through the brush. Even so, it must have taken an hour before a shout came from Tinsley's direction. Mose and his troopers fought through the brush toward there and waded their horses up to a muddy patch of bank near where the Crees had been found hiding. *Damnation,* he thought as soon as he saw them. Only a woman and two children. *This all we're gonna have to show for it?* He shook his head, letting his troopers know what he thought of their ability at pursuit.

"This don't sit right. Where's the mister?"

"These are all we seen any sign of," Tinsley managed to protest and sound subdued at the same time. He pointed down at the batch of hoofmarks in the mud along the creekbank. "Tracks are a hellish mess, can't make anything of those. Could all be theirs, Sergeant."

"Or could be the man of the bunch rode into the water here." Mose on his horse pushed in close to the Cree woman on hers. "Your husband. Your man. Where is he?"

"No man."

"Like hell." Mose had been through something like this before, the Crees making a sort of game of it: the man sneaking back to camp later to create a disturbance by spooking the horse herd and spiriting his family away again. He spun around to the squad. "Tinsley, you and Squint and Roscoe take these back. Bovard, you're coming with me. The rest of you, start sifting through this brush. Two on each side of the creek and what I mean, give that brush a looking. He's in there somewhere."

Mose applied the spurs to his horse and headed up onto the nearest rise to where he could take in more of the creekline ahead, Bovard barely managing to keep up. From the height of the benchland, Noon Creek could be seen winding into the foothills a few miles off, jack-pines joining brush there for the Indian to hide in, and between here and there beaver dams complicated nearly every course of search along the creek channel. Not too far ahead, though, there was an oxbow bend, and a wide-open stretch of water beyond that. Mose somehow knew. "C'mon, knothead," he growled to Bovard, "he's holed up in that clump by the bend."

The Cree had seen them coming. He sat motionless on his pony until the two soldiers forged through the willows to the stand of cottonwoods that grew large in the bow of the bend. Then, looking straight at them, he swung off his horse in a tired way and went over and sat crosslegged by the trunk of the biggest tree.

The sergeant and the private stared. Maybe the Indian was played out, maybe he had given up on it all, maybe any number of things, but it was plain they would have to handle the man like a side of beef, truss him up and sling him on his horse, to get him back to the line of march. Glaring at him sitting planted there, Mose had the awful supposition that he had more than likely rounded up this particular Indian three or four times before, and if the Indian was everlastingly sick of it, he was, too. He did not even think about what he did next. He slid his carbine from his saddle scabbard, drew down on the Cree, and shot him in the center of the chest.

Bovard surprised Mose by having the presence of mind to grab the reins of the Indian pony while the sound of the single shot still echoed off. The horse would have to go back with them as proof to show to Black Jack. Not necessarily the deceased over there, though, Mose decided in a hurry. He wasn't about to ride back into several hundred Indians, even Indians as whipped as these, leading a horse with a dead brave draped across it. *Be just my luck he's some kind of Indian Jesus.*

He started instructing Bovard. "Let's tuck him under the brush back of that beaver dam, best we can do." He had no doubt that Bovard, already in enough trouble, could be made to go blind and dumb about this. He knew how to handle it with Pershing, too. *"Must've been another one of those wanted ones, Lieutenant. Took care of himself, same way as that one pulled the trigger in front of you, sir."* And that would be that.

᳡

BY THE second month after Mose mustered out, there were times when Angeline sang as if wondering to high heaven where he had vanished off to now.

> *"Sometimes I feel like a feather in the air,*
> *A long ways from home."*

Standing there ironing her way through the summer—taffeta floated to the top of the officers' wives' laundry this hot time of year—she wondered how long she dared let this go on, a husband jangling loose in the world. At first Mose had crowed about being quit of the cavalry and its stand-to reviews on perfectly fine mornings for going grouse hunting. It did not take long, however, before he was under the steady inspection of her eyes. Without saying much, she added him to the rest of her chores, let him roughhouse with Montgomery probably more than was good for either of them, tried to make allowances for the fact that he still seemed more at home with his horse than his family. She could tell he had not liked the move to servants' quarters here in back of the hospital, not that she could see it was any step down from married men's quarters over by the barracks; quieter here. She was much relieved when he latched on with the fort's horse contractor as a wrangler. But being bossed in the breaking corral by men he had once been over did not sit well. Angeline had real cause to fret when he tossed over that job and began to spend a good deal of time at the roadhouse, a mile from the fort and handy to the thirsts and other wants of the cavalrymen. Doing odd jobs there, he described it as. She did not want to hear how odd.

> *"Sometimes I think I'm neither here nor there,*
> *A long ways from home."*

Switching a cooled iron for a heated one, by habit she used the brief trip to the stove to peek in on Montgomery in the next room where he was absorbed with his little zoo of tin toys. *When Papa coming home?* the boy kept pestering her with and she didn't have the heart to scold the question out of him. Lord knew, she asked herself it a hundred times a day. Ever since he took his discharge, Mose did not let her in on his thinking, just as he wouldn't say scat about that whole long last march to pitch those Crees back into Canada.

Something about that bothered at her. All his other times in the field, he came home with stories that would not quit. Now it would take an advanced mind-reader to get anything out of him. Off in hunt of work, was as much as he told her this time when he saddled up, tickled Montgomery into a frenzy, kissed her that way, then rode around the back of the stables before heading out the west gate of the fort. That had been a week ago. She'd had an uneasy feeling, watching him avoid the road along the parade ground and past the barracks where any of Troop D might have been encountered.

"PAPA!"

Angeline nearly dropped her flat-iron in startlement as Montgomery flung past her knees and sent the screendoor whamming open. "Papa, what that?!"

How Mose could ride a horse up to a house that quietly she never would understand, but here he was, practically on the front stoop, down out of the stirrups and unkinking himself by the time she could rush to the doorway. Montgomery had bounced to a halt and was turning into a solid fidget of excitement as he gazed up at his father.

"There's my Monty-tana!" came Mose's parade-ground boom. "C'mere, son. Brought you a persuader." He knelt and outfitted Montgomery with the miniature horsehair quirt. "Put the loop over your wrist, then hold it, so. Now you can give your stick pony what for, make him go as fast as you want. Off you go."

As the boy cantered away, quirt whizzing, Mose rose to his feet and swatted dust off himself as if in Angeline's honor, standing there akimbo the fresh way he did when he first came courting her. He all but had canary feathers on his lips, she saw.

"Found us work, Angel. Over in the Two Medicine country. Working for somebody rich. Goodbye, Fort Ass-in-a-Bone."

"Hush with that!" She looked past him for little ears, but Montgomery was busy rampaging in and out among the clotheslines in search of further air to be whipped. Besides, this was no time to let herself be scandalized, an improved mood around here was worth taking any amount of her husband's teasing. She smiled her best and said gently: "Mose, that's good, about the work. But you look done in. You need food?"

"I could handle some."

"It'll be ready by the time you put your horse up."

Hotcakes and sidepork, his favorite any time of day, sizzled on the griddle when he came slamming back into the house. He slapped Angeline on the hip and sat down to address himself to the food. Angeline served it up, then watchfully moved over to her mountain of ironing. She had to figure he would tell her the rest of it in his own good time, whatever calendar that was.

Mose ate and ate, still saying nothing, sitting there in something like a state of daze, as if the success of his journey was just now catching up with him. By damn, it had worked. You could never tell whether a white man would even look at you sideways, second time around. He had stood on the porch of the big ranch house waiting with his still respectable campaign hat swatting nervously against the leg of his best civilian pants. Then all at once Warren Williamson practically came flying out the door, over to him in a second and appearing monumentally annoyed at having been summoned to deal with this kind of caller.

"If you're looking for a meal, you ought to know enough to come around back and the cook will—" Something about Mose registered then, maybe the hat.

"You're that sergeant." Just that fast, Williamson's expression went from clouded to amused and suggestive. "Not still looking for that runaway Cree, are you? I believe I saw you and your private come back without him, just his horse."

"That one?" Mose had come three days' ride to take this chance. "Just between us, sir, he got cured of that with a lead pill."

"I figured he did." Now the ranch owner looked at Mose man-to-man, and any hesitation in him didn't last much longer than a couple of heartbeats. "I'll tell you what. If you're on the grub line now, I could maybe use a man who knows what he's doing on horseback."

Just like that. It still confounded Mose: you just never knew how things would work out. There on that porch he'd had his good piece of paper ready in his shirt pocket, but Warren Williamson never even asked whether he was discharged or had deserted.

Angeline realized she was swiping back and forth across the piece of clothing in front of her with a cold iron. She drew a breath and took the plunge:

"Mose? Two Medicine, you say? Isn't that over by where you threw those Crees across the line?"

"General vicinity, is all. I'll be riding for a big ranch, Angel. Be herding cattle instead of Crees."

Nose against the screendoor, Monty peered in at the grownups, impatient with their talking and eating. He could not wait any longer for the best thing about his father coming home, the moment when he would be grabbed up in those big arms like he didn't weigh anything at all and tossed in the air, way up by the ceiling, and caught and tossed over and over again—he knew it scared Momma, and for that matter it sort of scared him, but it was a treat from his father, catching him up like that. He slipped past the screendoor into the kitchen where they were, and when the two of them looked around at him, he raced headlong before Momma could stop him. "Papa! Papa! Make me fall up!"

UPTOWN AND DOWN

· 1925 ·

AS USUAL BY this hour of morning, Monty was out onto the street for the third time.

Habit stirred him awake early to do the chores even here, two-thirds of the continent away from the Double W, and even though the nature of the doing had changed beyond recognition. His first excursion, embarked on while it was still too soon to tell what the pinch of sky between the rooflines held for the day, always was around the corner and a few blocks over to the public school and its playground space out back, where he cinched up the roadwork shoes and ran to keep his breath built. At that hour only a few of the more fly types— Harlem never seemed to have any shortage whatsoever of types—out early or in late on activities that did not bear inquiring about were around to levy looks at the heavy-shouldered man, long way from a kid, bounding across the skip-rope scuffs. Back to the apartment for a washup after that, then gratefully to his big feed of the day, breakfast. He took his meals by the month at the E & B—Earl and Bea's 24-hour Buffet—in a nightlife district nearby; the Eat 'Em and Beat 'Em, if you could put away enough grub in the course of thirty days, and he had brought his appetite with him from the ranch. Ham and eggs and unlimited cornbread to set him up for the day, quite the life if he did say so himself. *Steak* and eggs, for two bits more, on concert days like yesterday.

He was getting his teeth into New York life in other ways, too. Each day he felt less like some sort of permanent tourist as he strode through the well-heeled neighborhood called Strivers Row. The tree-lined street brimmed with morning-faced people by this hour. Harlem, he was finding, operated as if every little while some signal was given to open a floodgate and it became the turn of this ten thousand or that to pile out to go to work, to school, to church, to nightlife, to wherever there was maybe another rung on the climb from dun beginnings. Every one of those street-set faces, the astonishment still struck him as soon as he hit the sidewalk, somewhere on the same prism of color as his. Oh, there were white countenances even here—harness-bull cops on the beat and bowtied owners of stores and theaters, mostly—but hardly any in comparison; white raisins in the dark plum cake, all they amounted to in Harlem.

He thought about this at some level even when he was thinking about everything else. Sometimes after breakfast he would linger on his counter stool just to watch through the big cafe-front window the start of the morning rush, the domestics and elevator men and street-cleaners and dishwashers and myriad other doers of chores heading for the elevated railway station in order to be on the job downtown when the white world there cranked open for business, and he could not help but marvel at the way things had swung his way. Last year at this time he had been in their shoes, even if his came with cowboy bootheels and milk-cow manure on them; and the Klan trying to cut his tracks, besides. Now he put on a suit every day of his life, and the fanciest of black cloth to perform in at night, and was it any wonder he felt far enough up in the world to tingle when he took his morning constitutional along Strivers Row and beyond?

Still, there was something more that kept trying to register in him on this particular outing. *Feels like the day it'll hit,* the rhythm of the notion came to him as steadily as his stride. *Feels like the odds are saying to hell with theirselves today.* He realized he of course did not have a whit of fact to back that up—luck doesn't let you know beforehand that it is about to change, like the more generous weather—but the impression tingled too much to ignore. It was somewhat like the jangle that went through him back there on the boat at the Gates of the Mountains, that incredible first day. He clenched one hand, just from nerves, as he navigated from one block of toney addresses to the next. His mind played with the idea that maybe there was such a thing as odds mounting up to the point where they vibrated like bees in a hive, sending something off into the air. In any case, he could not shake off the feeling of good fortune about to alight and start tickling him silly, did not want to even try to shrug that away; he had too many years of his life invested in finally reaching the vicinity of luck.

But maybe it was just the atmosphere. Strivers Row, after all, knew its stuff about prosperity. This later crowd stepped smartly into the day according to Harlem's own clock rather than downtown New York's, and while Monty had clued in that this given neighborhood carried a justifiable reputation for being snooty—it was swankily confident enough to joke of itself as being the home of America's leading second-class citizens—the evidence of the eyes was that this particular canyon of brownstones was indeed Harlem's hit-it-rich gulch, where the shared color was of a different luster than gold but at this time and place panning out just as nicely. Well-dressed men so dark of face that they made him look like a moonlight shadow nodded a respectful good morning to him and forged off to put fillings in people's mouths or plead their cases for them or align their voting habits. Kids dressed as spotless as little royalty flashed down tall sets of steps from the rowhouses and bounced one another in the general direction of their schoolday. Now and again a boy spilling over with mischief would skip in behind him and walk the cowboy way Monty did, toed in and just enough bowlegged to suggest horseback heroics, until the mother on sentry at a window called down in a well-modulated voice not to be pestering Mister Rathbun like that, hear? Monty knew better than to grow spoiled by such circumstances, but it gratified him every time to walk along here as recognized as a man chalked down the back.

His mind on all this and as always somewhat on tonight's music as well, he nonetheless grew leery as he approached the corner where the fancy stoops gave out and opportune storefronts suddenly lined up like they were clothespegged to the second-floor windows. Strivers Row could be as grand as it wanted, but the enterprises beyond were as forthright as a trapline. Even the fruit stands posted prices that seemed to want argument—the elocution-schooled wives from the rowhouses would be along to do their shopping any minute now, primed for debate—and somewhere on any block an apartment-room church with Eureka or Oasis in its name waited to reel in your soul and take it to heaven or Africa, and within a bottle's throw of those were cabaret speakeasies aswim with bootleggers, con men, cardsharps, touts of this or that, women with their hooks out, and other manner of lowlife ready, he well knew, to drain off what his singing was bringing in.

Making sure to sharpen up his eyes, the way he used to start watching out for the Loomises as soon as he lit onto Clore Street, he arrowed ahead past all the diversions. Tut-tutted sympathetically to the well-rehearsed hard-luck stories that cadenced from the strategic scatter of beggars and kept on the move. Even the accents of the blandishments were tricky here, the gumbo lingo of the cottonbacks up from the South and the lullaby intonations of the Caribs and the rounded declamations from the diction wallopers who might be genuine street preachers and might be something else entirely. This flange of Harlem struck him as remarkable in its way as Strivers Row, with its absolute necessity to keep your wits about you along here or there were just all kinds of pockets they could fly off into. Fortunately, within a couple of blocks his daily destination poked up like a smudged thumb out of all this concerted grasping, the newsstand where the ink of headlines practically obliterated the gray-napped proprietor within.

Exchanging greetings, Monty shopped the array of front pages the newsstand was wreathed in until he spotted the particular one he wanted today. The *World;* that ought to be ample enough. He handed the vendor the pennies for the newspaper, then a paper dollar for the number he wanted to play. "Three-oh-six again, how about."

"Straight or combination?"

"Straight again."

"A man can strop a razor on what you pick, Mister Rathbun." The old vendor jotted the number and Monty's bet on the cheatsheet, then handed him his slip of paper. "How'd it go last night?"

"I'm about to find out."

Back in his apartment, though, he took his time about that. Over and over he had told himself he shouldn't still be, but he was smarting from Boston last week, where he'd had a cold and his performance suffered accordingly. Some of the reviews there worked him over practically down to his shoeshine. "The crickets," J.J., his manager, pooh-poohed the critics; "you leave the crickets to me, Montgomery." Good sound logical advice, as far as Monty was concerned, just impossible to follow. Wasn't a person always going to be curious about what was written about him? Half the people he'd met in New York lived on that precise curiosity.

But he didn't have to let it smack him in the face this very moment. He did his voice exercises first. ("Make that such a habit you'll feel absolutely undressed without it," one of those precepts cross-stitched into him back at the North Fork and the Fort Assinniboine auditorium by you-know-who.) Straightened up his bed. Did some mindful dusting, wary in the vicinity of radiators and doorknobs where spark shocks lurked when a person lived on carpets all the time. Recalled that it was rent day, and the tab at the E & B had to be covered too, and his walking-around money needed an infusion as well. Humming, he dug out his bankbook, sneaked a look as if checking a hole card, and gave the kind of whistle he had been waiting a lifetime to give when holding his financial worth in his hand. How it did add up, each whopper of a deposit after one of the big performances, and even the smaller steady take from the Saturday-morning jumps, held at the Plaza Hotel and the Barbizon and those places. Cecil tickling the piano, him putting forth maybe half a dozen songs, eight tops. All due respect to the Double W and life as the Rathbuns previous to him had known it, but this beat looking at wet sheets on a clothesline or the back ends of cows.

Contentedly stashing the bankbook away, he came across yesterday's number slip in the dresser drawer, under his socks. He wadded it into a tiny ball and put today's in its place. To tell the truth, he would not be surprised if the number never did hit. But it was the luxury he allowed himself, a dollar a day to play the numbers; as much as his month's wages had been on the ranch, and here he didn't even miss it. Other than that buck-a-day bet, he had himself staying so tight to the straight and narrow he could have taught ropewalking. *If I don't know by now not to blow it all, how many hard knocks does it take?*

Still holding off on the newspaper, he could not help glancing toward it, its masthead *New York World* expectant on the table. Quite the world, all right. Last night he had walked onto the stage in front of a packed audience of twelve hundred, and tonight's would be no more than three dozen at best. Another musicale. The take wasn't great, but J.J. scheduled these with as much care as he did the big-hall recitals. People on the in; *sassiety,* J.J. called such gatherings.

Pulling out his song sheets to make sure they were in the right order, he tried to picture the probable musicale scene. (Another of her prescriptions.) A number of Strivers Row's own movers and shakers always adorned the evening's chosen living room, to be sure, but right in there with them mingled the fairhaired downtowners who came up here on the lure of the music or their own highly honed curiosity or just because it was the thing to do. The Rabiznaz, turnabout of the Zanzibar, he couldn't help but think of those as: cluster of white folks who stuck out oppositely in Harlem like the dark-skinned habitués in off Clore Street did there in Helena. Which was to say, reverse to the overwhelming color around them, the way faces show odd in the negatives of a photograph. Not that it bothered him—he had been mingling, to call it that, since the day he and his parents entered the pearly kingdom of the Williamsons—and it didn't visibly bother the Rabiznaz or the Harlemites, but he did find it close quarters compared to dealing with a stage audience. Close and elevated. Women who were said to have diamond-studded garters (not that he had chanced onto such a phenomenon himself yet). Men with books to their names, or handed-down money they hadn't bothered to count yet. Conversation that circled as mercilessly as the rims of their gin glasses. *"Oh, there's Blanche and Alfred, I'll bet he's scouting. . . . Oh, look, the Sitwells are over from London. Did you hear Heywood say, 'They don't with me'?"* It helped that the Major sometimes was on hand, providing some force of gravity. At the last one of these even his wife was there, looking as if the presence of other people was a strain.

Couldn't count on seeing him there tonight, though, it occurred to Monty, given what time of year it was. He thought a moment and rearranged the order of the night's songs, putting the Medicine Line one last so that he would have some guff about Montana and the Tenth Cavalry and so on to give out with when he had to be on his own to make conversation afterward. He fondled the stack of songs as appreciatively as he had the bankbook. *Talk about luck, having these.* They couldn't have squired him along on this any better, them and the Major.

By the time the whirlwind of success on the radio stations out West had carried him all the way to the big job in Chicago, he'd known it was prudent to consult with a higher authority about the step beyond that. The Major gave one of those smiles of his and said, "You need to get together with Phil Sherman." The heart-hammering trip into New York, the session of the three of them in Phil's fashionably run-down office in the theater district. There barely had been time for Phil at the upright piano to rack the accompaniment sheets into place and attempt to follow him in a few of the songs, when there came the knock at the door. In walked the slenderest man Monty had ever seen, in a duck-foot strut. His complexion was dark honey and his suit was fashionable London brown, both accentuated by a carnation of nearly blinding whiteness in his lapel.

"Philip," the man greeted Sherman, "tell me you have a theater owner who still knows how to spell vaudeville and would give his left one to book Butterbeans and Susie for, oh, six weeks at scale."

Who? still written on Wes's face and *Which?* similarly all over Monty's, they tried not to look like fish out of water as Phil, chuckling, steered the arrivee to them for handshakes. At Wes's name, the already taut man all but twanged with attention.

"The Major Williamson, do I gather? Philip here has been holding out on me. First Sergeant Jace Jackson, sir, 369th Infantry."

"The Harlem Hellfighters." Wes looked instantly at ease and shook hands with him a second time. "I never did understand why we wasted you by attaching you to the French. In the thick of it at the Argonne, your bunch?"

"Us alongside the Senegalese," that was answered. "A matched set, I presume the thinking was." J.J. at last zeroed in on Monty, who had a hunch he had deliberately been left for last. "And this is the talented gentleman you think I need to hear, Philip?"

"The very one. Allow for my piano playing, okey-doke?"

"Before we start," J.J. stated. "One thing." Up stood his index finger, illustrating the imperative. "Could save us all some time." He sent a warning gaze to each of them in turn. "This isn't going to be jazz, is it?" Or *jass*, as J.J. pronounced it with a wince. "Because, no slur on our singing friend here, that is not a field I will have anything to do with. You can tell me as much as you want to that jazz is all the thing. But the ambience, gentlemen, the ambience. Blind men, hopheads, scatty women—how's a person supposed to do bookings around menageries like that?"

"Relax, will you. Nobody's going to accuse this music of being jazz, it's more . . ." Phil came up short.

"It's a bit *different*," Wes tried to pitch in, "but—"

"Easiest thing to call it is spirituals," Monty confined things to.

Which made J.J. wince even harder. Delicately as a ballet performer he spun to Phil.

"Philip, if you don't mind my saying so, this is not up your alley. I can throw a fishline into any congregation between here and Mobile, and come up with a spirituals singer."

"Since when are you so overrun with performers you can't even listen, J.J.?"

His bluff called, J.J. parked himself across the room. Wes went over by him to complete the audience. Monty stepped to the piano beside Phil, and approximate as the keyboard work was, "Mouthful of Stars" roared to life.

In the silence after Monty's last wall-shaking line of song, J.J. appeared perplexed. "I don't know that one, and I have two uncles who are reverends."

"Then you have one more chance," Phil swiftly set the hook. "Shall we try him on that 'Jones' number, do you think, Monty?"

"Unless you want to save it for that other manager you have in mind," Wes made up on the spot. Monty could have kissed him.

Phil getting a bit more hang of it at the piano, "Just Another Praying Jones" went even better than the first song. J.J., all three of them could see, was almost sold.

"Maybe this is the real deal here," he weighed what he had heard as if the rest of them were not in the room. "An authentic." As if reluctantly rousing from that vision, he looked around at them and came to business. "He does have a voice on him, and something about those songs—Montgomery, I can undertake to represent you. I would put you together with Cecil—no offense, Philip, but he's the best around at churchy piano." He paused, turned back to Monty, and the index finger was there like an exclamation point again. "But coming from amateur, you need to know what you're letting yourself in for, back here. You have to nail it in every performance."

Nail it? Amateur, at what? Monty resisted asking the man if he had ever been in front of a rodeo bull that wanted his hide. Instead he said, with all the heft he could put into his voice: "Can't back up and start over on the radio either. You can ask a million or so people all the way from Spokane to the Twin Cities to Chicago—nobody has heard me mess up yet."

Six full months since then, and that *yet* still hadn't even come close to occurring, and Monty was determined it never would. He put aside the song sheets, ready for the musicale. *That's that.* All right: it was time. He went over to the table where the newspaper waited.

He folded the paper back, scanning until he spotted the review. Read it, chewing his lip. Read it again, a lot more slowly. Shaking his head to try to clarify the imprint of the words, even though he knew what they meant, he ripped the piece out of the paper as though it would get loose in the room and do something more to him. Then he caught his breath and sat down to write to Susan.

Downtown, at about where the measuring stick that was Manhattan Island struck fortunes made before the Civil War, Wes was picking out railroads. He'd had a wall rack installed behind his office door with slots for all his passes, now that he was of the gandydancer fraternity, and as perquisites went, this one bemused him more than most. *A lifetime ticket or one to bankruptcy, depending.* Each elegantly printed pass entitled him to highest privileges—which was to say, a private car—when he traveled on the rails of his fellow moguls. And should any of his ampersand-endowed confreres from the Chesapeake & Ohio or the Chicago, Milwaukee & St. Paul or the Atchison, Topeka & Santa Fe wish to ride the twenty-two miles of the Two Medicine & Teton, naturally he would be only too happy to reciprocate.

A rap on the door broke his cross-country train of thought, but still in a prime mood he moved aside and called out, "Open, Sesame, or Hilly, as the case may be." Hilfiger, his secretary, came in looking as if his Teutonic dignity had something spilled on it. "Major, I cannot at all account for this. But Mister Gardiner is downstairs with some new things."

"Now? I don't understand. You know I'm getting ready to go away."

"I somehow overlooked him when I cleared your schedule. Shall I tell him it will have to wait until after Montana?"

"Use your head, man. Whatever he's come up with will be gone by then. Send him in, but—" he looked pointedly at the wall clock. "And go ahead and make my arrangements, will you. I'll be taking the Pennsy to Chicago, and let's make it the Milwaukee on the next leg." It went without saying that Wes's own railcar and red-carpet treatment from the Great Northern Railway, which profited handsomely at the Montana end of things each time a trainload of Williamson cattle was shipped to market, were to be ready for him at the St. Paul depot as usual.

"Absolutely, Major."

"Oh, and Hilly, see if you can ring up— No, never mind," he canceled that with a wave of the hand that happened to go in the direction of Harlem. Lord knew, he was no expert on the owl-like life of a singer, but Monty very well might be sacked out, resting up for another night of performance. What was there to be said, anyway, welcome to the *World*? Wes wondered how he was taking that review. He should have picked up the phone to him first thing, but with all the hurry and scurry of putting house and family to rights for the summer . . . Too late now.

The only sound for a moment was the repentant slipslap of Hilfiger's soles as he hurriedly pattered down the stairs. The quiet was like a housewide trance, the machinery of mansion life stilled to only the occasional rustle of a distant maid. Making the most of the almost sinful spot of time, Wes virtually tiptoed over to his desk and sank into the lush silence. *Funny. The house has the best of it this time of year.*

We clear out, and the walls get to rest their ears. Since having to bow out of Montana politics, he had spent more of each year here—the vast old pile of a place had been imposed as part of Merrinell's dowry—and hoped he was not growing too used to its granitic grandeur. Guide-books to this venerable neighborhood called it "captivating," and he supposed that was right if a person took it back to Latin: *captivus,* captive—clarity in the root, as usual. Evidently conceived on the architectural conviction that a man's home was his Bastille, this ancestral bastion of his in-laws permitted only peeps through high narrow windows to similar slit-eyed neighboring mansions.

While he waited for Gardiner, Wes busily packed things into his attaché case. By this time tomorrow the place would be like a ship frozen into an ice floe, sheets over all the furniture, inhabitants scattered to different latitudes. Not more than an hour ago Merrinell had left with the girls for her mother's summer place at Saratoga; time to break them in to that circle of society. Inasmuch as Merrinell's mother was a living refutation that a female could not be a pope, Wes had sympathy for his daughters in the immersion into parasol sodality ahead of them but nothing of real help. It was all he could do to keep his own head above water in the fathoms of family.

Gardiner padded in with his portfolio case, its leather as softly sumptuous as his manner. "Major, thank you for working me in."

"What's on offer today, Timothy?"

"A find, I can safely say. I think you'll be pleased with it."

Wes stayed expressionless, his guard and his hopes both up. This was not like Gardiner. As a rule, the rotund old dealer managed an elegantly diffident approach, as though strays from the orphanages of literature and history somehow simply showed up on his doorstep. Their longstanding arrangement was for Wes to have first look within the range of his interests, and if he didn't buy, Gardiner had merely to pop over to the Morgan Library. But the item the dealer took out of his portfolio case now and lifted from its wrappings, he was handling as if it had come home to stay. The not very sizable journal he deposited on the desktop looked weathered from time rather than passage from hand to hand. Wes recognized that it was bound in elk-skin, not buckram-backed nor standardly done up in cow leather nor even deerskin, and he felt an anticipatory tightness in his throat.

He studied the cataloguing slip. "Joseph Field, Joseph Field. Why do I know that name?"

Looking wise but saying nothing, Gardiner let it sink in.

Wes's head snapped up. He threw away the first rule of haggling, he couldn't help himself. As if wishing, he asked: "The one with Lewis? In the Two Medicine country?"

"You anticipate me."

Wes wiped his fingertips on the serge insides of his thighs, then drew the journal to himself and opened it ever so carefully. Officerly skepticism still was uppermost in him. With astounding copiousness Lewis and Clark each had kept day-by-day account of the expedition they captained, as did their sergeant, Gass. The enlisted men had been told to do the same, but naturally few did. And those random contributions from the ranks supposedly were all archivally accounted for, long since. Prepared for all manner of disappointment from desultoriness to illegibility, Wes dipped into the age-crisped pages of the journal, and there the words stood startlingly clear. *Drewyer and self sent hunting for sage hens. . . . Capt Lewis & Reuben let our horses graize. . . . The visinity was a plesent level plain but for one butte poking high and a lake stinking of alkali. . . .*

Alkali Lake: on the Double W's Flag Butte pastureland. Wes stared into the crude slants of the ink as though seeing a treasure map suddenly come clear. Joseph Field and his brother Reuben and the hunter-scout Drouillard, he knew as if by rote, were with Meriwether Lewis on the exploration of the Two Medicine country. Just before nightfall at some hitherto unknown site along the river, they encountered a small band of Blackfeet, gave presents, and made wary camp with the Indians. *We must wrisk the night with these persons Capt Lewis told us & so we decended to the river in company with them & formed a camp in the bottom where stood 3 solitery trees in a simicircle . . .* Holding his breath, Wes turned the page to July 27, 1806. *I was on post & laid my gun beside me to reach & wake Reuben when one of the indians—the scoundrel Capt Lewis bestoed a friendship medal on during the night's parley—slipped behind me and took the gun.*

To Wes the rest unfolded with the familiarity of *The Iliad:* in the tussle that followed, Reuben Field stabbed one Blackfeet to death and Lewis shot one in the belly. The exploring party famously had to make its escape in a marathon one-day ride to the Missouri River, but the tilt of history was against the Blackfeet and other tribes from then on. Wes now had no doubt that he held in his hands the eyewitness account to the first blood spilled by American soldiers in the long contest for the West's upper prairie. This had gone missing for nearly one hundred and twenty years. "Gardiner, how did you come by this?"

"Oh, things sometimes surface, Major."

Wes realized he was breaching protocol front, back, and sideways. Collectors at his level necessarily embraced the pretense that provenance was a region of France. "Forget I asked. How much are you going to hold me up for, on this?"

"I must tell you, Harvard has expressed an interest in it."

Wes steepled his hands together, then ever so slowly lowered them until they pointed directly at the dealer. "Speaking of telling, drop a word to Pearson from me"—making it plain that he was letting it bounce here on Gardiner first before it reached the Harvard keeper of collections—"that as a donor I don't appreciate his bidding up materials he's eventually going to get anyway, damn it."

"I'll see that your concern is made known," Gardiner all but trilled. In contrition, he quoted a figure twenty percent too high instead of the usual forty, Wes batted that down to a semi-reasonable asking price, and they reached the deal.

Gardiner still hovered over the journal with avuncular tenderness after Wes handed him the check. "Timothy? Is there something else?"

"I understand that you're pressed for time, but if you could spare a few minutes more—"

"Given the going rate so far today, I ought to call an immediate curfew."

"It's been on my conscience that I can't come up with that Cheyne item you asked for some time back. But if you're interested in that period, I just happen to have a few interesting items with me."

"You just happen to." Wes smiled. He didn't believe in runs of luck, but fifteen minutes ago he wouldn't have had any faith in the existence of a vagabond Lewis and Clark Two Medicine journal either. "All right, lay them out."

A brief letter to a weekend hostess from Lord Byron, standardly flirtatious. A set of poems in the florid hand of Wasson, the Flemish Romantic. Wes shook his head each time.

"This is rather nice," the dealer said. "An original of a verse by Pushkin. He must have copied it out fresh to look it over."

Wes knew the military legend—Pushkin's forebear an Abyssinian prince who became a general for the Czar—better than he knew the poet's attainments, other than the customary one. "Fool for love, wasn't he?"

"Quite, Major. Sufficient to get himself done in, in a duel over it."

"Russian isn't quite Greek enough to me." Wes scanned the boldly penned couplet in Cyrillic lettering. "How does it read?"

The dealer checked the accompanying translation.

> *Not all of me is dust. Within my song,*
> *safe from the worm, my spirit will survive.*

Wes sat unmoving. Monty's singing at that last musicale flooded back to him. That's what Monty had seemed: *within* the Medicine Line song. The people there at that musical evening had turned to statues, not even the click of a glass, at his almost holy rendition of his father's prairie soldiery. Even Merrinell, who kept all her matters of the spirit confined east of the Palisades, remarked afterward how struck she was by it.

"Damn the poets," Wes said softly. "They tattoo all the way through. I'll take this, too."

The dealer left, a discreetly happy man, and Wes sat in the quiet company of this day's collected prizes, his thoughts once again on their way toward the West and Susan.

These pages went a bit lame during my regency in Angus's schoolroom, and now they threaten to gallop the hand off me to catch up. I find I can barely move the pen fast enough to keep up with the race of thoughts. I wonder what ninny it was who so blithely said a diary must be a servant—

Thunder sent another casual tremor through the loft room, the arriving storm dimming what should have been the peak of the day, and Susan got up from her desk and with guilty pleasure put on all the lights. After Scotch Heaven life the Helena house still felt unfamiliar and for that matter wastefully voluminous, the size of a factory, but to have electric light again was a treat she practically sprinkled behind her ears. She would not have traded all the gold of Last Chance Gulch for the teaching year she had just put in at the South Fork, nor would the same sum persuade her to do it over again. Her smock crackly with the weather's contribution to the atmosphere of energy, she sat back down to the pages brightly awaiting her continuance:

—not a master. Ho ho. As if the habit of summing one's days into ink could be as lax as whether to dust the top of the cupboard or not. I can no more ignore the need to keep track of life—as much of it as can be made to fit in these pages—than Wes could his confessional booth. And I find that there is the odd benefit that with the passage of time the words hold more than I knew I was putting there. I look back not even a year—she flipped pages; an eyebrow went up and stayed that way—*and I find Monty in despair, Monty persevering, Monty exasperating, Monty in magical voice.*

As she composed her thoughts at pen-length, the rain din built second by second. Merciless rods of it determined to puncture the roof, from the sounds of it. "Lord, if ye happen to be of a mind / Send us rain," Angus's inevitable appropriate weather couplet rattled in the back of her mind, "And if so be it ye spill some / Send it again." When the roar on the roof hit such a pitch she could not hear herself think, she gave in and quit the desk again, this time for the gable window and the rare sight of excessive moisture in Montana. Hollyhocks in the yard were rocking madly in the wind, rainwater puddling into small swamps around them. There was a smell of great freshness in the air, and the temperature was vigorously dropping. The only thing feeble about thundershowers this time of year was duration; hoping against hope she checked the sky, and while the stormy section looked like black sheep's wool, already on both sides of it were patches of bland blue-gray. She watched at the window until the sharp-edged squall rumbled off across town. Then returned to the diary and noted in brackets that not a drop of this worm-drowner would have reached far enough to do the Two Medicine country any good.

She paged back some more, under the spell of the inked words and their curlicues of memory. Maybe it was the ozone, but everything today seemed sprung out of the usual sense of passage of time. It felt curiously like adapting some foreign custom, this diarying in the middle of the day. Siesta in reverse. The role of woman of leisure did not come naturally to her, but she was working at it. Her hair was down—no pupils today, of course, and none in prospect until she could get the music school resurrected and a number of miffed mothers soothed—and the shawling effect on her shoulders was another sumptuous diversion from usual. As she read back over entry after entry, moments leaping out at her, she twiddled strands of the tresses she had let grow all her time at Scotch Heaven, idly judging their distance from gray. Reaching the point of doing that, was she. *Vanity, thy name is human.* Automatically she reached down a music sheet and jotted that in the margin in case it could be made to fit into the operetta somewhere.

Suddenly the pen had a mind of its own again: *What odd bits we remember,* she found herself resuming on today's marathon diary catching-up. *Monty's letter mentions Mrs. Gustafson's fearsome hotcakes— the plop of them hitting the griddle was in itself almost tough enough to chew—and I have thought back time and again to that X on the stage, to flatter it by calling it that, there that first day at Fort Assinniboine. What a nerve I had, chalking that mark and letting on to him that standing right there would solve all stage woes. I recall him looking long and hard at it (and doubtless at the proposition of myself as teacher). When he stood his ground to that barn of an auditorium and my asking of him, I knew we would get somewhere.*

Susan fidgeted the pen, rolling it contemplatively between the fingers of her writing hand, while she worked back to the page of that first day of scouring traces of cows out of the homestead house, the one about Scotch Heaven not amounting to much as a site but unbeatable as a sight. She tried to think back with exactness. Had she meant for those words to carry a whiff of epitaph for Scotch Heaven even then? They would have had to be astral as comets to predict the final human sum of the old valley: Adair Barclay McCaskill and Susan Duff its last residents. And Adair only until she had Christmased with Varick's family. At the new year she had gone to Scotland on a visit that showed no sign of ending. Susan had spent the full winter—fortunately an open one; only for a few nights had she put up at the Hahns', nearest family to the schoolhouse—and the swift spring in a Scotch Heaven that was as much apparition of its homestead decades as it was creek and valley. Varick had not decided yet on the disposition of the McCaskill homestead, ghostly indeed now without Angus and the sheep. For that matter, she still was making up her own mind what to do with the lower end of the valley. Ninian's land. With more than grass and hay attached to it.

That decision would keep for now. She read back over what she had written so far today. It constituted singing the scales, warming up one's voice. With a considerable intake of air, she commenced to the next:

Wes and I are like flighty children playing with matches. One of us ignites . . . and the other in scaredy-cat fashion stamps it out. Then the turns are reversed.

She wrote in that vein until her hand began to play out.

Well, at least there was one of them who had life's ground solidly under him at the moment. She plucked up the review Monty had sent, for the sheer savor of reading it over, every blessed word:

Fate lent a hand, or in this case an appreciative ear, to the inspired program of "spirit" songs performed by Montgomery Rathbun at Aeolian Hall last evening. To this hearer, and an audience unanimous in clapping and stamping for encore after encore, the setting was as apt as if by divination: in Mr. Rathbun's wondrous presentation it is as if hitherto hidden songs have always existed just beyond us, tingling in the air, and through him they sing forth like windtunes through some great Aeolian harp.

This he achieves in a voice of dimensions that are hard to measure. His is not the welling bass-baritone of Paul Robeson, deep as the keel of a slave ship, but a built-from-the-bottom-up tone that casts long shadows and etches the ground of life under the travels of his restless songs, qualities that can perhaps be traced to his background as a man of the prairie. That repertory, be it said, is fresh, no mean feat in this heaven-sent-by-way-of-Harlem season of resurging spirituals, when almost weekly new arrangements of timeless field songs can sometimes resemble musical chairs.

The songs he brings are only an added gift, however. Montgomery Rathbun could sing the pages of the telephone directory and lift your soul. His is the latest and perhaps most phenomenal troubadour's role in the renaissance of "sorrow songs" heralded in the pre-war recitals of Harry T. Burleigh, enhanced when Roland Hayes added spirituals to his classical presentations, furthered by the innovative scorings of the piano-and-tenor duo of J. Rosamond Johnson and Taylor Gordon, and burnished to a luster now that the profoundly gifted Paul Robeson has turned from dramatic roles to musicianship. At the onset of an earlier generous artistic flourishing, Ralph Waldo Emerson proffered to Walt Whitman: "I greet you at the beginning of a great career, which yet must have had a long foreground somewhere." Harlem's chorus of spiritual-singing virtuosos must similarly now pay their respects to Montgomery Rathbun, who stands forth as their latest compatriot and rival.

All that and the reviewer did not even have an inkling of how rocky that bottom had been. Reading back, finding the diary days when some bit of coaching or coaxing had worked and both of them felt another breathworth of soar in his song, Susan was starved all over again for that experience of the lessons with Monty. *Don't I wish there were another one where he came from.* Leading the South Fork schoolchildren in "Flow Gently, Sweet Afton" in preparation for the program all the parents were invited to, there had been times when she thought she would break off into a maddened howl. Very well then, face up and admit it, she had been spoiled by the particularities of Monty's voice. At least she was not totally bereft of it. One more time she picked up the letter the review had come with. *I did not pay the man to write this, honest.* The handwriting, in pencil, was welcomely familiar from the greetings he sent from wherever he sang; they amounted to postcards mailed in envelopes, safe from small-town post office eyes. She could picture the jackknife-sharpened stub, the earnest crouch over the stationery—somehow the words even stood slow and careful on the paper—and found it that much more reward-ful that he thought she was worth the diligence. This letter was almost warm to the touch. *Something, isn't it? To think that the spirit songs are having a heyday? And that the foreground, they call it, was the old wagontrack where you about made me run my legs off?* She smiled a moment at his growing penchant for question marks—he seemed determined to make punctuation count as much as it could, too—and skipped to the bottommost sentence: *I hope the old town is ready for me?* He was coming to Helena on his concert tour through the West. She circled the day on her calendar. Ahead of it by a week was the X'ed-over set of days she was to spend with Wes in the Two Medicine country.

U NDER the highstanding sun the cattle were mothering up. Their mode of reacquaintance was repeating itself a couple of thousand times at once, every cow moaning anxiously and making sure with thorough sniffs that the calf trying to raid milk from her udder was entitled to it.

Next to Wes in the shade of the boss tent, Susan speculatively watched the bawling scene along the lakeshore. Hers was not the only appraisal of what was being done to a calm noon at Lower Two Med-icine Lake: around the reflecting rim of water, sphinxlike mountains with manes of timber seemed to draw in closer to frown down over the intrusion.

She glanced at Wes, still busy checking his tallybook before he and whoever was sent out from the Blackfeet Indian Agency counted the cattle onto this reservation allotment, its rugged foothills practi-cally in the lap of Glacier National Park. Simply by eye the massed cattle seemed to Susan an excess of livestock for any summer range. But mob of feeders though this might be, she knew it was only a por-tion of the Williamsons' growing Deuce W herd. Thousands more were out in the coulees of Fort Assinniboine and the other outposts of the new ranch. Greater thousands than that were spread as usual on the home range of the Double W. The tallybook in Wes's hands had him knitted in study, flipping from one page to the next, back, further pages on into the black-and-white arithmetic of herds and necessary grass; it must be like trying to stay ahead of locusts, she thought. Next to everything the Bible had to say, the one saying she had grown up hearing was that the Williamsons always had more cattle than country. Wes, she was seeing for herself on this cattle drive, dealt not only in ranchland and beef on the hoof but the attic space of geography; nooks and crannies of pasture like this under the planet's eaves.

A series of whoops and orders being shouted above the mooing drew her attention back to the trail herd. Perhaps stuffing this many cattle this high into the timbered foothills of the Rockies went against the human ear and common sense, but she couldn't deny that it made quite a picture. Several day-herders now slaunched in their saddles at strategic points around the milling herd while the main file of riders headed in, their roans and sorrels and pintos mirrored in the bowl of lake like rich dabs of color on a clear blue palette. As they dismounted around the chuck tent for the midday meal, the bearded cook directed the traffic of Stetsons and batwing chaps with an imperial ladle. Susan tickled behind Wes's ear to make him look up and take in the scene. "Even I admit it's like a Russell, except nobody is bucking a bronc through the pork and beans."

Wes gave an appreciative wisp of smile. "Charlie apparently never met a horse that wasn't snorty at chow time."

"He portrays schoolmarms as a pernicious influence, too."

"While I think they are nature's highest achievement."

"Do you really? I'm afraid we have loftier rivals, right around here." She took in again the glacier-scarved mountains, augmented at this time of day by puffy clouds with flat, gray bases as if they had been sponged against the earth on that side. "Doesn't it remind you of that time in the Alps?"

He swung around to look at her, losing his place in the tallybook. "We were never in the Alps together."

"Just testing how well you keep track. And your ability to tell me from a Heidi. And how many yodels you've never yodeled."

"Not to mention your capacity to tease the life out of me."

"I hoped I was teasing it into you, Wes."

"All right." He laughed as if to demonstrate he hadn't forgotten how. "Guilty as charged. I'm more wrapped up in the travels of cows than I want to be. Whit has always been trail boss." At the moment Whit was in California, sorting out Wendell after some scrape frowned on by the college authorities. Getting the bearer of the Williamson family escutcheon through Stanford was requiring increasingly strong doses of fathering. "I'll make amends," Wes promised while he reached and took Susan's wrist as though he were a penitent who just happened to have a glint of another sort in his eye. "What would you say to a basket supper and sunset at the upper lake, when I'm done with the agency people? Whit would never spoil you like that, but if he hears about it and takes my job away, so much the better."

Susan had to smile back at him over that. She was no expert on trail drives, but she knew Whit also would never have shoved a couple of thousand head of cattle miles out of the way, as Wes had done the day before yesterday, to keep them from trampling the vicinity of the site of the Lewis party's fight with the Blackfeet, and then spent all afternoon bumping over that prairie in the Duesenberg, navigating from one landmark to the next in the Field journal with her in wonderment at his side and Gustafson peering over the steering wheel for badger holes. When at last the ill-used automobile nosed along a particularly precipitous brink of white-clay bluff, Wes let out the shout, "There!" Directly below, in the colossal rupture of the prairie where the Two Medicine River twisted through, stood the three huge old solitary cottonwood trees, like ancient attendants minding the campsite. With wild roses on the face of the bluff blowing in the wind, Wes and she had sat there gazing down into the century before, retrieved by a single witnessing pen. She had a diarist's feel for the quirks of opportunity it must have taken to set the Lewis and Clark explorations down onto pages at all, but an unearthed journal fresh from midtown New York still seemed to her as randomly propitious as lightning illuminating a safari map. She had tried to wheedle out of Wes the cost of such a piece of historical luminescence, but he wouldn't tell. "Beyond price," was all he would say. "Like you."

"Supper that way sounds grand," she responded now, along with a return squeeze of his arm. "This is rude of a guest, but will you clear something up for me? Why are you putting cows and calves onto rough country like this, and for that matter why isn't Whit throwing a fit about it? These cattle will have to work uphill for every spear of grass. Not to mention that the timber up here is full of blowdowns, and probably bear."

If her line of inquiry hit home, squarely in the tallybook, he didn't show it. "The Deuce W needs shaping up before we run the full number of stock on it," he said almost idly. "Some windmill watering holes, fencing to be done, that sort of thing."

"Short grass again, you mean."

"Your father's daughter." That drew him enough of a look that he hastily tacked on: "When it comes to grass. What was I thinking, trying that on you." Suddenly serious as could be, he folded his arms on his chest and contemplated the herd already starting to munch its way up a slope that turned to timber just ahead of them. "If we ever have anything but a dry summer, we can quit being cow conductors. For now, these bossies are going to have to pretend they're mountain goats."

He paused, then returned to her question. "Whit will just have to put up with the fact that I no longer can buy acres as fast as he can buy cows. You're right that we'll be nicked on a lease like this. A considerable number of head will end up inside grizzlies or at the bottom of gulches with broken legs. Probably more will end up in stewpots— we have to see that as a tithe." He gave a slight shrug.

Susan was surprised he could be that casual at the prospect of losing cows to enterprising Blackfeet. Rustling was rustling, wouldn't you think? Particularly if you were a Williamson?

"Speaking of fathers," she got in, still trying to follow his thinking, "let me be more rude yet while I'm at it. What would yours think of paying good money for land this time of year and then having to walk away from it in the fall?"

That turned Wes dramatically philosophical. "Why do you even ask?" He tossed a hand of futility in the air. "He would think Whit and I have taken screaming leave of our senses, as the old always think about the young. As Whit and I think about our own offspring."

"Oho. Old now, are we."

"It's only a masculine trait. Women grow more fascinating."

"Especially in a cow camp," she whittled that down. "Your riders look at me as if I have two heads." She mimicked a cowboy gape. "But you, oh no, you don't get that from them even when you chase off across the prairie in the Doozy after Lewis and Clark. I hope, my dear Major Williamson, that doesn't mean they're used to seeing you with a woman who isn't your wife."

At first she thought he wasn't going to answer, but then as though it were a duty to report this sort of thing he told her: "They seem to expect something of the sort of me, actually."

"Really?" Susan's tone was as if she were taking a scientific sounding. "It has come to that? Where there's a rich man, there positively has to be a mistress tagging along?"

"For God's sake, Susan. You know there's more than that to it, with us."

"No, this interests me. Shouldn't I see myself as a kind of collectible, like that journal you can barely stand to put down? And you as the connoisseur of sufficient means I've been lucky enough to be plucked up by? Privilege has its rank, we both recognize that. If you were one of your cow chousers squatting around the bean pot over there, we never would have had the least chance at one another, now would we."

Wes studied her thoughtfully, then stepped over and kissed her for as long as it took.

Susan brought up a hand and ever so lightly ran a finger back and forth along the side of where their lips met, as if saving it to taste. Eventually she stroked free and drew a breath. "I suppose you think that's a way of ending an argument. It's not bad."

"High praise. I can hardly wait until we outright fight. Add that to supper, can we?"

The words were no sooner out of his mouth than she gave him a soft biff to the collarbone, as if to announce her readiness to trade love taps any time he wanted. Wes chortled, and stepped away to collect his tallybook. "I hate to cease hostilities. But I'd better go down and run through things with Petrie"—his foreman—"so we'll be ready when the agency people show up."

"Wes. There's something on my mind—surprise, surprise, right?"

Reluctantly he pivoted to her and stood as if braced for the worst. Only to hear her say:

"How would it be if I let you have my piece of the North Fork?"

His face lit up, but she had anticipated that. Only in his eyes did she catch the flicker of the chain lightning of his mind.

"On lease, I mean," she stipulated. "This year, and we could see about next."

She could see the calculations flying in him, cows into acres, acres into cows, the capacity of the North Fork as an ever-running watering hole, the tonnage of its hay—"Susan, it would help on the Double W herd. In a big way."

"I want you to put a fencing crew in there first. I won't stand for cows mooching onto the McCaskill place from mine, I don't care if Whit has to sit out there himself shooing them away."

"I'll see that the fences are so tight not even a wee sleekit cowering tim'rous beastie could get through." Wes took an eager step toward her, although he knew better than to kiss her this time. Sticking to business if that was where she wanted to be, he vouched: "Of course we'll pay you top dollar."

"You'd better."

"I'll tell you what, I can bring the papers with when I come in for Monty's concert."

That wasn't her preference, but she held to the mood: "Two occasions for the price of one, why not?"

"On that. I'd like us as much together there as we can—you'll see, he's gotten astounding." Susan waited, knowing what was coming. Managing this was the one thing that seemed to throw him, and he was no better at it than ever when he awkwardly asked: "You'll be able to come in the warm company of Mrs. Gus, won't you?"

"I wouldn't miss the chance for anything, even Mrs. Gus."

Looking buoyed, Wes went off to muster the cattle for counting. This time Susan did not watch the panorama of herd and riders and wary mountains. She sat in the tent, distractedly leafing through the valuable journal Wes had given prideful place on his portable desk. *Beyond price. Like you.* Such woo from a Wes with infinite cattle on his mind. *I'll see that the fences are so tight not even a wee sleekit cowering tim'rous beastie could get through.* Passable Robert Burns from the man who ordinarily fumbled the Scottish tongue, no less. Where did he summon that from, even given his knack to perform up to what nearly any circumstance asked? She should know something about gauging that capacity in him, and it bothered her that she did not. Rehearsals were her field, but run those clinching sentences of Wes's over and over in her mind as she would, she could not decide whether he had rehearsed those lines.

H ATED to ask you to come all the way across town, but I didn't know how else—"

"All that way, tsk. This is a treat. I'd have been happy just to poke my head backstage and say hello after you floor them tonight."

"Couldn't let you off that easy. Get you something? Tea and honey?"

"You. Inflict my own medicine on me, would you. But thank you, nothing. Monty, this— I have to say, I'm impressed."

"Not exactly Fort Skin-and-Bone, is it." He followed her gaze around the parlor of the Broadwater Hotel, Helena's finest, complete with posh grounds and natatorium. Now that he and she were established in the plush chairs, nicely out in the open but far enough from the lobby not to have every word overheard, he felt relieved. Even yet this was not easy to make happen right, not here, not anywhere that he knew of. From the window of his room he had watched like a hawk, if hawks are ever nervous, until she pulled into the grounds in her car, its doors and fenders still peppered with what likely was Scotch Heaven mud. Then made himself hover out of sight at the top of the stairwell while she announced her purpose to the desk clerk, to see how it went before he would need to go down and try to bluff the clerk. *Damn it. All we want to do is visit with each other like human beings.* They lucked out on the clerk: the man turned out to be the father of one of her pupils in years past, and Susan's sweetly put "here for a musical consultation with your famous guest Mister Rathbun" did not stand his hair on end. Here then they sat, decorous amid the nearly smothering decor of velvet and Victoriana and tasseled rugs. Monty could tell she meant surprised along with impressed. "Year ago, they wouldn't have let me in here," he said what they both knew but it helped clear the parlor air by saying it. "Maybe even now, but the Major put in a word."

"Tell me whether I'm seeing things. A man out in the gardens looks all the world like Bailey."

"None other. I had him hired. There's a bruiser or two around somewhere, too." He rushed through that as if it was an ordinary part of business, but Susan was looking at him so pointedly that he broke off and made a small patting motion in the air. "Nothing to be excited about. The people I'm with are sort of spooked by what the clucks tried on you and me, is all. I thought they were going to back out of town when I told them about the Confederate Gulch gold and the Johnny Rebs who turned into galvanized Yankees out here as soon as they had money in their pockets. Took the pair of them around to Clore Street and that settled them down some." His turn to put a point to her with his eyes. "Life been treating you all right, I hope?"

"Atrociously. I haven't been around a world-beating voice for what seems like ages. Until the one I'll hear tonight."

"More what I had in mind was you being out there alone at Scotch Heaven all that while. It's been bothering—"

Surprised at the urgency in his voice, she cut in with what she always said when people got going on how much time she spent with herself: "Don't fret, 'alone' isn't spelled the same as 'lonely.'"

"Maybe around the edges, it's not," he said as if his experience did not jibe with hers.

She made a conceding murmur and ducked onto surer ground. "At any rate, you can quit worrying—I'm going to lease out the homestead. Helena has me on her hands again, poor old town."

Now Monty was the surprised one. "The Major didn't say anything to me about you giving up the place."

"No? Did you check the reflections in his vest buttons?" Fanning a hand and holding it with her other, Susan expertly mimicked a person playing cards close to the chest.

He acknowledged that with a slow nod. "I'll need to do that when he comes in from the ranch tonight, you think?"

"Whit's, too, while you're at it. You knew you're going to be honored with his presence, didn't you?"

"You must be kidding. He's setting foot off the place when there's no livestock involved?" It was on the tip of his tongue to say what next, the ghost of old Mister Warren showing up along with them tonight at the Marlow Theater and growling out *I take it back, Monty, go ahead and blow your bugle, boy.* But her and the Major, as close or apart as rails of a railroad track, depending on when you squinted in their direction—right now she was really up on the doings of the Williamsons, and he didn't want to tromp flatfooted into whatever that meant. He switched back over to his original intention. "I started to say, it's bothered the living daylights out of me that you were where the Klan hoodoos could have got at you. I know you wrote that the Williamsons made it too hot for them, but—"

"Scalding, was more like it." Departures in the night. Examples made by Whit and his ax-handle crew. Sheriffs and county attorneys suddenly rigorous. Wes and the influences he could bring to bear had taken the Klan out of the prairie heartland of Montana like lice soaked out of sheets. "My neck never felt at risk, any of the school year," she maintained. Monty watched the familiar way she arched that neck, ivory as a carved rarity, as she pronounced on that chapter of the past. "No excitement except the boys tipping over the girls' privy, and that's eternal. No, I've done my bit in memory of Angus and helped Adair close up their place, and now I'm tucked back into the house here and the Double W's cows inhabit the North Fork." Susan made a gesture, that was enough of that. Looking across at Monty, she sent him a mock teacherly frown intended to let him know she was inspecting his progress. He had filled out somewhat, but solidly, no jowls or paunch. His fetching blue pinstripe suit would not give any of Wes's a run for the money—whose would?—but it had a tailor's touches. All along the line, so far as she could see, he looked as if New York life agreed with him. Still, he was here, not there. "Somehow I didn't expect to see you back this soon."

"Denver is next on the tour." He grinned. "I convinced my manager this is practically on the way."

Susan's eyebrows were up. "I must have left geography out of those lessons of yours."

"That'd be about the only thing. Say, you know what works slick? That music stand." He had particularly wanted to ease her mind about the audience problem. "Can't explain it, but I don't get choky with the songsheets right there, even if I never need them."

"Told you." Her face lit, she urged: "Now your turn. Those fancy-pantsy musicales of yours—tell all."

From there on their conversation kept jumping its banks. He told her about hobnobbing with the Rabiznaz, wanted to know how her own music was coming. She told him she was within shouting distance of the end of the operetta if the shout could be a better song than she had managed to come up with yet, and what were his living arrangements in Harlem like? They were back and forth at this a mile a minute until they heard a notifying cough. In the doorway of the parlor stood J.J. and Cecil, fluffy bathtowels over the arm of each.

"This is my poor put-upon teacher I told you about," Monty reeled off the introductions. "Wasn't for her, the most I could look forward to would be changing sparkplugs every three months."

"Ah? Then the ears of the world are in your debt, Mrs. Duff," J.J. said with something between a nod and a bow. Cecil's wordless acknowledgment of her certifiably amounted to no more than a nod.

"It's Miss."

"Mizzz Duff, excuse me all hollow." J.J.'s sibilant antic made Monty want to bat him one.

"Sorry to interrupt," J.J. swept on, "but we were just passing. We are off to the waters," meaning the natatorium across the hotel grounds. "Cecil here needs to cook like an egg to thaw out from this Rocky Mountain air, he claims. We are told we will have a generous portion of the pool to ourselves." J.J. smiled as if at the wonder of that. "Roped off for our very own use, I gather the procedure is. Western hospitality is really quite something."

"We did give the world Monty, from out here," Susan offered as though it were a neutral observation. "We may be coasting a bit much on that."

"That was generous, I can't help but admit." J.J. fussily checked his watch against the parlor's grandfather clock as if two opinions were needed on the hour of day, then recited: "Keep an eye on the time, Montgomery, don't forget to catch some rest."

"It's as good as caught, J.J."

"Good day, Miss Duff. Been our pleasure."

Monty watched the pair of them go, shaking his head. "See what you and the Major got me into? They both know their stuff, but—what're you laughing about?"

"I just realized. Here you are in the Broadwater with a manager and an accompanist and Bailey and bruisers, all the trappings I could have dreamed of for you, and I've never even heard you in front of an audience."

"You have so. Not their fault they were pigeons. Toughest critics I've had yet, though."

Susan surprised herself as well as him by giggling. Monty chortled at the scale-like run of that, which tickled her some more, and then they were both in helpless gusts of laughter, two Two Medicine ragamuffins carried up past Fort Assinniboine's pigeon droppings and all other mires to make their marks on life by the glorious force of music.

Susan at last wiped her eyes. "Stop. Halt. Enough. I really should be going."

"Not before I put you to work a little." Before she could blink, he reached something out from behind his chair and rested it in his lap. "Do you mind? Wanted to show you a change in 'Mouthful of Stars'—I think I misremembered how the holy rollers used to do the chorus of that." As he dug out the piece of music she saw that he carried the songsheets in a leather case embossed with the initials M.R.; cowhide had a different place in his life now. "I think it should go"—at the back of his throat he deeply crooned down, then up, up, instead of up, down, up.

Susan hesitated. Was this something he needed done, or a pat on the head for her? He had not been the butter-spreading type before, but that was before. The question lasted no time before giving way to the spell of music in his throat and his hands. "Let's just see," she said, a bit out of breath, and was up from her chair and confronting the upright piano, its teeth yellow with age, that claimed a corner of the parlor.

Plinking until she found a reasonably reliable run of keys, she coaxed out an amendment to the tune, Monty at the end of the piano listening keenly. At her nod, he sang the chorus that way atop her playing. She knew she probably shouldn't—the justifiable wrath of his manager was somewhere between there and the natatorium—but she plunged into the whole song, Monty's voice all but taking down the walls of the parlor.

"There, then." Past the ache at the back of her heart for more of this, she made herself quit, saying she would fix up the follow-sheet for his accompanist if he liked. Monty dug in his shirt pocket, came up with a stub of pencil. With great care she wrote in the notes, guided by her own hum now. One last thing and then she would go. "Could I take a peek at the songsheets? It would be fun for me tonight to know the order of songs."

"You bet." He gravely handed her the sheaf that represented all their work together. "That's how I've got it put together for here. Oh, and over Cecil's just about dead body, I always stick in the Medicine Line one wherever the program feels like it needs a lift."

"Why doesn't he want you to use that one?"

"Because he doesn't like it."

"So then why do you use it?"

"Because he doesn't like it."

That set them off riotously again. Susan sobered an instant before he did—*what am I doing, this man has a performance tonight*—and resolutely stood up from the piano stool. But invoking a teacher's privilege, she took a last memory-book look at him, storing away the prospering dark features that were as heightened and polished as his voice now. Not much more than an arm's length away Monty was looking at her as if trying to remind himself of something. She held still, waiting for whatever it was. Finally he said: "You're wearing your hair down. It's nice." Hesitantly he put out his hand for the songsheets.

"Trying to keep up. Speaking of hair, it's really time I get out of yours."

Taking the music from her, he fumbled it back into the leather case. Then gestured as though he would change things if it were in his power. "We have a rehearsal, after J.J. and Cecil finish their soak. I'd have asked you to come to that, but—"

"Monty, I would have turned you down flat," she said fondly, sadness in there, too. "I'd be one too many irons in the fire there. Seeing you this way meant more."

* * *

All those other Saturday nights in town, and I never even made it through the door of this place. He moved back and forth in an arc across centerstage there in the afternoon-empty Marlow Theater, singing the two lines "When I was young and in my prime, I dabbed my X on the Medicine Line" over and over as he sought the spot where it felt right to stand. The massive chandelier out over the seats scintillated as if beaconing him to step this way or that. He grinned, just from general joy at treating this fancy stage like a parade ground. *No way this was in the running with the Zanzibar, back then. Some of those scrapes, ow. It's a wonder I'm here with my guts still in me.* He kept an eye on J.J., audience of one, who was prowling the empty seats, nodding when the sound reached him just so, shaking his head when it was not so good. Monty wheeled, tried it from closer to the lip of the stage. Took a step the other direction, cast "When I was young . . ." into the air of the theater from there as though flyfishing into promising water. Right from the start of the rehearsal he had been feeling exceptionally fine, as loose and full of jingle as when he was a much younger man challenging the rodeo bulls. The stage manager stood off at stage left patiently plucking his sleeve garters until Monty called over, "I think I found it here."

The man came out and chalked an X where the toe of Monty's shoe was indicating. "I'll be right back with your music stand and we can see how the lighting suits you," he told Monty and disappeared backstage.

Cecil had been sitting in wait at the piano. Now that Monty's voice was not claiming the theater, he noodled at the keyboard of the Steinway, apparently without satisfaction. "They call this a piano in this burg?"

Monty and J.J. exchanged glances. They might have been concerned about Helena's taste in pianos if they had not heard Cecil make this same complaint about Boston's. Before J.J. could say anything, Monty observed: "Looks to me like it has all the keys, Cece."

"This new follow-sheet, man, I don't see why that chorus goes—"

"Because now it's right," Monty said easily.

Frowning, Cecil tugged at the cuffs of his tux and looked to J.J. for justice.

With a show of judiciousness the manager sized up the two of them. Poor Cecil, eagerly waiting for fame to devour him. Monty was a different breed of cat. In off these wide open spaces. Monty reminded him of the Senegalese, when they stood there blank and calm sharpening those three-sided French bayonets as the attack barrage poured down only yards away. J.J. still could not put his finger on it exactly, but there was a solo quality about Monty that ran deeper than what issued from his mouth. In all his time as a manager, he had never come across a talent who climbed so fast yet kept his head about him. And that white woman, whatever she was about, had given Monty over readymade for stage work. "They're his songs, Cecil. Ours not to reason why if he feels better primping them."

"Probably be an audience like an icebox, no matter what I do," Monty by now had reached the trouper's point of courting good luck by invoking bad.

"You're sounding first-rate," J.J. told him, more than ritually. "A little more geared up for this than you maybe need to be, though. You don't have to bust a gusset for these people just because you're back home. They'll clap if you so much as step out there and clear your throat, you watch."

"Nothing doing," Monty retorted firmly. "All out, tonight. Goes for you, too, Cecil. Don't be on bad terms with that piana, hear?"

Just then the stage manager called him for the lighting check, and the other two retreated to backstage.

Cecil was still steamed. "Jace?" He was the only person in the world who called J.J. that, particularly with a permanent question mark. "What gives, anyway? I was kidding around about the piano. But messing with the follow-sheet without even talking to me about it, that's something else. He's been acting high and mighty since we got here. I know these are his old stomping grounds, but—"

"So let him stomp for the folks," J.J. said tiredly. "We'll sort all this out in Denver."

The bromide for the unspeakable is, "Words fail me." I vow they will not.

Susan was panting markedly with the effort this took. When she caught up to realization of it, she drew a careful series of breaths to steady herself before writing the next.

Tracing in ink what happened last night is the only way I know to tell the world ahead how one thing followed another, each piece of time a shard streaking lightninglike to the next.

This night she had come to the diary in something like a daze of duty, the rhythm of obligation as insistent in her as the tides of her heart. Her hand was fixed to the page before she made herself pause and review everything that had danced out of place since the last time she had seated herself there. The past twenty-four hours were a jumble, at every level. She blinked hard, barely staying dry-eyed, as it registered on her that Samuel's photograph had been toppled. Might she just now have done that herself, in her reach for ink, pen, and pages to testify on? Or—? Whether or not it was her own doing, she picked the photograph up off its face, stood it where it belonged, and again put herself for all she was worth into her pen hand.

Mrs. Gus and I had arrived to the theater together, bookends that don't match but surprisingly few people seem to notice. An audience huge for Helena was pouring in and the lobby was a crisscross of former pupils of mine grinning at me as if they had good sense and mothers on the warpath about my absence for the past—dear me—year and then some. I fended as well as circumstances would allow, promising probably too many of them that I now would be giving lessons again and if they dreamt of their child one day filling a theater this way, lo, that chance awaited in my music parlor. I could not account for why I was such a sudden celebrity until someone said in near-awe "You've met Montgomery Rathbun then, what is he like?" and that quick it dawned. Word had spread from Milly Tarrant's father, the desk clerk, that the famous Mr. Rathbun had sought me out for advice on a point of music; the image of us meeting like heads of state of the musical world there in the parlor of the Broadwater would have bowled us over at Fort Assinniboine.

Of course every stitch of a performance night interests me, even the straggly processional of the audience sorting itself into place, and we were going in to our seats early when Mrs. G. looked back over her shoulder and said, "The misters are here."

There was a last nimbus of sun going down behind Mount Helena and a moon like a globe lantern waiting to replace it as Wes and Whit climbed out of the big car. Lilacs bloomed, their color deepening with the day, in the hillside neighborhood across the street from the Marlow Theater. Summer on such an evening was slow to step down from the longest day, a week before; dusk and warmth would linger as if night had been temporarily postponed. Because of the time of year Monty's performance was set for eight-thirty so people could do the necessary for their gardens and lawns, come in from fishing or porch-sitting, round up the musically inclined members of the family, and stroll down the gulch to the theater, men carrying their suit jackets carefully over their arms.

Whit, though, lodged a complaint to the evening air that seemed to have come in on a tropical tradewind. "Damnedest weather. Still feels like the middle of the afternoon."

"Is there any weather you do like?" Wes inquired, genuinely wondering, while he gestured that Whit's tie was riding cockeyed. "You came back from ten days of California sun complaining it didn't give you anything to get your teeth into."

"This is about as balmy as it was there, and you can't tell me that's natural. Gus, I need to fix my choker. Would you——?" As Gustafson held the door of the Duesenberg open at an angle that provided enough reflection, Whit bent down and used the car window as a mirror to adjust his white tie.

Waiting for him beneath the modernly elegant vertical marquee of the Marlow, Wes took the chance to scan the streets and was reassured to find policemen posted where they ought to be—some up at the corner of Broadway and Last Chance Gulch, others down here at the intersection by the theater—just conspicuous enough. Whit was in the Knights of Columbus with the Helena chief of police, and it had been decided that any dregs of the Klan who showed up to shout epithets were going to find themselves charged with spitting on the sidewalk. Privately Wes believed last summer's crackdown had sent any of them who counted slinking off to safer climes, tails between their legs, but an extra shift of police should make Monty's entourage feel better. Right then a lantern-jawed man stepped out of the lobby, took a look around, and nodded to him. One of Bailey's. They probably were unnecessary too, but wouldn't hurt either. "What do you think then," Whit was asking as he gave a last tug at his tie and straightened up, "will Monty add 'The Palm Trees Sway When You Say I May' to his list tonight?"

Wes looked at his brother in surprise. Whit getting off a thighslapper over a song of the day was about as likely as Al Jolson making a joke about Herefords. But Whit himself would have been the first to say he was an improved person since the North Fork was offered up. For his part, Wes had stuffed the lease papers into his attaché case before they left the ranch as if the document were any other transaction. Which, pretend to himself as he was trying, it in no way could ever be. He still was working on tomorrow, when the two of them were to meet with Susan in the morning and signatures were to go onto dotted lines. When they pulled up in front of the theater he had glimpsed her for a moment there in the lobby and knew he would be aware of her during every note of Monty's performance and it still seemed beyond reckoning that a bumpy encounter in France had led all the way to this. And Monty at the heart of it. In tribute to that he started into the theater, but Whit rerouted him with a shoo of the hand.

"Let's hold on out here a minute—we're in for more culture than I can usually sit through. Condemned man always is given a chance to roll a last one, isn't he?" He pulled a tobacco pouch and pack of rolling papers out of the pocket of his evening wear, did a judicious sprinkle, and licked together a cigarette.

While Wes withdrew into his thoughts, which he never seemed to want company on, Whit let out a silent whistle of smoke as he studied the theater placard studded with the most glowing phrases from the review in the *New York World*. Half the newspapers in Montana had picked up that review. He shook his head at having had so famous a choreboy. "Do it all over again, would you?"

Wes chose to misunderstand. "What, every particle of my life?"

"How about one or two of the main chunks here lately?" Whit invited.

"What's turned you philosophical?"

"Ahh, who knows. Told you it's funny weather." Whit tossed down his cigarette and demolished it under his patent leather shoe. "All right, let's go get music in our ears. Here's hoping his Montana debut turns out better than his mother's."

Wes said flatly, "It's bound to."

You can sometimes tell what an audience is like beforehand. This one was curious, perhaps a bit—Susan waited, pen nib poised, for the right sharpening of word—*anxious. Monty's songs would be as new to them as an underground stream suddenly pouring up out of the ground. My sense was that they wanted Monty to be the real thing, to be someone who had made it to on high, from their midst.*

There was the curtain motion, the flutter, that happens not long before a performance.

"Five minutes, Mister Rathbun," came the call and short rapid tattoo of rap on his dressing room door that seemed to be delivered by the same set of vocal cords and knuckles in every theater in the land.

"Be right there, thanks," Monty responded and checked in the mirror one last time. Meeting there a version of himself so fitted out in distinction and determination that the apparition looked primed to perform the concert from that spot in the dressing room and be heard in the dusk-curtained canyons of the Rockies all the way to the Two Medicine country. Out across the reach of prairie, bounded only by the moon, to Fort Assinniboine. Into the winding country of memory, where his mother lifts from her laundress chores and prepares herself to sing at the statehood celebration, in a yesterday that never came, three dozen years ago. He nodded satisfaction at the personage in the looking-glass as if catching up with him after all this time.

Exultant, he went on out to the back of the stage and around to the wing and the stage manager's roost. Even yet he didn't care much for the feel of backstage, it amounted to about the same as the chute area in a rodeo: you hoped nobody did anything back here that would have untoward consequences to you out front. But he thought of how Susan loved every guy rope, dust mote, and gizmo trunk of it, and had an abrupt word with himself for not working it out to invite her to watch from the wings tonight. Could have asked the Gustafsons and she'd have been included as if attached to them, that would have been the way. *Can't get it all right all the time.*

Within whispering range of the stage manager, J.J. was at his usual perch on a high stool too big for him, like a natty flagpole sitter. A figure planted in the shadows beyond J.J. and the stage manager and a couple of stagehands was as unmoving as a costume mannequin, but the set of its hat identified it as Bailey. Monty knew that one of the bruisers was stationed at the back door, and if all this didn't reassure J.J. and Cecil, he didn't know what would.

"Good house tonight," J.J. recited to Monty as he always did, whatever the audience size.

Monty stepped out onto the curtained stage to check that his music stand was on the mark, then made a beeline for the stage manager's peephole.

J.J. was not stretching it tonight; a sellout crowd, packed from the front row to standees along the farthest wall. What seemed to be Clore Street intact filled one entire balcony. He spotted Susan beside the Gustafsons. A row behind and a few seats over, the Major and Whit Williamson in full evening regalia, one slick and one mussed but otherwise drawn by the same hand.

"One minute," the stage manager called, nervously watching Cecil, who was still fussing with his music sheets in the rack for them on the piano, moving them an inch one way and then the other, although Monty seriously doubted music racks differed very much from piano to piano. But as he always did, with seconds to spare Cecil sashayed over into the wing alongside the rest of them as if the curtain could not rise without his elevating presence, the first bow of the evening deliciously his.

The accompanist sopped up applause somewhat overlong, Susan jabbed the comma in as if it were a thumb in Cecil's ribs, *bobbing like one of those toy birds that dips its beak in a glass of water. But then Monty made his appearance, and the real applause started.*

As he came out I saw that he had been right to resist my attempts to cure his walk—that cowboy saunter of his lets the audience know this is a person who has come an extreme way to reach this point. He handles himself notably in every other way that counts, too. It has been long years since I sang on the Marlow stage myself, but I thought I remembered its particularities, and Monty did me proud when he took his mark exactly where I had guessed. As if the stage belonged to him. As if he had inherited it from the most royal line of singers.

The applause poured over him until he steepled his fingers in a gesture of thanks and readiness. He had decided against saying anything first, just hit them with the first song. Now he nodded ever so slightly to Cecil, who piously unclasped his fingers from his lap as if raveling out a prayer, and the piano music rippled out with a parade-ground prance.

> *"Forty miles a day*
> *on beans and hay.*
> *Scenery all the way*
> *on cavalry pay.*
>
> *When I was young and in my prime—"*

Monty with controlled power held the note on the last consonant, setting it up to chime with the even more resounding one in the next line—

> *"I dabbed my X on the Medicine Line."*

As he hit that note, round and perfect, the chandelier above the crowd began to sway.

He froze, the cut-glass constellation in motion even more now. Cecil shot him a confused look, trying to decide whether to keep playing so Monty could pick the melody back up or wash the tune out and start over—and then his hands halted on the keys as if a message was coming up through them. The music stilled, the only sound now the gentle tinkling of the chandelier. Then a rumble, like thunder down in the ground.

The theater floor vibrated as if it were the deck of a steamship leaving the dock. Pell-mell, the crowd came to its feet and started piling toward the doors, not a stampede yet but definitely a clogged surge.

An earthquake gives a person a jolt in more ways than one. It causes your basic assumption of life, the ground on which you exist, to quiver. I had been through one before, the time I took Samuel to Yellowstone Park. But we were outdoors there, the sway of the trees like fishing rods in truth rather interesting. Here the question was whether the theater would shake to pieces with us in it. I thought something already had fallen and bruised my arm when I realized it was Mrs. Gus's grip on me.

Willing his bad leg to match his good one in the effort, Wes was up and clambering into the next aisle, fighting past eddying audience members to reach Susan and Mrs. Gustafson. He always hated pandemonium, he would rather take his chances in a shellhole. Now he banged over seats until he was within reach of Susan, a vexed expression on her that seemed to wonder why people needed to be so contrary, as she tried to make her way toward the stage. His instinct supported that: "The stage steps! Out that way!" No sooner did he have Susan and Mrs. Gustafson plunging that direction with him than the Marlow Theater gave another shudder and the lights went out. In the sudden interior dusk, plaster dust making them all cough, he muscled a path for the women to follow him. Whit and Gustafson, each puffing harder than the other, caught up with them.

At the first ripple of motion under the stage Monty had bolted for the shelter of the nearest wall, in case the roof was coming down. He hung on there, peering out into the spilling aisles of the theater, in spite of Bailey tugging at him and J.J. and Cecil shouting at him from the backstage door. When Susan and the rest of the group came stumbling up the steps in the dimness he grabbed her by her free arm, and between them he and Wes, and Bailey somewhere in there, too, half-shielded and half-levitated her in a crablike scramble.

It is the nearest I will experience to traveling by sedan chair. Behind me Mrs. Gus was similarly scooped up by Whit and Gus and the bruiser.

A chunk of plaster the size of a garage door fell and shattered on the stage. They heard a rain of glass as windows rattled to pieces. As they ran the obstacle course of backstage, the building seemed to think it over, whether to settle back from its restlessness or curtsy to the mastering earth.

We came out in the sidestreet. The quake seemed to have shaken the clock mechanism of the universe, it had been only a few minutes yet it was as if we had passed through some entire season of life.

J.J. and Cecil were there to lend a hand when they flooded out the door. The rumbling and shaking quit as abruptly as it had started and that was disorienting too, not knowing when the earth's case of the quivers might start up again. The group of them clambered away from the back of the theater, Wes counting heads as they skittered out into the sidestreet like a handful of dropped marbles. He halted everybody when they were safely out of range of walls that might crumble. Dazed, they peered around as if surprised that the moon still hung in place, that there was the same air to breathe as before the thundershake of the earth. Except for the population out in its streets, most of whom would spend the night in their cars, downtown Helena at the intersection a block away from them appeared remarkably unchanged. "Gus, if the car is in one piece, bring it around here, quick," Wes directed. Bailey said the same to his man, then sprinted up to the corner to see if the streets were passable out of the Gulch.

No one else moved much, as though the surface under them was delicate. Susan had taken to gripping Mrs. Gustafson's considerable biceps reassuringly rather than have that muscle applied to Mrs. Gustafson's gripping of her. All the while, the only sound besides everybody's tentative breathing was Mrs. Gustafson softly moaning in a hiccuping way. The cluster of them stood waiting there, dressed like aristocratic refugees amid the tipped ashcans and broken window-glass. The night was staying warm. "Earthquake weather," Whit accused, from his familiarity with California. "Damn it, I knew it was up to no good."

Monty numbly stared around at the city pocketed now in the moonlit mountainscape. *What does it take,* the thought came at him from every direction, *a million tries?* Rodeo getup or tuxedo, this place was determined to leave him in the dirt. Two more shakes and every one of them would have been buried in bricks, all because he had been determined to put the postponed anthems of his family into the air here.

Watching the look on Monty with apprehension, J.J. cursed under his breath. He edged up to Susan and whispered, "Can you do anything with him?"

No longer holding back, she was at his side in an instant. "Monty, you can't let this get you down," she heard herself saying, something they both knew the words to. She rummaged desperately for anything that might count as consolation. "Caruso was in San Francisco in that earthquake, and he went on to—"

"I'm no kind of a Ca—"

Just then the Duesenberg nosed into sight, Bailey riding its run-ningboard. He jumped off before the car drew to a complete halt.

"I grabbed onto a newspaperman who's on the line to his office," he reported. "Most of this was around Three Forks, Sixteenmile Canyon, in through there. Streets look like we can get through." Wes nodded along as he worked on the logistics of delivering everyone out of this. While Bailey was speaking, Gustafson climbed out and planted himself beside a fender, evidently wanting his feet on the ground until the other car got there and things were sorted out.

Whit came over to draw Wes's attention. "Maybe we've lucked out. This far away, any aftershock might not amount to—"

"HARM!" Gustafson shouted, startling them all. He broke from beside the car, making a run at the danger he could not name.

Wes whirled, but saw he was too far away. The man had charged out from behind the lilacs here on the residential side of the street. He targeted Monty before the others saw him as anything but a blur detaching from the dark, swinging the ax handle with both hands, like a baseball bat. Monty tried to duck while Bailey pushed Susan out of the way and kicked at the assailant.

Wildly the ax handle swished in the air as the man bulled in on Monty like a crazed woodchopper. Just before Gustafson barreled into the attacker and upended him, a backswing caught Monty as he tried to turn his head away, the blade-end of the wood cracking him across the base of the collarbone and up onto that side of the throat with a terrible sound. He fell backward to the street with one hand splayed toward where he had been hit.

The other men boiled around the pinned-down attacker as Wes tried to minister to Monty and Whit chucked his rolled-up tuxedo jacket beneath his head for a pillow. There over them, Susan stared, sickened unto stupefaction, at the Williamsons with all their powers and Monty on the ground like something slaughtered.

Wes looked up at her when he had Monty's tie undone and his shirt plucked open. "The collarbone took it worst. But the throat, along that side—"

J.J. and Cecil and Bailey scrambled over to help lift Monty to the car. Bailey's men frog-marched the assailant off to turn him in to the police. "Ned recognizes him," Bailey choked out, near tears, "hanger-on who didn't even make it into Potter's bunch. He's the dimwit brother of somebody Whit's boys gave a going-over. I guess that's why an ax handle instead of a gun."

The hospital was a nightmare. Miraculously few were injured by the quake, but there were hysterics, and it took some doing to make it understood that we had a man out in the car who had been beaten with a club. Wes prevailed, of course, and a doctor and stretcher crew went out for Monty.

In the hallway of the hospital after the patient had been installed in a room and was being examined, J.J. came over to Wes to make the matter clear. "Just as soon as he can be moved we'll be taking him back to New York, Major. Had enough hospitality out here."

"My railcar is in the yards over there. It's yours."

"That would help."

Nightmare does not begin to say it, about this. People wake from nightmares eventually. Monty may never, even though his eyes came open when I last saw him, being carried from the hospital. That creature from out of the dark could not have hit him in a more severe place if he had sighted in with a rifle. I—

Susan stopped writing. Downstairs, the snick of a key in a lock, the sound of the front door opening and then quietly shut.

She knew it would be Wes.

The train howled out steam, white whistle blast beneath the plume of locomotive smoke, at the latest cattle that had broken through the right-of-way fence. Cecil took such shrieking personally. "Can't they train those cows to keep off the railroad, like dogs are housebroke?"

J.J. trimmed him to silence with a single glance. To him too this prairie seemed to go on forever, and heifers or whatever they were roamed in shocking freedom. But in his considerable experience grumbling had never been known to make a train go faster.

Cecil vamoosed to the front of the Pullman to read his breviary. J.J. went back to the paneled-off sleeping compartment to look in on Monty again, not that looking helped much either. The doctor whom the Williamsons had sent with them, Walker, told him at the start: "The collarbone, that's nothing. I've set hundreds of them on rodeo riders and ranch hands. But that business with the throat—all I can do is keep him quiet and turn him over to somebody who knows what he's doing."

Monty and the doctor both were dozing, the one in the bunk half mummified with the cast across the upper part of him, the other in a chair with his head propped by an arm in a way doubtless learned by waiting for babies to come. J.J. had stepped in here steeled, but the sight of sleep as the only reliable truce that life let anybody have made him wilt as much as it had during the shooting war in Europe. The catch in his throat he recognized as the fear he had carried through the Argonne forest of hell: of a living death, the kind of wound that took away eyes or testicles or a leg or an arm. He hadn't even thought of the voice.

Feeling the train slow a notch and then another and another, he backed out of the sleeping compartment to watch what happened at this stop.

It had started at Harlem, the Montana depot version of it. Some railroad magnate went goofy, J.J. had noticed on the way out, and slapped names on the stops along the tracks the same as real places of the world—Malta, Zurich, you'd think you were on a royal tour instead of some toot-toot prairie train. He and Cecil had razzed Monty about that particular little burg, asking why he'd figured he had to go all the way to 135th Street when here was a Harlem in Mon-tan-i-o, just look, it even had a skyscraper: the grain elevator taller than the main street was long, the two of them had thought that was funnier than anything. This time when the train made its quick stop at the tiny town, there by the telegrapher's office waited an overalled man nearly as dark as the shadowed area he was standing back in: the depot swamper, pushbroom in hand, in respectful attendance. A couple of hours farther on at the depot at Glasgow, the same ceremony of witness by a colored church congregation of ten or a dozen; there was no mistaking the preacher with the dignified wool under his homburg. J.J. realized that stop must be a division point on the railroad, to account for such a number, and from that he figured it out in a hurry. The trainmen. The yassuh telegraph, silent polite ebony-faced servers of railroad food and dark distant caboose-riding brakemen who some mysterious way were spreading the word ahead.

Wolf Point, the weather-scarred sign on this town less than royally said, and J.J. saw that this time it was a colored family, probably the only one in a place so small, presenting itself on the depot platform, the father pointing past the Great Northern coaches to the Two Medicine & Teton railcar and saying something to his children in a tone obviously hushed.

Back at Glasgow the first newspaperman had been waiting, too, and J.J. knew there would be packs of them at the big-city depots ahead. That was the only good thing about this, he thought grimly, and set to work on his statement about the one more form of lynching that would be on the conscience of this country if Montgomery Rathbun was never able to sing again.

Why didn't that sonofabitch just kill me and get it over with?

Somewhere around Minot, Monty came more or less awake again. He felt as if something terribly heavy was sitting on his windpipe, with its claws dug in. Not to mention his collarbone hurting like fury all the way out to the point of his shoulder, and the skin under the cast starting to itch.

The bastard had to really hate hard, ride out an earthquake to get at me. Godamighty, is there just no end to—

"Here," the gruff voice was back. "Just try some."

Hovering over him the same as the last time he had opened his eyes was Doc Walker, after him to take some soup down. Monty started to shake his head, and found out what a bad idea that was.

"Goddamnit," the doctor reasoned, "if you don't want to eat for your own sake, do it for mine. How's it going to look if a patient of mine starves to death?"

To get Doc Walker's spoon out of his face, he opened wide enough for a sip of the soup. It hurt all the way down.

A LL lyrics seemed leaden to Susan, in the days after, and she hastily abbreviated the rendition of "When the Roll Is Called Up Yonder" that the redheaded girl had been proudly prompted into by her mother.

"I can take it on faith that you kept her voice up, Mrs. Quinton," Susan pasted on her best expression again. "Very well then, we will resume Lily's lessons. I regret that I had to go away for that while, but Lily is so much more mature now that we'll make up for that bit of interruption in no time." One version or another of this she had recited five times already today, and she was almost prayerfully grateful for the rescuing knock on the front door.

But when she answered it, what the threshold held was Wes. *Keyless? And if so, why?* her eyes interrogated before a rustle of impatience at the side of him manifested itself as Whit.

"Sorry to intrude, we thought you would be done by this time of day," Wes put forth a politeness that carried like cologne toward Mrs. Quinton and her daughter. "Really, our business matter can wait if—"

"Not at all," Susan interjected, her eyes still working him over and delivering a few swipes at Whit as well. "We were just finishing off ours. Come in out of the summer."

Mrs. Quinton simpered past the man who would have been governor and his cattle king brother, Lily managed to look everywhere except at the gauntlet of grownups, and off down Highland Street they vanished, leaving Susan with her next tableau.

"My, the brothers Williamson. Thinking of becoming a duet, are you?"

"I'm needed to co-sign," Whit for once kept himself to the minimum.

She studied him as though wondering whether he was fit for such a task. When she had him sufficiently unnerved, she turned toward Wes. "And Monty? Any fresh word?"

Wes hesitated. The side of his face could feel the press of Whit watching him at this. "He's out of Presbyterian Hospital back there," he kept it to. "J.J. has him in his apartment, a nurse with him. The medicoes can't tell about his voice yet."

Susan would rather have taken a beating than do the arithmetic of *yet.* A week after the drunken roper at Havre had done her such damage at her neck, her voice had begun to respond. It had been ten days now since Monty's clubbing. Equivocation by the doctors at this point was worst news, she knew.

Wes ached to go to her. Which only would have postponed the next hard part. "I—we don't like to bother you with this, honestly. But another dry summer— Whit tells me tomorrow wouldn't be too soon to start watering cattle on the North Fork."

"Yesterday," Whit husked as if his own throat was parched.

Susan stood there uncommonly pale, as if keeping a moment of silence for Scotch Heaven. After some seconds, she murmured: "Then let's get it over with."

The signing of the papers didn't take time at all, it seemed to Susan. Whit had capped the pen and handed it back to her with awkward gallantry when she became aware that Wes was studying her speculatively. "Now that we're past that," she caught up to what he was saying, "this came just as we were leaving the house." He handed her a telegram.

MUST REACH MISS DUFF. PLEASE.
—JACE JACKSON

DOWNTOWN AND UP

· 1925 ·

WHY GIVE THEM another run at me?

The pencil point nearly pierced the paper as Monty jabbed the question mark onto that. Behind the angry fuse of line was explosiveness tamped tight by ax handle. What else was he supposed to do with the fundamental fact of life that some loony would pop out of nowhere swinging a club or worse and leave him like this, beaten halfway to hamburger and rooked out of his singing career just when he had it made, no matter how he watched his step. And it was always going to be that way, because that's the way it had always been. He turned the tablet around and shoved it across the table to her as if they were trading turns in a furious grudge match of tic-tac-toe.

Susan leaned to the table again, trying not to let her apprehension show as she took in the writing. The tablet traveled on the veneer with a sandpapery whisper each time Monty whipped it over to her. She held back for a few moments, as if waiting for the paper to quit rasping, before she spoke. "You can't just let them wreck you. You certainly don't have to worry about another run at you from that cretin with the ax handle—the Williamsons will see to it he'll be in the penitentiary until he comes out in his coffin." Monty was grabbing the tablet back to himself, pencil at the ready. "I know," she tried to head off the agitated scribble, "that doesn't put you back to what you were. But *he's* going to be out of commission from now on and there's every chance that *you're* only out of commission until you heal up."

The tablet scooted back toward her as if of its own accord. *You don't savvy,* it read, *it hurts to even breathe deep.* Before she could respond, he swung the paper again and jotted: *& I sound like death warmed over, you heard that yourself.*

There, she would have had to admit under oath, he had chisel-hard truth. Her ears still were trying to recover from when she stepped into this stuffy apartment with Jace Jackson and heard like a croak from the crypt: "Why'd they have to bring you back here?"

"Such a greeting," she had forced out, for once in her life certifiably scared. "Are you supposed to use your voice yet? I don't think you should." In disgusted answer he brandished the writing paper. She had stood rooted there, trying not to stare at the purple splotch of bruise that was the side of his throat, and below that the turtleshell of plaster cast showing through his dressing robe. A sleeve of the robe hung empty, that arm sling-fixed in front of him to immobilize the shattered collarbone. By then J.J. was fleeing to the kitchen with the excuse that he had to tend to business by phone.

"Monty," she tried again now, "all I am saying is that when the doctors decide it's all right for you to try your voice, we can see how it handles music. I helped with that once, I may as well again." The pencil was twitching in his fingers as if he couldn't wait to stab at that. Whatever the medical prognosis turned out to be, the mood she was seeing across the table showed the opposite of hope. "You have every right to be down on life," she felt she had to resort to, "but what happened back there was a chain of bad luck. If we hadn't all been shaken out of our boots, Bailey and his men would have been able to keep that creature off you. That's behind, now, and when we have you so you can sing again and audiences flock to hear the man who withstood the idiots of the world, life will even out again."

He shook his head, slight movements that still looked as if they hurt like fury. He held up his hand as if to say wait a minute, then set to work on his next message.

She sat there trying to dab her wrists and brow into some semblance of dry, but perspiration popped back on her within seconds after each swipe of her handkerchief. The living room of the apart-

ment—rented furnished, she could tell; Monty would not likely have
smothered the couch and every stuffed chair with matching magenta
antimacassars, nor invited in the retired-looking piano that took up
more space than anything else in the room—was close and dense as a
chick hatchery on a day like this. She remembered these kinds of summers from her first time around in New York, with a heatwave haze
over the city for days on end, a gauzy coverlet on top of the blanket of
humidity. She felt doped with the heat, and rocky yet from the three-
day train ride that had deposited her at Pennsylvania Station that
morning. "Could we have a bit of air, do you think?"

Monty lifted his pencil long enough to gesture impatiently that he
did not care one way or the other, although the upper part of him
must have been sweltering under that cast.

She shoved the window up as high as she could. The air of Harlem
felt only marginally less hot than the incubating apartment.
Nonetheless she pushed aside the lace curtains and stood at the window trying to will the atmosphere into some cooling motion. What
she got was commotion. Iron-wheeled clatter of a knife-grinder's cart
going by, along with a chant she could not understand a word of. Peppering in and out of that was the rackety putt-putt of an ice truck.
Background to both was the pervasive locust hum of automobile traffic over on the avenues and main cross-streets. The steady clamor it
took a mammoth city to produce, and she was fifteen years out of date
at coping with its energies and mystifications.

When she turned around to Monty, bracing herself for the treatise,
he was sitting back as if spent. Slowly he sent the tablet her way.

*Miss Susan—I am taking your name in vain, but I need to make the point
as strong as I can—I know you think you can fix anything but the break of
day. But this isn't anything a music stand or running to keep my breath up or
anything else will help. The man who beat me is only one of who knows how
many, and that's what there is no cure for. You know and I know that I didn't
pick out my skin, like it was the one suit of clothes I'd ever get. Yet that's how
it is. The singing does not work out for someone like me, we have to face up to
that. I'll maybe end up back milking cows, but at least I will be in one piece.
Believe me, I hate to say this, it goes against everything the both of us have
tried to do. But I wish we had never started.*

Susan read it over, then motioned for the pencil. "To save both of us hearing me say this over and over like a cuckoo clock, I may as well write it down where it'll be handy." She flipped to a fresh tablet sheet, jotted briefly, then tore the page out. "I'll put this over here and simply point to it every time it's needed, all right?"

He saw she had written: *I categorically disagree.*

"Mr. Jackson, something bothers me." Striding beside her through Strivers Row and its inventive margin of enterprises, carrying the same small black case that he had met her at the el with, Jace Jackson looked for all the world like one more snappily dressed postulant of success out on his professional rounds. Which, Susan reflected, he in a way was, if escorting an outlandishly white woman in and out of Harlem counted as a professional endeavor. It was nearly noon and as far as she was concerned the heat had turned the streets into block-long griddles, but people were flashing by as if they were ice-skating. Obviously a midday flurry of people heading home from visiting or shopping, the sidewalk traffic every step of the way was overwhelmingly female and except for Susan, unanimously dark in complexion. The whole sashaying caravan of them, as far as she could see, in frocks of colors that seemed to have come from heaven's candy jars. When a particularly well put together woman, dusky as Nefertiti and suggestive, rhythmic as the Song of Solomon, sailed past her like a luscious vision in peppermint, Susan felt like a pillar of chalk. Yet all the passersby's glances that slid off Jace Jackson and stuck to her pale self seemed not to convey hostility or racial grievance, but something more like cold hard clinical curiosity. Distracted at being constantly gone over as if she were an eye-chart, it took her a number of strides before she managed to find her way back to what she had been wanting to ask. "As I understand it, if I were to come up here at night with other whites and party until dawn, that would cause no stir. But you say I hadn't better show up alone in broad daylight."

"I do not make the rules for the game of skin, Miss Duff."

"Then tell me this. Why is it all right for you to walk in and out of here with me?"

J.J. sighed. "Second time I've been asked that today—my wife claims she is married to a crazy man all of a sudden."

"Well, then?" she pressed him. They were only a block or so now from where the elevated railway stood like a steel-legged aquaduct into Harlem, and an arriving throng was pouring down from the platform to refill the street, every eye of them, naturally, on her.

J.J.'s low response was drowned out by the departing train. She waited, watching as the train cars caused the shadow-and-light pattern beneath the elevated track to flicker like giant piano keys being madly played, until the rumble passed them by. "I'm sorry. What?"

He gestured at the teeming street and said only loud enough for her to hear: "People think you're a doctor."

Susan snorted a laugh, saw he was serious, and stopped short in the middle of the sidewalk.

J.J. reluctantly hove to beside her. "Throat specialist from the West Coast," he rattled off in the same low tone. "Studied in Vienna. First woman admitted to the Royal College of Surgeons. Please don't be looking at me that way, people have to be told something." He handed her the satchel. "I'll meet you at the el again tomorrow, same time. Be sure to bring your doctor bag."

Monty grimly plowed at his brought-in meal. It was a mess, one-handed eating. He still was on milk toast, but even so, the bowl and spoon had minds of their own and his throat did not want anything to come near it. He had made it clear to J.J., practically in block letters, that he did not want anyone around when he had to tackle food like this. The kitchen helper from the E & B who lugged in the hot-water caddy three times a day and fished out the bowl of sick man's grub always cleared out anyway as soon as the dish was on the table. Couldn't blame him. Tongue-tied invalid propped up by plaster of paris and tablet paper; who wants to hang around in that sort of company?

He negotiated another mouthful of milk-sopped toast as carefully as he could, slopping some of it even so. Damn, but being a patient was hard work. He was unbelievably tired all the time with this. At least he would be able to sack out again this afternoon. Sleep was the one thing he could look forward to. Bed rest. Read the newspapers J.J. brought. Take it easy, was everyone's prescription for him. He wished he could find anything about this that was easy to take. J.J. was being an absolute ace, but he couldn't run his business by way of the kitchen telephone forever. The Major was pretty much out of the picture, it was his Montana time of year for months yet, and he couldn't be expected to hand-hold a person endlessly either. Meanwhile the bankbook with the name *Rathbun, Montgomery* on it was going down as if a plug had been pulled.

Which only brought the worries as far as the medical side of things. Tomorrow he would be put through another round of doctor appointments over at Presbyterian Hospital. How many ways were there to say "inconclusive"? So far the sum of their diagnosis was that his damaged shoulder would only be an inch lower than his other when it finally mended and somewhere down the line he would have his voice back; but a voice that sounded like what?

And on top of it all Susan Duff had materialized, right in this room. Didn't she know when enough was enough?

"Going on six years, how can it be," Vandiver was saying, as if marveling at how calendars took flight, when he and Susan faced each other across the light-grained expanse of his desk; mahogany, she noted, not true oak. She knew that much of his job was as official greeter, and right now he was addressing her as if she had just descended the gangway from one of the ocean liners down there at the Hudson docks framed by his office window. His was a bracing style, a conscious bit of brine to it, like the air here so close to the working river. People came into the headquarters of the Over There Memorial Committee expecting a war poet, some consumptive stick of a soul who had glimpsed humankind's worst fate in the reddened mud of Flanders and dedicated himself to making sure the waste of so many lives would never be forgotten. But Vandiver looked like Tom Mix unhorsed. His big impressive hands were clasped on the desk in front of him as if they were a gift put there specially for her. "Life has been treating you well, I hope?"

"As well as I have a right to expect, Van."

Vandiver canted into a pose of appraisal. Odd woman. He knew from something she had mentioned back there at the St. Mihiel event that she had once partaken of Greenwich Village life, before the war, in its storied era of longhaired men and shorthaired women. A blunted singing career, the way he heard it, that not uncommon souvenir of New York. But after she was dislodged by family obligation or the whim of changing her vocal vocation to teaching or the lure of the suffrage movement in the West where it had seemed to be doing some good—the particular story that followed Susan Duff wandered back and forth over all of those—she had chosen to burrow herself away in Montana ever since. He had to wonder about that. Her efforts out there for the committee had been miraculous, and every autumn she could be counted on to subscribe for a contributor's ticket to the Armistice Day observance; at Carnegie Hall going rates, that was not a negligible amount. Before her last trip to France he had written to persuade her to stop over here and for once attend the great event, he and his wife would be glad to put her up and show her around for a few days afterward, but she replied that she had already arranged to sail from Montreal to have a headstart on French, thank you very much. Now, though, here she sat, running a caretaking eye over his view of the ocean liners and the docks they were nuzzled to, as if they were her personal aquarium. He cleared his throat. "Susan, may I ask—what brings you to New York at last?"

"Recuperation."

When she realized Vandiver had no idea what to make of that, she tacked on: "A friend's, after a bad accident. I came to help with the care."

Vandiver waited, but that appeared to be all. After a bit, he ventured: "You're available to us, do I gather?"

"I apologize, Van," she said with a start. "Talk about out of practice—it's been an age since I was any kind of job applicant. But yes. I need a steady wage while I'm here, and I thought—"

The big hands spread apart on the table as if measuring out the invitation. "We can always use your talents," Vandiver delivered it along with the practiced smile, "I've told you that before." He cautiously ventured a salary figure. "It's not as much as I'd like to offer, but—"

"Fine, then," she responded. "Oh, did I mention, I must have mornings for myself. The, ahm, recuperative chore. Although if you'll furnish me a typewriter, I can take any amount of work home and do it at night."

That set an executive nerve to twitching in him, she could tell. But when he spoke, it was to say he supposed they could work around that, since it was her. As if that reminded him of something, he cocked his head to one side again. "You'll need to find lodging, I suppose? Miss Cooper or Mister Lehrkind could go around with you. Or, my wife's mother knows Mrs. Maeterlinck in the Village, she might take in—"

"That's quite all right. I'm taken care of."

Susan's return glance having firmly sealed off that topic, Vandiver cleared his throat more extensively. "It's really quite lucky, for you to show up just now. I know you have a particular interest in the archive. It's become a struggle to keep up with it." Hearing what was coming, she resigned herself to sorting paper; cataloguing, to put the most elegant job-name on the dryest task. Well, she told herself, somebody had to do the chores. "Susan, I spend what seems like every minute of my life raising funds," Vandiver seemed to be going a long way around to get to the point. "The monument, the Armistice Day observance— they take everything we've got. The archive collecting, I'm ashamed to admit it, has had to be neglected. Other chapters weren't as quick off the mark as you were in Montana." He gave her another of his off-angle looks, but this time she didn't care, she could already tell she was being spared from paper-sorting. Vandiver got up as if it was time for both of them to go to work. "I would ask you to apply your knack at rounding up war letters and diaries and what-all for us."

I T WAS a week later, although to Monty it seemed a lot more than that off his life. The doctors had counseled that he not use his voice for one more week, and all they could do then was to test his windpipe capacity. He couldn't help thinking that while they were waiting on a medical miracle that way, they ought to try to come up with one that would take the pester out of Susan.

There she sat, same time, same place, those simmer-brown eyes of hers giving him no rest. Behind the closed kitchen door J.J. could be dimly heard trotting the virtues of one of his other acts past some theater owner or another. Monty started to write, made an impatient face, and scratched out the first word of the salutation needed for him to frame this the right way. With quite scholarly care he formed down onto the paper a fresh version:

Susan. Can I call you that? Saves words.

"You may. You'd better."

Susan, listen for once.

"I take it you mean, don't spout back until you're good and done."

He nodded with more vigor than had been possible the week before and went to extended writing.

J.J. and you deserve all the credit there is for thinking I am worth one more try. But what's happened is something I don't think my voice can ever get over. I don't much like the idea of going out in front of an audience and wondering if somebody out there is going to clobber me, either. You have your own notions of what a person can and can't do, and good for you, but I can only tell you how it feels in my windpipe and for that matter the rest of me. No good.

"You've had worse."

Worse? The pencil was nearly burning holes in the paper. *Worse than an earthquake worse, and a crazy SOB trying to separate my head from my shoulders as soon as the shaking quit?*

"That bull's horn. I didn't see any reason to tell you at the time, but that goring should have finished you as a singer, before you even started." She watched him rock back from the table at that, staring at her as if she had put over a swindle on him. "And somebody gave you an earlier working-over in Helena, I remember," she kept right on. "Those bruises?" She mapped them out on her own ribcage and chest frontage as if he needed reminding of each contusion.

Monty absorbed with interest her pantomime of that particular pasting the Zanzibar Club had handed him, then went to work on the tablet again.

Any of that, I brought on myself. But this—it's like terrible weather that just never quits.

"It'll clear up when—" she began, and he threw down the pencil at having handed her that opening.

Susan dry-scrubbed her face with her hands, then peered blearily at him over her withdrawing fingertips. "We are both overly touchy, it's the fault of the situation. But you're being too leery. I don't care what the doctors say, I wouldn't think of inflicting voice exercises on you after that examination next week."

Cautiously he retrieved the pencil.

You wouldn't? Promise?

"Not until you have your cast off."

He gave up.

*O*UR *routine must have half of Harlem wondering by now whether we are testing foghorns in that building,* she made her way back into the diary three weeks after that.

Monty had yawned miles' worth, feeling ridiculous, their first day.

"Again," she coaxed unmercifully, "but tongue flat as a rug this time."

Dubious as he was about the amount of control anyone could exercise on the human tongue, he willed himself to give her another gape if that's what it took. The jaw-hanging yawn this time drew her in on him. "I need to see in there, hold it open . . . hold . . . yes, that's good, your palate is lifting nicely."

As she backed away he closed up like a man who'd had a toothache explored. Rubbing his tired muscles of face and jaw, he said in the hoarse tone he hated to hear coming out of himself: "Susan, he didn't hit me in the palate, you know."

"Now then," she marched right past that, "trap shut, please. You're relaxing that jaw nicely, so you're ready to hum. Have at it until I tell you to stop. Lips together, tongue flat in there, *quit gritting!* Your teeth need to be apart enough so they don't vibrate against each other—*tsee, like zis,*" she showed him as if holding a pencil between her teeth. "Ready? One, two, three, hum. That's it, *hmmm mmm mm,* keep it going, work on the resonance, make it carry all the way up to here." She tapped each side of the bridge of her nose indicatively. "Put your fingers up there by your eyes, feel the vibration?"

For whatever it was worth, he could.

* * *

So we have proceeded, these first weeks, from the bottom of the barrel of music up to the spigot where fully rounded sounds must come out. The work needed to bring the sounds from his voicebox up and resonating out as they should is chore, chore, chore, translated in musical terms into ah ay ee oh oo and the like. While it is too much to say that Monty finds any pleasure in the endless pitch exercises I make him do, he did smile just a smidgen when I threatened that any time he let his voice break on a vowel I would yell, "Timbre!"

"You're unbelievably lucky to have someone Scotch for this," she was assuring him, "vowels are the currency of our realm." He could have sworn she brought the scent of heather into the overstuffed apartment by the way she uttered that. He'd heard her slip into her inherited burr before, but this time she was laying it on as thick as if she was fresh off the boat. "All right, we've been over the drill," she pranced her voice as if his was bound to follow, "now let's go through it a few times. I'm the customer, I come into your dry-goods store looking for, oh, let's say a new shawl"—she glanced around and felt of the hem of the nearest antimacassar—"and I'm not just sure what material it is I'm finding. Remember, you answer only with the vowels like a temporary Scotchman. I ask," and now she trilled, "Wool?"

"*Oo,*" he dutifully confirmed in a resonant drone.

"My good man," she sang, the vowels of each word so sweet and rounded he thought something would break inside him, "you are sure it's wool?"

"*Ay, oo.*"

"All wool?"

"*Ay, aw oo.*"

"All ewe wool?"

"*Ay, aw ew oo.*"

"All one ewe's wool?"

"*Ay, aw ae ew oo.*"

"We're getting there," she briskly dusted her hands of the exercise. "Tomorrow we'll do 'eel oil.' Now let's work on your—"

In from the kitchen came J.J., showing stress. He brought his arms up like a man in a holdup and pointed to both his ears. "Nothing against what you're at, mind you, but I'm going to cut, over to the Lincoln. They'll let me set up shop at the backstage telephone this time of day. Quieter there." He gave Susan a mingled look in which the only clear sentiment was that he hoped she knew what she was doing. "I'll be back in time for your noon train. Bring you anything, Monty, besides the usual?"

"No. Don't forget that, though. You did yesterday."

"That was yesterday," J.J. said breezily, and left them to themselves.

Her pen paused in mid-page as if listening. The first metallic wheeze from across the street was always as if the siren was gulping in enough breath to last, and now the firetruck howled off as if baying on the scent of smoke. *So much for my cosmopolitan airs,* she twitted herself for not nearly the first time during this New York residency. On her hunt for housing, it had taken her only one transit of Greenwich Village to convince her that its changeover to teahouses and poseur garrets would be too depressing, and she opted instead for a set of rooms in a reminiscently scented neighborhood nearer the docks where French silk merchants once clustered. Smitten with iron-trellised balconies and creeper vines and the air-promised presence of bread and cheese, she had managed to entirely miss the presence of the firehouse in the middle of the block.

As the siren wound away, she glanced at the clock. Nearly the middle of the night already. The city ate her time when she wasn't looking. Visitational as a cat, it sneaked pawfuls of hours away every time she turned around to do something. Its appetite for her nights was insatiable; now that she had taken up membership in a light opera group that met once a week, somehow two nights or three went to its persuasions. An evening at the Vandivers' or an occasional Broadway show, and she was abruptly short of portions of the week for Over There work. The morning trips up to Harlem, distinct as a picnic during her hours with Monty, turned into an agonizing nibbling of her time all the long ride back downtown on the el. Held in the sway of the train, she perpetually had to try to make up for the lost top of the afternoon by composing in her head that day's plea to the state chairman in Georgia to get in there among the peach crews and harvest their war letters, or to coax the one in New Hampshire that *some* Granite Stater must have overcome reticence enough to write home during the hundreds of days the American Expeditionary Force was in the frontlines.

She and her chronic escort were at the foot of the station stairs when it occurred to her. She moved to one side as the usual trample of Harlem home-goers came heading toward the two of them. "Before I go, Mister Jackson—"

"Could you please stop with that? Mister Jackson is my grandfather the undertaker—I'm used to answering to 'J.J.'"

"J.J., then, here's what I need to ask. I don't know what Monty says about me, but when he wants to grumble about you in this, he'll always say you treat him like a boot recruit. Do you come by that because you were in the war?"

"To the gills."

"You keep in touch with the others from here, do you?"

J.J. halted at the top of the first ramp and turned to consider her. As he stood there, slim as a clarinet, Susan wondered how *he* felt navigating these streets beside a white woman who could have picked him up under one arm. She saw curiosity getting the better of him, until he decided to provide:

"To some extent, sure. There's a bunch of our old regiment in James Europe's orchestra—we run into each other at benefits and such. Plenty others work at the post office. Redcaps down at Penn Station, you practically trip over Harlem vets there. They're around, why?"

"Because to me you're all men of letters."

Yet I made time again today, didn't I, the pen picked up her chronicle of all this, *to go hear the confusion concert.*

It was not many blocks out of her way on the walk home from

work, and the first time she heard it in the middle distance she laughed incredulously and made straight for it. The neighborhood was a few away from hers, but she knew that was only by luck of the moment. Back in her younger experience here, she had learned that New York perpetually colonized itself. A stretch of street that was a lens grinders' district the last time you looked would have turned through some cosmic New York logic into a major center of the making of lampshades, and the spot on the river where you bought imported perfume was all at once where the banana boats came in. She couldn't remember what these precise blocks of ironfront buildings had been before, but now they were unmissably the radio district.

No, that almost inaudibly said it; Babel and Bedlam freshly seeded with Radio Corporation of America amplifiers, was more like it. Trying to face one another down across the contested air of the street, a couple of blockfuls of these fresh enterprises chorally dinned out the samples of their wares. The ebonite loudspeaker over the entryway of one radio store blaring out Paul Whiteman's jazz band at the St. Regis Hotel, the tin glory horn out the transom of the one next door dizzily trumpeting the fanfare of *Carmen,* the noise emporium across the way countering both with Madame Ernestine Schumann-Heink in grave Wagnerian matinee mode at the Metropolitan Opera—her first time through, Susan couldn't believe her ears, but only a stone-deaf person could doubt this. Turn her head toward New Jersey, and she received the WOR chant of Bernarr Macfadden calisthenics. Incline in the general direction of Brooklyn, and some boy baritone reached forth all the way from the WAHG studio to present her "Roses of Picardy." As best she could tell, there was an inviolate pact among the stores that none would play the same radio station as any other one, but beyond that anything went—banners, installment plans, money-back guarantees, free aerials, complimentary shrinelike bamboo stands to set your set on. At least once a week she feigned interest in the infinite varieties of radio cabinetry, store window by store window, to walk slowly through the mad glorious gauntlet of confusion and attune herself to how zealously the world was enwrapped in voices. To imagine each time one more soar of sound into the atmospheric mix, from up in Harlem.

* * *

"Good as gold but hard to hold—"

The blues had been trying to get Monty by the ears, and failing. *The man sounds like that and probably gets paid plenty for it. Me, if I was to do my songs that way, everybody would just say my voice is shot.*

He had been listening offhandedly—all right, enough to scoff—in the dim of the apartment to the program drifting into his cabinet radio from someplace where shoeing mules and tending moonshine stills seemed to be pretty much the constants of life. Harlem and the prairie both beat that, at least. But he sat up, disturbed now, as the Delta growl made wavery by distance found something remembered in him.

> *"Flat to stack and round to roll—*
> *Silver dollar, lift my soul.*
> *Silver, silver, silver,*
> *silver dollar blues."*

That old ditty, he knew every step of the way. The Zanzibar Club on Saturday nights had been as much education of that sort as any one person could stand, hadn't it?

> *"Hard to bend but easy to spend—*
> *Flat to stack and round to roll—"*

I get the idea. He reached over and snapped off the radio. Blues singers were really something, they could get by with about twenty words and repeating ninety percent of them six times. The ditty out of nowhere had put him up against himself yet again, though. Now that his shoulder was mended and the purple blotch of the blow was gone from the column of his neck, he seemed to be back to what he had been, in any way that he could see. The staves of his legs, the arch of his foot, the slight pink of his heel, all those seemed the same. Hands, fingers, nimble as they ever were. His same darkly durable skin over the same basic arrangement of bones. The workings of his head, he had to hope that even those were not drastically different. But a stranger was living downstairs in his throat.

He wished Susan was right about coaxing back the voice he'd had. He also wished she was out of reach of the stretch of his imagination.

There is an awful distance to go, summation came to Susan's pen, *before Monty has his music back. But so far neither of us has swerved from that.* She folded the diary closed, and in midnight ink began her weekly letter to Wes.

T HE mountains stood taller than ever in the magnifying summer air, but the Scotch Heaven homesteads had gone to their knees.

The places are folding in on themselves, Susan, as if you and the McCaskills were their last mainstays against gravity. The least he could do, Wes told himself as if it were an order to a subordinate, was to make this reconnoiter of the ways of water and grass and time into a salutation to Susan.

If you were here you wouldn't let me get away with calling the separated chapters of your life on the North Fork long arithmetic, would you. But that is the sum of it by any adding up I know. Girl you were, when that father of yours out-stubborned mine for this land, and beloved calamity you've been to me these half dozen years, unto who knows when. It has to be said, Susan, it is a length—one I have gone to, haven't I.

The creek, subdued by this time of the summer, prattled at the stones of the crossing just enough to be heard at the brow of the benchland where he sat in the buckboard studying the vee of the North Fork. He had been perched there for some minutes now, totting up what lay before him. The creek-twined line of homesteads showed pockets worn through by the past winter. Half the roof of the long sheep shed between the Duff and Erskine homesteads had been brought low by one too many loads of snow. Midway up the creek, the Allan Frew homestead appeared to be without chimney. Nearer at hand—*closer to home, you would have me say*—off to the side of the Duff house the root cellar had caved in, the dirt of its crater fresh, not grassed over. He calculated back: it was no more than a year since he wheeled in there with the makings of a picnic in the johnnybox of this wagon, and given the quantity of time he was weighing today, he had to think that was not much. The seasons here were even more ruthless than most calendars, though.

He flicked the reins to start the horses toward the creek crossing. The day already had the hot crinkly feel of August, the peak of haying season, the one month of the ranch year when lack of rain was a blessing. Not until now had he found the right morning to intercept Whit on his way out to boss the stacking crew and let him know he would be gone for the day, over to the North Fork to check on the fencing. Whit, suspicious, told him, "Wes, that fence would hold in elephants," then corked up at the look he got back.

As the buckboard trundled decorously down off the benchland, Wes once more went over the genealogy of the double handful of homesteads to make sure he had them straight in his mind. Thinking this out beforehand, he had made the disturbing discovery that he could not put names, let alone faces or memory traces, on more than half the homesteaders of the North Fork. Accordingly he'd had Gustafson take him in to the county courthouse so he could go through old assessor's records. Then when business next required him in Helena, he went up to the capitol grounds and over to the state office where birth records and death certificates were kept. He topped off the compilation by delving into the proving-up files at the federal land office for naturalization papers and dates when each parcel of homestead land was filed on. With those and a quadrangle map, he had Scotch Heaven on paper now. *It's the margins, where the coffee cups get put down or someone doodles a figure, that require imagination to fill in.*

When the wagon pulled out of the creek, he headed it west past Breed Butte, not bothering to trace along the strands of barbed wire and new cedar posts that now stitched across the valley. He knew he could trust Whit's word on something like a fence.

The road along the creek passed in and out of the dapple of stands of cottonwoods and the wheeltracks were firm from the accumulated heat of the summer. The going was not as easy on the eyes. One after another the homesteads met him like a ghost town that had been pulled apart and scattered, the sun-browned boards of a barn or a shed or a picket fence cropping into view at a bend of the creek or an inlet of meadow. The houses as he passed them were a gallery of gaping window casements and empty doorways.

Susan, I honestly don't mean to sound like a coroner touring through. But examination is the spine of the three of us, in this. Your intense attention to music. Mine to parcels of earth and those who happen to hold them. Monty frisking himself, with a timely patdown or two from each of us, until he found his voice. Whatever we add up to separately, we at least are linked in that.

His conversational "Whoa, we're there" to the grays as they pulled into the yard sounded loud in the still air. More lately lived on than the others, the McCaskill place seemed evacuated, walked away from, rather than undermined by age. In front of the house, he levered himself down from the wagon and knotted the horses to a hitching rail which visitors had probably made scant use of over the years, this far up onto the ruggedest edge of country that broke from the prairie in rising waves of ridge and reef. He knew he shouldn't stay here long, technically this was trespass. Varick McCaskill still had not sold this place, nor would he offer it in the direction of a Williamson if he ever did. But among the compulsions of this day was the need to view the North Fork as had the angular man who dwelled here for thirty-five years in the unashamed harems of his head, half the poems ever written living it up in one corner, calculations of the heart always ongoing in another. *What a haunting figure Angus was, even in life, I'll say along with you, Susan.*

The mountains practically at the back of his neck, Wes perused this pocketed-away homestead at the top of the valley, catch-basin of snow in the winter, gentle swale the color of cured hay at the moment. The silence over everything was as if a spell had been cast, and in a way it had, although it had taken nearly three dozen years to register. The North Fork valley was all as empty as his father ever could have wished it. Which was to say, occupied only by Double W cattle with their heads down in the good grass.

So there I stood, in the tracks of a man who once told me my father had been such a sonofabitch toward the people of Scotch Heaven it was running out his ears. Angus McCaskill had an everything-included romance with the language, did he not. I know as well as anything that you had a sort of crush on him, from girlhood on, and there is a side of me—opposite the green latitude of jealousy—that commends your taste for that. Given it all to do again, he is a man I would have tried to explore a lot more deeply.

He gave it his best there in the shadeless blaze of midday. Guilty of trespass perhaps, but for once innocent of motive beyond the quest into another man's divided soul. About the third time he fanned himself with his hat, the appropriate voice formed in his head: *Man, there's no law against thinking in the shade.*

Smiling to himself, he untied the team and moved the wagon down toward the creek and a grove of cottonwoods. Under their canopy he waited out the heaviest heat, listening to the sentinel rustle of the cottonwoods at the touch of wind, no other sound like it. After a while he unpacked his lunch from the box beneath the wagon seat. The hurry-up sandwiches the insufficiently notified cook had made for him dried in the air faster than he could eat them.

It was a noon of absent company, Susan. No sooner would I set a place for Angus at the arguing table than some part of me would be in the way between us. Wes counted back: the last half dozen years, no night here would ever have known a neighboring light, not a sign of a larger world beyond the fate-inked dark of this valley. Days, what would have begun as necessary settler solitude would have turned into emptiness, nothing out there past the walls of these buildings to angle away the wind, no prospect except the mountains and ridgelines which simply went up at one end and down at the other, with only the neutrality of nature in between. *In short, try as I would to see with his eyes, what stayed with me was the visual evidence that the lines of settlement long ago began to buckle in the gnarled contours of the foothills up in back of Scotch Heaven. And Angus was the westernmost of the people who hurled their lives against those hills.*

He climbed back in the buckboard and began to work his way down the creek, homestead to homestead, for the afternoon. Each time, carefully tying the team to something stout; it would be utterly in the temper of this chafing summer for the horses to run away and leave him afoot over here. Then he prowled, seeing what suggested itself. He knew that out of the volume of lives here he could discern only flecks; but from such glints of memory we try to make out what we were, do we not. The patterns built into everyday homestead life still were there at each place. The barn never more than two lariat lengths from the house, because no sane person wanted to have to follow a rope farther than that to feed the workhorses during a whiteout blizzard. The outhouses always astutely downwind from the living quarters. Colossal runaway molten-orange poppies, tall as he was, marked the flowerbeds the women long ago put in under their kitchen windows.

He found bachelor thrift at the Tom Mortenson homestead. *His kitchen cupboard he built from his leftover flooring, how's that for being honorary Scotch?* Indolence at the Spedderson place. *Not even a garden plot, Susan, nor a decent stanchion for the milk cow.* Overreaching at the Barclay quarter-section, up on Breed Butte nearest the McCaskill place. *This you must have seen with your own girlhood eyes and heard your elders tut-tut about: the spring on the slope under a small brow of land, like a weeping eye, and Rob Barclay chose to build a reservoir there rather than site himself and his sheep along the creek with the rest of you.*

Finally he was brought again to the Duff place and the neighboring Erskine habitation, the earliest two homesteads of Scotch Heaven. He walked the Erskine place first. Donald and Jen they had been. She a thrushlike woman, by report; Wes could not recall ever having seen her. Donald a quiet block of a man, well remembered. The death certificates showed that both had perished right here in the influenza epidemic. It still was unfathomable to Wes that he had been safer in the trenches of 1918 than these homesteaders in their own beds.

Turning slowly in the yard, he took in the structures fashioned by the hand of Donald Erskine, even yet standing foursquare. You could tell by the way he built: he was not one to run.

One to go now, just across what was left of the section-line fence that Donald Erskine and Ninian Duff probably had not needed between them except by habit. "They were a pair to draw to," Wes's father had said more than once, the saying of it a bitter grudging admiration in itself. With reluctance but knowing he had to, Wes hoisted himself into the wagon, fixed the bolster to his leg one more time, and went onto Ninian's land.

As he pulled into it, the Duff place seemed to him the emptiest of all, without Susan's presence. New York, and her mending of Monty there, was all but unimaginable from here. He half-wished she wouldn't write him the letters she did. The other half of the time, he yearned to hear from her every mortal day.

Climbing down into the yard, he at least took a wry pleasure in the house of Ninian Duff having been turned into a music parlor, there at the last.

Angus McCaskill at the top of the valley, Ninian Duff at the bottom of it. I know both of them better from their proving-up papers than I ever did in life, Susan. But if I were in office I'd have been on the speaker's stump at the Gros Ventre picnic on the Fourth, extolling the way people such as them historically bent their backs on ground such as this. Without saying anything approaching the full of it: that the particular pair of them make a parenthesis of onset and conclusion, of the sort that clasps around dates in an epitaph. You know how I love the wit of words but am not in favor of irony—indeed, you have swatted at me when I picked up your copy of Forster and said he would be a less rusty writer if he would scrap irony. But even I have to admit to a portion of the ironic in the beginnings and endings enclosed by your father and Angus. Plus a bit.

Her own sharply missed residency here at the old Duff place of course was the bit. Wes again felt it come over him, the emptiness that had driven him to undertake this day. Without Susan to go to, he was enduring the summer as a season with the sameness of an uneasily dreamed trek, going from sun to sun, never done. Until today.

Talk about parentheses. Susan, if you look at it along class lines, these Scotch Heaven families—McCaskill, Mortensen, Spedderson, Frew, a second Frew, Barclay, Findlater, Erskine, Duff; see, I can recite the names from top to bottom now—were bracketed by a significant pair of others in the Two Medicine writ of life, back then. My own stands first and most imposing, I suppose, we Williamsons possessors by nature. And at the other end, one of the almost accidental acquisitions we had picked up in our baronial way, the Rathbun family; man, woman, child, coming to us out of a past a couple of cuts below the life of you here on the homesteads, which was to say not appreciably above the way tumbleweeds existed.

And here is the "what if," Susan. What if, when Mose Rathbun, shaped by emancipation (to call it that) to be a soldier, which is to say a follower of orders—what if when Sergeant Mose came hat in hand, my father had put him here among you as a homesteader. Had unobtrusively shepherded him through filing the claim where old Mortenson eventually came and put his name on, let's say. Had privately counseled, one old cavalryman to another, the now landholding head of the Rathbun family through the proving-up years with necessary patience and perhaps a dab of man-to-man loan. Had provided him some seasonal work, at calving and at roundup. Had created an occasional wage for Angeline, too—Lord knows, the house at the Double W could stand spring cleaning any number of times a year. In short, had neighbored the Rathbun family as ours easily could have afforded to. There would have been ways. True, Scotch Heaven was as whitely Protestant as we were whitely Catholic, but Ninian Duff—I give him this much—cared only about the complexion of a man's work. The others here, grudgingly or not, would have hewed to his example toward the Rathbun family.

And that brings us to Monty. Imagine him, as I have been, tuned to the best of his abilities in the school of Angus over here. One great thing Angus knew, and put into you and Samuel and others of any talent, was that chore-sharpened ambition could aim itself upward from the narrow acres here. Think of it, Susan, although your emotions on the matter would be necessarily mixed: a greatly earlier start in life for Monty, a less fettered chance for his voice to find the glory it deserves.

Wes gave the Duff homestead one last looking at and turned away.

Well, that is my letter back to you from what was Scotch Heaven and now is leased cow pasture, Susan. Or it would be if I ever dared to put the words down on paper, let alone mail it.

It was growing late, but he stayed on at the lip of the valley, as if to experience the full of the day he was seeing back into. The gleaning flights of swifts over the homestead remnants traced the change of air coming with evening. The high enfolding land to the west was starting to take the color of dusk. He watched in particular the shift of light on the business part of the continental rise; the grassy ridges under the rockfaces, the precious green skirts of the mountains. Two Medicine National Forest land, it was now, but back at the beginnings of Scotch Heaven it had been a last beckoning rumple of open range—free grass—in behind the North Fork. At this time of day, Wes knew as surely as the Bible passage that Ninian Duff would have quoted as justification of Scotch Heaven, the homesteaders would have lifted up their eyes unto those hills where their livestock grazed. Cattle, at first, those would have been, with Duff and Erskine brands on them; he had checked the old tax assessments to be doubly sure of that fact, even though he knew it almost by the rules of drama. The Double W and its most durable adversaries started off with at least that much in common.

As he watched, the shadows grew down off the cliffs of the Rockies, and then came spear-pointed out of the timbered bottom slopes, and at last put a curtain of definition—evening's unarguable edge—down from the grassy ridges to him, as though something old as these hills had been concluded.

W E HAVE an announcement, J.J., hold on to your hat." Susan had saved this to spring on him as soon as he delivered her into the apartment today. "Don't we, Monty."

"Doesn't seem to be any way around it." He sounded on guard, but not about to challenge.

"We're ready to start on songs," she gave J.J. the big news. "Actual music, no more *oo ee ah ah*." She swept over to the reclusive piano. "Ta-da!" Pinging a finger down onto a key to underscore that, she elicited a broad flat *brang* as keys either side of that one stuck to it.

"I'll get a tuner in here," J.J. said hastily, "first thing in the morning. I'm slipping, I should have cottoned that you were about to creep up on the real singing. Montgomery, this lady will have you top-billed at the Aeolian again in no time."

"I've been meaning to ask how we're going to work this," Susan broached. "I'll tend to all the voice matters, but accustoming to the music will take piano playing. Shouldn't his usual accompanist—?"

"No can do." J.J. seemed less concerned than she would have thought. "Cecil's up at New Haven, filling in on the organ at Yale. He's in choirboy heaven. You did the piano work the time before, didn't you? That'll serve."

"I get the pudding beat out of me," Monty husked, "and Cecil gets to go to Yale. I hope you don't have any more good news."

"Actually, I do. I copped the follow-sheets from him before he left."

"There, see?" Susan didn't know why she felt so celebratory, when all they had to work with was a raspy voicebox and a rickety piano, both in sore need of tuning; but she did.

As soon as J.J. took leave of them, Monty turned her way. With a bit of panic she remembered that first time at the North Fork house, his second thoughts adding up faster then than she could subtract them; from the look of him, the arithmetic of this could go the same way. But he merely said, "All right, Susan. How do we start at it this time?"

"By changing clothes."

His eyebrows questioned everything about that, but she thought she saw a slight expression of yearning make a quick visit on him. "Performance getup, you mean."

"The whole kit and caboodle," she said as though she told men to put on tuxedoes at ten in the morning every day of her life. "It'll spiff up the session, start us off right."

"One thing about it," he more or less assented, "if I sound like I think I'm going to, I can go over to the Bronx Zoo and live with the penguins." He disappeared into the bedroom to change while Susan attacked pieces of furniture, clearing space enough for singer, music stand, roving vocal coach—she was wrestling a chintz chair when J.J. popped his head back in the door, casting around for Monty.

"He's dressing up," she explained. "We're going to try it in full rig."

"Never too soon. Pass this along to him, would you? He gets sore at me when I forget to give it to him."

The pregnant trio of numbers on the unfolded slip of paper he handed her, a fatly printed three and an ought and a six, caught her eye. "J.J., humor me a second. Is this what I think it is?"

"We all do it," he sounded surprised as could be at having to defend the numbers game in its own fertile habitat. "Like whites are with racetracks, is all it is. He's careful with it, he only lays two bits a day on it now."

Next she startled him with a sharp laugh. "I don't care about that, Monty is free to make whatever bets he wants. I just hadn't seen one of these before."

"Seen one of his, you've seen them all," J.J. shook his head. "I keep telling him he ought to try to spread his luck around some, but he plays that same dumb number all the time."

Abruptly Susan felt so singled out it went through her like a fever tremor. Of the endless thousands in Harlem, of the millions in all of New York, she was the one person who understood a man playing a number commemorating as close as he could the 30.06 rifle that escorted him to the sanctuary of the Medicine Line.

"Too bad he didn't beat me deaf, too. I hear what I sound like."

"Your voice is somewhat different, a bit clouded, but—"

"Nowhere near the same, is what you mean."

"With work, maybe we can get past that, I still say."

"No sign of it yet."

He had a point and she knew it. They had just tried "Praying Jones" for what seemed like hours on end and the song not once showed any of the magic-lamp burnish of old. She crossly plucked up the follow-sheet and re-creased it, as if the trouble lay there in the music on paper. For the first time she considered surrendering. These weeks of runthroughs, every song in the bunch tested and circled back to and all but sung into the ground, were not getting them anywhere except on each other's nerves.

Monty sagged out of singing posture and leaned against the end of the piano, torn. Susan sat there two feet away from him oblivious to anything but the direction of her thought. She was one of those people you could see the wheels go around in. Fascinating as he found that, he was determined it was time—probably past time—to put it at the inevitable distance. Maybe, he thought wistfully, they could go on writing to each other when she was back West.

"It'd be a mercy to the songs," he delivered in a soft tone, "if we just let them drop. The whole thing. I hate to, as much as you do. But I'm doing my best and you're doing more than that, and they still come out sounding like—"

"Madame Schumann-Heink."

Put off, he folded his arms as sternly as she'd handled the music sheet and waited for her to make sense.

"Her voice famously changed because of the war," she was thinking out loud, enthusiasm starting to dig its spurs in. "It just now hit me. Monty! Before, she sang every opera as a contralto. But now, and

I've heard this with my own ears if I was only bright enough to know what I was hearing, her tone goes in a direction where she could nearly do tenor parts. There we go! If—"

"How do you mean, 'because of the war'?"

"She had sons in the thick of it on both sides." Monty watched her struggle past the war words. "And lost two of them." She gathered breath and hurried on: "What she went through came out in her voice. To the benefit of her music, don't you see?"

"Susan, I know you mean this the best in the world," he had sympathy for all this, who wouldn't, "but I am no Madame Hank. Broken heart, it sounds like in her case, but on me it was a busted voicebox, and those two just aren't—"

"I apologize to you up, down, and sideways," she broke in earnestly. "You've been in the hands of an impostor. An imbecile. An incompetent. An—"

"A little hard to deal with, now and then," he readily granted, "but—"

"No, no. I call myself a voice teacher, and here I've been going about this like a deaf woman. Clouded, I've been saying. *Shaded!* We need to work with the shadings in your voice now. The catch, the bee in the bottle, whatever we can find in there."

This, from the person who had drilled him the length and breadth of the North Fork and Fort Assinniboine on enunciation and rounded tone? What about all those Scotch vowels? Mustering all the calm he could put in his speaking voice, he asked:

"Susan, excuse me, but since when is that any way to be a singer?"

"Since jazz. Since the blues."

He blew up. "Take a look at me, will you? What I mean, really look. I'm a choreboy, a cowboy, a Fort Skin-and-Bone little colored boy—there's no way you can sic me on jazz or blues and have me be anything but a freak from in off the prairie. I don't have any feel for any of that kind of jive, it's all I can do to keep up with one old lame piana. Besides," he whapped a hand downward as if flinging, "J.J. would drop me like a hot horseshoe. And if I know anything by now, it's that it's hard to pick yourself back up in this business."

She waited to see if he was done.

"Who said we're going to graft jazz or blues onto you?" she started in. "We'll keep doing your songs, of course we will. But a bit differently . . ." She fingered the piano in a lower key than usual, then a higher, already on the search. "We'll bend the music, no matter, we'll know the right accompaniment for this when we hear it. The main thing is to bring the songs to your voice, not the other way around like we've been. If how you sound happens to have"—he watched her to see just how she was going to describe a voice that had been beaten lopsided; she caught his look, steeled herself against all the angry evidence in it, and managed to continue—"some woe in it, let's make full use of it."

Monty shook his head, started to say something, then stood there working on what she had said. He chewed at the inside of his mouth long enough that she hoped he wasn't doing himself damage. At last he provided:

"You think?"

"Give me a few minutes with the follow-sheets. Can you scare up some tea and honey while I'm at that?"

They clattered sustenance into themselves and started the day over. She coached him on letting the edges of his voice work on the words like pumice, roughening then smoothing. They tried "Praying Jones" again.

The song still was uneven, but *vexed* had a haunted grandeur to it now. And *hexed* matched it like the second word of a dark secret. The phrasings shaded uncannily into one another.

They looked at each other as if afraid to say it out loud. They were beginning to get somewhere.

D ELIVERY for Miss Duff."
   Somehow she knew that voice. She opened the door of her cubbyhole office and was met with a tower of hatboxes. They descended onto her desk, and the most dapper deliveryman on the North American continent emerged from behind them.

"J.J.," Susan threatened him, "you had better not be teasing." She tore into the string of the top box and snatched the lid off. Letters, packets and packets of them, all with the American Expeditionary

Force postmarks that she could have recognized in the dimness of a coalmine. Amid them here and there like agate outcroppings, the spines of diaries.

Dazzled, she murmured as if afraid to break the spell: "I've shaken a whole state by the ankles for the past six years and never come close to this. How—who—"

"Couple of the boys from the regiment look after things in the neighborhood for Tammany, and I had them put out the word," J.J. said with becoming managerial modesty. "The stuff is probably rag-tag and bobtail, but there it is." He hesitated, then finally produced another packet from inside his suitcoat. "Here, before I lose my nerve. Love letters to my wife, the ones the censors let pass."

"I wouldn't really say I can tell, J.J., but I suspect you're blushing."

T HE days sailed, now that they were unmoored from any fixed notion of the songs. Line by line, alphabet curlicue by curlicue, note by note, the two of them finicked with each piece of music, her jotting, him resonating. A day, a week, whatever it took, tune and lyrics were coaxed around to the shadings of his voice. The development of each song, as Susan later thought to put in her diary, was like snapshot upon snapshot, in more ways than one: they worked upward from negatives. So Monty's voice could no longer prance through *"Sometimes I feel like a feather in the air"*? They let the line waft, drift in on the listener unexpectedly like a sun-caught mote of memory. Nor could he echo, any more, his mother's ascending carol of "Mouthful of Stars." They brought it down to the horizon, its drumbeat line-endings of "Heaven" searching off to the corners of this world.

Then came the morning when "End of the Road" resisted everything they tried, until Susan looked at him and said thoughtfully: "I think you need punctuation."

Blank with the effort he had been putting into the song, Monty could only murmur: "Better run that by me again."

"Let's see, let's try"—she scrabbled among his lyric sheets—"here, and here. Let it break, a beat, maybe two, where I've dabbed in com-

mas, all right? And Monty, make me *hear* those commas. Like this."
As he tilted his head to make sure he was taking all this in, she
demonstrated amply:

> *"You know how you get, at the end of the road.*
> *Trying to stand up, under—"*

"No, wait," she corrected herself in mid-lilt, "right there we want—
oh, never mind what it's called, just—"

"No, put a name to it for me," he said firmly.

"*Arioso,* then, it's what opera singers do in arias when they phrase
to a certain word, not necessarily the one you'd expect." Excitement
lit up her voice. "Here, sneak it in like this, a word early:

> *"Trying to stand, up under life's load."*

Monty caught on like a house afire. She was barely done with that
line before he was over by her, plucking up the sheet of music and
producing on first try:

> *"Done in, and done up, and down, to a speck."*

And knew, before she could say anything, to let the last line flow
uncomma'ed out of the pent-up confidences of those first three:

> *"That's when the right word will lighten your trek."*

Susan couldn't help herself. She clapped, once but resoundingly,
whirled to the keyboard, and pounded out the opening bar of an ode
to joy, da-de-*dum*-de-da-da-*dee*. For his part, Monty crossed the room
as if dreamwalking and collapsed in an easy chair, arms flung in
wonder.

"We're there!" Susan was the first to recover enough to speak. "You
have your whole set of songs now. I'll bet anything this will be a
stronger program than the way you sang them before." With that, she
settled her hands in her lap, reaching that point every teacher does
where the tools of instruction reluctantly need to be put away. She

smiled gamely. "We can let J.J. know he won't have to ride herd on me anymore. Oh, a brush-up session every few weeks until you're back performing all the time wouldn't hurt, but beyond that—"

"I could probably stand once a week," he surprised her with.

"Very well. If J.J. will go along with that, next Friday I'll put you through the paces until your tongue hangs out, how's that?"

"Susan? You know how I'd like to celebrate?" The request came out shy but determined. "You play something."

"Mental telepathy. I hoped you would ask."

With a flourish she turned around to the piano again, and sitting very straight, she caressed the keys as if reminding them to trust her touch. The music at once rose in suggestion, a sudden glide of reprise of what she had played for him in the Fort Assinniboine auditorium, then the tune soared, turned in flight, soared again. It fit. That was Monty's first thought: this piece found its way gloriously to the opening part of her music, as if time was cutting its own circle on itself and the past was hooking on to something lovingly recalled. He listened with all his might, so glad for her he could feel his heart run itself up.

When she had finished, he let the eloquence of silence match the echoing memory of the notes. Then, to make sure: "That what I think it is?"

"Mmm hmm. The ending of *Prairie Tide,* which I was always afraid would end me first. It even has words, but I'll spare you those." Now she turned full around to him on the piano bench and gestured as if the music flew in from hiding places unknown. She was as aglow, he registered, as whatever the most valuable white gem was. "The operetta bunch I told you about kept after me, I had to write and write in self-defense. And working the way we did here—it must have been catching."

"It's a beauty. Makes me homesick, if that was home."

"High praise, I think." She laughed a little. He didn't.

"That brings up something," he said huskily. "The day we're done, rehearsals or whatever, you're off back to Helena, aren't you."

"Not just that quick," she did what she could to sugarcoat the inevitable, "you make me sound like I have one foot on the train. But soon enough after, I'd better. The house is there waiting, the mothers with my pupils dribbling after them. And that 'consultation' you sprang on me back at the Broadwater will be better than money in the bank. 'Montgomery Rathbun himself asked *her* for musical advice'— they'll tell that story forever in Helena." Monty's brows were drawn down. The ability to start a frown with his forehead was a marvelous stage attribute, but not one she wanted to see at the moment. *Why didn't I stick to business and not set things off by playing around on the piano, today of all days?* She ran out of pretense. "I'm set in my ways—that's hardly news, is it," she resumed unevenly. "But you and your music have been good for me."

He watched her square her music sheets together and lay them away in the black bag. She snapped the clasp shut, then looked at the door as if it were a long way off. "Monty, I can't tell you how much this has meant to—"

"Don't, please," he heard a voice he scarcely recognized as his own. He pushed up out of his chair and strode over to the window, the farthest point of the room from her. Stood there like a confined man wanting to take a sledgehammer to every building-stone and brick in Harlem. Eventually, as if his head was clearing, he turned around. "Let's get out of this place. Come on, I'll stand you to coffee and pie. Give me a minute to ring up J.J. and tell him we're rehearsing extra today."

Susan did not bother to ask whether he was sure such a stroll together was a good idea. Rightly or wrongly, it stuck out all over him that he intended for it to happen. Still, she was surprised when he told her firmly: "No, leave that ridiculous satchel."

They walked out into Harlem as it went about its midday business. Kept pace for a block or so with the yam man's pushcart, Susan's head turned in astonishment as usual at the pitch of the man's voice: close her eyes during his chant and she could have sworn he was somebody's sister from Spain. Kept on the move past the exhortations of the soapbox preacher Monty identified to her as the Reverend Skypiece— "Ambassador hat on him, you wouldn't know to look at him he delivers ice, would you." Veered around children lost in sidewalk games. The whole way to the Eat 'Em and Beat 'Em, people on the brownstone stoops or congregated at storefronts would call out to Monty to ask how he was doing by now and he ritually answered

"Much better" and "Getting there." All of them were used to seeing J.J. businesslike at the side of this exotic white woman doctor, but now second looks seemed to be in order.

"Finally I know a little what it's like for you," Susan murmured. "It's as if they're counting the pores on us."

"That's what people do. Gets old in a hurry, doesn't it."

He held the door of the eatery for her, and the eye-flicker atmosphere of the street accompanied the two of them in. Monty was greeted by the regulars, but a person did not have to be a vocal expert to hear false notes in the greetings. He made directly for the presiding waitress.

"Nolene, think we could use the banquet room? High-powered medical consultation. No reason we can't do it over sweet potato pie and couple cups of joe, though."

Her eyebrows inched up, but the snake-hipped waitress automatically slid into motion toward the pie cabinet. "It's available, Monty," she provided over her shoulder.

Not "Mister Rathbun," Susan took note, along with all else that was registering soundly in her from this excursion. She had the absurd feeling she was leaving a trail of phosphorescence through Harlem, but she squared her shoulders and marched in what she hoped was medical fashion beside Monty to the banquet room at the back.

In the large empty room he gestured wryly to a table that would have seated twenty, and they were barely in their chairs when the waitress, looking pouty, sauntered in with mugs of coffee and pieces of pie. As the woman's hands flashed cups, plates, and utensils into place, Susan saw that her skin tone was the same strong cocoa color as Monty's. Gravely the waitress asked if that would be all, and Monty allowed as how it was for now.

"Well," Susan said with forced brightness when they were alone, "here's to *arioso*." She plucked up her fork and tried the pie, which was not as suffocatingly Southern sweet as she had expected. Wordlessly Monty watched her while he toyed with his coffee cup. Three bites ahead of him, she was about to point out this repast had been his idea, when he finally lifted his fork and plowed into his piece of pie. When he was no more than halfway done, though, he dropped the fork to the plate and sat back rigidly. Susan glanced up and froze short of the next bite. She had never seen him this grim, even in the worst of despond after his beating. What he was saying sounded as if he had to half-strangle it to control it at all:

"This ought to give us enough of a taste, hadn't it? Of what we can't have?"

She knew this had nothing to do with sweet potato pie. Thank goodness his words stumbled out low, wrathful as they were. "You saw for yourself how it is. Just on our little jaunt to here. People looked at us like we're out of our minds—'Oh oh, black man and white woman together, the world is about to end.'" She winced as he fiercely rubbed the side of his neck. "And this is nothing," he flung his hand out to indicate the front of the restaurant and beyond, "to what would happen if you took me into a Schraffts, anywhere downtown."

She made her own words surge before he could go on. "It is the saddest thing, yes. That people can't see past that aspect. But Monty, we've done miraculously, you and I, given all that's against us. Your voice is unstoppable now, and as for me, this experience with you has been the best thing that could ever happen to a drying-up voice teacher. And," she tried to maintain momentum despite the catch in her throat, "onward we each go, in spite of—"

He cut her off with the force of the expression that had come onto his face.

"Susan, I—I'm stuck." He knew he had to get it out if it killed him, even though this was the sort of thing that could. "With telling you how I feel about you. I chickened out of doing it," he faltered on, "that time at the Broadwater."

. . . *chickened out of doing it, that time at the Broadwater,* she was equally shaky when she recorded it in the diary that night.

"I wouldn't do it now, neither, if I felt like I had any choice," Monty had gone on brokenly. The anguish in his voice jarred her. She felt like a raw nurse facing a patient who had something she could not afford to come down with. As she held her breath, he mustered his and gulped out the hardest kind of words. "But it works me over, night and day. That I can't even begin to say how far gone I am over you." He spread his hands, palms up, as if their emptiness spoke it better than he could. "I couldn't stand to not tell you, ever. What the hell kind of way is that for people to have to live?"

It tore through her. "Caring about me, it sounds like you mean."

"Worse than that. Bad as love gets, if I have to put a name to it." Bleakly he stared across the table at her. "I was hoping it would wear off, Susan, honest. Was I ever hoping that."

She knew she had to try to slip a different meaning over this. "Working close as we have on the songs and all, there's naturally something emotional about it," she said as if she had been around such cases before. None too successfully she tried to force a chuckle. "I take it as a compliment you've come out of this feeling the way you do rather than wanting to box a bossy teacher's ears."

"It's not just the music," he responded so intensely it came out bitter, "even though I've tried like everything to hold it to that."

"Monty. How long have you been putting up with this?"

"Since sometime back there at the fort," he said as if saying *forever*. "When I saw how far you'd stick your neck out for me, that couldn't help but draw my attention, could it. Then everything else"—his features spoke such wrenching effort that she realized what it had taken for him to work up to this—"the music together like you say, the hay-wire Klan keeping us cooped up with each other, the two of us up against it all, next thing I knew I was stuck on you. Sparking on you to myself like some fool kid. Tried not to show it. I guess I hope I didn't."

"Then when I showed up here," she said slowly, "I wasn't doing you any favor."

"Of course you were!" he leapt to defend her against herself. "Only trying to save my neck in more ways than one, weren't you. Don't do yourself dirt about coming back East. I couldn't get you off my mind no matter where you were. Had ever so many conversations in my head with you. 'Wish she could see this,' I'd think in Boston or Chicago or any of those. 'Wish she'd been on hand for last night's do.'" He sunk his face in his hands as he had in the Williamsons' office at the Double W, then slowly brought them down and away, saying so low she could barely hear it: "'Wish she was here to talk to.'"

It was her turn to falter. "Monty, we shouldn't go too far into this."

He wiped the corners of his eyes with his fingertips. "Let me just

toward one another since the reunion afternoon at the Broadwater in ways beyond the power of music. Safe word, *fond.* But a certain kind of fondness after long enough, she wrote decisively, deserves another name. Somewhere she had read the inlaid words: *The beautiful contradiction of love is that it is a fidelity beyond truth, which is merely occasional.* She had no idea what came after that. But on the evidence of the feelings she was at last permitting herself to admit about Monty, there wasn't going to be anything the least bit occasional about it.

And then there we were, alone together but with everything changed. The fact of attraction had been admitted into the apartment and they both knew it. Each of them had been through enough life to recognize how a situation sharpens on this category of craving. Susan was acutely aware of her nipples budding, natural convergence of blood to the vicinity of the warmed heart. Opposite her, Monty crossed his legs urgently. She had every desire to rush over to him and knew, plain as that door over there, that would jinx this and J.J. would walk in on them. Monty, she saw, shared that precise intuition. Staying desperately planted in his chair, he struggled past the moment to the calendar of complications ahead of them now. "This isn't real bright of either of us, is it."

"Sometimes that can't be helped. Right now we have to think about something else. If I'm seen with you anymore, if we're seen as a couple, it will throw your career off."

She could almost feel his grimace across the room. "About like beating it in the head with an ax handle, you mean." The worse pain of truth was written on his face as he looked over at her and slowly spoke. "They wouldn't go easy on you either. You know that."

She was there ahead of him. "I've faced it before." A pause. "With Wes."

"Susan, I don't think you have. Not like this."

Just then came J.J.'s usual shave-and-a-haircut knock on the door, she wrote in smaller hand to make the last page of the diary entry come out even, leave a fresh one for whatever next. *Before letting him in, Monty looked at me as we both fixed our expressions and said, "Painted in a corner, aren't we. Two coats."*

* * *

J.J. did a skip-step to keep in stride with her. Whatever Susan was marching to today, it didn't know slow. They were already bearing down on the el station and he still was trying to catch up with her surprise prognosis.

"Really ready?" he persisted. "Enough that I can put him up in front of people and they won't mob me for their money back?"

"His voice is ready," she repeated.

"Well, then, amen," he made his decision. "I'll set up a musicale or two, sprinkle him around town that way at first. Let Montgomery tune himself up without the whole world listening."

"And then?"

"Maybe tour him some before letting the New York crickets at him. One thing, Miss Duff." He halted so abruptly at the base of the el stairs that Susan flew past him a couple of steps before she could attend to his next utterance. "You have to understand, you probably won't see us in Helena again," and he handed her the black bag in the usual ritual of goodbye.

A T THE office in the days after, Susan plunged her mind as far into work as it would conceivably go. She came in very early, now that there were no journeys to Harlem these mornings, and in no time was well on her way to wringing extra effort out of every Over There chapter on the eastern seaboard. This day, with the watchmen's barrel bonfires barely quenched in her window-framed view of the awakening docks, she just was starting rapid-fire typing when the jangle of the telephone joined in. She let it ring a couple more times while she gathered her mental forces. At this hour chances were it was either the New Jersey state chairman who could not wait to howl about the stiff letter she had sent calling attention to the collecting prowess of the Tammany political machine versus his in Jersey City, or—

"This is the *Amsterdam News*," came the sweet voice at the other end, "wondering if you might be interested in our introductory subscription price for downtown folk."

"Monty, it's all right. I'm here alone, except for a crazy man on the phone."

"Not seeing you puts me that way. Maybe we both ought to check ourselves into the loony bin, where things make more sense than this."

"You first. I feel like I finally have a head on my shoulders."

"Mine's still spinning. Listen, why I'm calling—you find out how you stand with the Over Theres?"

"They can use me until after the Observance. That gives us a bit of time."

"Take what we can get. Guess what. J.J.'s lined up a musicale. Wait, don't say anything, here's the rest of it: even if I have to hogtie everybody involved, I want you on hand there."

"That's dear of you, but—"

"Never mind *dear*. It'd buck me up to look out over Cecil's pointy head and see you. Besides, you deserve to be there as much as I do. We don't have to be, what's a nice way to put it, obvious—but I want you in that room hearing the music we've put together."

"Don't think I wouldn't give a year off my life to be there. Really, but no. You've told me yourself how swank those evenings are, and I'm only the voice teacher. That's no leg up at all on the roost back here," she spoke from experience.

"You're going to be there, depend on it," he decreed. "I know somebody you can show up with, it'll look just fine. Don't be a scaredy-cat, Susan. I'm enough that for both of us."

Her spirits shot up at the sudden chance to hear him in front of people. "If you're that sure. When?"

"Before I know it, almost. Friday."

"You'll knock the ears right off them, I know you will."

"There's something else." He measured out the words. "J.J.'s booking me and Cecil a tour. Across the pond."

"That's wonderful," she said, sick underneath.

"One end of Europe to the other, what he tells me. He's not saying so, but I expect he wants to break me in on big audiences where nobody in this country can hear. Can't exactly blame him."

"How long?"

"That's the catch. Half a year. I hate it like blazes, but J.J. claims that's what it takes to cover the ground, over across."

"That sounds right." In that instant, Bristol, Cologne, Brest, the tens and dozens of provincial stages where she had toured, came alight in her memory like a stained-glass window; and the greater halls, the leading cities, would be thrown open to his voice. "You have to write me from everywhere or you're in for it," she tried to sound full of anticipation.

"That's a ways ahead yet. Friday, though—"

"You're right, that's almost in sight. Down to business, you. We'll put off that session to save you for the evening," she made the decision a voice teacher had to. "You feel perfectly ready to sing at the musicale, don't you?"

"I wouldn't say perfectly. But do I want a chance to let the songs out, Godamighty, do I ever."

"Party bunches, those can be uncomfortably close quarters."

That produced a significant silence at his end of the phone line; one more instance when she had hit the nail on the head in the dark. "Funny you say that," he mustered after a bit. "Let's just say I'm not overly comfortable with these sassiety shindigs, but I can swallow them."

"Bigger crowds," she said as if speculating. "You told me back at the Broadwater that having the music stand took care of the nerves you had about those."

"That could have been truer."

"Monty, wait, you aren't still bothered by having to face a genuine audience, are you?"

"Sometimes."

"Often?"

"Just about always. Susan, I get myself by the scruff of the neck and make myself face those audiences, okay? Did it before, every damned time, and I have to figure I can again. Question for you now," his voice warmed. "Do you ever let a poor beat-up singing pupil alone?"

"In this case, not until he's perfect. You're within a spoonful or so."

"Right. Try several shovelfuls. Susan? It's only been a few days and I already miss you like everything. Any hope for the patient, you think?"

She responded as if he was not the only one who needed steadying. "Cures like this always take a while."

After the silence that followed he said he had better get going on his daily constitutional or Strivers Row would be sending a search party for him, she said she had absolute mountains of work to do, and they hung up. Both of them were wet-eyed.

J.J. boiled into her office the next day.

"What's this about our Harlem letters?" He flung down her message. "'Problem' with them, what kind of all of a sudden 'problem'? The color of our stationery, maybe?"

"Insufficient recognition."

"Say that again?"

"The Harlem collection deserves—what do you call it when you want notice for Monty or one of your other performers—push?"

"Push it till it smokes, if that's what you want," he responded, crinkled with puzzlement. "I can help you pitch it to the newspapers some, if that's what you're after, but—"

"I have to wonder, J.J., if your sense of push is working the way it should these days." She had spent nearly all night thinking this through, and even so she found herself desperately having to ad-lib it all. "Scooping Monty out of the country before you put him in front of a real audience, for instance."

For a moment the impatient manager went still but alert, as if figuring out the crossfire she had him in. Then he moved to the side of her desk, leaning in a bit to deliver each sentence piece by articulated piece. "All right, Miss Duff. Feel free to tell me my business then, why don't you. Where would you book a colored singer who has every right to have the heebie-jeebies after what's happened to him?"

"Carnegie Hall. On November eleventh."

J.J. went back on his heels ever so slightly.

"It would all fit," Susan wouldn't let him get in a word edgewise or otherwise, "the Harlem letters would have their fanfare at the Observance, your veterans would be there to be honored better late than never, Monty's songs would be a natural, and Over There would gain push galore."

"You mean this? I don't question that you want to do it, but can you?"

"I know where the ears are located on those who can."

J.J. looked like a man who had been given a fast horse and a race-track to go with it. His index finger came up and simply stood there, his mind so busy with her.

"One thing," she prompted.

"Right. Have you spoken to Montgomery about this? Because I don't want his hopes up and then—"

"It should come from you. I haven't said a peep to him about this."

"I think it's a leading idea," Vandiver gave her notion his blessing at the planning session the next morning. "It does put us on a different footing with the Carnegie Hall people, however," he informed the two of them across his desk with just enough chief executive sorrow at lack of perfection. "They take a radically different view"—he rubbed his thumb and fingertips together in the universal suggestive sign for money—"if it's a performance rental rather than a benefit speaking event."

Susan sent her *Well, then?* gaze to the other person on her side of the desk. He returned her an appraising look, as though weighing where she fit in the Table of Elements. She'd felt vastly relieved when, for all she had heard about him from Wes, he walked into the office not seeming to know her from a potted plant. Even freshly shaved and pomaded, Phil Sherman had some of the grizzle of his redoubtable family line of generals and senators; he looked like he could take your head off in one bite.

But he sounded as plummy as the runaway to Broadway that he was when he finally spoke up. "Maybe you missed your calling, Susan, if I may. Van puts the touch on all of us for the Observance every year, but it's usually like going to church the second time in the same week. This has some ginger to it. Let's count on our fingers first, though. One, you're sure J.J. is game to book Monty into a show for our rather fancy but not that lucrative downtown benefit crowd? And two, Monty is thoroughly fit to be back onstage again?"

"Absolutely, both of those."

"Then I'm in. Monty is an incredible talent, this could be a ripper of an event." He shifted his gaze to Vandiver. "I'll agree to be the pro-ducer if somebody with actual money will come up with the backing.

I'm tapped out, Van—everything but my gold fillings is in Flo's next show."

"We thought perhaps Major Williamson—"

"I thought that's what you thought." He served them both a veteran backstager's grin. "Serves Wes right for being out there with the cows instead of in here defending his back like a civilized man. He'll be back in town when?"

Two hours from now, Susan knew to the minute and also knew better than to say.

"I'll have Miss Cooper ring up his secretary and find out," Vandiver took care of that. "So," he delegated by habit, not skipping himself, "I'll put a toe in the water with the Carnegie people. Susan, if you would be so good as to handle the speaking arrangements, work up the presentation of the Harlem letters, and so on. Phil, you'll pull the rest of it together, bless you. Anything we've missed?"

Sherman spread his hands. "That should cover it. All we need now is Wes, so we can clap him on the shoulder in congratulations on being the honorary chairman of the Observance and catch what falls out of his wallet at the same time."

Vandiver stepped out to instruct Miss Cooper, and Susan sat thinking ahead to Wes as she gazed out the window at the docked ships. As casually as an old flame, Phil murmured: "What time would you like me tonight?"

She gave him a look barely short of a scalping.

"Didn't Monty get word to you yet?" he asked, furrowing up. "He put the arm on me to escort you to his musicale."

Sunlight poured in the mullioned window, tendrils of vine shadowing onto her bedroom wall.

Their breathing having barely settled down from the first time, he was increasingly aware of the warm cup of her hand, already urging him to hardness again. In most of his waking moments all summer he had wished for just such a scrimmage of desire, but she seemed to be ahead of him in every way. Wes could not actually have said who led whom to this, but Susan was performing like an Amazonian guide on a mission. The sun playing on the disgracefully mussed bedding, their entwined bodies made a memory duplicate of their 1919 spell together, but this time as if caught in the hot light of an explosion.

He managed to pause long enough in what they were at to ask: "You're supposedly where?"

"Mmmh?" She had to think for a second what she had told Vandiver. "Oh. Carnegie Hall."

"You rate it."

Afterward, the surprise on her this time, he took her to supper at the dining room of the Brevoort Hotel. Quite possibly on the basis, it looked like to Susan, that this was the nearest palace he could think of. The headwaiter fussed them into place, chanted *Monsieur* and *Madame* while enthroning them at the nicely placed table which one glance at the cut of Wes's suit evidently had entitled them to. Something was whispered in Wes's ear that made him nod gravely, menus were conferred on them, and then they, like the other dining couples, were by themselves in the sea of ice-white tables. Glancing around at the murmuring class that obviously frequented here, Susan wondered how far back in history the rule ran that as the caliber of the family name goes up, the velocity goes down. Wes could be counted on to be the exception.

"Too bad Montana doesn't have a seacoast," he was saying as if something should be done about that. Running a finger rapidly down the seafood side of the menu, he chose clams, specifying *à la crème*.

She ducked her head to the menu, not fully trusting her expression in front of a man whose version of eating fish on Friday was clams prepared in cream. "I'm hopelessly carnivorous." In French probably better than Wes's and the waiter's combined, she ordered loin of lamb, cooked *à point, s'il vous plaît*. "Back home we never ate the little dickenses, you know, or maybe you don't," she rattled on to Wes to be saying something. "Mutton, yes. Religiously. So to speak." She didn't want to babble at this, but words were not the surest part of her at the moment.

Wes felt around under the draping tablecloth and pulled out a champagne bottle. "Louis informs me the only available wine is on the order of glycerine, but this isn't bad." He poured the sparkling liquid in their waterglasses. Susan was constantly astonished at the hiding places of alcohol in the public venues of New York.

While they sipped and maintained a patchwork conversation, she kept on questioning what she had done back there in the sunlit bedroom even though the answer always was that she'd had to. A holding action: Wes himself doubtless had employed such a maneuver sometime or other, in whatever manual of arms men resorted to. That he had to be held, until Monty's opening note resounded at Carnegie Hall, was nobody's fault but fate's, she was quite sure. Well, not that sure, really. But at least she had herself sorted out about the afternoon's particular declension of *fond,* which she was relieved to find was the one that wears itself out naturally. She had launched into their bout of mutual want as if driven to prove something, and while it no doubt could be said better in French, proof was there to take its turn when the bedsheets cooled. The afternoon with Wes had not changed anything but her pulse rate.

The soup course was bestowed before she gave in to curiosity: "Versailles-on-the-Hudson, here—is this safe for you?"

He realized that she didn't know—how could she—that the snoops and tattlers of his and Merrinell's set were universally at summer places yet; for the gilded ilk, October brought the social season back to New York as inexorably as the tides of Fundy reversed themselves. Across the next ten days or so the pair of them could cavort around and around the ankle of Manhattan if they so pleased, then suddenly the Puritans would land again. Rather than go into all that, Wes gestured around at the palatial roomful of couples. "We're nicely hidden in plain sight here. Snowshoe rabbits in a drifted field."

But Susan said, as if she knew more than that about the nature of camouflage, "Won't they pick us out by the pink of our eyes?"

He was about to laugh and hoist his glass with the remark that pink champagne was more likely a dead giveaway in such circumstances, when she said: "Pink is the color of guilt, isn't it?"

Wes put his glass back down. "I've just hit town, so I'm running behind on the guilt issue." Although, he caught himself at, he was staying conspicuously silent about his exegesis of Scotch Heaven. He gazed over at Susan to try to stroke away her mood. "I suppose we did heat up things to the color of blushes this afternoon. Just when I wanted to try to do better by you in one way, at least." She leaned forward in listening attitude but tautly enough that he knew he needed to be on the mark with the phrasing of this. "Knowing you, I have to calculate that you'll take yourself back to Helena as soon as you have Monty put right and the Observance out of the way."

"I ought to, yes."

"Don't deprive us that way. Stay in New York. We've hardly been together at all this year. I don't like the sound of 'arrangements' any better than I know you do, but something could be managed that would let you be on your own—take on pupils back here, why not—and we could just call it our way to be together."

"That's a big step. If I were a certain someone, I'd call it a major step."

"That's short of a yes. But I'll take what I can get. I'll break my back to set you up some way like that, Susan, if you'll stay."

"I need some time to think about what all that would mean, Wes."

"Of course. Think it over from every direction of the compass, but I can't see how you'd be worse off by trying me out on this."

The meals came.

"Fair warning," said Susan after an approving mouthful of lamb done just pink. "Your wife." He went still. "Van is going to put the arm on you to coax her and her circle, he calls them, in on the Observance. He seems to think she hobnobs with the governor's wife, among others. A slum relief committee together, is it, the Cardinal and some others thrown in?" Her face was perfectly straight.

"You know how that is, committees make"—just in time he backed off from the cliff where the sign read "strange bedfellows." Something like a chuckle came along with the realization that a conversation with Susan still was next thing to a blood sport. He could feel a stirring in his lately underused capacity of verbal thrust and parry. "Van knows how to turn a circle into a round number," he polished that off. "I'll see that Merrinell's phalanx pitches in on the event, don't worry."

"I wasn't, particularly. Now I have a better surprise for you."

"Isn't there a limit on them, in one calendar day?"

"Monty's first musicale, since."

"Already?"

"And we're going to it. We're expected."

"Are we. When is this?"

"Oh, around ten."

"Ten when?" Then it dawned on him, or whatever the noctural equivalent is. *"Tonight?"*

"Of course tonight."

"I've been on a train practically forever, not to mention—" he did not have to cite their bedroom workout to have it active in both their awarenesses again. As Susan started to say something, he managed to beat her to it. "Of course I'll come hear Monty, after everything the two of you have put into this summer. A musical interlude, just what the doctor ordered." He sat back to compose himself for a moment. "I hope you're not going to tell me next it's at my house."

"Even J.J. wouldn't pull anything like that, now would he. It's what he calls 'a Park Avenue do.' Who did he tell me the people are, Baxters, Hatchers, Thatchers—*voilà,* Brewsters!"

"Susan, this is pushing it. I do business with Howard Brewster, and Lord only knows who else like that will show up."

"Don't fret, we're not strolling in together. Phil Sherman is squiring me. You can make your appearance when you like, only don't you dare miss any of the songs—Monty and I worked ourselves to the bone on them."

"That Phil. I'm going to have to keep an eye on him."

"Actually it was Monty's idea. I still have never heard him sing in performance, you know."

"That's purely silly," he said as if just noticing that state of affairs. "Of course you need to be there, it's only fair." They both busied themselves with their food. When they were nearly done, Wes felt he should smooth this part of the evening away a bit more. "I'm sorry to have sprung that on you so quick, about wanting you to stay. Forgive me that, all right?"

"All is forgive," Susan resorted to a comic-tragic accent that could have got her hired on the spot at the Brevoort. She felt a last genuine pang for Wes, and what might have been if they had dined together here when she was in her Village days and he was unattached, but left that for the diary page to handle and went to fix her face for Monty's musicale.

* * *

The grand piano at the Brewsters' had the type of gleam to it that comes from that assiduous polishing agent, old money. Cecil hung around the great dark lustrous instrument looking as pleased as if it was his to take home. *Run your hands under hot water before touching it, did you, Cece?* Monty stood by, anchoring himself into what seemed the best spot to sing from, watching as Cecil enthroned himself on the piano bench and began manipulating the follow-sheets, and along with them his third beer. Prohibition, in Cecil's opinion, had made brewing an uncertain art, and as usual he plopped a cough drop into his glass to give the beer some snap.

J.J. was down at the far end of a living room that at a minimum had to be called sumptuous, making chitchat with the heir to something or other. Monty never liked taking it on himself where Cecil was concerned, but an accompanist who was not up to the mark was the last thing this night needed. He pattycaked a brief drumbeat on the piano top, leaving fingermarks that drew Cecil's instant attention. "Easy does it, partner," he issued. "Those cough drops can get you."

The pianist glanced up, irked, and just as quickly learned he had better not be. Cowpoke or wrangler or whatever he was, Monty had a set to him that suggested you really ought to start herding yourself in the direction he wanted you to. And he hadn't come out of that beating any less determined to have performances done his way and no other. Privately Cecil had figured Monty was headed for the scrap heap. But that woman, whatever kind of music witch she was, and him, however they did it, the pair of them had come up with renditions that made his fingers itch, they were so choice.

"Only oiling up enough to be loose, Monty," he soothed. "I'll be right on soon as we start."

"That'd be good," Monty said deadpan.

He turned away from Cecil and scanned the party-comers as they gathered in flocks of four or six. Pompadoured men and bobbed women, about like the last one of these all those months ago, but none of these evenings quite mirrored any of the others; he was pretty sure that was their point. Costumes, sometimes—once there had been a hat night, with half the crowd in sombreros and hawkshaws and he sang in his tux and Stetson—and more generally some ins and outs to the mix of the invited each time. High society constantly put itself through a strainer, it looked to him like, and keeping track was J.J.'s job and thank heavens not his. He did know that without coming out and saying so J.J. had wanted tonight's do to be out of Harlem, to see how the resuscitated voice and redone songs went over with white hearers. *Got his wish on that, for sure.* Tonight's guest-list sift had shaken out like pure flour. The only dark skins in evidence anywhere in the room were J.J.'s and his and Cecil's, except of course those of the serving staff, as carefully distant-faced as Eskimos.

At the point now where his music was ready in him and the waiting had to be got through, Monty occupied himself by watching the faces, all the rituals of expressively widened eyes and laughing lips and butterfly kisses on cheeks. Tonight's host and hostess were the type who pollinated the party by staying on the move, shunting this famous couple over to meet that notorious one, bringing a hipper-dipper with the ladies over to meet the newspaper versifier who had recently left her husband. Monty knew there were places in the world where people like these would be taken out and shot, but at the moment he found it hard to hold much against anybody whose worst quality—at least out in public—was trying everything in order to have a good time. Quite a few of these, he figured, were the sort of person who would be fun on a picnic, if it was a short enough picnic.

At last he saw Susan come in, on the much-used arm of Phil Sherman.

Here we go, hon, his thought cried across the room to her. *Someplace we never thought we'd get to, let alone in a bundle.*

Two-faced as I have been today, do I have enough left for this?

Looking at herself in the abstract, which was currently the only way she could stand to, Susan believed herself to be as revealing and moment-by-moment duplicitous as a mirror with multiple panels. The first reflection showed a man her heart went to, across the room there. Somewhere on his way up Park Avenue to join the picture, a man whom every other part of her had been entwined with that very afternoon. As she stepped into the stratospheric evening where they would both be, she had to hope this divided version of herself would not fall apart.

First of all, though, she had to survive the onslaught of hospitality. "Delighted to make your acquaintance . . . welcome to our little evening," was luxuriantly drawled at her from both sides before either she or Phil could put a name on herself. When he managed to, the hostess and host beamed expertly while they tried to place it. Even the muscles of their smiles, Susan sensed, had pedigree. Susetta Brewster was of an old Virginia family, Tidewater roots as far back as the first anchor splashes, and slender and decisive as a sceptre. Her husband, older, possessed a high stomach, on the style of a pigeon, and had a way of leaning in on whomever he was talking to as if offering the comfort of that hearty bosom. As the Brewsters' gracious hovering elongated into hesitation, though, Susan realized that her showing up with Phil Sherman did not fit expectations, rather like a kangaroo print in the snow. She fixed a shielding smile against the determined attention Susetta Brewster was giving her—with just a tiny stitch of wariness at the corner of each eye—as Phil yattered an introduction that didn't make much sense until he invoked Susan's work for the Over There Committee.

At once that pegged her for Susetta: doubtless a war widow, tragic as a mateless eagle from the look of her, most likely an heiress from the West on top of it all or why else would Phil Sherman bother to be convoying her around town? With relief she burst out to her husband: "Oh, then, Howard, you must see to it that she meets Major Williamson."

"Shall!" promised Brewster.

Until that could be made to happen, she and Phil were shooed into action in the crowd. Phil did not abandon her, but in this atmosphere of excess money and women with telltale sidling eyes, he had trolling to do and often worked with his back to her.

In the course of the evening she jumped whenever Howard Brewster shouted "Sooz!" which each time turned out to be robust abbreviation of his wife rather than the start of summons of herself. Maybe it was the marinade in the Brevoort lamb, but in this gathering Susan felt temporarily French. The slightly wicked but of course apt salon saying over there could just as well have been stenciled on the penthouse wainscoting here: "On the ladder of life one must climb like a parrot, with the help of beak and claws." Tonight's rungs were perilously close to the top of New York. She drew on resources she hadn't used in a dozen years. After all, a certain pang kept reminding her, she had been through this before, in the Village; there had been nights then when she was the one standing ready by the piano. So, tooth and nail, she set to socializing in this altitudinous throng. She had a good pithy conversation with an old growler who had started as a rigger in the Oklahoma oilfields and wildcatted his way next door to the Rockefellers. Next she was trapped in one that spun in circles, with a cottontopped young actress who had been the stand-in for Jeanne Eagels in *Rain*. Susan politely peppered her with questions, but what she really wanted to know was what it was like to play a role off a piece of paper instead of from the scraps of one's self.

Wes paused in the doorway. In the bit of time between the butler spiriting his hat from him and Howard Brewster hoving to, he performed a rapid surveillance on the room, best chance to do so on evenings of this sort. Utrecht velvet on the near wall, making that statement in a hurry. The newer decorating touch was paisley shawls adorning the backs of all the furniture, as if peasant women the size of gnomes were stationed throughout the crowd. Over the fireplace blazed one of Nikolai Fechin's Taos paintings, a pueblo woman in a dress of many colors and holding out a golden peach. The rest of the significant interior decoration was wall-to-wall people. His scan sorted them in a hurry. Half a head taller than nearly all the other women, Susan, intently mingling. And poised beside the piano, Monty. Seeing them both here, Wes had a moment of he wasn't quite sure what: abashed self-congratulation? Then Howard Brewster clamped his arm and swirled him into the party.

"Wes of the West!" Phil greeted him. "Welcome back to civilization." Phil was languidly sandwiched between Susan and a flushed woman with a feathery little headpiece in the assisted red of her hair. His practiced hand, Wes noted with due relief, was in the small of her back rather than Susan's. When presented to each other, once again he and Susan exclaimed for everyone else's benefit that their families had been acquainted. Brewster hung on with them, proud of his prowess at putting people together, until he could not resist foisting other couples into the conversation.

Wes took the chance before the impending blizzard of introductions to say in Susan's ear: "I meant what I said, at dinner. Stay in New York and see the world."

Just then the piano announced itself. Not trusting herself to say anything, Susan brushed fingertips across the back of Wes's hand and slipped off to listen from the far side of the room.

As he squared up for his opening number, Monty knew the work cut out for him. This wasn't a particularly hard audience, but not an automatic one either. Gin had made its inroads in attention spans. Right off, he let them know what they were in for with the newly sneaky "End of the Road," his voice effortlessly peppering the song just enough. He was relieved to see heads begin to bob in rhythm with his sly phrase breaks by the second verse. Song after song caught them by the gills the same way; the crowd seemed to be breathing the music rather than air.

Listening, watching, exulting, Susan knew with secret pride that he could sing his way to the top of anywhere when his voice was on, the way it was this penthouse night.

He was happily readying himself for his finale when a hand plucked his sleeve. "Excuse me all to hell, Montgomery," J.J. whispered, holding on to a tiniest inch of fabric to show he was interrupting only to the absolute minimum. "But I have to hit them with this before the night goes to pieces."

Monty backed up, knowing J.J. would not do this if it didn't count.

"Good people," J.J. raised a hand as if swearing an oath, "I need to make an announcement. Would you believe, I get paid to spill the beans and these are some delicious ones. On the eleventh of November, Montgomery and Cecil have another little do." He gave an indicating nod to one and then the other of them. "They're hearing about it for the first time along with the rest of you, look at their faces. They know something is up, all right, but they don't know it's going to be them. They will be performing that night," he bulleted the news with pauses, "at a place . . . called . . . Carnegie Hall!"

An *ahhh* like an ascending run plucked on a harp zephyred through the room. Skillfully J.J. went on to make the pitch on behalf of the Observance, singling out some in the room who had cut their teeth over there in the trenches—Major Williamson, Phil Sherman, "and for that matter yours truly"—and who now felt prepared for Carnegie Hall. "So come be with us that night, hear? And need I say, bring any money you're tired of having laying around. Now for another good cause, the way these two are flying high here tonight, back to our music."

Monty had barely heard the last of J.J.'s spiel, swept up as he was into the thin air at the peak of the announcement. *Carnegie damn Hall, whoo. About the next thing I better do is check myself for nosebleed.*

Instead he squared up again to sing.

"Forty miles a day . . ."

Something phantasmal came into the room now with the first words of the Medicine Line song. Wes felt it as a chin-level chill, up around where his officer tabs used to be. Hauntingly, tinged with rhythm beyond mere tune, some note of the ancient fate-haunted trade of being a soldier came through in Monty's voice when he sang that song now; Homer sang so in his epic lines, and kilted foot-sloggers in accompaniment to bagpipes. Monty's every previous performance of the ballad, Wes had listened to with something like fascinated reluctance, but never with the thought that "Sergeant Mose and old Black Jack" would force a way into musical canon. But this evening, knowing that his was not the keenest musical ear in the room by far, Wes with a shock understood how the earned magnificence of Monty's voice elevated the tune from the Fort Assinniboine barracks. Until now, the classic parade song of the prairie wars was that of the Seventh Cavalry, Custer's outfit, the spirited "Garryowen." Until now.

When Monty finished and stepped back with a bow, the applause beat and beat against the walls and city-spangled windows of the penthouse. Then it was time to circulate, take plaudits, make modest conversation. Without seeming to, he managed to work the route around to the vicinity of Susan.

She had been cornered, no small feat in the middle of a room that size, by the big Dutchman he had been warned about. Artist of some kind, no one seemed quite sure on what basis. The man's wife was across the room, although her hard dark eyes were not. She watched, Monty watched, as he leaned intently in on Susan. "So you are from the wilds of Montana, ha. Had you heard of this musical gentleman out there? His singing is amazing. So—so natural."

Over the man's shoulder Monty traded a sneaking glance with Susan, knowing she had caught on in the same instant he had as to how close that was in the alphabet of fate to naturally so-so.

"Only barely," she answered about Monty's voice having made its way through the wilds to her, "over the sound of the tom-toms. Wouldn't you say, Mister Rathbun?" The Dutchman sputtered a laugh and moved on.

Watching his chance, Monty caught her alone for a minute at the extensive table of food.

"Carnegie Hall, that's pretty foxy," he said low and offhand as though consulting her on whether the Pecorino cheese carried any advantage over the Stilton. "Wonder where the Over Theres might've got that idea."

"I'll never tell."

"Susan, good Godamighty, you know I'm sort of leery on big audiences yet and you're going to plop me in front of—"

"You'll get over it," she assured him, confident enough for both of them. "You'll have to." She slipped him a smile that went to the heart of things. Love was her silent apology for what she had done this afternoon. It had to be. "Now shush about being leery. Your following wants petting, here come some now. And just so you know—you were everything I could have hoped, tonight."

Past one in the morning the evening began to break up, as raggedly and inevitably as floes calving off an iceberg. The noisiest contingent wanted to go up to Harlem. Cecil immediately enlisted as guide. When they swept by Monty he declined by rote, saying the only place up there he wanted to see this time of night had a bedpost in each corner and a pillow to welcome him. From her windowseat

Susan sat watching what happens after the finale, content to her core that Monty's music—their music—had reached this gathering.

Before long, Phil detoured over and manfully asked her to come along with a bunch he had assembled to go to the Kit Kat Club where the liveliest hoofers from *Flapper Revue* congregated after the show; there would be dancing—"Phil, I'm sorry, but I don't flap." He offered to flag her a taxi for home, and out they went, she once again on his arm, past the indefatigable cordialities of the Brewsters.

Wes had waited for the party to thin out before going up to Monty.

"Major, how you doing, how's the ranch? Hoped we'd have a chance to shoot the breeze," Monty fended industriously while thinking *How over is it with her and him?* Susan would do her absolute best, he didn't dare doubt, but—*Williamsons don't any too often say "uncle."*

"I'm calling it a night," Wes surprised him with. "I just wanted to add my bravo to all the rest. You and Susan have done wonders."

"She's one of a kind, for sure," Monty testified, feeling he could afford to say that much. "The Lord Himself wouldn't know how to put a price on her, don't you think?"

J.J. was in a purring mood when he met with Susan to work out the Observance details from his side of things. "The newspapers will lap it up. 'Negro singer shrugs off Klan beating, reaches heights of Carnegie Hall.'"

"As you say, vitamin P," she said, meaning the power of push.

"You know, I can sort of see the audience that night in here," he palmed his forehead like a phrenologist. "You ever do that?"

"Only before every time I ever performed."

"Then let me tell you the kind of thing I see there in great big gorgeous Carnegie Hall." He sketched dreamily in the air with his hands. "People dressed to the nines, Vandiver and the Major's people wearing their money on their backs, they got every right to. Lots of medals catching the light, I may even put on my set. Montgomery and Cecil up there onstage, looking so fine—oh, by the way, since it's the finale, we'll hold them to half a dozen songs, tops. Double encore that way, if the whole crowd isn't out there sitting on their hands."

"Right," Susan muttered, writing down the six-song stipulation on her list.

"All that, then," J.J.'s voice pussyfooted on, "I can see just as plain as anything. And all of us of a certain shade up, ever so high, up there in . . . peanut heaven."

Susan's head yanked up. Cinnamon eyes to almond eyes, she and he stared to a draw. After a while she said, "No one has told us the seating has to be that strict."

"There is a way to encourage it not to be."

"J.J., I'm no good at mind-reading."

"Round up the cripples."

Susan had to swallow hard. She kept still, so he would go on.

"Ours and yours both. Crutchers, one-lungers, blind beggars, any of the wounded vets." He clicked these off like an abacus. "Make them honored guests, put them in the front row, mix them up. Speckle the place with them, that way. How can Carnegie Hall make a fuss about where anybody else sits if those are up there together, I ask you?" He didn't even stop for breath. "Another thing. Welcoming speech from Major Williamson. Hero and big giver and all, it would be good for the crowd to see him gimp across the stage."

"But he doesn't—" She realized she had never thought any gait of Wes's could be called that. "I'll see that he's asked."

After the last musicale—it had been at the Dutchman's place on the Upper West Side; the man went around sputtering like a tea kettle, but he knew how to throw a party—Monty was already fondly missing them when J.J. gave him a lift home as usual. He didn't even much care that the weather had turned nasty. November had come to New York as if colliding with it, rain pouring down like the clouds were being punctured by the high buildings, but slick streets were nothing new to J.J. Monty sat back perfectly glad to be gliding up to Harlem on a night such as this as a passenger instead of a chauffeur.

"Good do tonight," J.J. was musing out loud over the working of the windshield wipers. "Nice and speckled," his term for a mixed audience. "Your better class of ofays, but you couldn't swing a cat in there without hitting a hushmouth poet either." He added a short knowing laugh. "Not to mention the fine assortment of brown honeys. Wouldn't hurt you to get yourself one of those."

Monty made an amused sound at the back of his throat and was about to rib back by asking him what sort of manager he was, trying to push a poor angelic recuperating singer into the clutches of wild women, when J.J.'s next words hit:

"Because you ought to lay off the white lady."

Monty swung his head around the guarded way he used to when there was trouble in the vicinity of the bull chutes.

"Goddamn it, J.J., where's your evidence on that?"

J.J. tapped his temple impatiently and then went back to squinting past the wipers into the torrent of taxicabs the rain had generated. "Too careful says something, too, you know."

"I thought you got along with her."

"Getting along with her isn't the same as getting in deep with her. Montgomery, the last time I looked half an hour ago, that woman was white, white, white. Mingle with them, chin to chin, elbow to elbow, that's fine. But draw the line where the skirt starts, okay? You got no business up there anyway. Whatever you may have heard, that pink thing of theirs doesn't run sideways in them. At least not in the French ones, I can speak from experience. So don't go being curious."

"She's—the music—" Monty fumbled for how to say it. "We've gotten to be friends, her and me. Been through damn near everything together, trying to bring the songs up out of nowhere and me along with them. Godamighty, J.J. You know most all of that. I don't see why—"

"You are not seeing, that's why I have to bring this up. Godamighty yourself, Montgomery. You can't count on the rest of the world going around blind. Cecil's noticed, too."

"Cecil is going to be counting his teeth in his hand if he—"

"This isn't about Cecil. It's about the fact that you and her can be mental kissing cousins over the songs, if you have to, but you're still of the colored persuasion and she's still Miss Pond Cream. Bruise around among the ladies if you want, you're entitled. But you're plenty bright enough to tell black from white." J.J. delivered the next with the finality of slamming a door: "Don't let these lah-de-dah musicales fool you. This is still a country where they run one of us up on a rope every couple of days, and making eyes at their women is one of their favorite excuses. Didn't that ax handle give you enough taste of that?"

Helpless on his own part, Monty tried to defend hers. "You wouldn't be creaming off your cut of the take, every time I sing a note, if it wasn't for her."

"That's as may be. I figure I'm doing her all the favor I can by trying to clout some sense into you." J.J. changed lanes as deftly as a jockey. "You got to watch your step, man. You'd be better off shoveling coal to Major Williamson than to her."

Now that rehearsals and musicales were at an end, meeting without drawing notice was desperately hard. They resorted to the bridle path at first light.

"Any trouble?" Susan asked as her horse caught up to his, the countless seagulls and pigeons staking early claims to one of Central Park's nearly countless monuments their only spectators.

"They figured I was looking for a job as a stable hand, is all." Monty cast an eye over her riding outfit, a purple velvet divided skirt. "Bet they didn't ask you that, did they."

"Grace Vandiver loaned it to me. It makes it, but it's snug."

His evaluating grin said all that was necessary.

"They'll maybe think I'm your—what's that the French have?"

"Equerry," she rolled the word. "A Two Medicine equerry, first of its kind in the world. You're rare enough for it."

They rode without saying anything for a few minutes while they accustomed themselves to the feel of their rental saddles and fit of their stirrups. True daughter of her father, from the side of her eye she studied Monty's potbellied mare and its plodding gait. Son of a cavalryman, he dolefully eyed Susan's broadbeamed bay as it waddled along.

"Nags," he said it for both of them.

"And they call these silly things spurs."

They cantered along as best they could make the horses move, well ahead of other horseback denizens of dawn and those were few. At that early hour, the stilled park seemed something central to not merely the metropolitan island of Manhattan but all the kingdom of autumn, the ramble of its gravely outlined barebone trees and subdued lawn greenery and quiescent waters where even the mallards still dozed a portal between the summer that had been and the winter well on its way. *Let dark winter come its worst / we minor suns were here first,* Susan's memory was jogged by the rhythm of the hooves. *I'm getting as bad as Angus,* she told herself, and brought her thoughts back to the immediate calendar. Ten days into November now, and tomorrow one of history's steep ones.

"More newspaper people coming this afternoon," Monty was saying in a fog of breath. "I feel like one of your records." He slowed down his voice as if a mighty finger rested on it: *"Leht Cahrnehgie Hawl gahthur uss toogehthur . . ."*

"It all helps."

"Something you better know," his tone dropped until it was all but lost in the clop of the horses. "I'm catching hell from J.J."

"About us, naturally."

He nodded. "Funny how we can get on people's minds in a hurry." He started to say something more but held it as a mounted policeman on his morning round crossed the riding path ahead of them. Susan gave the officer a look of such imperturbable ladyship that he may well have figured Monty was along to help her on and off the horse. As he rode away from them, Monty retrieved what had been on his mind:

"Susan? J.J. does have a real question there," he was trying to put it delicately, "whether two like us belong together."

"I categorically—"

"—disagree, don't I know. But that doesn't change—"

"Skin and hair," she said as if heartily tired of hearing those words, "that's not all we're made of—why should those rule all else of life? We are not some kind of a stain on other people's notion of things, we amount to more than that."

"You're sure as you were that first day? About us keeping on?"

"I'm set in stone."

"Just checking. Wanted you to have a chance to cut me loose with no hard feelings."

"Put that in the poorbox," she told him warmly. "We each have a fair idea of what we're getting, Monty."

"I hope you're right about that," relief and rue mixed in his voice. He glanced over at her as if making sure one last time. "J.J.'s not the only one who's ever going to have an opinion on this, you know. I'll bet the Major wouldn't figure this is what he bargained for, either."

"He's the one who went out of his way to toss us together," she said speculatively as if the words would stand clear in the chill air, "he must have figured he was getting something out of it. The Williamsons generally do." She turned her head and met his look with one that said that was as far as she should go on the topic of Wes. "We have to give this some time, Monty. Tomorrow night will carry you a long way. After that, let's—let's see what happens after your tour of Europe. That's the vital thing. You should be fine over there. There won't be any—" she gestured toward the side of her throat.

"That's what J.J. keeps saying," Monty shook his head as if it was too good to entirely believe. "Of all damned things, colored performers are—how's he put it—at a premium in those countries. Tells me they practically made Robeson the second king of England last winter, and the French upped the ante. Bricktop, Jo Baker, they're all learning to eat snails." He was silent for several moments, then said as if putting that away: "Doesn't help us any here, does it."

They rounded a last seasonally solemn grove of trees at a bend of the path, a clear stretch ahead. Susan leaned forward in her saddle and held her horse back until his was even with hers. "Race you to the stable."

"Think so?" His sudden grin expanded into his voice. "You know I wouldn't have a chance against a fancypants rider like you, I'm just the eq—"

She whipped his horse across the flank with the end of her reins, then swatted hers on its bountiful rump.

The horses seemed to shudder into life. Grunting in alarm they bolted down the riding path, eyes wild, hooves pounding, prairie warriors clinging to their backs.

"It's on me today." Phil palmed the meal chits almost before they had settled to the table. "If you don't look back in your checkbook, you can pretend it's a free lunch. Cheap enough for me, too, considering you've roped the governor into the Observance. I kowtow to anyone who can get Ashcan Al inside a concert hall."

Wes grabbed up a fork in one fist and a knife in the other and sat posed like a trencherman ready to attack the feast of a lifetime, then dismissively clinked the silverware back into alignment with the crimson crest on the tablecloth. "Honesty is a costly policy," he said with a tired smile of admission. "The ones you really ought to be tucking oysters and slaw into are my wife and the Honorable Mrs. Smith."

"The club isn't ready for that," Phil gestured idly around at the wholly masculine roomful of alumni in protectorates of three and four, "and I doubt that those particular ladies are ready for the deli-catessen behind the Garrick. You have to be the stand-in. Pile on the chow, you can probably use the nourishment for your Carnegie debut. Everything down pat?"

"I'm so rusty it's pitiful—it's been five years since I made a speech, can you believe? I used to reel them off almost without thinking. This one is giving me fits. I can see myself tomorrow night, I'll end up reading it from a piece of paper like a town crier."

"Maybe you should have Susan Duff rehearse you for a change."

Wes examined his oldest friend. The start of a chill came into him at hearing Phil, cunning about women, make a point with her name on it. "You aren't just telling me that to see if the silverware will jump again, are you."

"Hardly. I don't like what the side of my eye has been seeing at our man Monty's musicales." Now Wes felt the frost of apprehension fill in fully within himself. "Susan is as clever as a woman can be about it," Phil's tone betrayed nothing and granted nothing; he could have been discussing a character turn in a script that had come in over the transom, "but she and Monty keep crossing paths a tad too often. Let's hope they haven't come down with a case of each other."

Afraid of how he would sound, Wes didn't say anything. He sat all the way back in his chair, pinned as a butterfly, waiting for what else the suddenly prosecutorial friend across the table would come out with.

"You've backed Monty enough it ought to earn you sainthood," Phil went on making his case, "but it's reached the point where you need to bend his ear on what goes and what doesn't. It's a fact of life, is all—the two of them are asking for trouble if they so much as make eyes at each other. If I've noticed they're on the brink, others will."

Of necessity Wes found words, for what they were worth. "Phil, really. Aren't you reading rather a lot into a couple of people simply working up music together? I know you're a professional noticer, but in this case I think you're jumping to conclusions."

"And you're dodging them." Phil leaned in, diagnosing as he came. "There are times when you don't see what you don't want to, Wes. Probably that saved your skin where the odds of getting past machine-gun nests were involved. But it can cost you everything you've put into Monty's getting somewhere, if you don't snap to." Pup of the historic old wolves in his family, Phil Sherman knew how to nip when he had to. When he was satisfied that his words were sufficiently under Wes's skin, he settled back again. "Don't I wish I were misreading," he said more leniently. "Seeing the way he lights up around her—I thought at first it was gratitude, on his part. Missy from the nice house, helping him up in the world—why wouldn't he feel grateful? He's feeling more than that, though, I'd bet anything. She doesn't show any signs of allergy to his skin either, if you know what I mean. If that doesn't bother her, why wouldn't she set her cap for a man on his way to being famous?"

Incalculably more irritated than he dared to show, Wes managed to say by the book: "My family knew hers. She's from different circumstances than you and I. She doesn't work that way."

"That makes it worse then," came back implacably. "A steel heiress or a countess with enough money to be naughty might get away with a fling across the color line. Not someone whose name only carries the letters it has in it." Phil tapped the tabletop in emphasis. "Susan Duff throws everything out of kilter. I'm not poking my beezer into this for the fun of it—you of all people know me better than that. I like Monty, I'm all for him. Nothing against her, for that matter, if you like them on the tall prickly side. But I'm not entirely disinterested in how they behave with one another. The sky is the limit, for a voice like his—I can imagine him someday in the right kind of Broadway vehicle. *Green Pastures of the West,* why not? If the gossip columns take in after him, though, that fries that." He raised a cautionary hand. "We don't want to upset our main act before the

Observance. But the minute that's over, somebody had better land on Montgomery Rathbun with both feet about this."

"Damn it," Wes struggled to keep his voice down, "I'm not his lord and master. Something like that ought to come from—well, from his manager."

"If I know J.J., he'll weigh in strong on that, if he hasn't already," Phil conceded. "But a manager is just another kind of hired hand, you know about those. Monty is used to listening to you. Wait until we have tomorrow night over with, then do us all a favor and take him aside and straighten him out about white women." He signaled as though just remembering the purpose of this noon at the club. "Ready to order?"

Something that outwardly resembled Wes made its way to his street address, handed over his hat to the usual serving hands inside the voluminous front door, somehow navigated stairs and hall and thick silence of office to slump into the refuge of his desk chair. This hollow version of himself echoed without stop with what he had never expected to hear. The Harvard Club conversation, to call it that, tortured all the more because its initiating voice was next to his own. *Damn you, if you brought this up and are wrong, Phil, and double damn you if you are right.* But here in the terrible honesty of aloneness he took over the interrogation of the creature who bore his name in all this and made correction after correction, now that it was too late. What a crude mechanism the mind is, he savagely notified himself. He hadn't foreseen, hadn't headed this off in time, hadn't calculated that their courage could be greater than his. *More fool yet, I hadn't a clue I was being one, did I.*

Eventually what he had left to work with began to come to in him. Clock, social calendar, the footstep chronometry of the household, such reminding taps of time impelled him, however reluctantly, to unmoor from the chair and go through the motions necessary. This next semblance of himself managed to put in an appearance downstairs. It roused considerably at the news that Merrinell was out for hours more, enmeshed in the fitting of the necessary new gown for the Observance gala. Then it mystified Hilfiger by discharging him for the rest of the afternoon. This was not behavior expected of the Major, and every eye of the downstairs staff watched the muted figure climb back up the stairs.

But he was enough himself by now to go about this methodically. His bedroom the first stop, he winnowed through his closet until he found a shirt slightly yellowing with age and tux pants with a wine stain on them, the nearest thing he had to workclothes. The change of costume usefully occupied him; he decided against risking cufflinks up there and rolled back the shirtsleeves, then glanced down at his usual good shoes and shed them in exchange for his old pair of army field boots. Looking more like a propbox from Carnegie Hall than someone who was going to appear there the next night, out he went into the upper hallway and tromped on up to the mansard attic, the sight of him freezing maids in their tracks all along the way.

Taking care in dodging under the rafters—he had been conked enough for one day—he surveyed the family flotsam stashed there. An attic was always the overhead catch-basin of life's leavings, but he was surprised to see how things had bubbled up here strictly according to generations. Presiding over upright clothes trunks was a lineup of dressmaking forms, successively more slender than the proportions of Merrinell that were being swathed this very moment. In a gathering of their own were the girls' jilted playthings: rocking horses; menageries of puppets; their dollhouse period. Farthest back in the eaves, galleon-like under sagging sail-riggings of cobwebs and most of a decade of dust, rested his brassbound Harvard trunk handed down from his father and in which the old man's mementos were mixed with his. He hadn't known what else to do with his father's last effects.

Grunting, Wes went down in front of the trunk in an angled half-crouch. The accumulated grime and spider output made him hesitate; he had forgotten gloves. With mental apology to his daughters, he pulled on a sleeve puppet of a giraffe with coy eyelashes and batted away the cobwebs. Then he cautiously blew the dust off the trunk and lifted its lid.

His father's things were the top few strata of its holdings. Brittle mummy-brown scrapbooks; on the first page of the first one that came open, a Miles City newspaper account of the inception of the Montana Stockmen's Association in 1885. Wes could not help running his finger down the list of the men who possessed the prairie then: Granville Stuart, the bookish cattle king chosen as president; James Fergus, who had a county named after him; among the others, the invited ranch operators from just over the Dakota line, including one T. Roosevelt. Wes knew enough of the story; certain members of the cattlemen's group had evolved immediately into vigilantes with pedigrees. Secret lynching crews—Stuart's Stranglers—had been set loose against suspected rustlers in the Missouri Breaks and across the eastern plains of Montana. He ran down the founders' list again, even though he was as sure as anything can be. Notably missing was the name Williamson. *That was like him.* Whatever else might be said about his father, Warren Williamson had always had his own way of doing things in the Two Medicine country.

He stacked the scrapbooks aside, then with soldierly care lifted out the holstered horse pistol that young Lieutenant Warren Williamson had used with effect in the Union cavalry corps, and never after. It took Wes over for a moment, the antique pistolry of his father's war compared to the mammoth-caliber barrages of his own. *A peashooter like this to Big Bertha—there's progress for you.* He stuck the gun aside with the scrapbooks and dipped again into the trunk until he could reach what he was looking for. There, beneath it all, the box that he and Whit had long ago agreed they wanted off the ranch.

Surprisingly light but awkward to handle, at least the thing had a carry-string, as such boxes do; he wouldn't have to go there holding it in both hands like something that was about to spill. *Not that it's anything that will ever wash out, no matter how careful I am.* The box had risen, in his grasp, only to the brass-edged rim of the trunk, insecurely resting where the corners lipped together. Holding it there he stayed in the half-crouch, still deciding, bothered raw both ways. There would have been a time when he'd have prayed, in such a position, to work out what to do; sought some justifying snippet of code in the holy accumulation of teachings, some overlooked affidavit of motive that would spell out whether to keep the silence or let this box speak its piece. But, in a wealth of confusion as unsortable as the attic around him, faith had entirely too many meanings in this situation. The word was as shifting as bits of alphabet shaken into a kaleidoscope: a twitch back or forth spun up a different color-stained letter of faith that one or another of them had put full belief into.

Wes drew a deciding sift of breath through his teeth. He hadn't become who he was by letting others put their spin on things. Lifting the box on up, already he was fashioning his route out past Merrinell for the evening. Benny Leonard's bout tonight; he would say Phil had happened onto ringside tickets. Lightweights usually went the full fifteen rounds, that would give him ample time. He could cover with details from the morning paper, if she showed curiosity. That wasn't likely.

He lugged the box downstairs and stashed it at the back of his closet, cleaned up and changed into clothes for the evening. The preliminary with Merrinell aside, the worst he faced now was killing time until dark. *It doesn't stay killed, that's the problem. It lies around in us in piles until something like this fans air into it.*

It was full night when he emerged from the taxi, stood stock-still on the sidewalk to see if he was going through with this, then pushed off on his good leg and approached the door.

Quicker than he had figured, Susan was down from her quarters to answer his rap. Abruptly she stood there only the distance of the sill from him, angular but poised, still magical in the nightframe of light, which made this even worse. Surprise came and went on her face, and something else settled in as he watched.

"What's wrong?" Not that she had to ask.

Everything. Us. The two of you. The history that our skins are the descendants of. The fact that life wants to be so strict with us that we only have to strike a match to catch a whiff of Hell. The skirmishes of desire that we fall into blind, and make worse. The list could go on. Wes waited, not ready to try to put any of it into words while perched on a doorstep.

Susan gauged him some more, his elegance at odds with the thing on a string dangling in his hand as if he were an unwilling participant in a scavenger hunt. "You're not just taking that for a stroll, I suppose. You had better come in, come up." She led the way up the stairs, glancing at him over her shoulder. He still carried what he came with. "A bonnet box? Collecting Easter finery now, are you?" He simply trudged up after her, tread by tread, still wordless.

They came into the organized muss of the room she used for work. Correspondence files were stacked, state by state, on the trestle table along the wall. With the typewriter on its traveling stand neatly drawn up beside the raft of paperwork, that end of the room looked scrupulously secretarial. The writing desk by the window, on the other hand, had a strew of music sheets as if a whirlwind had gone through a concert hall.

He stood as if brought in on inspection, she stood watching him. Neither of them showed any inclination to sit. "Major," she said as if trying out a word in another language. "You're in, you're up, and you have a captive audience. Has the cat got your tongue?"

"There's talk. About Monty and you."

"And not much of it for," she estimated forthrightly. "Except your own spirited defense of our normal adult right to such conduct, I'll bet anything."

"Susan, don't mock, not now." He gave her a gaze crimped with pain, then looked off from her unyielding eyes. Whiter than the music sheets on the desk were the coupled pages, open, with the fountain pen in the seam between them like a bookmark. It was the time of night, he realized, when she did her diary.

"It's all in there, I suppose? If I had any sense I'd probably make you an offer on it. Maybe that would make this go away."

"Wes, not even you can buy ink back from the page."

He felt the cut of that, but would have let parts of him be lopped off rather than betray it to her just now. As solidly as if on guard duty, he stood planted to his chosen spot of the room and challenged: "Can you drop it, this with Monty?"

She shook her head. "Even if I could, I'm not sure I would scoot away from him on anybody else's say. All people have to do is look the other way if they don't like the shades of our faces together. You look all too bothered by it yourself." Her eyes were penetrating now. "Cuba? You never?" She trailed a finger on the black leather cushion of the desk chair. "You didn't even once touch a woman this color? Or this?" She touched the mahogany-brown corner of the trestle table. "Or this?" The warm walnut tone of the window ledge. "You really must have been an exceptional soldier if you never resorted to a woman darker than you when you were a young buck on leave, furlough, whatever. Didn't even your Saint Augustine ask for virtue only when he was ready for it?"

"Please, Susan, don't—what race Monty is, isn't the direct reason I—"

"No? Indirect? Just a little something that sets you off like this? Wes, I suppose you're entitled to a man's usual hissy fit because I'm drawn to someone else and you couldn't imagine it happening. But this other—you'd better tear that out of your bones."

"There's more in back of it than that." He undid the lid of the hat-box and brought out an old cavalry hat, battered and less than intact.

SOLDIERS

· 1889 ·

A FROWN WAS not something you wanted to see on Ninian Duff, particularly when it was in connection with his trigger finger.

On the horse beside his, Donald Erskine also sat looking as peeved as a parson whose Sunday dinner had been interrupted, which in a sense it had. The two of them were out after deer, and there near the upper pasture salt lick where their small herd of red cattle was congregated, a sly three-point buck and his dainty does were picking their way ever so gradually to the lure of the lick. Tempting as the presence of venison was, Ninian kept on tapping his finger against the walnut grip of his rifle but made no move to draw the long gun from its saddle scabbard.

Finally his words bit the air:

"I don't see my brockle-face."

"Nor my cow with the one horn," Donald said bleakly.

This was the third time since calving that cows of theirs had gone missing, no matter how anxiously one or the other of them rode up here noon and night from the labors of their homesteads to check on the livestock, and they long since had absolved bears, wolves, and other four-legged suspects. Much the greater likelihood, they were by now convinced, was a hidden corral somewhere considerably to the north of here near the agency for the Blackfeet reservation, where a few cows at a time were butchered, their hides burned, and the cheap rustled beef doled out as tribal allotment by some conniving agent who booked it at market price and pocketed the difference. Scottishly numerate as they were, Ninian and Donald had worked out that the economics of someone stealing their cattle only by twos and threes must necessitate a regular wage somewhere for the riders involved; rustling as an encouraged sideline, a bit of a bonus. It weighed constantly on both men: encouragement of that kind had only one logical home in the Two Medicine country, and its address bore a double set of the letter W.

Donald dourly glanced across at the thundercloud that was his oldest friend's bearded face. These were men who at the best of times were not happy with the thought that they were being toyed with.

"Ninian, are you lighting on what I am, though? That obstinate brockle of yours—"

"Ay, her natural element is the brush, isn't it." Ever a verifier, Ninian glanced behind them at the North Fork's coil of cottonwoods and willows where the brockle-face herd quitter liked to lurk, fly season or not. He and Donald had had to fight her out of there to bring her to fresh pasture with the others. Now he turned his eyes in the direction that led to the reservation. "Let's just see if our callers are earning misery by trying to drive her."

"Old Williamson thinks it's so easy, walking over us," Donald mused. "Sheriff in his pocket, and us thin on the ground."

"One day he's going to have another think coming." Ninian rose in his saddle as if testing the air. "Just possibly today."

The two men rode north at a quick trot, into a carrying wind that they somehow knew would aid their cause. Beside them but a mile loftier, the Rockies already showed early snow, November's first bright ash of the dwindling year, the third one these determined men had expended on the landclaims that drew them and theirs to America. They used the uneven ground to advantage today, riding in short order to familiar timberline on Breed Butte so they could see across the swale of Noon Creek and all the way onward to the kettle hills between the next creeks, Birch and Badger. No horsemen nor abducted cattle out in the open, near or far. Exchanging looks of satisfaction that their objects of pursuit were not making a run for it, Ninian and Donald urged their horses down toward the jackpines and brush that hemmed the foothills.

* * *

They came onto the rustlers not far into the gulch country at the head of Noon Creek. The bawling brought by the wind sent them off their horses. Each man jacked a shell into the chamber of his rifle, then slid another into the magazine to have it fully loaded, and side by side they maneuvered up the low hogback ridge that the creek bent around. Just below the brow of it, they removed their hats and cautiously looked things over from behind an outcropping. The commotion was beyond a rifleshot away but, as they had figured it would be, was happening at the tangle of the creek brush. Taking her stand there in the diamond willows, the brockle was lowing like a mad thing. The pair of men on horseback who, by chance, were trying to drive the worst cow ever created kept circling her vicinity as if they were on a frustrating carousel.

"One's a black fellow, Ninian."

"Thieves are plaid."

The lay of the land was not bad for their purpose, they decided. "I'd say let's try them from that coulee," Ninian provided in the same low murmur they always used when hunting.

To make sure they were playing the same hand, Donald countered: "And then?"

"It's still the old drill, isn't it. 'Ready, steady, fire.'"

"Hurry the hell up, Rathbun, dab the rope on her," Flannery encouraged or jeered, it was hard to tell which, while he more or less hazed the one-horned cow away from joining the brush expedition.

Mose flung him a look that would have taken a trooper's head off, but had no apparent effect on his fellow taker of cows. Flannery's qualifications for rustling apparently amounted to his having been in a scrape of some kind in Texas. *Not that mine are a hell of a lot better,* Mose had to admit to himself as the brockle-faced cow went one side of a willow clump and his lasso toss caught only wood. Easy money for a bit of hard riding, this was not turning out to be.

"Roping was not in my schooling," Mose rumbled back, but on his next throw his loop flopped over the cow's neck. Immediately she bellowed and lurched deeper into the willow thicket before he could manage to dally his rope around the saddlehorn and get his horse started on dragging her out of there.

"Better see this," he heard Flannery say as if he was at a sideshow. "Couple of honyocker fools think they're an army. Ready to take 'em?"

Still cinched to the creature in the brush by the lariat, Mose dubiously turned half around in his saddle. Flannery for once wasn't just woofing. The pair of men at the mouth of the coulee were a great deal closer than Mose liked to see. One figure like a mop, the other like a chopping block, both of them in antiquated infantry kneel that he had only ever seen in tattered manuals. And probably were shaking in their boots, but even so—Flannery carried just a pistol, the idiot, and right now he was a lot slower with it than advertised. Plainly it was up to Mose. In the matter of instants needed for all this to register, he kick-spurred his horse forward to take the tension off that rope while simultaneously pulling his carbine from the scabbard.

Before Mose's rifle was clear of the leather, Ninian shot the horse from under him.

Donald's rifle echoed an instant after his, and Flannery went out of his saddle backward, hit at the base of his throat.

In the brush, the horse on its side kicking out the last of its life and the alarmed cow trying to crash its way free of rope and willow, Mose scrambled on all fours to dodge them and the prospect of hanging for rustling as well. He panted raggedly, most of his breath knocked out when the ground flew up and met him. When he had cover enough he flopped low, trying to clear his head. Bonus on these damnable cows or not, this wasn't anywhere in the bargain with Williamson, for a person to get the life shot out of him like had just happened with Flannery. Where'd these sharpshooting fiends show up from? Opponents came and went, in soldier life, but surprise was forever the enemy. Dry-mouthed, and not liking the taste of that, Mose ever so slowly began to wriggle through the brush. The rifle he had lost in his hard spill was somewhere right here, and he hadn't yet seen a situation he and a cavalry-issue Springfield couldn't deal with. The damn thing could not have flown very far when he hit the dirt. As he crept in search, it was on his mind that the honyockers were not firing wildly the way a person had a reasonable right to expect, not mowing down brush every time a willow swayed. They would not be anywhere near out of ammunition, the devils. He would have to deal with that as it came, if he just could ever find the damn—

There. He spotted the Springfield behind a thatch of willows about twice the length of his body away. Counting on the screen of brush to give him enough hiding place to get into action and make quick work of these down-on-their-knees scissorbills, he gathered himself and scooted low and fast to make a grab for the weapon.

Ninian dropped him with the next shot, and when Mose went on thrashing, shot him again for good measure.

The sound of the rifle fire repeated from gulch to gulch, then rolled away at last into the timber at the base of the mountains. Rising as righteous bearded men had from the plains of Jericho, Ninian and Donald at once began about the next of this messy business. As he stalked cautiously toward the creek Ninian worked it out in his mind that they would have to hope to get into those deer on their way back, to account for all the sounds of shooting. Not that he at all liked the prospect of alibiing that they had banged away at venison for half a day until finally hitting some, but there was no choice.

Even with the echoes of the shots at last stilled, the silence seemed to ring. Ninian looked everywhere around. The two cows were hieing for home, the lariat still dangling from the brockle-face. Without expression he examined the hunched-over dark man he had killed. Nearby, Donald's victim lay toes-up, an incredulous expression on his face and a red stain over his entire chest. The one in front of Ninian at least did not look as if this was never expected.

By now Donald had coaxed the riderless horse and tied its reins to the trunk of a young cottonwood. He came puffing over and in his turn studied down at the two riders where they lay, then blew out a long breath. "Old Williamson is going to be cross toward us."

"I doubt that he will," Ninian spoke in his most considering tone. "I would wager that two empty beds at the bunkhouse will give him more than he wants to think about. No, it seems our man Williamson shies away from all-out war on the likes of us or he wouldn't have spent so much care trying to just peck us to death, a few cows at a time. The Williamson way is to work around the edges, I'd say. At any rate, he'll know now we're not so easily done away with."

Donald's round cheeks still were the color of cottage cheese.

"Donald. They had guns, we had guns. The race is to the swift, man."

"I know it is. Still, this isn't like when they chaired us through the Castle grounds while we waved the shire targetry trophy around, is it."

"Edinburgh or here," Ninian was giving no ground, "marksmanship in a good cause is no sin. Let's get cracking. We'll use the other horse with ours to drag that one into the beaver dams there, then do away with it." He studied down at the bodies, his beard moving with the grimace beneath. "As to our adversaries, I'm afraid their graves are going to have to be coyotes' bellies." Luckily there was plenty of country, back in here, and the pair could be disposed of in one timber-thick gulch or another. As a known man of the Bible, Ninian had spoken at more funerals than he could count, but this occasion necessarily lacked holy words. Before starting on making the dead vanish to the extent that they would, Ninian put a hand on the shoulder of his companion. "Never a word, Donald. You understand that? To anyone. We never can."

"Jen knows my every breath."

"Jen will need to forbear, this once. As will Flora." A grim light of idea came into Ninian's eyes. "Williamson, though. Let's give him something further to think about. We'll leave a hat on that wood gate of his. A bit of homesteader glue"—a piece of barbed wire—"will hold it until they find it."

Donald scooped up both hats and, one in each hand, asked punctiliously: "Which, for the occasion?"

"It doesn't much matter. I suppose the one with the play-pretty on it stands out a bit better." Donald handed him Mose's hat with the crossed-swords escutcheon of the Tenth Cavalry pinned front and center.

For a moment Ninian held the well-worn hat as if it deserved better, then hung it on the barrel tip of his lifted rifle. "Just so there won't be any doubt about how this came out." Pointing the gun off across the prairie, he blasted a hole through the hat with one last shot.

FINALE

· 1925 ·

"THERE'S NO OTHER way it could have been," Wes concluded, after his necessarily bare-bones version. "A shot-up hat doesn't barb-wire itself to a gate. Especially the gate squarely between our holdings and Scotch Heaven." His voice had gone unusually soft. The telling of it had taken long enough that he'd had to rest his weight against the trestle table. There beside him, as if on fashion-of-the-season display, the battleworn hat reposed atop the hatbox. "Whit and I—we were the ones who found it."

Dry-mouthed, with the hard corners of the story still bruising in her as she thought it through, Susan could see the rest of it as if it were taking place now as puppet-play on that table. Royal cubs with the run of the ranch, he and Whit bringing the hat to their father in excited curiosity. The old manipulator, out-manipulated, his guns outgunned, pulling back to a waiting game. Angeline Rathbun and Monty, casualties of Mose's disappearance, reduced to charitable charges. And coming home to Scotch Heaven, that day, with a blood-writ added to their landclaims there, her father in his Jehovan determination and reliable Donald beside him, their silences deeper than ever and their spines stronger than Warren Williamson's.

When she could manage, she asked harshly:

"This couldn't wait? Past tomorrow night?"

For an instant, Wes's facial muscles backed away from the ferocity of her tone, but his flinch just as quickly fell before the resolute expression he had worked up to, coming here. "I thought it might be harder on you to find out then."

"Harder?"

Her voice ripped him. "Oh, let's travel round more such Christian ground," she tore onward. "A kick in the heart is better a day early than a day late, is that your thinking? Wes, damn you, if you've pulled this stunt with Monty too. *Tell me! No, look at me and tell me!* If you've thrown him, with everything riding on tomorrow night—"

"I haven't said word one to him. We never have." The Williamson *We,* embedded in Wes since the christening moment when it was made part of his name. Susan struggled with the ramifications from that answer, him and his. Do the Double W's of life, principalities of the prairie and other swaths of the earth, entitle themselves to their own rules? Take unto themselves the privilege to use the Mose Rathbuns like poker chips, then when their bluff is called, convert the washhouse to sanctuary for the widow and orphan? Ever so charitably never saying word one, of course, letting silence hide the past, and does that wash them clean? Does kindly deceit count as a charity? In this blooded instance, was she in a position to say it didn't?

Amid all that was raging in her she had to marvel at Wes, she couldn't even make his eyes drop. She shook her head as if bringing herself out of a spell. "So it's up to me, is it. You spring this on me. And now I'm supposed to what—swear off Monty as if I were taking the temperance vow? Or hand this along to him: 'By the way, my father one time did away with a rustler who happened to be your father—more tea, my dear?'"

"Susan," he pleaded, "you and I haven't been able to line out any kind of life together, don't I know that. But if you try it with Monty, just by the nature of things you'll be up against worse trouble."

"I wonder, Wes. I wonder."

Her words were like pepper in the air. "All this. You backing Monty once he saw how to make something of himself. Then coming to me—'I have the pupil of a lifetime for you,'" she mimicked with sad accuracy. "All that expense and involvement. What did you think you were doing, rinsing out your conscience or the Williamson family conscience, such as that might be? Or buying yourself forgiveness for being a Williamson, were you? Granting yourself an indulgence, was that it? My understanding is that went out several dozen popes ago." If that drew blood on him somewhere, he did not let it show. "Monty has had his own reasons to wonder what you're up to, did that occur to you? Even if you didn't outright think of him as bait for the Klan"—Wes's lips parted, but no sound issued—"weren't you glad to rub him in on them, boost him to show them how little they are? And luck or design, have it work out that you had your whack at them, in the end?" With a catch in her throat she relentlessly went on down the list. "Or was it all to coax me around. Did you want Scotch Heaven, what's left of it, that badly?" Her last charge was the calmest and therefore the worst. "Or do you even know what you were playing at, anymore?"

"Are you through?"

Her glare said no, but she compressed the rest into an accusing silence for him to try to fight out of.

Wes made the effort. "Tomorrow night Monty steps onto the stage at Carnegie Hall. He *is* the pupil of your life, Susan, you can't get around that, unless you manage to take Chaliapin under your wing. Maybe I didn't know precisely what I was setting into motion, but where was the push for any of it if it hadn't come from me? Monty didn't look you up on his own, did he, and you didn't come scouting the woods for his voice that I know of." Susan said nothing to that, an acknowledgment of sorts. For this next, Wes kept himself anchored with a white-knuckled grip on the table while he forced out the words: "Given that, I can ask as much as anyone—who's been up to what? I didn't do this to start a Lonelyhearts Club for Monty, you can bet on that."

"Well, there now," she said point-blank back at him. "Just that quick you're more sure of your motive than you've shown so far."

"This isn't getting us anywhere," he gave in to battle fatigue. "What do you say we wait until the Observance is out of the way and talk this over sanely."

"Which means you better leave now, while the wind is with you," her burr of anger sounding for all the world like her father's. She stalked back toward her desk and the still-opened diary, flinging a hand of contempt at the cavalry hat as she passed it. "And you may as well leave that."

N OT bad," J.J. sized up the nicely appointed accommodations the next afternoon, a discreet suite at the rear of Carnegie Hall usually reserved for performers whose travel arrangements nudged uncomfortably close to performance time, "the Carnies giving us out-of-towners' treatment." The three from Harlem shared out a grin that said *Pretty much what we are* and helped themselves to the atmosphere of luxury. Cecil adjusted the royal-blue drapes to his liking as Monty poked his head into a bedroom twice the size of the washhouse quarters where he had spent his ranch life. *Couldn't have whistled for this.* Susan at that moment was in the working part of the hall, he knew, on the early side to help oversee arrangements for the Observance. *We're both here, at the tip of the top. Take that, odds,* that particular observation warming him as if he and she had confounded all the laws of all the games of chance. With just enough of a smile, he took off his hat and skimmed it in onto the extravagant bed.

"They're going to want us spang on time for the runthrough, what with all the bigwigs," J.J. was getting back to business. "Montgomery, you going to catch some rest first, I hope?"

"Figured I'd sack out a while like usual, sure."

"Cece, you?"

"Not me, I have to see to my piano." He already was on his way out to company that better befitted Carnegie Hall, his expression said.

After the slam of the door J.J. chuckled. "He'll settle down, always does. I see here"—he flapped a hand on the rehearsal schedule—"there's quite a set of speeches before your turn. If you want, Cece and I can hold the fort until they're about done practicing those, then I can come fetch you."

Monty gave a short sharp shake of his head. "I want to be there for the whole works." *She's there.* Now he said in easy fashion but meaning it: "While Cecil's playing with his piana, I hope you're going to polish up your medals and slap them on."

Trying not to look embarrassed and pleased, J.J. tucked away the schedule in the handiest pocket and muttered: "Polish up Phil Sherman, more like. I better go see if there are any kinks in the production, be the first time if there aren't. I'll roust you thirty minutes before the rehearsal." Monty nodded to that, and turned to follow his hat to the regal welcome of the bed.

"Montgomery?" J.J. sounded as if a kink had occurred to him. But something in the way that the lanky figure tautened to hear what was coming put a pause in him. Swallowing, J.J. said only: "Sweet dreams, man. You've earned them."

There on the soft raft of bed, borne by tides he couldn't have forecast if he had tried when he and she and the Major first embarked on this, Monty let himself drift, half there, half in the latitudes of yearning: Susan and the night's music, the night's music and Susan. Not so much a nap as a trance, this time of waiting. Susan he had made up his mind on, and to keep from battering himself endlessly on the nerve ends of that, he mentally worked through the songs, the imaginary flow of piano keys beneath them, even though he knew them as well as his own skin. Maybe better. Always there was going to be a mystery in that, why the fairly puny human range of colors—nobody was cat-puke green, were they? there wasn't any race that was an aggravating eggplant purple, was there?—didn't register all the same in the basic human eye.

"We are not some kind of a stain on other people's notion of things," she had said. No, he thought, but we're not the pattern they show any sign of picking out to like, either. Her own decision, as far as it went: "Let's see what happens after your tour." That was the trick, all right, seeing ahead when life kept stretching over the curve of the world.

Restlessly he rolled onto his side, but a moment later he was on his back again, half-spreadeagled with an arm over his eyes as he tried to imagine tonight. What J.J. had started to say and didn't, he perfectly well knew, was some sort of encouragement about the audience. *Right, J.J., just the usual riffraff that wanders into Carnegie Hall, hmm?* Words were no help on the audience question, the stomach juices were what made the statement. All he could do was to gird himself—he'd been doing that since he first set foot into the soft soil of a rodeo arena, hadn't he. By now he ought to know pretty much all there was to know about girding. He put his hand to where the scars were, his ribcage and then the column of his throat, reflexively tracing those near misses of death in a manner as old as when warriors of *The Iliad* touched places where their armor had shielded off a blow, as thankful as when a cavalryman stroked a brass buckle that had turned a bullet. Oddly, he found that the grievous harms he carried on himself put him in a calmer mood for tonight. Plenty of company coming tonight, when it came to bearing wounds: the shot-up veterans, like—well, like the Major; the busloads down from Harlem, unpenned for one night from the segregation line at 125th Street. Everybody who would be here tonight was a survivor of something. His voice would need to reflect that.

"Whatever patient clock ticks out there in the night of the universe has brought us again to the eleventh day of the eleventh month, which holds the moment of stillness when the Great War stopped. Into that holy silence of the Armistice we bring, on this night of observance, the greatest vows of which we are capable, some in spoken word, some in glorious song, all from the heartsprings deepest within us."

Wes broke off reading and stepped away from the microphone. "And it goes on like that for a further four minutes and thirty seconds," he notified the stage echelon of command congregated in the wings. He was truculent about the rehearsal, Susan could tell. Of all of them, Wes was a maestro of impromptu, his political years having given him a natural ease at climbing up in front of any gathering and speaking his piece. *I can think of one I wish he had choked on.*

The stage manager hastily clicked his stopwatch off, Phil Sherman looking bemused beside him. "Major, we have plenty of rehearsal time, you are free to go through your whole speech."

"What for?" the shortly put question answered itself. "You requested five minutes' worth and that's what it will be." Wes all but marched off the stage, the slight hitch in his gait made increasingly plain as he covered the desert-like distance from centerstage.

Been around the man since he came back with that in '18 and never noticed it that much. That told Monty something about the proportion of matters here. One more time he studied around at the amplitude of

Carnegie Hall; the place was the definition of big, all right. Extra-tall fancy-peaked doorways with what looked like lions' forelegs carved high up on the frames, huge columns of some Greek kind set into the walls, atmosphere of a mansion about to be toned up for a party—and all that was simply on the stage. Out front, the gilded horseshoe balconies were banked, up and up, like decks of a topheavy steamboat. Not long from now an audience would squash into that expanse like the representation of everything on two legs; even here at rehearsal this place had a couple of rows full, as if the listening level always had to be kept going like a low fire. J.J. had whispered to him that Vandiver had salted the rehearsal with any of Over There's big givers—"the Major's crowd"—who wanted to come and gawk, and the Carnegie Hall management was there in force as a mark of respect to such wallet power. In his performance tux as he waited with the others in the wings to step out in front of this chosen bunch, Monty felt very nearly underdressed.

Susan and he were not standing near each other in the gaggle in the wings, they were mutually showing at least that much common sense. Cued now by the stage manager, she stepped out, heart pounding in spite of her willed poise, strode smoothly to the microphone stand there beneath the proscenium of all American prosceniums, and delivered a ringing recital about the Harlem letters. She made way for Tammany's man in Harlem, whom no one expected to follow Wes's example of deferring a speechmaking chance until the house was full. Nor did he.

In the comedy spot, Butterbeans and Susie strolled on and traded contentious married-couple wisecracks. Then Susan once more, to introduce the Lincoln Theater house announcer, Charles York, for the reading of selections from the Harlem war archive in his basso profundo.

Vandiver was to follow this with his spiel for Bonds of Peace and as he zeroed in on the microphone, J.J. slid over by Monty and murmured, "You're up next."

Everything else necessarily came to a halt as Monty sighted-in his voice from various spots on the stage to choose his mark. The first time he sent "When I was young and in my prime, I dabbed my X on the Medicine Line" soaring out into the hall, he glanced upward for a moment, then turned his head enough to wink at J.J.: no swaying chandelier.

Susan had slipped away into the main-floor seats to hear this. As the bell-clear tone shimmered through the air of the hall each time Monty tested the line, she moved from one spot to another, momentarily pushing all else from her mind for his music. From any velvet-seated sector, he sounded simply glorious.

It took more tries than usual—this was Carnegie Hall, after all—but when he indicated the place on the stage he was settling for, stagehands wheeled out the grand piano and its spot was duly tape-marked as well. Over by the curtain Cecil went up on tiptoes and serenely down again, part of his ritual before presenting himself. As if reminded of something, Monty turned to the stage manager. "There is one change I need to make in the program."

Busy making his lighting notations on a clipboard, the stage manager said aside: "You're getting a bit ahead of us, Mister Rathbun—we can deal with that as you run through the music."

"Can't either," Monty genially contradicted him. "It has to do with the music right from the start. I would like for Miss Duff to be my accompanist tonight."

J.J.'s head jerked around from conversation with Phil Sherman. Cecil looked sucker-punched. Down in the front rows, the well-dressed givers sat up as if now they were starting to get their considerable money's worth.

Where she was roving the main floor, Susan heard Monty's words like a firebell and sped for the doorway that led to backstage.

"Seems like it'd be fitting," Monty offered around generally, as if the frozen onstage group had asked for his opinion and here it was, "what with all she's done to bring in the Harlem side of things for tonight."

The stage manager straightened up as if bracing to be struck by lightning next. Seeing that Monty appeared serious, he said in a carefully juggled voice: "I'm afraid that's not on. Miss Duff may be a perfectly capable musician in her own right, I'm sure. But tonight has been advertised as you and Cecil—"

"—and of course that's the understanding with the radio hookup," Vandiver inserted swiftly.

"—that's the way we're set up," the stage manager said with a conclusive shrug, "that's the point of this rehearsal."

"No, the music part of the rehearsal hasn't really got under way yet, has it," Monty pointed out, all reasonableness. "That's why I figured this is the time I better let you know she's the one I want at those keys." He called over consolingly, "Just tonight, Cece."

"I'm sorry, but I don't see how—" The stage manager searched out the house manager with a despairing look.

The house manager, crisp as the point of his Vandyke beard, knew how to handle a tiff of this sort: "Speak up here, Phil, you're the producer."

"Monty, as long as Cecil is in good health, we're obligated to do the program as advertised," Phil called out. "If we haven't given notification of a substitution three days before the performance, the management has the right to—"

Monty cut him off. "Rights are sure cropping up here all of a sudden. Where've they been hiding before now? The way I savvy it, Harlem didn't get invited down here much, before tonight. Before this lady pitched in." He looked around as if marveling. "And you know what, I thought the acoustics would be better in a place like this. Everybody? One more time: I would like for Miss Duff to be at that piana."

From where he was watching in the wings, Wes in spite of himself had to grade Monty right up there in tactics. *Maybe he did learn something in those Clore Street scuffles. If you're going to run a bluff, why not run a big one.*

Abruptly Susan flew past him, giving him a look that forgave nothing of last night but shared an understanding of how things avalanched, and charged onward to the group moiling at centerstage like a troupe having trouble remembering its lines. She caught her breath and pierced the circle of disputing men.

"Van, Phil, let me—Mister Rathbun, that's wildly generous of you, but we haven't even practiced for this."

Monty let that sail in one end of his smile and out the other. "A musician of your experience can catch on to these songs in no time, I'm sure."

"Gentlemen and all," J.J. spoke up. "Give me a minute with my client. Montgomery?" Not quite plucking Monty's sleeve but plainly wanting to, he indicated with his head toward the nearest stage door.

"Excuse me, everybody, I have to smooth some feathers," Monty said to the assemblage as though J.J. had come down with a raging disorder. "Miss Duff," he called over, his eyes saying to her *Susan, Susan,* "don't let them talk you out of this, none. It's going to work out."

As quickly as Monty and J.J. disappeared through the stage door, Phil set about talking her out of it. "A performer sometimes gets this kind of bee in his bonnet," he said as if confiding a truth learned the hard way on Broadway. "Nerves, I'm sure."

"Maybe the singular of that in this case, Phil," she retorted.

"Whichever. It would help like anything if you were to go over to Monty and say you're honored, but you're just not up to playing to a packed house"—he feathered that in as though it would be rude to outright say a Carnegie Hall packed house—"on such short notice."

Beside Phil, Vandiver nodded with vigor to encourage her in that direction. The Carnegie Hall staff one after another looked at their watches discreetly. She stood there as if the stage had taken hold of her. Not one of these glorified supernumeraries counted any more than the ushers when it came to the making of the music, as Monty wanted of her. All at once the words arrived to her, cool and clear:

"I *am* honored. And I don't know that I'm not up to it."

She knew wondering looks were being passed behind her. She swung her own gaze to Wes. He looked away.

Backstage, J.J. cut loose on Monty: "Are you that far out of your mind? The Carnies are never going to go for that woman, and even if they did the Over Theres won't—you see the look on Vandiver and Philip, and even your buddy the Major? They don't know whether to crap in their hats or go blind."

"I'm the one going to get up there and sing at this Observance of theirs," Monty said dead-level. "Let me have the say, this once."

"Be reasonable here." J.J. himself was frantic. "We both know Cecil is a prune, but he's the best in the business."

"Not my business, he isn't," Monty retorted with equal force. "You forgetting that every one of those song arrangements are hers, are you? That woman, as you call her—the bones in her fingers are the same color as ours, J.J. She savvies the music, that's what counts."

J.J. sucked in his breath. "Don't be doing this, Montgomery. How many ways do I have to beg?" He cast an indicating glance through the doorway at the huddle of Carnegie officials. "They'll snake out on us—the 'professional standards' clause. You and Miss Pond Cream can sort yourselves out however you damn want, but not here. You say one more time that she has to be at that piano and they'll be on the telephone getting hold of Robeson's manager, or Roland Hayes's, or haul in Blind Mortimer from the streetcorner, if it comes to that. Somebody to step in while we're thrown out. You're asking for it, my friend."

"Let's just see."

The onstage bunch and the now keenly attentive front-row onlookers saw in a hurry: Monty coming back out looking serenely stubborn, J.J. saying with a shake of his head that was that.

The house manager looked at his watch again, nothing discreet about it this time. "Phil, J.J., I'm sorry but as of now we're giving notice—"

"Let's be clear here." Wes's voice took command of the stage. He heard himself saying: "Notice is being *given,* all right, but I don't hear it noticeably being *taken.*"

In the massive silence that met that, he mechanically strode out onto the apron of the stage, contriving as he came. "I don't see what the commotion is about," he boomed, casting a glance at the piano as if even he could play it. "I particularly asked this of Monty. He was simply trying to carry out the favor."

Even more so than Susan, Monty had experience of the ungodly capacities of the Williamsons, but this stretch from the Major startled him to the absolute limits of his ability to keep a straight face. He gazed at the Major—rescuer, rival, sugar daddy in all this, in-over-his-head debtor to somebody in all this—with thankful wonderment. *I figured something would give if I could stay dug in hard enough here. Never thought it would be him. Who knew he'd lie for us like this?*

As Wes's sentences added up, Susan felt the agony of last night leave her and something like prospect come in its place. *Wes, you holy fool or whatever you are. Not even you can calculate the cost of this act.*

Front and center, Wes looked all around, as if to make sure everyone present was wide awake. He needn't have bothered. Several dozen sets of the most appraising eyes in New York were taking this in. His glance passed over Susan, over Monty, a flicker of resolve in it for each of them. *If each other is so damn much what you need, this is the one way I can give you that.*

Pivoting toward the group mid-stage who had thought they were in charge of tonight, he split the cloud of speculative staring, drew the lightning onto himself. "Miss Duff is—someone I've admired from afar, during our time together on the committee. And out West, she has great standing as a musician herself. I thought this would be a way Over There could repay her for her services a bit. I don't like to throw my weight around on this, but the rest of you are busy doing it. So I must insist. If she isn't at the piano tonight, I cancel my backing. What I'm putting up for the Observance, what I've pledged for the Bonds of Peace, any annual giving ever again to the Hall—the works."

The house manager had no trouble reaching his decision. "Van?"

"That does put a different light on things, Major," Vandiver said tightly. "We appreciate your forthrightness. Naturally, now that we know the full circumstances, we can accommodate a special request of this sort. Can't we, Phil." Expressions, masked as they were, in the semi-circle there at centerstage spoke a good deal more in Wes's direction than Vandiver's words. *Stage door Johnny. Overage schoolboy with a crush. Lothario with more money than sense.* Phil's face simply said, *Bye-bye, old friend.*

Head and heart high, Monty stepped toward Susan and gestured her toward the piano as if it was an atoll of refuge. "If you'll excuse us briefly, gentlemen. Miss Duff and I have our music to go over."

I T IS in gatherings such as this that the man of war—man in his armor, in his uniform of whatever color—must change his stripes and be created anew, in the magnificent pinto skin we form when all our human hues are displayed together." As Wes stepped away to a thunder of handclaps, he had to concede that even the applause sounded better in Carnegie Hall.

He stayed just offstage now that his part in the evening was over. He ached like fury from standing so long on the hard flooring but he kept to his carefully planted stance there and watched Susan radiantly deliver her lines about the Harlem letters collection to perfection, endured Tammany next, then the mid-show comedy and its counter-face of tragedy in the letters and diaries, and as Vandiver began making his pitch for Bonds of Peace, he knew he could delay no longer and moved off to the hallway and stairwell that would take him to his seat up in the box circle.

He stepped with care into the darkened box. Nodded a series of apologies for his lateness as he squeezed behind the retinue his wife and Mrs. Smith had assembled in the seats there. Automatically shook hands with Governor Smith in passing. Merrinell, in whispered conversation with the governor's wife, gave a little acknowledging whisk to where he would sit. His bolster chair was installed at the angle needed to favor his knee, and he settled into it facing a bit away from Merrinell, which he figured he may as well grow used to. From her flutter of gesture, word had not yet reached her about his rehearsal declamation. But it would be told as many ways as there were tellers. When she heard, whatever version she heard, Merrinell with her active history of suspicion would do her best to make his life a ceaseless purgatory. Not that it much resembled anything else to him from here on anyway.

Straightening up, forcing his mind to the moment, Wes looked out over a Carnegie Hall such as he had never seen before, a marbled crowd, rows of colored faces and immediate other rows of pale ones and mixes in between. Below, in the front row and the space between there and the stage and out into the side aisles, were the veterans clutching crutches or armrests of wheelchairs or in the case of the blinded ones, an arm of the person next to them. Their array reminded him of a field hospital, the one place he had seen troops of both colors quartered together in either of his wars.

Up on the stage Vandiver finished as he had begun, with a flourish. Now out they came, one from each wing, Susan to the grand piano and Monty to the music stand near it. A ripple of programs, and more, met her entrance. In what applause of welcome there was, though, Monty walked toward her and extended an arm of introduction. They did not quite touch. Wes fully knew that if they hadn't already done so in private, they soon would.

With one finger, then two, then the fan of his hand as if in pledge, Wes pressed lightly on the breast pocket of his suit where Susan's diary rested. "You'll know the proper cubbyhole for this," she had whispered as she slid it into his hand, backstage, before she went out to speak. In the half-light of the stage manager's nook he had done what anyone would do, gone to the pages of the last few days. Lord, should earthly existence cause a person to laugh or gasp? He wondered how long it might take—into the next century?—before some delving scholar burrowed into the papers of the Double W and the Williamson family, flipped open this stray item as far as the flyleaf and Susan's elongated handwriting there, and be drawn into the diary to its final inkdrops of sentence: *I hope never to be forced into harder deciding than that brought on by Wes's visit tonight, but life being life, who knows. The cavalry hat, and the knot of harm carried in our family lines, are turning to ash in the fireplace as I write this. Needless to say—no, perhaps this is precisely what does need to be set into permanence here—Monty will know from me only the same silence Wes has vowed over this. Some truths stand taller than others, and the one that I am betting the rest of my life on is my love for Monty.*

Monty stepped to the microphone.

"It's my pleasure to bring back onstage Miss Susan Duff, who has kindly agreed to accompany me tonight. She is an A-1 musician in her own right—as we say uptown, she knows how to negotiate the numbers." Laughter spread, dark to white, at that. "The particular number of hers," he played off the line while the audience was still in chuckles, "that we're going to perform for you is the finale of a fine piece she has written. The tune has something of a nocturne to it, and seeing as how we're all nocturnal enough to come out this evening to this particular hall, I thought it might fit the occasion." He paused for a moment to gaze out at them all. "Any of you who have been caught in range of my voice before will know that I've been in the habit of starting things off with an old song of the prairie, where I am from—

and would you believe it, Miss Duff too. Who knows, this one may kick that one aside." Turning his head toward Susan, he nodded just the fraction needed, and the music came.

> *"A tide of grass runs the earth,*
> *The green of hope there in birth,*
> *And where we've together been and how we'll together be*
> *Is all in the rolling song of that prairie sea. . . ."*

Monty could feel the lift of his voice, the lilt of Susan's song, as never before. He was going to sing his way off this earth. The America patch of it, anyway, and not alone. Susan was coming with him on the Europe tour.

At the piano she delicately put the melody under his voice, her every ounce of musicianship focused on Monty at his music stand. He showed no sign of needing to look down.

Her hands knew all there was to do on the keys, and her mind flew ahead. Europe. The join of their lives, which their own country would never let be easy. In asking her if she would come with him, Monty with heartbreaking fairness also had offered her every way out, making her know that all they would be able to count on besides each other would be trouble for being together, until she put the stop to that by saying: "There's no better trouble we could have."

Before coming onstage with Monty, she had peered out past the curtain to spot Wes in the audience, angled apart from the others in his box. His to bear from here on, too, the story as set down. The thought went through her again now, as she knew it every so often would. Then she lost herself into the playing as Monty's transporting voice and her rippling keys combined into the crescendo, the music reaching out over the footlights into the great dimmed-down hall and its unmoving audience, the medaled and the jeweled, the plainspun and the Sunday-clothed, the war-stricken and the spared, the shadow-like faces and the pale, raptly in place out there in the levels of the night as if each in a seat assigned in some dark-held circle of a heaven or a hell, Wes's own as usual custom-made.

ACKNOWLEDGMENTS

Fiction always takes some sleight-of-hand, and in this novel I occasionally bend the corners of time to fit the makings of plot:

—Although the "buffalo soldiers" of the Tenth Cavalry figure here several years earlier, the regiment arrived on assignment to Fort Assinniboine in 1894. John J. Pershing's term of service with the regiment began in October of 1895 and lasted a year; his command of Troop D in evicting Little Bear's band of Crees into Canada occurred in the summer of 1896. The repeated rounding up of the Crees and putting them under military escort to the border, however, was under way in the 1880s as I portray it, and continued sporadically until the displaced tribe obtained land on the Rocky Boy Reservation in northern Montana in 1916.

—The Zanzibar Club, as a sometimes rowdy center of nightlife for Helena's small nonwhite population, had its license lifted by an indignant city council in 1906; I gave it a new lease on life for Monty's purposes in these pages.

—The city of Helena was indeed shaken by an earthquake on the Saturday night of June 27, 1925, but I have conflated the much more severe effects of the big Helena quake a decade later—the evening of October 3, 1935—into my rendering of the disaster.

—The Klan-related killing at Crow Agency that my characters allude to occurred in actuality in 1926, when James Belden was shot to death and burned in his cabin after a fatal exchange of gunfire with the Big Horn County sheriff, who was said to be an official of the Klan.

Similarly, the vow against Klansmen by the sheriff in Butte, to "shoot them down like wolves," was issued in the year 1921. (The insufficiently known story of the Ku Klux Klan's surge westward in the 1920s is provided an overview in *The Invisible Empire in the West: Toward a New Historical Appraisal of the Ku Klux Klan of the 1920s,* edited by Shawn Lay. There also has been some state-by-state examination by historians, most prominently: *Hooded Empire: The Ku Klux Klan in Colorado,* by Robert Alan Goldberg; *Blazing Crosses in Zion: The Ku Klux Klan in Utah,* by Larry R. Gerlach; *Inside the Klavern,* a rare set of minutes of a Klan chapter [in LaGrande, Oregon], annotated by David A. Horowitz. In the instance of Montana, the most comprehensive studies are Dave Walter's article "White Hoods Under the Big Sky" in *Montana Magazine,* Jan./Feb. 1998, and Christine K. Erickson's M.A. thesis at the University of Montana, "The Boys in Butte: the Ku Klux Klan Confronts the Catholics, 1923–1929." My specific description of a Klan membership card is from the records of the 1920s Klan chapter in Harlowton, Montana, archivally held by the Montana Historical Society and the Upper Musselshell Historical Society. I also wish to thank Rayette Wilder, archives librarian of the Northwest Museum of Arts & Culture/Eastern Washington State Historical Society, for information from the society's Montana Ku Klux Klan manuscript collection.)

—The dust storm that overtakes Monty and Wes in the summer of 1924 may seem more characteristic of the drought-stricken 1930s, but one of the most detailed memoirs about the Montana homestead period—*Traces on the Landscape,* by Kent Midgett—recounts dust storms on the sod-broken prairie as early as August and September of 1917. The U.S. Weather Bureau's climatological data for the summer of 1924 in Montana includes a term which prefigured the rural disaster on the northern plains in the Depression years, "a pronounced shortage of rain."

—In a remark by my Broadway character Phil Sherman, I have shuffled Marc Connelly's 1930 spirituals-inspired play *The Green Pastures* into production five years earlier.

—And for purely dramatic purposes I have promoted Varick McCaskill to forest ranger at the fictitious Indian Head station about a year earlier than alluded to in my Two Medicine trilogy about the McCaskills and their times.

Students of the Harlem Renaissance will notice a resemblance in Monty's arc of career, from approximately nowhere to the heady neighborhood of Strivers Row, to that of Taylor Gordon, my fellow townsman back where we were both born, White Sulphur Springs, Montana. The late Mr. Gordon provided his own sprightly telling of that rough ride to New York, and in his case, back to White Sulphur, in his 1929 book, *Born to Be*. But while the example of Taylor Gordon's splendid tenor voice inspired me in the writing of Monty's singing career, the background and personal path of life I have given Monty is as different from his as I have been able to make it. In my attempt to sketch what life might have been like in a tiny community of the early-twentieth-century American West for a person whom we now would call African-American, I have restricted myself to a handful of crystallizing details, and a few sparkling turns of phrase, from the Gordon family itself as told to me by Taylor and his sister Rose in an afternoon-long interview in 1968. Examples include: the passed-down tale, from the time of slavery, of their mother minding the white horse in the woods, which I considerably embellished; Rose's unbetterable phrase about the rough knocks of life, "this old pig-iron world"; the highly appealing recounting of "Angel Momma" when they referred to their mother, which chimed in me with Roland Hayes's term of endearment for his mother, "Angel Mo'"; and Rose's recounting of the joke back on the world she and her brother found themselves in, their habitual pause just out of hearing before joining in on the otherwise all-white gatherings in town, to remark wryly to one another: "Well, the two colored persons are here."

Of the songs I've conjured for my characters to possess, two were born of intriguing phrases in other genres. The "ballad" sung by Susan at Angus's funeral takes its inspiration from a line of "The Making of a Poet," John Davison's haunting poem about the Clydeside port of Greenock: "this old grey town . . . is world enough for me." And in Monty's Medicine Line song, the phrase "forty miles a day on beans and hay" is an irrepressible jingle evidently picked up from a pair of 1875 vaudevillians by various U.S. cavalry units and tailored into their own songs about various campaigns; this musical background and much other lore of the cavalry regulars in the West is told by the late Don Rickey, Junior, in his military history that also used the phrase as its title.

The splendid murk that is the past posed me a couple of spelling puzzles. "Assiniboin" is the customary spelling of the tribal name in the northern borderlands where a portion of this book is set, but the U.S. War Department of the time dubbed the military post established there in 1879 "Fort Assinniboine"; I've used the military spelling because it preponderates in historical references to the once-massive fort. And in the instance of the private whose last name is given in half the histories of the Lewis and Clark expedition as "Fields" and the other half as "Field," I've followed the lead of Gary Moulton, editor of the most complete edition of the Lewis and Clark journals, in calling him Joseph Field.

Devoutly as it might be wished to exist, no journal account by Joseph Field nor his brother Reuben nor George Drouillard of the Lewis party's clash with the Blackfeet in 1806 has been unearthed. The isolated battle site on the Two Medicine River is in its own way everlastingly eloquent, however, and I am grateful to rancher Vernon Carroll for providing my wife and me the doubly poignant journey across ranchland where my father and grandmother once worked.

In library holdings that I have drawn from, those of the University of Washington library and the Beinecke Library at Yale University were particularly vital for the period of the 1920s. At the Montana Historical Society, once again I owe all kinds of thanks to specific members of its peerless staff: Brian Shovers, Angela Murray, Jody Foley, Vivian Hays, Charlene Porsild, Lorie Morrow, Ellen Arguimbau; and Marcella Sherfy, for always smoothing the way. And Dave Walter as ever could be counted on as a remarkable human storehouse of Montana history.

From Harvard days to lore about Western vigilantes, historian Richard Maxwell Brown generously lent me his transcontinental insights. I'm similarly indebted to another estimable historical delver, William L. Lang, for sharing his pathbreaking research on the black community within the city of Helena.

In every realm from hospitality, encouragement, and information to the nitty-gritty of publishing, this book has had a cadre of friends in the right places: Marshall J. Nelson, Gloria Swisher, Denyse Delcourt, Katharina and John Maloof, Margaret Svec, Jan Mason, Clyde Milner, Lois and Jim Welch, the Arnst-Hallingstad-Payton extended family in Great Falls, Ken and Phyllis Adler of the Duck Inn, Liz Darhansoff, Susan Moldow, Nan Graham, Brant Rumble, and Karen Richardson. And Carol Doig, always a ten, my loving companion and sharp-eyed photographer on all the travels for this tenth book.

PRAIRIE NOCTURNE

DISCUSSION POINTS

1. The Overture to the story is an excerpt from Susan's diary, ostensibly discovered in the year 2025: "A story wants to be told a certain way, or it is merely the alphabet badly recited. At the right time the words borrow us, so to speak, and then out can come the unsuspected sides of things with a force like that of music. This is the story of the three of us, which I am more fit to tell now than when I was alive." What do you suppose the author intended to convey with this statement? Did it hold different meaning for you after you finished reading the story?

2. Did the passages from Susan's journal give you further insight into her character? Does keeping a diary give her greater clarity about her own life and the people in it? Why does Susan give her diary to Wes?

3. The reader first sees Wes when Susan does—when he lets himself into her house in the middle of the night with a spare key he has been keeping for four years since they last parted. What does this opening scene reveal about Wes? How about Susan? Why does Susan so readily allow Wes back into her life?

4. Do you think Susan is the strongest character in the novel? Why or why not? Wes muses that "soldier Samuel Duff was too fearless for his own good" (page 110). Can the same be said of Susan?

5. Wes not only encourages Monty's dream of becoming a professional singer but also provides the means for him to fulfill that ambition. Discuss Wes's motivations for aiding Monty. Did your opinion change when you read the story's ending, specifically Wes's conversation with Susan about Monty's father?

6. In one instance Wes laments that "once more he was helpless against too much memory" (page 103). Cite examples of how events in the past continue to impact the characters.

7. Compare the two main settings in the story—the Montana prairie and New York City. Aside from geographical ones, what are the major differences? Do the characters act differently in each place?

8. Discuss the issue of race in the book, particularly in the context of the time. Monty has to deal the most obviously with racial prejudice, but

are there other instances of prejudice in the book? What accounts for Wes's vehement dislike of the Ku Klux Klan, which Monty in particular notices? In Harlem, how is the race issue reversed?

9. A writer has to make various decisions in the creation of a book. One is the method of narration, whether to make the "voice" of the story the invisible author's own or first-person by a protagonist. How might *Prairie Nocturne* have been different, in each case, if Wes, Monty, or Susan had been made the narrator?

10. Susan's relationships with both Wes and Monty go against the standards of society—Wes because he is married and Monty because of the color of his skin. Why do you suppose Susan enters into these relationships that are destined to have complications? In what other aspects of her life does Susan defy convention?

11. Susan and Monty share a love of music and singing. What else draws them together? From their first singing lesson to the concluding scene at Carnegie Hall, how does their relationship progress from student and teacher to something more?

12. Why do you suppose Wes and Whit never told Monty the truth about his father's death? Why does Susan also opt for silence about it, even burning Mose Rathbun's hat? Does Monty deserve to know the truth?

13. Discuss the arc of Susan and Wes's relationship. In one instance Susan "felt a last genuine pang for Wes, and what might have been if they had dined together here when she was in her Village days and he was unattached" (page 323). If they had met before Wes's marriage, do you think they would have had a more sustained relationship?

14. Phil Sherman tells Wes there is speculation that Susan and Monty have romantic feelings for each other. "[Wes] hadn't foreseen, hadn't headed this off in time, hadn't calculated that their courage could be greater than his" (page 339). How, as Wes believes, is Susan and Monty's courage "greater than his"? Does this apply in any other ways in the story?

15. When Monty suggests during the rehearsal at Carnegie Hall that Susan act as his accompanist, Wes is the one who tips the scales. Does he realize what he's setting in motion, both for Susan and Monty as well as repercussions he might encounter?

16. Ivan Doig has said, "If I have any creed that I wish you as readers . . . will take with you from my pages, it'd be this belief of mine that writers of caliber can ground their work in specific land and lingo and yet be writing of that larger country: life." How does the land and lingo in the world of *Prairie Nocturne* reflect larger, more universal themes?

Look for more Simon & Schuster reading group guides online and download them for free at www.bookclubreader.com